Praise for *Expect Me Tomorrow*

'It features the brilliant concepts and literary sleights of hand
we can expect from the author of *The Prestige*, but there's also
a warmth and emotional urgency that makes it one of his best'
The Guardian

'A subtle, resonant, impactful tale that is both urgent and time-
less . . . captured in Priest's typically elegant and understated
prose' *Locus Magazine*

'Christopher Priest is another author who writes with an illu-
sionist's skill about shifting realities and identities'
Gary K. Wolfe

'In *Expect Me Tomorrow*, decades of writerly craft are honed
to produce not the great British novel, but a deadpan, darkly
comic anti-novel' The British Science Fiction Association

'Christopher is a master writer, in setting out stories that are
puzzles . . . It is by turns twisty and turny, but always mesmer-
ising' *SFFWorld.com*

'As a powerful and challenging work by one of speculative
fiction's key voices . . . It is an uncompromising and thought-
provoking novel that will stay with the reader long after the
final page' *Fantasy Hive*

T0286377

By Christopher Priest

Indoctrinaire
Fugue for a Darkening Island
Inverted World
The Space Machine
A Dream of Wessex
The Affirmation
The Glamour
The Quiet Women
The Prestige
The Extremes
The Separation
The Dream Archipelago
The Islanders
The Adjacent
The Gradual
An American Story
Episodes
The Evidence
Expect Me Tomorrow

expect me tomorrow

Christopher Priest

First published in Great Britain in 2022 by Gollancz
an imprint of The Orion Publishing Group Ltd
Carmelite House, 50 Victoria Embankment
London EC4Y 0DZ

An Hachette UK Company

This edition first published in 2023

1 3 5 7 9 10 8 6 4 2

Copyright © Christopher Priest 2022

The moral right of Christopher Priest to be identified as
the author of this work has been asserted in accordance
with the Copyright, Designs and Patents Act of 1988.

All rights reserved. No part of this publication may be
reproduced, stored in a retrieval system, or transmitted
in any form or by any means, electronic, mechanical,
photocopying, recording, or otherwise, without the
prior permission of both the copyright owner and the
above publisher of this book.

All the characters in this book are fictitious, and any resemblance
to actual persons, living or dead, is purely coincidental.

A CIP catalogue record for this book is
available from the British Library.

ISBN (MMP) 978 1 473 23514 4
ISBN (eBook) 978 1 473 23515 1
ISBN (audio) 978 1 399 60788 9

Typeset by Input Data Services Ltd, Somerset

Printed in Great Britain by Clays Ltd, Elcograf S.p.A.

www.gollancz.co.uk

To Anne and Garry Charnock

I

John Smith (1877)

i

In May 1877 a trial took place at the Central Criminal Court in London, and became the first act in the story that follows. The other people in this narrative knew nothing of it, being involved in more urgent matters. Even if they had been told about the trial they would have shown no more than a passing interest. Professor Adler J. Beck was living in London with his wife and a small baby son, and working full-time as a lecturer at a naval college. His brother Dolf was travelling and performing opera in South America, apparently successful and contented but not communicating well with Adler. Neither of them would even hear of the accused man until several years later. As for Charles Ramsey, his wife Ingrid and his brother Greg, they would not be born for more than a hundred years.

The crimes the defendant was charged with were minor, but they had a devastating impact on his alleged victims. Sections of the press took an interest in that, and for a few days the social injustice revealed by the case became a matter of concern. Events moved on, though, and within a few days the criminal was under lock and key and his unhappy victims were forgotten. But for the system of justice the case was to loom large, with a lasting influence on the way criminal trials were heard in British courts.

The importance of the trial lay in the nature of the evidence that was given to convict the man, and his questionable identity.

The year 1877 was the fortieth of the reign of Queen Victoria, widowed by the death of Prince Albert and now living in seclusion. It was the year in which Tchaikovsky's ballet *Swan Lake* received its initial performance in Moscow, the first lawn tennis championships were held at Wimbledon (delayed by rain), President Rutherford B. Hayes was inaugurated as President of the USA and Thomas Edison invented and patented the phonograph.

The criminal trial was of a man who was accused of fifteen offences, all much the same in detail, and all despicable in motive. His real name was never known to the court, but he called himself 'John Smith'.

ii

Smith was a confidence trickster and swindler, who preyed on vulnerable women he met on the streets. Most of these women would be described in the word of the day as 'fallen'. There were many such women in London during the second half of the nineteenth century. A fallen woman was in most cases one whose husband had left her: sometimes inadvertently by his death, or more deliberately by divorce or abandonment. She, blameless, and often with children in her care, would be left with nothing. If she came from the middle classes she would often be disowned by her family. Society would discard her, suspecting immorality or dishonesty. She would resort to desperate measures, somehow finding a place to live and sleep, somehow making enough money to feed herself and her children, somehow maintaining pride in herself, and often surrounded by a few remaining tokens of her past life, which she treasured: a wedding ring, a necklace or earrings, a wrist-watch, perhaps even a picture in a frame. John Smith set out deliberately and ruthlessly to cheat these unfortunate women of such harmless mementos.

On May 10th 1877 John Smith was produced from custody at Court No. 1 in the Central Criminal Court, the Old Bailey, in London. He appeared before the Common Serjeant, the second most senior judge in London. The Common Serjeant was then Sir Thomas Chambers QC. A jury of twelve ordinary citizens, all men, were empanelled for the hearing. John Smith had the fifteen charges read out to him, to every one of which he pleaded not guilty.

There were no unusual features to the case itself and justice was efficiently dispensed. Smith's defence was paid for from the public purse, and he was represented by a dock brief called Mr Montagu Williams. The prosecution on behalf of the Crown was led by a barrister named Mr Forrest Fulton.

The court first took evidence from Louisa Leonard. Mrs Leonard told the court she had been stopped in a street near Charing Cross by a well-dressed gentleman, who appeared to have mistaken her for a certain Lady Harridge. The man himself had aristocratic manners and spoke with a faint accent she thought might have been German. He told her his name was Lord Winton de Willoughby, and lived in a residence in St John's Wood, known throughout London as an exclusive suburb. Once the mistaken identity had been cleared up, Lord Willoughby mentioned that his housekeeper had just departed and he was seeking a replacement. He said he thought Mrs Leonard could be ideal and asked her if he might call on her the next day to discuss the job. The woman told the court that because she was at the time in desperate need of money, she agreed. She gave Lord Willoughby her address. Overnight he sent her a letter of confirmation written on the headed notepaper of an expensive hotel in Mayfair. He included the phrase, *Please expect me tomorrow.* She received the letter the following morning, and Lord Willoughby called on her later in the day.

He told her he was particular about the appearance of people who worked for him, and gave her a letter of introduction to Redfern's, a well-known couturier in Bond Street, saying she should order whatever she wished on his account. He wrote down a list of garments she might like to try on for size. He then offered her a small advance on the proposed salary, and handed her a cheque for fifty pounds, drawn on a branch of the Union Bank in Pall Mall. Mrs Leonard told the court she had never imagined that she would ever again see so much money, which would radically improve her reduced circumstances.

Lord Willoughby went on to point out that she would need beautiful jewellery for a job which involved greeting and serving famous and important guests, so he said he would order some new jewellery for her, including a replacement ring. She lent him her existing ring, to match the size, and her wristwatch. He finally asked her if she happened to have any cash, as that morning his valet had laid out his clothes and forgotten to put money in his pocket. She handed over what she had in her savings, which amounted to £13.10s.0d (thirteen pounds and ten shillings). 'It was all the money I had in the world,' she told the court, weeping.

She never saw Lord Willoughby again. When she went to Redfern's they denied ever having heard of him, and had no account in his name. When she tried to take the cheque to the Union Bank she could not find it at the address in Pall Mall. Another branch of the same bank refused to cash it, saying it was forged. She later discovered from the police that her jewellery had been pawned.

Asked in court if she could see the man who had claimed to be Lord Willoughby, she pointed directly at John Smith, who was ordered to stand up in the dock.

'That is the man,' she declared.

John Smith in 1877

A total of fourteen more women, of a similar background to Mrs Leonard, told their stories to the court. Some details varied, but the deception was the same. All the women positively identified John Smith as the man who had swindled them.

A police constable called Eliss Spurrell gave evidence as the arresting officer. PC Spurrell said that the only name the defendant would give was 'John Smith', which had raised his suspicions. 'John Smith' was a name sometimes used by criminals as an alias, but in addition 'Smith' spoke with what seemed to be a German accent. Since he would admit to no other name, and there was no other means of identifying him, he was charged as John Smith. When the verdict of the court was known he was sentenced as John Smith, and served his time in prison under that name. He was sentenced to five years' penal servitude.

Smith was released from prison on licence in April 1881, his period of incarceration reduced because of good behaviour.

Not long after his release he went abroad, where he was to remain for several years. However, John Smith would eventually return.

2

Adler and Adolf Beck (1868-1904)

i

Yesterday I put the finishing touches to the galley proofs of my new book, and this morning a messenger from the publisher's office called round to the college to collect them. If all goes to plan the finished edition should be in the bookshops in the spring of next year, 1905, and then we shall see. The publishers, Messrs Sherratt & Hughes, say they will be arranging for extracts to appear in one of the daily newspapers. They are treating it as the breaking of a news story, which of course it is. The announcement that the world will soon end and civilization will be destroyed has been often made by fantasists, but none of them so far has backed up their dire warnings with the unarguable reality of science. At last the truth will be available to the reading public.

The publishers rejected the title I chose for it, saying insensitively that it sounded too stodgy and academic. They are now calling it *Take Heed! – A Scientist Warns of the Terror to Come.* I can't complain because the publishers need to make back the money they are investing. I still should have preferred a less catchpenny approach in the title.

There is, though, no toning down of the content. While I

was working on the book the facts I was uncovering often kept me awake at night. It is sensational stuff.

With the book complete I now at last have time to set down the extraordinary background to my discoveries.

ii

My story begins nearly four decades ago, in 1868, when I was waiting impatiently in London for the delivery of my files and instruments from Bergen in Norway.

When I left Norway five years earlier after my graduation, I placed everything for safekeeping with the Department of Earth Sciences at Bergen's Technical University, my alma mater. Since then I had been living and working in London. I was now planning my next move, this time to New York City, where the opportunity of a research position at the Haddon Institute of Biological Study had arisen. I needed to take everything with me.

Two members of the faculty staff in Bergen assured me my property had been despatched – I knew the identity of the shipping agency, and the name of the ship on which they had been loaded, but it had still not berthed in London. I had an onward journey to make. I was due to travel from London to the seaport of Liverpool, where I had already booked passages for myself and my brother with the Star Line.

My subject at university was the study of glaciers, and if pressed to define myself I would use the modern word glaciologist. However, since I left university events and experience have widened my interests. I would now say that I am a generalist on the special subject of climate, or sometimes the other way around.

I became interested in glaciers as a young boy because of

8

my father's work. He, Joseph Beck, worked most of his life for the various mountain authorities who in those days monitored glaciers. He concentrated on Jostedalsbreen, the largest glacier in continental Europe, in Vestland. He reported regularly on size, depth, movement, moraine, meltwater levels and snow capture. As soon as I was old enough he would sometimes take me with him on his research trips, and it was because of those long days on the ice that I formed my permanent respect for glaciers.

I am now wary of their sluggish moods, brutal as they sometimes are. Like my father I have measured many of them, climbed several, I have lowered myself into their frigid blue crevasses to take samples of the deepest firn ice. I have slept fitfully in bitterly cold tents beside them, listening to them creak and grind in the night. I still sometimes dream of glaciers.

I lost my father to Jostedalsbreen, when he was alone on the mountain, a routine visit to collect certain measurements. Two colleagues saw him before he departed, and said later that he had been in his normal good spirits. The three of them intended to meet for dinner at the end of the day – instead, those two, together with others, spent days searching for him after he did not return. They never found his body. It must have been encased and crushed somewhere deep inside the glacier, never to be recovered.

His death affected me profoundly but less so my twin brother Dolf, or so it seemed.

Dolf and I were alike, physically identical in fact, but our outlook on the world has always been at odds. I loved clambering up the mountains with Pappa, cold and terrified, enthralled by heights and steep slippery slopes and expanses of deadly ice. Dolf went quiet whenever Pappa proposed a new expedition to the mountains. He pretended to be reading, or to have hurt his leg, or would simply leave the house to avoid any more persuasion. He was clearly distraught when the news of the accident came down the mountain from the rescue team, but he would never speak to me about it. I was desperate to vent and share my unhappiness, and for a time I wanted Dolf close to me so I could relieve that feeling. But Dolf shut himself away emotionally, causing me to do much the same, expressed differently. I started exploring glaciers alone as a sort of tribute to Pappa.

One day, when I was about fifteen years old, I was clambering around on a jagged part of the lower ice sheet, not far above Jostedalsbreen's snout. I discovered a wall of ice which had apparently become exposed only recently. I was intending to take a sample of the firn, the compressed ice and snow that makes up the depths of the glacier. It was a risky thing to do – at that age I took less care than I would now. Using only one tethered rope and an ice axe I crawled slowly down.

Then I was stricken by what I later came to call an incursion. I was to experience incursions many times over the years, but this time, this day on the terrifying ice wall of a glacier, was the first. I did not try to describe it by any name. It simply happened and it almost killed me.

I was suddenly paralysed – my limbs became frozen, my eyes remained locked on wherever I was looking at that time. I stared at blank ice. I could still breathe, but only with great effort. I could certainly not shout or call for help. There was no one around anyway. By chance I had moments before secured a foothold, and the rope from above was tight. I did not fall, but had this incursion started at almost any time before or after it would have been the end of me. I held on, but there was no choice. My hands were clamped immovably in the handholds I had taken. I stared at the firn before my eyes, barely breathing.

Then came the voice. It sounded so unnaturally close that for an instant I thought someone must be there beside me, or behind me. But I was alone in the mountain valley, clinging to a wall of ice. The voice was in me, within me! Nothing could be closer. Who was it? How did it speak?

More to the point, what did it say? That I do not know. I heard what I thought was my own name, spoken aloud, questioning. It was not fluent, seeming to stutter. It said 'Ad' several times, but I was so taken by surprise: the 'Ad' sound could have been meant for me, Adler, or my brother – Dolf as I called him, Adolf as he had been named at birth. What was the voice asking? It spoke in English, a language I knew enough of to be able to recognize when spoken, but not enough to understand. The voice spoke quickly, urgently, as if stressed. It was not a normal sound.

As suddenly as I had been seized I was released. My body relaxed, once again within my control, but my handholds also relaxed and for a moment I felt myself falling backwards, away from the firn wall. I managed to grab a spur of ice, corrected the fall, then reached out to regain those precious handholds. Soon I was safe again, but shaken by what had happened.

It was the first incursion of its kind, and as I later discovered it was not to be the last, but I was fifteen, an age when you tend to treat survival as less of a mystery than the cause of the accident. I did not dwell on the incident.

I never forgot it, though.

iii

And now to describe Dolf, my brother.

I have always loved Dolf, but from around the time our father died he became increasingly difficult to understand or live with. He became restless, unfocused, irrational in arguments, petulant, annoying. He would leave the house unannounced, stay away for too long, involve himself in escapades of which I knew nothing and which he would never talk about.

Perhaps my own adventures in the mountains meant I was over compensating in a different way. We were both in distress. We had never known our mother, Astrid: she died two days after our birth. All we had of her was a small painting made by our father shortly before they married. And we had the excuse of being just boys. We were only twelve years old when Pappa died, and soon after we were going through the complex and sometimes awkward process of adolescence.

I was in London, waiting for my papers to arrive, waiting for Dolf. Once again I was being forced to wonder where he had gone and when he would turn up. He had wandered away from the lodgings we were renting together, leaving no message. I had heard nothing from him since. If he was away longer than two more days he would find me gone and the apartment closed. I usually put up with his feckless behaviour, but this time I was determined not to let him interfere with what I wanted to do. The appointment to the Haddon Institute was too important to let slip away.

Dolf is twenty minutes younger than me, and I believe he has always resented the fact that I was first to be born. When he is angry or feeling guilty he treats me sulkily like a much older brother, or even a parent. But we are twins, identical twins, born in the hospital on the island of Christianssund, in 1841. After the death of our mother we were brought up until we were twelve by our grief-stricken father and his sister, our Tante Helena. She had a house in Bergen, so all three of us moved from the island to be with her. After Pappa died we stayed on with her, of course. It was Tante Helena who encouraged both me and Dolf to learn to speak and write English. I took to it better than Dolf, another source of friction between us.

I felt I was honouring the example of Joseph, my father, by

following a scientific career. He had tutored me in scientific method. Look at the facts, Adler, he would say. The facts provide evidence of what might follow. Collecting and understanding evidence is a first priority.

All this was lost on Dolf though. He has never shown much interest in that sort of thing. He has gone his own way, in his own fashion. When I wanted to move to London he did not put up much resistance, travelled with me and soon found a job he seemed to enjoy, at least for a while. He worked as a clerk in a merchant's office, similar to the work he had done in Bergen. When I landed the appointment in New York, he acceded to the idea more quickly than I expected.

But his sudden absences went on. Even in the weeks when we were preparing for the journey to the USA, his drifting around town continued as before. He had a circle of shadowy acquaintances unknown to me. All this was a minor annoyance and I was always glad when he returned nonchalantly, usually taking to his bed for a couple of days to recover from whatever he had been up to.

iv

I could not give too much attention to worrying about Dolf. My time in London was taken up with scouring through climate records, of which a huge archive was maintained at the Royal College of Science in Kensington. I travelled to and from the college every day, noting, recording, analysing, trying to make sense of what history could tell me about the climate of the past. It is my belief that understanding the patterns of the past would reveal possible developments in the future.

Although the Royal College's records were extensive, consistent and well catalogued, and even the very old entries were legible, they represented only a fraction of the information I wished to extract. Nearly all the records were concerned, understandably enough, with the weather in the British Isles. The British were interested in local effects, in temporary weather events. Hours of sunshine, depth of rainfall, maximum and minimum temperatures, all were faithfully and consistently noted, as were exceptional events: heavy rain leading to flooding, blizzards and deep snow, long periods of summer heat. I needed that data, but I wanted to know about the weather the same day in, say, my home town Bergen, or for that matter in Paris or Baghdad or St Petersburg or Peking, or anywhere else in the world. What had been the weather at sea? What depth of cloud cover had there been? In short the British were interested in weather while I was concerned with the climate.

I corresponded with colleagues in other parts of the world. By following contributions to learned journals about such matters I picked up more interesting information. In this way I opened contact with fellow climate investigators in New York City. This was how my research appointment to the Haddon Institute came about. It included visiting and archive rights to the Haddon Marine Center in Florida.

The Haddon specialized in oceanographical study of currents, and the impact of the annual release of organic matter from the depths to the warmer waters closer to the surface. This process had been proved to have an influence on air temperature in certain areas, which was exactly the kind of information I needed to measure and evaluate.

v

Two days before I was due to take the train to Liverpool I received notification that the ship had arrived from Norway.

My luggage had cleared excise checks and could be collected from Rotherhithe Dock. I went directly there and hired a cab to bring everything back to the lodgings. To my surprise and pleasure my brother Dolf was waiting for me there. He helped carry the instrument cases and document files up to our rooms.

We embraced in a brotherly way, then I said, 'Where have you been, Dolf?'

'*Jeg har sunget med en ung kvinne jeg traff, som håper å bli tatt opp i Det kongelige operahus.*'

'We must always speak to each other in English,' I said.

'There is no one to overhear us, Adler. Why does it matter?'

'Because English is our language now. We agreed this before we left home. No one here speaks Norwegian. When we arrive in New York you will find it is the same there.'

'English is not the language of opera.'

'Neither is Norwegian, but that's another matter. Your English is good enough.'

'Your English is better than mine.'

'But you don't need me to speak for you.'

'And I find it difficult to write in English. The grammar is horrible.'

In fact Dolf's spoken English was as good as mine. Tante Helena had always instructed us together, but there was still a difference. Dolf spoke English with a more distinctive Norwegian accent. One or two of our English friends said they had thought Dolf was German when they first met him, or at least had a German accent. He said he did not mind. What did it matter?

I continued with my packing and made sure Dolf did not leave the apartment again before our departure. He seemed genuinely excited by the prospect of going to America. I wondered how involved he might have been with the lady opera singer he mentioned, but he never told me her name and did not speak of her again.

vi

We boarded the steamer *Star of Albion* from Canada Dock in Liverpool. The next morning, on the high tide, we slipped our moorings and set off down the Mersey estuary. I was excited by the knowledge that the ship would be sailing against, or more accurately across, the Gulf Stream, first charted by Benjamin Franklin a century earlier. Once we had passed the northern extremity of the Irish island I spent most of a day on the foredeck, staring out at the ocean, hoping for some visible sign of the current.

On our third day out the captain warned the passengers that he was expecting a gale to blow up. This interested me and I headed up to the deck to watch. For an hour or two the increasing wind and the height of the waves caused movement of the ship, fore and aft and side to side. Dolf, sheltering in the cabin, suffered mal de mer for a day, while I was excited. It turned out to be a rough sea rather than a full-blown storm, but even so.

I was sympathetic to Dolf's sickness, but it also intrigued me. He sometimes claimed to be a seasoned sailor. One of his past adventures, when he was twenty-three, was running away to sea. He had impulsively signed on as a deckhand on the *Snøjeger*, a merchant ship docked in Bergen harbour, and when she sailed he sailed with her. He was gone for about a year, while the ship tramped around the Far East. When he was home again he never told me much about it, but it was clear his seafaring days were at an end.

The passengers with us were a mixed bunch: a few were

16

Americans returning home, the majority were English or Scottish, and there were several Italians and Spaniards. Most of them remarked in a friendly way on how physically alike Dolf and I were – our two blond heads, our blue eyes, our slight stature, made us seem different from the others. Dolf and I played a harmless routine we knew people found amusing, so we willingly demonstrated mannerisms we shared, and so on.

As the ship approached the densely clustered buildings of New York City, everyone gathered on the upper deck to share the thrill of arrival. I had read many accounts of travellers in which they described the supreme experience of sailing slowly up the Narrows to the greatest port city in America, and perhaps in the world. I said this to Dolf.

'Entering Sydney Harbour is better,' he said, and moved away from me, shading his eyes.

New York did not disappoint me: we were arriving late in the afternoon and the sun was low across the land, dazzling us towards the west but magically lighting up the buildings before us. A light atmospheric haze, which I attributed to a low-pressure system the captain had told me was stationary across the eastern seaboard, softened the stark, rectangular outlines of the modern buildings. The thousands of windows glittered in the rays of the sun. For several minutes the privations of the long voyage felt worthwhile. We had arrived in the new world and the future at last lay ahead.

vii

Dolf sprung one of his unwelcome surprises when we were in the Port Authority arrivals shed, waiting for permission to enter the country. Because I was carrying letters of approval and introduction from the Haddon Institute the officials accepted me, but Dolf encountered more of an obstacle. He told me in London he had prepared the necessary paperwork for our stay, but now it turned out he had done no such thing. After a long wait in the arrivals shed, and after offering what assurances I could, he was granted permission to stay in the USA for one month only. There was no guarantee of renewal. The immigration officers finally waved us through.

While we were still inside the noisy and crowded customs building, trying to agree how to divide up our luggage for carrying, I said to Dolf, 'As soon as we have settled down we must apply to get you permission to stay in America for more than one month. I have a lot of work to do here.'

'A single month will be enough,' he replied, raising his voice above the racket that filled the cavernous building.

'It is nowhere near enough.'

'That might be true for you. But I am planning to leave.'

'Planning what?' I said. He had the evasive look I was so used to. He was trying to get me to agree to something he knew I was against. 'Why didn't you say anything about this before? What are you going to do?'

'I thought I would travel. I have had enough of living in a large city.'

'Once I have established myself at the Institute I am intending to travel to their marine laboratory in the Florida Keys. Would that be travel enough for you?'

'That's still in the USA,' said Dolf.

'Then make your own plans,' I said, annoyed with him. 'You always do.'

He turned his back on me.

I went in search of a porter or cab driver, to help us with our luggage, leaving Dolf to guard the pile. Two hours later we were inside the apartment provided by the Haddon Institute, both of us excited to be in New York at last, but also fairly worn out by the journey. We were now a long way from any-where we might think of as home.

viii

I came into the apartment one evening, returning from my workplace at the Haddon building. Dolf was waiting for me, looking restless. I was glad to see him – he had been away for a few days, another of his unexplained absences. I had grown used to them in Bergen and London, but New York was a city on a different scale. It was so much larger, so exciting, so full of unknown dangers. I worried about him when he was gone.

However, there he was, apparently unchanged and unaffect-ed by whatever he had been doing or wherever he had been. I prepared a meal for us both, and we sat down together to eat. He asked a few harmless questions about the work I was doing.

'I shall be researching here in New York until the end of summer,' I told him. 'Then I hope to take a train south to Florida, where I expect to stay for a few months. It all depends on how much I can get done while I'm there. I have to be back here in New York before the end of next year, as I am expected to put in a report of my findings.'

'Do you have any findings?' Dolf said.

'Nothing of substance so far. For now I am exploring the archives in the Institute, trying to familiarize myself with the work that has already been done.'

'I'm never sure what you are hoping to find.'

'I am trying to measure the growth and expansion of glaciers.'

'I didn't know there were glaciers in Florida,' he said, but he sounded as if he was already bored with the subject.

'Never mind.'

19

'My visa expires at the end of next week. I have to renew it soon, or leave the country. You said you would come with me to do that.'

'I will, of course. I have already located the office where we can apply for an extension.'

'Yes, but I have been thinking. I am planning to go away for a while, out of America.'

'Not back to London? Or Norway?'

'No – why should you think that?' Dolf said. 'There is nothing for me in Norway except your fjords and glaciers, and my boredom. I want to go to South America.'

I was astounded. Indeed, I was lost for words. Finally I said, 'Where would you go to in South America?'

'At first I would travel to Uruguay. To Montevideo.' He obviously saw the incredulous expression on my face. 'There is an opera house in Montevideo and I am told they are always short of tenors. That is my true interest, Adler.'

'I don't dispute that. But why go all the way to Uruguay? There are opera houses everywhere. In fact, where we are staying is only a short distance from the New York Met.'

'I have tried the Met, and I failed even to be offered an audition. They claimed they had no need of tenors.'

'Chicago?'

'I haven't tried, but I have no contacts there and from my point of view Chicago is as far away as Montevideo. I know the long journey to Uruguay would be an adventure, while going to Chicago might not be. And Chicago could turn out to be another disappointment. I can't face that. I have a friend in Montevideo who can give me somewhere to live. He says he is well known to the opera company and will introduce me.'

'You have a friend in Uruguay?' Almost everything he was telling me was coming as a surprise.

'He is a performer. A virtuoso pianist. His name is Louis Moreau Gottschalk, although you almost certainly won't have heard of him.'

'I haven't.'

'Mr Gottschalk is an American, born in New Orleans. I met him briefly while he was performing in London, and since then I have exchanged letters with him.'

'You say you never write letters!'

'I have a friend here who writes down for me what I ask. It is easy work for her, but really useful to me.'

'Another friend of yours I have never heard of. Does she have a name?'

'Yes, she does. It is all arranged with Mr Gottschalk.'

'Exactly what have you arranged?'

'I shall contact him when I arrive in Montevideo. He will accompany me to the most important salons in the city, and he will introduce me to the opera company's artistic director.'

'How do you propose to travel to distant Uruguay?' I said, thinking of the distance and the expense.

'That is what I need to discuss with you, brother.'

ix

Dolf and I survived on a small trust fund our father had set up for us before his death. Tante Helena had become its trustee, and she managed it well until we reached the age of twenty-five. Then it was released to us. We were twenty-seven when we arrived in New York – I knew Dolf's taste in clothes and wine was expensive, and that he had a habit of visiting drinking and entertainment clubs. I often worried about him wandering around city streets at night, vulnerable to thieves and others who might see him as a soft touch, but so far no perceptible harm had come to him. I did notice that whenever we were together we usually spent my money, not his.

His singing voice was his golden asset, a pure tenor with a good vocal range. I found it exciting and charming to hear him sing, although I always suspected that trying to make a living from it would be perilous. While we were in London he had taken regular lessons from a tutor, and I know that he and a group of other young singers had formed an ensemble who occasionally found recital work.

Like many people who are not especially artistic I was sympathetic to his ambitions while privately doubting he would ever be successful enough to find fame and fortune. I knew that if he were to travel to South America it would be for him a final release into adult life. Much as I cared for him, and grew irritated with him every now and then, I respected his independence. I was soon certain that the trip was not a foolish or passing whim, so I gave him what support I could. This meant, I was in no doubt, that I would have to pay his way.

'All I need is the cost of the passage south,' Dolf said. 'I would not, will not, trouble you for more. Once I am established in Montevideo I am certain I will be able to live by my own efforts. If I become rich and famous then perhaps one day I will pay you back.'

'I would not let you do that,' I said. 'You are my only brother, my only relative in the world.'

'And you are mine.'

For once we embraced with genuine warmth.

We immediately started making plans for his journey, finding a transportation agency that worked out an itinerary for him: some ships, some trains, departure, arrival and transfer times. A complex plan, but overall the financial cost was not too great. Dolf was extremely excited.

Two days later, with an unexpired week remaining on his

United States visa, Dolf departed New York City. I was moved and saddened to see him leave. Whatever Dolf said or promised about returning and our reunion in the future, I did harbour a dread suspicion we might never meet again. No sooner had he left than I was missing him.

x

In 1869, a year after Dolf and I moved to New York City, I finally achieved what I had wanted all along. My research project was confirmed by the Haddon Institute and the agreed funding was released to me. I travelled south to their Marine Center in the new southern state of Florida. For many months I had ploughed through the weather and oceanographic reports filed in the New York archive, gradually forming a complex scientific picture of the importance of the Gulf of Mexico to the climate, not only to the region but also to Europe and the eastern seaboard of the USA.

The Gulf resembles in outline a wide, safe, circular harbour, and because of its enormous diversity of plant, animal and sea life it acts as an almost inviolable ecological refuge. The climate is mostly benign. The only serious weather disruption, which happened not to occur while I was working there, is caused by the violent storms that brew up over the warm waters of the South Atlantic, and which then move west against the Gulf or the placid Caribbean to the south of it.

The Florida Keys are hundreds of small islands that make up a long east-west archipelago off the most southerly extreme of Florida. Haddon Marine Center was situated on Key Largo, one of the islands closest to the Florida mainland and accessible to it by a ferry service.

As soon as I was settled in my lodgings I reported to the

Center. The people I met all commented, not unkindly, on my obvious need for clothes better suited to the warm climate. Coming from Norway and London, and latterly living through the harshness of a New York winter, I habitually wrapped myself warmly. That had suddenly become nonsensical.

On arrival at the Center I learned that a polite young technician from Michigan had been assigned to showing me around. His name was Ed, and he was to be my research assistant for the duration of my stay. Ed had earned a degree in hydrology, at that time a discipline new to the studies of ocean, but now he was training as a marine biologist. He spoke enthusiastically about his work: he said he and his supervisor were concerned with research into the physical properties of the waters, both on the surface and in the depths, the distribution of nutrients, the effects of tides, the circulation of the currents.

He told me he knew I was concerned with the Gulf Stream, but from the quizzical tone of his voice I knew he could not think why. I was a glaciologist – he was a warm water man. What might we have in common? There was time enough ahead for us to discuss these matters, and no doubt each learn a lot from the other.

Ed took me to a big store on the island, where it appeared possible to buy almost anything imaginable. There was a dazzling array of foodstuffs, cooking implements, writing materials, tools, books, magazines, firearms, medicines, alcoholic beverages and clothes. Sorely tempted by this cornucopia to buy all manner of American things that were a novelty to me, I confined myself to the sort of casual garments I had seen Ed and some of the other men at the Haddon wearing: workmanlike jeans, light shirts and canvas shoes. I was glad of the informal and attractive way Americans dressed in this climate, and tried to throw off what I think they might have seen as my stuffy, over dressed European attitudes.

My pale Norwegian skin was already suffering in the Florida sunshine, so I bought some unguent to soothe where I was turning pink.

As we left the store, stepping out from the cool interior into the glaring heat of the sun, it occurred to me that wearing a hat might be a better way of habitually protecting myself. I had seen some broad-brimmed straw hats on sale. I paused, thinking I might go back into the store for one.

An exactitude: Ed was already a few paces ahead of me. I thought I should call to him to say I had decided to go back inside. I was carrying under one arm a paper sack the store had given me, with my new purchases. But I also thought: I could come back another day, without bothering Ed. It was this that had made me hesitate.

For some reason I raised my free hand to my forehead, perhaps anticipating the feel of a head covering. I was looking towards Ed, who was walking ahead of me. Beyond him the straight and smooth track that led past the store, beyond that a line of trees and a couple of low buildings, beyond those the bright mirror of the sea glittering under the sun. In that moment of exactitude I experienced another incursion.

I froze in position, one foot ahead of the other. All my senses remained: I was staring towards the sea, I felt the heat of the sun, I became aware of the sounds of the breeze rustling the leaves of the trees, and the store's metal sign swinging overhead. I could see, hear, feel, think, but I was incapable of movement. Breathing became a silent struggle. I was suddenly swept back to the memory of being trapped on the wall of ice.

The voice broke in. Again it seemed to emerge within me, again it sounded tense, straining. 'Adolf? I—' A short period of silence, with a soft and distracting, faint hissing noise. Then again, a bursting of words, 'Are you Adolf?'

I struggled to speak, to make some kind of reply. Ahead of

me I saw Ed suddenly turning back towards me. Some people went by along the track in an open carriage. I felt strangulated, inarticulate. Ed had a friendly smile, waiting for me. Then he took some steps towards me. At that moment the incursion suddenly ceased.

'Everything OK with you, sir?' said Ed. 'Did you forget something?'

Released, freed. I felt my body relaxing, but because unlike the occasion on the glacier I was at no risk, the transition back to normal movements was probably almost imperceptible. I completed the step forward I had been taking, then halted.

'I'm sorry, Ed—'

'I didn't mean to interrupt. You looked preoccupied.'

'Yes. Yes, I was suddenly remembering something that happened to me a few years ago. I was on a glacier—'

'A glacier?' said Ed, then unaware that he was repeating what Dolf had said to me a few months earlier, he added, 'We don't see too many of them around here, sir.'

'I was just thinking – maybe I should buy one of those wide-brimmed hats they have back there.'

'Sure – let's do it now.'

So we turned, went back into the store, found what I was looking for, then returned to the Center.

The moment of incursion had been a shock: it was so many years since that earlier experience in the glacier's crevasse that I had mostly forgotten it had happened, or assumed that I was misremembering it somehow. I was certainly not expecting it to happen again, not then, not on this semi-tropical island in the heat and bright sunshine.

I said nothing to Ed about what had just occurred and could only imagine how my frozen stance must have appeared to him.

Off and on I brooded about it for the next few weeks,

worrying about what it might mean for my mental state. Gradually, as nothing like it came upon me again, I felt reassured. It faded into my past.

Ed's training at the Haddon focused on sedimentary concerns. He explained to me that as the warm waters of the Gulf of Mexico swirled around, and flowed past the tip of Florida into the Atlantic Ocean, rich sediment from the depths of the sea floor was released or swept up. This provided nutrition at the base of the food chain for krill and other microscopic animals close to the surface, where larger fish and sea creatures consumed them.

The work of the Haddon was mostly academic, but they had a lucrative commercial sideline with the local fishing industry. Wealthy vacationers from the northern US states wanted guidance on where best to hunt for the big fish: the sharks, the barracudas, the tunny-fish. The scientists at the Haddon were pleased to provide reliable charts of the likely feeding and breeding grounds.

More seriously, they were also concerned that one day the source of primal food might through over use become unavailable. In this they were working with teams of marine biologists to try to establish the sustainability of the sediment and its food content.

I told Ed why I was there, to learn about the warm current flowing out of the Gulf, and its impact on the climate of Europe and the eastern seaboard of the USA. The next day I took my files with me to the laboratory, and spread out the charts and diagrams I used for my own research.

Ed and I leaned on the table side by side, to trace the matters that interested us. We had our different approaches, but we were united by the Gulf Stream.

The basis for everything was the chart drawn up by Benjamin Franklin, first published in 1786. Even though it had been constantly refined and modified by oceanographers over the years, it demonstrated the fundamental importance of the Gulf Stream.

We discussed the way in which the seawater, warm and sediment-rich from the Gulf of Mexico, flowed north-east after it had swirled around the foot of Florida. It followed the eastern seaboard of North America.

'I'm kind of well informed about sludge at the bottom of the sea,' Ed said. 'Broken shells, dead fish, you want to know about those? But anything going on around the surface – it's mostly news to me.'

'Warm water readily convects,' I said. 'So clouds form. The combination of warm water, humid air and ocean winds creates a propensity for storms. Every year this low-lying American coastline is in danger of flooding. Damage to the sea defences is frequent.'

Gradually, the direction of the Gulf Stream moves away from the relatively shallow water along the coast, and by the time it passes New York and the New England states it is streaming almost in mid-ocean. At this point oceanographers call it the North Atlantic Drift, which is how it is named on most modern maps and charts.

As the current travels further it not only widens, estimated to be in some parts of the Atlantic about seventy miles across, it also flows more quickly. This at first mystified investigators, but it is now believed that the pressure of the prevailing winds is responsible for this. Also, the rotation of the Earth causes oceanic waters to circulate in gyres, and as the stream passes close to the huge gyre in equatorial mid-Atlantic this too speeds up the current.

Sometimes ships sailing against the Gulf Stream were slowed or even halted by the current. Famously, the fleet of Juan Ponce de León, the Spanish conquistador, was sailing south along the eastern Florida coast in the early sixteenth century. His navigating captains discovered that in spite of a strong following wind and apparently good progress for a whole day towards their destination, the fleet had actually been propelled backwards. One of the smaller ships was swept away, and was temporarily lost to the fleet. This was the first known encounter with the strength of the Gulf Stream by ships equipped with navigation aids.

The quiet power of the Gulf Stream was of endless fascination to me. It is in effect a vast river flowing unswervingly through the ocean, but no landlocked river anywhere, not even the mighty Amazon or the Mississippi or the Nile, carries such a huge volume of water.

Ed and I approached the subject from different standpoints. He lent me some recent charts and depth maps from his days as a student, but his professional interest in the current ran out, as did his charts, somewhere in the mid-Atlantic. That was where my own involvement really began.

The Gulf Stream divides at the approximate latitude of the north of Africa. Part of it branches off and follows the gyre east towards the land, then swings southwards along the African coast. The rest of it, the greater part, continues in a north or north-easterly direction towards Europe. It flows along the western coasts of Portugal, Spain and France, then the British Isles, then finally to its destiny in the Norwegian Sea.

Most of France is at the same latitude as Canada, yet Canada suffers a continental climate of extremes: unbearably hot and dusty summers, with icy cold winters. France has a pleasant and mild climate: a median of cold and windy winters, but long summers of warm sunshine and, along its Mediterranean coast, endlessly hot days. The Gulf Stream passing close by its western shores ameliorates and warms the northern climate.

For the same reason the British Isles also enjoy an unexpectedly mild climate. London is at approximately the same latitude as Newfoundland and Labrador, level with Hudson Bay, where polar bears roam. Ireland is relentlessly temperate, the fertile soil soft with year-round rains. Britain's most northerly territory, the Shetland Islands, is at the sixtieth level, the same as the southern tip of Greenland, where icebergs and ice floes drift on the sea and walruses and polar bears hunt along the coasts.

This unexpected warmth is caused by the winds blowing across the Gulf Stream and being warmed by it. Those same winds cause the water to evaporate and cool, so on land they are often rain-bringing. The sea water's salinity and density become greater with evaporation.

As the current moves ineluctably northwards it enters the cold Norwegian Sea. Sea ice starts to form and this increases the density. Most of the water in the current does not freeze. A process called downwelling begins: the dense water sinks through the less dense water already there. This downdraft meets another current, deep in the sea, a southwards stream. It is the difference in density, not the difference in temperatures, that is the driving force of a sea current. In the deeps, the waters of the former Gulf Stream start the long slow journey south.

Although I was fascinated by the warming effect of the Gulf Stream, my own area of interest was another matter: those rain-laden clouds swept up by the west winds might bring the temperate effect of rain to Ireland, England and Scotland, but they also brought heavy snow to the mountains and valleys of Norway. That of course was where I began, learning the beauty and danger of the glaciers.

Glaciologists around the world, including myself, accept that the world is coming to the end of the Holocene, a warm interglacial period, an era of temperate and balanced weather, on average, across the world. The Holocene is just one geological epoch of many. So far it has lasted for about twelve thousand years, which in comparison with other epochs is a short one. Everything we know or have discovered about the human species has happened within the Holocene: all human history, development of technology, creation of art, building of civilizations.

Considered overall the world has suffered the grip of ice ages more often than it has not.

One thing that is certain about the climate is that it is always changing. For now, in the second half of the nineteenth century, the climate seems stable, the sun shines every day, the glaciers are quiescent, or that is how they seem to most people.

A glacier does not melt away, or at least in the modern age no glaciers are melting away. In fact, my interest in glaciers was reinforced when I was able to confirm my father's observations. Most of the Norwegian glaciers are gaining in length and height, expanding slowly but unstoppably down the valleys and plains lying before them. It is too slow a process for excitement or fear, but the truth of the matter is that the ice sheets of the northern hemisphere are spreading again.

Jostedalsbreen is of special interest to me, for obvious personal reasons. I can never forget, nor should I, that the body of my father is buried somewhere in its frozen grasp. The glacier is in a relatively southerly position in the mountains of Vestland, about one hundred kilometres from Bergen. Jostedalsbreen is unusual in that it is sustained by heavy winter snowfalls, followed by a melting through the short summer months. Its bulk is therefore maintained by precipitation, not by being in a permanently frozen zone. It has around fifty sub-glaciers, each with its own glaciated valley, each with its own snout where meltwater pours away. Year by year the new top snow accumulates, compacts the previous snow and ice into firn beneath it, freezes into a dome. Every year meltwater pours off it and from beneath it, but never quite as much water as has landed on it.

This is why I take an interest in the Gulf Stream. Should the ocean current divert for some reason, move further offshore, should its overall temperature reduce, even by a few degrees, a catastrophe would follow. The water would not evaporate so readily, the wind would not be warmed by it. The winter months would be longer and colder, the summer months shorter.

Because some snow would of course fall in the high mountains, that would build up on the glacier, compress the earlier snow, but the melting would be slower. The glaciers would start to expand more quickly. Northern Sweden and Finland would be colder. The great heights of Russia would harden under permanent snow and ice. Britain and Ireland would have weather comparable with the present chilly climate of the Canadian province of Labrador.

On the other hand, should the temperature of the seas, and the Gulf Stream in particular, increase in temperature the outcome would be just as catastrophic. More water would evaporate into the winds, the clouds would thicken and hold the warmth, over the mountains and high passes the snow would fall thicker and longer and would compress and harden more. The melting season would be unchanged. The glaciers' growth would accelerate. Warmer countries would flood, fields would become infertile. Forests would burn. But the ice would still be advancing at an ever increasing rate.

A climatologist seeks to find and be reassured by climate stability. What we are on guard against is the anomalies, the agents of abrupt or irreversible change.

I later returned to New York City, intending to arrange a posting, if possible, to one of the great observatories in the western mountains of the USA. Visiting a very warm part of the world to confirm my knowledge of some of the coldest places had given me extra insights.

I was grateful to the staff of the Haddon Center in Florida, because their different view of the oceans had provided my objectivity, but I had learned from them all I required for the moment.

And I had learned something about myself, more than just about the seas and their impact on the climate.

I realized I did not want disruption in my life. I was inherently conservative, content to potter about with charts and meteorological records, observing, noting, contemplating, perhaps preparing myself for more papers to write, or possibly even books. As I wished for the climate, I sought no sudden change in myself.

I had not, though, taken into consideration the doings and adventures of my wayward brother.

xiii

Imperator Hotel
Rua Valparaiso
Tiyuca
Rio de Janeiro
December 30th, 1869

My dearest brother Adler,

Your last letter was forwarded from my address in

33

Montevideo, and it has taken several weeks to reach me. It has also taken me some time to arrange for an English-speaking transcription agency in this town to draft this letter for me.

For today this address, this hotel, is the starting point for contacting me. I shall, however, be departing it soon. I cannot afford the expense any more of staying here, and the place has become imbued with sadness for me. For the same reasons, Rio as a whole is now associated for me with sorrow.

Even so, I have good news to tell you. These have been exciting and thrilling times. I have met and worked with celebrated artistes, and travelled to surprising, stimulating and beautiful places. I am in good fettle. There was briefly a medical ailment that I suffered, a terrible nervous attack of some kind, but I have fully recovered since.

I wrote to you from Montevideo, and in that letter I detailed the city much as I found and liked it. Monte-video is a busy but relaxed place, with an enjoyable climate. You would not be interested by it – there are no glaciers in Uruguay, and as far as I could find out very few snowstorms.

What I omitted to tell you before is that within two days of arriving in Montevideo I made contact with my friend Gottschalk, whom I first met, briefly, in London. He is the virtuoso pianist and composer in whom you seemed to disbelieve when I told you about him. His full name, the one under which he is becoming celebrated, is Louis Moreau Gottschalk. He was performing a series of recitals in London, and happened to be at a party where I was present. Everyone there that day spoke admiringly of him. I was introduced to him at the party, told him of my own musical ambitions and was grateful to receive his gentle encouragements. He spoke English with a charming French accent. I was impressed by him. He told me he was planning a visit to Montevideo, and invited me to contact him should I ever be there too.

I met him soon after I arrived. Gottschalk was an American citizen. He told me he had been born in New Orleans and grew up with French as his first language. The music of New Orleans enthralled him, and he drew on musical influences from diverse backgrounds. Many musicians came to the town to play, to meet and mix with others. Gottschalk soaked up all these rich sounds and harmonies and melodies. He learned to play the piano at an early age, and was quickly recognized as a prodigy. He gave his first public performance at the age of eleven, and at thirteen he and his father left New Orleans and travelled to Paris, where Gottschalk was to further his studies.

In Paris, while still only twenty years old, he had written and performed a composition called *Le Bananier*. This was inspired by the Creole music of his home town. It made him a star of the French music world, and enabled him to make many personal appearances at sold-out recitals.

One day he suggested I might sing for him and I did so, but it was a nervous moment for me. To be accompanied by a maestro was something beyond my dreams. We were in his studio, so the three songs I essayed were in private. Afterwards he applauded and congratulated me. He recommended me to a singing coach in the town, and paid for me to have a few lessons.

After that I accompanied him as he toured, and it was this friendship which brought me here, to Rio de

Janeiro. Once or twice he would invite me on to the platform at the end of his recital, to join him for a song.

There is more. While he was in Havana he was joined by a brilliant young soprano, Adelina Patti, who is even now still only fourteen or fifteen years of age. Signorina Patti arrived in company with her family, all of whom are musical. Gottschalk and the Patti family became close, mostly performing separately after they left Havana, but meeting up at regular intervals.

It was because of my friendship with Gottschalk, while I was still in Uruguay, that I came to know Adelina's older sister, Carlotta. She too is a coloratura soprano, training with her sister for leading roles in grand opera. She is of great beauty and immense intelligence, and I was smitten with her from the start. When we were alone she and I practised operatic duets together, and through the agency who arranged the Patti family's bookings Carlotta and I began looking for opportunities where we might sing together.

Then she and her family announced they were going on tour, and I was cast into gloom by the thought of not being able to see her. Three days before they departed, Signor Patti approached me himself at Gottschalk's rooms and much to my surprise offered me a temporary job as managerial assistant. That is how I came to accompany them, leaving Louis Gottschalk alone but well occupied in Rio.

My role as managerial assistant was in name only. My duties mainly consisted in being present to take on any errand or task that was needed, and helping out with all the various logistical problems that arise when a long and complicated musical tour is in train. We travelled first to Buenos Aires, where the troupe spent more than

36

two weeks rehearsing for and then performing a gala celebration of popular operatic arias. I was kept busy, dealing with a seemingly endless series of small practical problems. I saw Carlotta every day, but the opportunity of private time with her was virtually non-existent.

Then we moved along the coast to the next engagement, in Porto Alegre, and unexpectedly we had to wait an extra five days before orchestra rehearsals could begin. Carlotta and I rented a small studio, and there we chose a duet that we both enjoyed, loved to sing together. It was *Brindisi, The Drinking Song*, from Verdi's *La Traviata*, the opera about a fallen woman.

Carlotta promised me that once she started her public performances she would, if called upon for an encore, invite me on to the platform to join her for a duet. As misfortune would have it, the one occasion when this was possible was also when I suffered the malaise I mentioned. It struck me down. It came from nowhere. It was inexplicable, terrifying, ruinous.

The call for Carlotta's encore came on the evening of the third recital, which was mounted in Porto Alegre's recently built opera house. The orchestra was in good sound, the auditorium was packed, the night was warm, the singers were inspired. I stood alone in the wings as I had done at the two earlier concerts, dressed in finery, nervous beyond description. Carlotta's singing was wonderful in every performance, but in truth the audience, exalted by some extraordinary newspaper reviews, had bought their tickets to hear her prodigious sister, Adelina. She was a phenomenon, and she was presented as the climax to the gala evening, following Carlotta.

That evening, Carlotta's final aria was Donizetti's *Il Dolce Suono*, from *Lucia di Lammermoor*. I had already heard her sing it several times, and it was so beautiful it made the breath catch in my throat. That night she was superb. My hands were clenched tightly because I was certain the audience would demand an encore.

The aria ended in Donizetti's simple, unaccompanied phrases. Silence. Then a spontaneous outburst of stamping, shouting approval from the audience. Flowers were thrown from the stalls, the circle and the loges, showering down on the lovely young woman I so adored. Everyone was on their feet with excitement.

Smiling and gracious, Carlotta beckoned to me in the wings. I strode out, suddenly free of the nervousness that had been gripping me. As Carlotta held up her hand towards me the audience cheered and clapped. She nodded to the conductor, a pre-arranged signal, and he acknowledged her. Members of the orchestra opened their scores. I was standing next to her. The baton was raised, the conductor was waiting for quiet. Then it happened.

Somewhere deep inside me there was a voice. Not a voice anyone could hear, but a voice in my inner self. It was in me, around me, pressing down. I was paralysed by it. I could barely breathe. I was half-turned towards Carlotta, half towards the audience. I was smiling. Beside me, Carlotta swept away, towards the wings, where another member of the troupe was standing in readiness. He was carrying a small tray with two flute glasses of champagne. She took them both from him, and the audience, sensing the perennially popular duet we were about to sing, cheered loudly.

The inner voice said what sounded like, 'Ramssi? Ramssi? Is that you, Adolf *ramssi*?' The voice was urgent, but hesitant, tripping over itself.

For a moment I thought it must be someone unseen behind me, but I could no more turn than I could lower my hand, from where I had been holding Carlotta's. She now was walking back across the stage towards me, both glasses held aloft. Spotlights picked her out. The liquid sparkled magically. She was smiling in anticipation, a stage laugh.

The voice spoke again, strained, but in English. 'Where – are you? Is that a theatre?'

Then a sudden silence from within. It came so suddenly it was a shock, but in fact it was the shock of a sudden departure, a return to normality.

I came alive – I was stunned by what had happened, but I had been released from the paralysis. Carlotta passed me one of the flutes, and we saluted each other by raising them. The audience roared with approval. The conductor swung his baton, and the familiar first four bars of *Brindisi* rose around us. I had to open the duet! I had to sing!

I sang – by some amazing fortune I collected my senses, drew at last a deep breath, and sang. Dear brother, that was the end of the incident, the attack, at least as I remember it. The next few moments were filled with excitement, glorious music, in full public glare, the need to perform charging through me unstoppably – the familiar song, the happy audience, the smiling presence of Carlotta, her wonderful voice. The words from Verdi's libretto: 'All is folly that is not pleasure.' So direct, so appropriate, so many underlying special meanings for me and Carlotta.

In the days afterwards the excitement eventually slowed and finally left me. I had time to reflect.

Somebody had spoken directly into my mind. Who

would do that to me? Who could? Where was he and what did he want? (It was certainly a male voice.) Why should he call me Adolf? I never use my full name, and neither do you. And *'ramssi'*? What could that possibly mean? What language was it? It sounded something like Italian, perhaps a tempo marking – but one I had never heard before. I later tentatively asked Carlotta if she knew what it meant, but she did not. She said it was not an Italian word. Had I imagined the whole thing?

That, I am afraid, is the conclusion I finally came to – that I had suffered some kind of strange and threatening fantasy. But it has happened only once, and I can't imagine how or when it could ever repeat itself. My dear Adler, if you have any advice or reassurance I will be glad to receive it.

Finally, I must describe the source of sadness that has blighted my time in Rio. When I returned from the tour (the Patti family moved on without me, but I hope and expect to see them again soon) I was anxious to be with Louis Gottschalk. I saw him as my only, my closest, friend in Rio.

I came to this hotel in Rio, where I knew he would be staying. I registered. I went to my room, planning to change my clothes after the long journey, then seek out Louis as soon as I could, but exhaustion overtook me and I fell on my bed and slept through the night.

The next morning I learned to my horror of the disaster that had swept over my friend while I was away. Louis suffered intermittently from recurring bouts of malaria, but I was told that while I was travelling he experienced a major attack. He had died in a ferocious fever at the same time as I was on my way back from Porto Alegre.

I hope you will share some of my grief over the sudden death of this marvellous friend, and brilliant musician.

Write to me soon, my dear Adler. I should like to hear your news and where you are and what you are doing. I hope we might see each other once again.

While in this spirit of brotherly love I have one last request. I can only state it plainly, while bitterly regretting the need for it. Adler, dearest brother, I am soon to be abject.

I have enough local money to last me three or four weeks, if I live plainly. After that I will be destitute, unless I can find temporary work of some kind. Please will you help me?

That wretched voice in my head, unexplained and madness-making, has somehow destroyed everything I was living for. You might say it is a coincidence, but almost everything I had before it has gone. I have lost my two best friends within the space of days. Gottschalk is permanently gone, and I have only the thin chance that I can trace Carlotta and her family if I move swiftly across this vast land. I helped create their planned itinerary, so there is real hope. American dollars are the universal legal tender here. Anything you can send poste restante to Rio I will seize upon with cries of love and gratitude. You know of course that when my circumstances change for the better I will try to repay you.

From your warm-hearted and anxious brother, with love and admiration,

Dolf Beck

In the spring of 1872 I said my farewells to colleagues at the Haddon in New York, and set out north and west on the newly completed railroad running between Chicago and NYC. I had been invited to work with the Dearborn Observatory, built in the grounds of the Old University of Chicago. Here they had the largest refracting telescope in the USA, and one of the most powerful of its kind in the world. The Dearborn had recently become renowned for the discovery of a small companion star to Sirius, the brightest star in the night sky. This was both exciting and annoying to me, because suddenly the Dearborn was high on the list of sites to be visited by everyone interested in astronomy. I had to wait for a free slot in what had become their busy schedule. It was doubly irritating because my own interest in astronomy was, in the terms the people at the Dearborn understood it, only marginal. I had applied to use not the main telescope but a smaller instrument, which was set up to make observations of the sun.

It was an important year for scientific study of the sun. About a quarter-century earlier a Swiss astronomer and mathematician called Rudolf Wolf had studied the history of the appearance of sunspots. These had first been systematically logged by the German astronomer Samuel Schwabe, as far back as the beginning of the seventeenth century. Wolf calculated that the sun has a periodic cycle of approximately eleven years, during which sunspot activity steadily increases then decreases. He measured and tabulated the cycle in which he had made this discovery, other astronomers confirmed it and ever since then the solar cycles have been carefully observed and recorded.

The cycles are simply numbered. Solar Cycle 10 had come to an end about six years earlier, and the next, SC 11, was estimated to have started about a year after that, in 1867. A solar cycle is only identified and numbered retrospectively, so although in practice a new cycle is already under way it will not exist until sunspot activity has been thoroughly observed and recorded. Astronomers fix the centre period of a solar cycle as the Solar Maximum, that is, when sunspot activity is at its greatest. After that the starting date can be firmly established. The situation as I travelled to take up my appointment in Chicago was that SC 11 was proceeding but it had not then been formally identified.

The unique aspect of SC 10 was that sunspot activity was high. This was for an eleven-year period: three and a half thousand days with sunspots, out of a total of about four thousand.

Sunspots increase the heat reaching our planet. The years 1855 to 1867, covered by SC 10, had experienced several unusually mild winters in the northern hemisphere, as well as three exceptionally warm summers. I had my own survey of British meteorological records, where the daily readings accurately reported the upsurge, and I had myself endured the baking heat, the humid air and the dusty streets of New York City for three of those summers.

I also knew from local reports, which confirmed my own observations, that during those years there was a noticeable impact on many of the Norwegian glaciers. These had briefly retreated, with a flooding release of meltwater, although their steady growth had resumed since.

It was this mounting evidence that prompted me to send off the application to the Dearborn.

xv

I arrived in good time, was allocated a room in the residence hall of the university, and in due course I reported to the observatory. I was greeted by a senior member of staff, Meredith

43

D. Hawkhurst, a woman of severe attitude. So formal was she with me that I assumed she saw my arrival as an interruption to her work, and a nuisance to the observatory in general. She told me that because of the recent influx of visitors their regular schedule of work had been delayed. She was correct and courteous to me, though, and took me on a guided tour of the telescopes and laboratories, introducing me to the people who worked on the permanent staff. She answered all my questions, tersely but informatively.

Because of her prickly manner I was nervous of Meredith Hawkhurst from the outset, but I also became increasingly uncomfortable about my presence there at the observatory. Meredith Hawkhurst remarked sceptically on the fact that I was a glaciologist specializing in climate aberrations. She appeared to wonder what I might gain from a telescope.

At the end of the tour Miss Hawkhurst took me to the basement. This was the Department of Heliophysics, the solar observatory.

It is of course impossible to view the sun with the naked eye, and certainly not through a magnifying lens. Instant and permanent eye damage would result. A solar telescope is set up so that its filtered image is projected vertically down through a series of mirrors and lenses to a pure-white hard surface. The image can then be studied at will, and there are various controls allowing it to be brightened or dimmed, or filtered in different ways, or enlarged so that segments of the image may be more closely examined.

Once we were inside the heliophysics area Meredith Hawkhurst became more relaxed and communicative. This was her domain. She invited me to take a position on one of the viewing stools beside the screen, and showed me how I could modify the image as needed. I was stunned by the brilliance of the sun's projected image, the pulsing movement and energy, terrifying but somehow comforting. She placed a dime on the edge of the image, as an approximate representation of the Earth's size to scale. She then showed me how the telescope had to be constantly rotated on its mount to keep aligned with the sun, told me how they coped when the sun was obscured by clouds, and talked about the need to relocate the observatory to somewhere that was either further away from the smoky atmosphere of the city, or high up on a mountain. I only half attended to what she was saying, fascinated by the awe-inspiring sight before me.

Two sunspots were visible, close to what could be called the solar equator. Apart from using smoked glass to steal a fleeting glimpse of the sun's surface, when sunspots are occasionally visible to the naked eye, I had never before looked properly at the sun. I was familiar with drawings or sketches of spots, but to see the actual events going on before me was astounding.

There were two areas to each one: the umbra, the dark heart of the phenomenon, and a surrounding penumbra, a deep red or dark orange.

Meredith Hawkhurst produced a long measuring scale, marked to the dimensions of the sun's image, and laid it across the spots.

According to this the larger of the two was more than one hundred and fifty kilometres in diameter, the other being about half that. She said that these were actually minor spots, and that when the sunspot season was at its peak there were usually several spots much larger than these.

The rest of the sun's surface pulsated with devastating heat and energy, with brighter, lighter flashes appearing regularly on all parts of the visible sphere.

It was a disturbing and frightening experience to stare at the fiery image, and to realize that all life on Earth, from a humble single-cell organism to the most advanced human intellect, owed its continued existence to this body.

xvi

Meredith Hawkhurst was apparently not one for small talk, so after I had stared at the terrible image of the glowing sun for a few minutes she moved me to a desk space that had been cleared on one side of the room. She warned me that many more visitors would be coming into the heliophysics department, to gaze, as I had done, at the sun. She would ensure I had full access to the many records and charts she and her colleagues had amassed over the years.

With that she left me to my own devices, so I settled at the desk arranging my notebooks, and so on. Earlier, during our tour of the observatory, she had led me to the document area and introduced me to the archivist. I went along to see him again. He showed me the drawers where the daily sunspot observations were filed. I selected a file folder which looked as if the dates coincided with SC 10, then went back to the desk to start reading, noting and tabulating the records.

In the middle of the day I noticed that the telescope was no longer in use and that the other people I had seen around the department had left, so I went in search of something to eat. Someone outside mentioned there was a refectory in the main building of the campus. As I walked in I saw that Meredith Hawkhurst was sitting alone at a table laid for two, and she signalled to me that I should join her.

As food was brought to us by the refectory staff, we exchanged fragments of information about each other.

She was intrigued by my name, and like many people she had assumed I was from Germany. ('Adler means "eagle", does it not?' she asked. I replied, 'In Norway too, but in Norway the name Adler mostly means Adler.') I told her briefly about my long interest in glaciers and what they could tell us as a warning about changes in climate, then why I had travelled to the USA, where I would go after leaving Chicago, and so on.

I mentioned I had a twin brother who sang opera – she shrugged, uninterested.

She told me in her forthright and candid American voice that she had qualified for entry as one of the first students at Girton College, Cambridge, in England. She was unable to gain a degree, which was not available to women, but she had taken the final examinations anyway, just because she could. 'They're real naïve about astrophysics at Girton,' she said. 'More like proto-astrophysics. I learned more about astronomy in high school.'

Her appointment to the Dearborn Observatory when she returned to America was the fulfilment of a young ambition. She hoped one day to ascend to be head, or at least deputy head, of Heliophysics. 'Before that, I need to get a degree from some university here in the US,' she said.

She added, speaking in a low and confidential voice, that she had had to overcome many career obstacles as a woman, but was intent on her purpose. If advancement did not come her way soon she would move. She had already received covert enquiries from other universities and observatories, including an offer for a research position in what was currently the most important observatory in the world, at Greenwich, London. She was still weighing up her options, as she did not want to leave the USA.

After these admissions, the confidential tone of which I had not been expecting, she fell silent. I think she was suddenly afraid she had opened up too much to me. We had only just become acquainted. We concentrated on our food until our plates were clear.

Then I said to her, 'I'd be interested to know what you have learned about sunspots.'

'They're not my main interest,' she said. 'I'm more concerned with solar flares, what causes them and their effect on this planet.'

'But you have a huge archive of sunspot activity. That is the reason I am here, because of the collection.'

'Sure, but if you want to talk sunspots you should meet with my colleague Reynard Schultz. He heads up the sunspot team. And he's head of our department.'

'May I meet Professor Schultz?'

'Well, not right now. He's working in the Philippines, where the US government is building a new reflector telescope. He won't be back for a while. He asked me to meet with you on his behalf, and show you what you need to see. Will you still be here next year? He's expected back in March or April, depending how well work on the new telescope goes.'

'I don't know,' I said. 'I might be back in New York. I haven't planned that far ahead.'

'It's not that I'm uninterested in sunspots – once you start solar studies you realize they are a part of the whole mystery of the sun. Have you come across the theories of solar wind?'

'The discoveries of Carrington and Hodgson,' I said immediately, because their work had been the subject of several recent papers in the scientific world. 'Coronal mass ejection, related to magnetic field imbalance, Richard Carrington said.'

'Same as sunspots. But flares can happen any time. They don't appear to have a sequence like the spots. That in itself might be significant. What we're doing here at present is trying to see if we can establish a pattern, if there is in fact a sequence that we haven't picked up on.'

'And the solar wind?'

'That's a science in its infancy. What we know from Richard

Hodgson's work is that the sun radiates an immense number of particles, which are ejected at speed from the surface in all directions, like a constant gale. You only have to go outside on a warm day to know that the sun provides unlimited heat, unlimited light. But you can't see or feel, or have any way of detecting, the particles it throws out. We know they are real, but as yet all we have about them is theories. They can't be harmful to life because the sun has been emitting them for millions of years, but we need to show that, prove it. Maybe there is something in the upper atmosphere that protects us. So far we have traced a connection between solar flares and the auroras at the poles. We have a couple of colleagues working on that right now.'

I was aware that the tables in the refectory were one by one emptying as people finished their meals and headed back to their tasks. Soon Meredith and I would be the only ones remaining. One of the staff came across to our table and took away our used plates.

'I'm convinced that there is a relationship between sunspots and climate,' I said. 'But it's hard tracking down corroborating data. I found out recently that sunspots were being observed and noted in Imperial China – I don't know how I could ever get access. Two thousand years of records. So tantalizing, knowing the information is there. So I have to concentrate on observations recorded in Britain, America and some of the European countries.'

'What we have here isn't nearly as much.'

'Dearborn's records go back as far as 1610. That's good enough for now.' I looked around at the nearly empty hall. 'Shouldn't we be getting back to your department?' I said.

'Of course. I'll see if Professor Schultz left any of his notes in the library. I know he came to a similar conclusion to yours: that although sunspots are actually cooler than the rest of the sun's photosphere, they appear during periods of increased radiation.'

xvii

For most of the remainder of the afternoon Meredith Hawkhurst was busy, engaged with two postgraduate students who had presented papers for evaluation. I began the long process of ploughing through the many handwritten notes that constituted the archive for SC 10. Towards the end of the day, Meredith came to my desk and gave me two huge bound folders, saying they had been deposited in the library by Reynard Schultz before he departed for the Philippines.

The next day I left aside the files for SC 10, returned to the archive hall and selected the records that covered the final years of the eighteenth century and the early years of this. This period had always been of interest to me, and coincided with Solar Cycles 4 to 7. It includes an event called the Dalton Minimum, which was named after the English meteorologist John Dalton.

The Dalton Minimum, which was observed and identified from conventional weather records, is recognized by climate scientists as a period from about 1790 until 1830, when winters were harsher than normal and the summers were shorter and cooler.

SC 6 included the year 1816, which was known both to scientists and to the ordinary people who went through it as 'the year without summer'. There has never been another year like 1816, at least within recorded history. That year, the longest period of 'normal' warm weather in Britain and Europe lasted just two days, with a similar experience in most American states.

Overall the weather was so consistently bad that temperatures averaged three degrees centigrade below normal. To a lay person that does not sound much, but in climate terms it was an average cooling that meant dramatic and unprecedented troughs of low temperature readings. It caused excessive rain to fall when only light seasonal showers might be expected. Where this heavy precipitation occurred, calamitous flooding followed. Worse, there were repeated occurrences of frost and snowfall during the months of June to August when none at all would normally be expected. The wind was chill and persistent. Crops failed all over the northern hemisphere and food was in short supply, leading to famine. There were massive movements of refugees and migrants. A wave of religious fervour swept through many of the worst affected areas, and violent crime increased dramatically. An epidemic of typhus broke out, causing thousands of extra deaths.

Anecdotally, I had already read of Beethoven's unhappy life in Vienna during 1816. He was shivering and suffering from catarrh all through that chill and fogbound period, his deafness acutely worsened by congestion. The English poet Lord Byron, sheltering in a rented villa on the shores of a storm-racked Lac Léman, wrote one of his greatest poems, 'Darkness', in that summer: *The bright sun was extinguish'd, and the stars / Did wander darkling in the eternal space, / Rayless, and pathless, and the icy earth / Swung blind and blackening in the moonless air.* One of Byron's companions in Switzerland, Mary Wollstonecraft Shelley, wrote her novel *Frankenstein* at the same time.

As a climate scientist, I knew that scientific assumptions about the cold summer of 1816, and the Dalton Minimum, were to an extent misread by others.

In the April of the preceding year there had been an explosive eruption of Mount Tambora in the Dutch East Indies, which ejected a huge quantity of tephra: airborne ashes, pumice, pyroclastic gases and microscopic particles high into the strato-sphere. The mountain had been one of the tallest peaks in the East Indies, probably more than fourteen thousand feet in height. After the eruption what was left of the mountain was less than half that. The rest of it was blown catastrophically into the sky. Tens of thousands of people were thought to have died, and hundreds of thousands more heard the tremendous explosions at vast distances. It was one of the largest and most sudden volcanic eruptions in recorded history, if not the most destructive of all. The debris from the eruption was taken up by high winds in the stratosphere and distributed around the world.

This would undoubtedly have had an effect. The dense layer of airborne particles alone would have filtered the sunlight and cooled the climate, and almost certainly produced the chilly summer of 1816. Spectacular sunsets were observed all over the world. In the northern hemisphere a persistent murki-ness shrouded most countries. It was called at the time a 'dry fog', filtering the sun and causing many people to suffer from breathing problems. The dry fog was not dispersed by wind or rain, of which there was much.

However, this eruption occurred in the middle of the Dal-ton period. There were severe winters and cool summers both before and after 1816. To me, it seemed relevant to try to align the appearance, or more correctly the non-appearance, of sun-spots with that period. Most of the weather readings from that period are the ones used by John Dalton, but his data were based heavily on the British records. I already knew that SC 6 had a long solar minimum – it would be instructive to compare the Dearborn's mostly American records with that.

There were other records I was keen to examine. The notes kept in Imperial China, tempting though they were, seemed impossible to get to, for reasons of distance, expense, language and much else. But I knew that the ships of the Royal Navy took regular and accurate measurements of air temperature, wind direction, sea temperature, and so on, at least three times a day. They maintained this routine no matter what else was going on, or where in the world they happened to be, but from my point of view the naval records were scattered. The Admiralty was reluctant to release them, or even make them available. They possibly saw them as part of their operational secrecy. More likely, they were unwilling to devote the time and effort to hunting them down from various ships of the fleet.

The systematic recording at the Dearborn Observatory was for my purposes ideal. I began transcribing the data to my notebooks, trying from the outset to create then follow a consistent format.

xviii

Twelve weeks later I was still engaged in the increasingly dull task of tabulating the sunspot record. I was determined to finish what I had started, and kept at it. There were occasional benefits. Being so close on a daily basis to the projected image of the sun's fiery surface meant that I could frequently look at it, and in some instances take note of how a sunspot first appeared, how it developed and how it eventually faded away.

I did an exhaustive tabulation of the sunspot activity during the Dalton Minimum, and eventually confirmed that throughout the period it was indeed greatly reduced. There were no spots at all at the time of the Tambora eruption, and none followed for more than eighteen months. Even in the periods of solar maximum in SC 6, when spots would usually be observed in great numbers, the sightings were few and far between.

Meredith Hawkhurst became a valued supporter and kept me abreast of other research developments. Sometimes, when the observatory itself was quiet, she would sit beside me and copy over some of the data herself. I admired her small and neat handwriting, a contrast to my own more elaborate scrawl. We often worked companionably together into the evenings, when of course the solar instrument could not be in use, and most of the activity in the building centred around the main refracting scope under its dome.

One evening we were alone together in the half light of the laboratory. Everyone else had left, or was in the next building with the refractor. Meredith and I were working in silence, side by side in the pool of light thrown on my desk.

I had no warning of what was about to happen to me, and I was shocked and disconcerted by it. Another incursion suddenly began, the first since that memorable occasion on Key Largo.

There was no warning, but because it had happened before I was in that sense prepared for it. As I heard and felt that sinister background hiss, not in fact at all in the background but some-how also around me, I managed to retain a certain detachment. I wanted to try to understand it, as well as suffer it.

A slight nausea and a feeling of dizziness swept over me, but otherwise I did not feel ill or that I was about to lose my balance. I was in fact firmly seated on my hard wooden office chair, both arms leaning on the surface of the desk. My left hand was resting on the pile of reports. My right hand held my pen above the notebook. I was staring down at one of the records for SC 8 – I noted the now-familiar mark someone had made to indicate the observation of a sunspot.

I was physically paralysed. Breathing was a problem. I could not move either of my hands, and my gaze remained fixed on the entry. Meredith was of course beside me. She was writing something in one of the notebooks. My thinking was clear, but the sensation of dizziness increased.

I was suddenly released, and normality returned. I was determined not to react to that. I had an urge to gasp, or exclaim, but Meredith was close beside me. I felt pent-up by the paralysis. I breathed out steadily, a feeling of relief. It made Meredith glance towards me.

'You went very still,' she said.

'Nothing wrong. Just a thought. It sometimes happens.'

My left hand moved to the next record which I pulled into the well of light. Meredith turned away from me and bent once again over her own notes. How could I say anything to her about what I had just experienced? I could not describe it because I had no idea what it was.

Then it happened again. I was still placing the sheet of paper in front of me, but when my hand became paralysed it slipped through my fingers and landed approximately where I was about to put it. Meredith showed no awareness that anything about me was different, but once again I was physically paralysed. I tensed against it. With an effort I moved my hand to lie it down on the document. The strain made my hand shake.

The hissing noise around me had returned, but this time it seemed louder, more urgent. I was certain Meredith must be able to hear it.

A voice said in English, 'Ramsey? Ad— Adolf Ramsey? Is that you?'

I urged to reply. All I could manage was a guttural sound in my throat. This alerted Meredith.

'Mr Beck, what is it?' she said. She laid a hand on my forearm. 'Did you speak to me?'

I strained again to speak, but without effect.

Inside me, the voice said, 'This is – an experiment. Adolf Ramsey, could this be you?'

Two things happened simultaneously: I was released, and the effort to speak broke out from me as a dry cough. I stood up in a hurried movement, pushing back my chair. It fell on the floor behind me. I staggered, reorienting to normality, and reached to take Meredith's outstretched hand for support. She seized my wrist, holding it tightly. I leaned forward across the desk, resting my legs against its hard edge, facing down, my head drooping forward. Meredith took my arm with her other hand. I found this calming and pleasant, but also awkward because our relationship was strictly professional and we had never made any kind of physical contact before, except in the most innocent and formal of ways.

'A sudden attack,' I managed to say. I could think of no other way of describing it. 'A storm in my mind. Is that possible?'

'A storm? Are you in pain? There is a doctor on the campus. Let me take you to the surgery.'

'No! No! I have already recovered. It was just a surprise, a terrible incursion of some kind. I thought I heard a sudden sound. A voice.'

'Sit down, please.'

She raised my fallen chair and moved it back to its position. She helped me lower myself into it, even though I had not hurt myself.

As well as being embarrassed by the state of paralysis and my sudden release from it, I was uncomfortable because of the unexpected and intimate contact with her and what it had been caused by. Also, I was smitten by sudden feelings of tenderness towards her, which until this moment I had been suppressing.

After so many weeks at the Dearborn a clear but undefined position had been established between Meredith and myself, that of professional colleagues working alongside each other. I had always abided by that and so had she. I knew little about her life, the family she came from, even the town where she had been born and brought up. I had no idea of her wishes or plans, or the people she knew when she was not at work, nothing I had not observed of her within this observatory. There was no acknowledged space for personal feelings. Even so, I often thought warmly about her when I was away from the building, having harmless dreams. Now I stared down dumbly at the documents on the desk, my notes, her notes, our two different kinds of handwriting.

'Is the voice speaking to you now, Mr Beck?' she said.

'I think I am feeling better.'

For the next few minutes I tried to find the words to describe or explain what had just occurred, and Meredith was sympathetic and interested, but obviously she could not have the least idea of what had happened. Nothing could explain it. Nothing rational, at least. Everything I said to her sounded to me unmistakably like the utterances of someone losing their mind. I wanted to put the intrusive event behind me, not try to find an explanation for it.

Meredith brought me a glass of water which I sipped but which I did not in fact need. I was feeling normal and rational, the incident already pushed into the back of my mind. Whatever it was, it had brought an end to the work we were doing. We put away our papers and notes, then walked across the quiet lawns, the air scented by the summer-warmed pines, to the main university building. Meredith told me she needed to refer to a book in the main library. I went to my room.

xix

As the summer came to an end and many of the trees on the campus turned red and golden and brown, my annotation of the sunspot record was nearing completion. I had to make a decision about what to do next, and that of course depended on a suitable research place. The Haddon still had a position open for me, but it was only for a few more weeks. Another choice would be to return to London and start work on the theoretical essay I wanted to write soon.

During those final weeks at the Dearborn I worked more or less alone, with Meredith occupied by her own researches. As a member of the permanent staff she was under no pressure to complete a particular project within a certain time frame, but she was constantly busy. She sometimes came to my desk towards the end of the day, and helped me with the more detailed tabulation work. We concentrated on the task, maintained our professional demeanour, and neither of us mentioned the intrusive event that had briefly brought us together.

More often than I had in the past I thought about my brother Dolf, away somewhere on the southern continent, living in the world of opera that I little understood. The voice that spoke in my head was addressing him, not me. Adolf, not Adler. His life was certainly more interesting than mine at the moment. We were now unalike in so many ways. As we grew up we became used to the fact that most people could not tell us apart. Sometimes we played along with that, sometimes we resisted it.

When we reached adulthood the similarity began to wane. Dolf and I were still physically identical, of course, but we dressed differently, had different circles of friends, and most importantly we thought and behaved differently. Since then we had drifted apart, tied forever by our family and blood but otherwise living as two separate beings.

Dolf had sometimes mentioned in his letters that he too occasionally suffered incursions of a voice trying to speak to him. Details from Dolf were spare, as usual. My own instinct was to look for details, try to establish a pattern, so that I could try to understand.

Dolf's most recent letter had been mailed from a small town on the bank of the River Amazon, a place called Manaus. Unless you were prepared to cut your way through uncleared jungle it could be reached only by boat. I had never heard of Manaus, but apparently it was important enough to have an opera house. Dolf had gone there to sing. He was in love then with a woman voice coach who, he said, had transformed his career. All his letters were excited and brimming with names of singers I had never heard of, operas by composers I did not know, and arias and choruses which Dolf had sung, alone or with others.

None of this meant anything to me, except that I was pleased by his apparent sense of well-being. Our interests were at least the length of the Amazon apart.

I checked the local poste restante office every week, but his letters to me were scarce. When he did write he showed nothing more than a vague interest in the work I was doing. I assume the letters I wrote had the same sort of effect on him in reverse. In one letter he asked me if I had ever heard of El Niño (The Child). In my ignorance I assumed it was probably a reference to some kind of church idolatry, or yet another opera, and ignored his observation that El Niño was something many people in South America spoke nervously about. I did not pick up the reference at the time. We all make mistakes.

xx

I was thrilled by the feeling that I was forming a coherent theory of climate upheaval, of climate change. It frightened me. A pattern was certainly emerging, and as the evidence mounted I realized how terrible it could be.

It seemed to me the science was overwhelming. Meredith had already shown me how she and the rest of her team had discovered and monitored a long decline in the size and frequency of solar flares. From sunspots alone, admittedly only part of the picture, I knew that over the last hundred years the grand solar maxima had borne an increasing number of spots, some of them extremely large even in the context of the sun. Against that, the solar minima, when sunspots were rarely or never seen, were lasting longer. That trend was continuing. Extremes were being established.

Neither had a predictable outcome, but the historical record showed that a long solar minimum coinciding with some other extreme cooling event could have a drastic effect – there would always be the upheaval of another hurricane, another landslide, another volcanic eruption, another earthquake. They were what often interfered with the assumed stability of the climate.

Until the intrusion of some such cataclysmic upheaval the change in the climate would be gradual, it would be slow, it would perhaps even start imperceptibly, it would not be noticed at first by most people going about their ordinary lives, and almost certainly it would be contested by other researchers and by industries and groups with a vested interest in the status quo.

My scientific knowledge would be challenged, my sources questioned, my motives cast into doubt. I was ready for that.

What I found more difficult was a private thought. I was dogged by it, the sobering realization that the changes I foresaw would not happen within my lifetime.

Mount Tambora would not be the final major eruption. One day there would be another, perhaps even more catastrophic. Solar minima occurred every decade or so. Glaciers melted less quickly than they refroze.

The outcome was becoming certain. More research was needed to back up what I had already learned, but I saw that as necessary confirmation only. The Holocene was coming to an end.

I calculated that before the last years of the twentieth century glaciers and permafrost would have spread unstoppably across most of the continental land of the northern hemisphere. The Antarctic ice sheet would spread across the southern oceans. A new ice age would have arrived, a long epoch of freezing, destined to last for several thousand years. It would bring to an end the world we knew.

3

Charles and Gregory Ramsey (2050)

i

Chad Ramsey had not heard from his brother Gregory in several weeks. Greg was a political journalist, working on a freelance contract for British National News – BNN. He travelled abroad at regular intervals, out of touch with home more often than not, but this most recent trip had created an unusually long silence. Chad knew Greg had checked in to a hotel in Budapest about two weeks earlier, but after a text message to his wife Ellie saying he was going off-grid for a few days nothing more had been heard from him. The TV station had also lost their line of contact. They all started to worry, because Hungary was politically unstable and Gregory relished that sort of challenge. He worked with a producer called Angie Sayeed, and a crew who had filmed with him on and off for more than three years, but whether they encouraged him to go it alone, or tried and failed to get him to stay within the government-approved compounds, Chad did not know.

Chad was standing on an unbroken spur of the former sea road, staring out at the remains of the town's old seaside pier when he felt the phone vibrating in his pocket. The rusty upright piles of the pier managed to hold on somehow, still visible and prodding up at low tide, although low tide had itself become something of a rarity. The sunshine on the white foam of the breakers was dazzling. Greg's name was on his screen. He turned his back on the sea.

'Greg?'

The line was clear, untroubled by interference, but there was a delay of about a second. A strong wind blustered in from the sea, hot and enervating, throwing flecks of spray from the waves and buffeting in Chad's ear. He had been about to turn away and walk home. Now he moved to a patch of shade cast by an advertising hoarding, putting him temporarily out of the direct sun but still in the hot and muggy air.

'Hi, Chad. Where are you?' Greg sounded distant but clear.

'Standing here, staring at the sea. Wishing I wasn't. More to the point, where are you?'

'I'm back in Buda, waiting to get a flight home. Perhaps later today, or early tomorrow. We didn't want to spend another three or four days on the train.'

'Greg – you must call Ellie. She's been worried sick about you.'

'I spoke to her a few minutes ago. And the kids. We're good. I was out of network range for several days, but I called her as soon as we were back in the city. Everything's fine. I'll probably be home the day after tomorrow.'

Chad had last seen Gregory around Christmas, when he and Ellie and the children visited and stayed two nights, although it was probably the last time they would make that journey. The distance from Scotland was too great, and there wasn't enough space at Chad and Ingrid's for two growing children.

While Greg was away working Chad made a point of watching TV every evening, looking out for news despatches on BNN, or occasionally his brother's written articles that were found in online news. Those had ceased a few weeks before as a result of a change of BNN policy about freelancers working for other outlets.

Greg had received a compensatory pay rise from the TV channel but it meant his visibility while he was away was reduced. That always induced nervousness about what risks he was facing. News media crews from northern European countries often encountered problems while moving around. There were constant hacking and security breaches around their equipment, and more and more news organizations had started to cut back. Reports sent in by local journalists working for agencies were increasingly common. Only once or twice in the last few weeks had Chad seen his brother's reports.

'You should check in at home more often,' Chad said. 'No news is worrying news.'

'I know. I do what I can. But I'm in safe hands. Ellie said you called her a few times, for which she was grateful, but it was impossible to get a signal here most of the time. Angie had a chat with Ellie earlier, reassured her everything was under control. That made up for a lot. I was OK, and I'm OK now.'

'What are you doing at the moment?'

'I'm hanging around in the hotel room waiting to hear back from Angie about the flight. She's downstairs at the desk. But Ellie told me just now that you had been sacked from your job. You've been doing the same thing for years. What happened?'

'Not sacked. Well, they called it constructive redundancy, with a lump sum pay-off. But they basically kicked me out, yes.'

'How do you feel about that? Weren't you getting a bit sick of it?'

'No,' Chad said. 'It wasn't like that. It had its problems, but I hadn't given up on it.' Greg had never really come to terms with the idea that his brother worked for the police, even as a civilian technician. 'I enjoyed the job,' Chad said. 'I got a lot out of it. I didn't want to lose it, but it started being difficult. A new superintendent was posted to the station, and he was put in charge of me. I'd never had that before. I was hired by the Home Affairs Office, so although I was in the station every day I was independent of the operational cops there. Then this guy came in. We never hit it off. Probably time for a change.'

'It's a chance for you to move away from Hastings, though?'

'Why should we? Ingrid and I like it here.'

'What about the sea? Isn't that a problem?'

'No more here than anywhere else along the coast.' Chad said. 'Perhaps better, in fact. Most of the town is above flood risk. Our house is high up the hill. And I can come down here to the seafront and actually see the state of things. Knowing what the sea is doing is important. Another big chunk of the cliff outside the town centre went down last week.'

'You used to take the sea for granted.'

'Not now – it wasn't always like this. There used to be a sea wall, and Bottle Alley finally gave in to the waves.'

Chad and Gregory were identical twins. Uncannily alike as babies and small children, their physical similarities had become less obvious as they grew up. Now in middle age they looked like brothers, not necessarily twins. Chad was marginally more corpulent than Gregory, but working on slimming down a bit. Years of sitting in front of a computer had given him a slight stoop, and he was trying to exercise his way out of that too. His more physically active brother was fitter, but in adult life Greg had been hospitalized for removal of two lower wisdom teeth, and as a result his jaw was slightly displaced to one side. Gregory needed spectacles, while Chad wore contact lenses. Gregory and his Scottish-born wife lived in a house on high ground in east Scotland, and they had two children. Chad was married to a Norwegian woman called Ingrid – they had no children. The brothers sometimes argued – they had different political views. Yet they were still close, and both felt the odd and undeniable bond shared by many twins.

Gregory and Chad had gone their separate ways as adults. They went to college in different cities, made new friends, developed different skills and interests. At present, with Chad living on the south coast of England, Gregory north of the border in a village near Dundee, they were more than five hundred miles apart, and in separate countries.

In the current political atmosphere Gregory Ramsey was seen by many, particularly those in the Westminster government, as a significant delver. Their term for a journo who stuck to the facts, Greg said. His track record of investigative journalism had made him few friends in either Edinburgh or London. He was assumed to be sympathetic to the left – but he always claimed independence of view. The mid-twenty-first century was a time of nationalism and demagoguery, in Britain and many other countries, although not Scotland. Greg's political viewpoint was not just a stance. He believed in democratic socialism. He was always being detained and searched when he crossed international borders, his Caledonian passport still, even after twenty years, a document that almost invariably attracted unwanted interest and interrogation. This was especially true when he was travelling into or out of Britain, as England and Wales were now collectively known. Chad's job with the British police was something he and Greg had long silently agreed not to discuss.

'Angie has just come back in,' Greg said suddenly, his voice sounding muffled as he placed his hand over the pickup. 'I have to go.'

'OK. When will we see you again?'

'I'll call you when I've been home a few days. I want to talk to you about something. How are you getting on with the search for Uncle Adolf?'

'The trail went cold a century and a half ago,' Chad said. 'I told you this after my trip to Oslo. And I told you again this year. Now I've lost my job I probably won't be able to access the police files any more. Anyway, there was nothing to find.'

'Yes, there is. I've been passed some extra information about him.'

'Uncle Adolf doesn't matter any more.'

'Perhaps not to you,' said Gregory. 'But I need to know.'

ii

Chad and Gregory Ramsey were born in 2002 – they were now forty-eight years old. Chad was named Charles at birth, shortened soon after by his father to 'Chas', then as toddler Gregory tried to grapple with pronouncing his brother's name he became Chad to everyone in the family. It stuck.

In the empty days since losing his job he had begun taking long walks along the Hastings seafront. He was developing a new and immediate interest in the present dangers of the physical world, in particular the state of the coastline. His absorption in his job, which had involved long hours in a cramped three-room office on the top floor of a twentieth-century block, had made him neglectful of the larger world. He had taken the general worsening of the climate situation for granted, hearing on the media about one crisis or disaster somewhere else, listening to the warnings from international bodies of scientists about global warming, learning about the extinction of so many species of animals, birds and insects, putting up with petty new restrictions on daily life. But now his time was his own he had begun to see things in terms of more imminent changes, directly affecting himself and the people around him.

In a place like Hastings the sea was prime. The threat it held was clear and ever-present. The damage it had already done was still evident to anyone who looked. Bottle Alley, as it was affectionately known by everyone who lived in the town (a long-gone builder had decorated the concrete walls with thousands of shards of broken bottle glass), was a semi-underground passageway alongside the beach. Built in the 1930s, partly for people to stroll by the sea while protected from the weather, but latterly in a generally dilapidated state, it had become a useful frontline physical barrier against storms. Fifteen years earlier, not long after Chad and Ingrid moved to the town, a violent storm with a high tidal surge had demolished most of it. A long section of the sea road and some of the buildings along it had followed Bottle Alley into the sea in one tempestuous night – large chunks of the old shard-filled walls could still be sometimes glimpsed in the shallows. A new, high-tech sea wall was hurriedly erected in its place, but that also fell foul of the sea a few years later.

When he was in his house Chad could not see the sea, other than a distant glimpse towards Eastbourne from an upper window. Hastings and its twin town St Leonards were on the same stretch of coast. On most of the days he went down to the front the sea was surprisingly calm, innocuous wavelets breaking with hardly a sound. But nearly all the old beach was semi-permanently under the waves, except where piles of rubble remained, and most of that bore a huge crust of plastic waste. More plastic rubbish came in every day. The frequent storms helped break up the unsightly encrustation, but it came and went with the tides.

Hastings itself was a hilly place, which in recent times had been its saving grace. It was built up and developed in the mid-nineteenth century as a fashionable and expensive watering hole. It had existed as a fishing village since before the

68

Norman Conquest, but by the time the developers arrived the fishing boats were barely operating. The village was physically expanded as a planned new resort, a holiday refuge for the wealthy and their families. The newly opened railway line from London brought the successful merchants, the factory owners and the financiers, with their retinues of servants, for vacations that lasted a month or more through the summer. The relatively isolated position of the town, the surroundings of open countryside, the stunning sea views and a generally benign and sunny climate made it a popular place. The First World War put an end to that along with much else, but afterwards, until the middle of the twentieth century, Hastings enjoyed a more democratic and affordable reputation as an inexpensive family holiday destination. The stunning sea views remained. Then public tastes changed again, this time in favour of package holidays abroad. The town fell into decline.

By the turn of the present century Hastings had reinvented itself as a place that fostered the arts. Compared with London and other coastal towns, property was inexpensive to buy or rent. Writers and artists drifted to Hastings, attracted not only by the lower prices but also by the spacious old houses and the promisingly fecund aura of seedy and faded glamour. The formerly decrepit terraces and shops began to be refurbished and put to new use. Theatre groups were started, an orchestra was formed, and galleries, craft boutiques and bookstores opened in the picturesque narrow lanes close to the seafront.

Then the changing climate took a hand. Gradually, atmospheric temperatures rose. The unstable climate produced erratic changes of weather, so although sometimes the summer temperatures were killingly high, there were also violent storms and spells of freezing.

For a coastal town like Hastings, the focus was on what the sea would do. The level of the English Channel rose steadily and unstoppably. Glaciers in the Antarctic calved off chunks the size of islands into the southern oceans. Apart from a few short frozen weeks in midwinter the north polar ice cap had disappeared. The centuries-old ice sheet over Greenland's vast mountainous interior was shedding millions of litres of meltwater every day.

Once again the nature and physical appearance of Hastings was changing. Most of the lower areas of the town, the homes and businesses along the coast road and up the former main shopping street, had been abandoned for at least a decade and a half. Many of the old buildings were derelict or their remains had been washed away by storms. There were still some intact buildings and other areas boxed in by ad hoc flood defences, but even they now looked as if they would be effective only for the time being.

iii

Until earlier in the year Chad had been employed by the British government's Home Affairs Office as a civilian worker attached to the police. The officers in his building, an admin office for East Sussex Police, addressed him as Inspector Ramsey. This was a nominal commission he had been awarded by the HAO advisory panel when he was first appointed two decades earlier.

His work was technical, specialist, a skill, an intellectual and rational process, an addendum to routine police work. He had never wanted to be a police officer. In fact, over the years he had developed a reasoned dislike for many of the worst attributes of policing, a dislike which increased after he suddenly lost his job. His brother's views had played a small part in this, but it was mostly the constant insider awareness he had necessarily picked up of attitudes and prejudices within the force, normally disguised or controlled for public view.

Chad had been married for around twenty-five years. He met his wife Ingrid while he was making a visit to Oslo.

One of the lesser reasons for the trip was that he thought it would be a chance to investigate the background of a distant relative. This was a great (multiple levels of great) uncle who, according to family gossip, was said to have served a long prison sentence in Norway after being involved in a famous scandal. Few details were known for sure. When Gregory and Chad were children, Uncle Adolf was a semi-serious legendary figure, whose reputation was sometimes whispered about conspiratorially by older members of the extended family. To the twins he was made thrilling by an aura of distant wickedness.

In 2023 Chad had just left university, had time on his hands and was intrigued by the thought of a disgraced ancestor, a genuine family black sheep. Uncle Adolf gave him an excuse to travel to Norway, a country he was curious about in any case, as he was one-eighth or possibly one-sixteenth part Norwegian on his father's side, the Ramseys. At that time air travel between places like London and Oslo was still relatively affordable if the tickets were bought ahead on the grey internet market.

Chad knew almost nothing about the Norwegian part of his ancestry. He did not speak the language, and with a feeling of guilt knew little of the culture of the country. Once in Oslo, and with the help of cooperative staff, he started a search through newspaper and official archives. He began with court records, then police and prison archives, but there was nothing at all about anyone called Ramsey, assuming the possibility that at some point one of the ancestors might have anglicized the name.

He spoke to an official at one of the libraries and described his problem. When asked the likely birth date of the person he was searching for, the best Chad could estimate was that it was during the nineteenth century, not certain when, perhaps even in the first half. The librarian told him that was a long period of hardship for many Norwegians, and a great number of young people had emigrated. Most of them went to America, others to Britain.

Knowing of course that this ancestor must indeed have emigrated and eventually established a family in Britain, Chad gave up that part of his search. Next he tried newspaper archives, thinking that if there had been a scandal serious enough to warrant a prison sentence then whatever it was must surely have been reported in the press.

He quickly discovered Norwegian newspapers of that period maintained a policy of stolid respectability. Information about churches, farming, social concerns, governmental matters, but not a hint of a scandal anywhere.

Chad was a young man on holiday. A day was time enough to spend searching dusty archives. Two weeks later he left Norway no wiser about his ancient uncle, but having met Ingrid, a student of foreign languages in her final year at university. They were attracted to each other from the start, a chance meeting outside a bookstore. They spent the rest of his holiday together, renting a car, driving to Bergen then Alesund, glorying in the stupendous scenery of mountains, glaciers and fjords, falling irreversibly in love. At the end of the fortnight his non-transferable air ticket meant he had to fly back to Britain without her, but she followed him a few weeks later. Not long afterwards they were married.

iv

Gregory returned home to Scotland and the following week-end he and Chad made time to go online and chat. Chad wanted to try out the new hardware he had been supplied with in the final weeks of his job, just before the axe fell. This was something known as an IMC. He was wary of it, and in fact most of his time spent using the IMC had been during an introductory training session, which had consisted of several trial demonstration runs. He was still not completely familiar with its controls, and some of the effects he had experienced during the demos made him nervous of trying it out. The IMC was said to be capable of many advanced techniques: using it for interpersonal communication was one of the simplest. That suited Chad.

When Gregory called they made visual contact through their laptops. Once they had acknowledged each other, Chad patched Greg into the new system. He did not tell his brother what he was doing, but after the switchover Greg noticed immediately that the visual image on his screen was immensely improved and the sound was clearer.

'You've cut your hair short, Chad. What made you do that?'

'I didn't have much choice. Something for my job.'

'The job you don't have any more.'

'I had no idea they were going to dump me at the time. If I'd known—'

'Let me look at you again.'

Chad did not want to say much about the IMC. The officer who eased him out of his job had warned him that the technology he had been equipped with was government property, it had a security rating higher than his, and use of it was closed and restricted within the English police force. Because of what had happened soon afterwards Chad no longer felt much loyalty to the old job, but he still had the hardware. It could hardly be taken away from him. Perhaps they should have thought of that before they put him on the induction course?

He subsequently discovered, through his friend Pat

O'Connell, that there was already a commercial version being beta tested. Pat, who was an independent AI consultant, told him it used the same architecture as the IMC. Although early models would be expensive, if the system became popular the price would plummet. Pat had never seen or used this other version, but the very fact of its existence seemed to suggest that the police system was not unique, that the commercial version was almost certainly compatible with it in some way, and in the end would probably supplant it.

Chad had used the kit so infrequently he was still uncomfortable with it. Any contact made through it had an invasive, tactile feel. He did not like the sensation much. Whenever he switched off he felt drained by it, mentally stupefied, a feeling that usually lasted a few minutes. But the system had its advantages. Speaking to Gregory online had such an intimate feeling of connection it was like being in the same room with him.

He turned his head to and fro in front of the laptop's cam, so Greg could see the bareness of his cranium. They both normally had full heads of hair, thickly growing, sometimes untameable, and the idea of shaving it away had never come up before. Chad was still uncomfortable with the feeling of nakedness, and now always wore a hat when he was outside, even when the sun was covered by cloud. The bareness was already a detectable fuzz – soon it would look like a close haircut, and within a month his normal untamed mop would have grown back.

He asked Gregory about his trip to Hungary and wherever else he had roamed while filming.

'It's tougher than ever,' he said. 'Here in Britain we know or think we know what's going on everywhere else, but you realize how comparatively insulated we are by being an island on the edge of the Atlantic. You don't want to believe that, or even think it, but it's true. It's still just about liveable here.

74

Mainland Europe is mostly a mess. So long as you stay within a large city or town, things are OK, depending on how the place is run. Budapest is all right because of the endless rules they have. You've probably heard about the army running the city and a few other towns in the big swathe of the country towards Croatia. But if you head out east, or to the mountains, you realize the world is going to hell.

'From a journalistic viewpoint there's not a lot of fresh news to report: migrants, refugees, private armies, land grabs, endless disputes about water sources, paramilitary groups. There are rackets going on everywhere. All this is real, all terrible, but no longer newsworthy, which I hate to admit. How many more starving children do we have to film? Anywhere south and east of Budapest is open season on refugees, a killing field. So we follow specific stories. This time we were trying to track down a self-styled warlord, with a huge private militia around him, but no one would speak to us, except off the record. He was expert at eluding us, although the evidence of his crimes was everywhere. We did send back several filmed stories, some of them about the terrible plight of the migrants because there sometimes seemed no alternative, but most of what I filed was spiked by the guys at BNN. I'm still trying to find out why.'

'Were they deliberately suppressing it?'

'Spiked, not suppressed. I did four of those reports and each one was scheduled to go out, but something else came along which they broadcast instead. I think the reality is much the same as we find when we're trying to get to a story: they think nothing new can be said now that's different from the reports they've carried for the last two and a half decades. One of the line editors actually said as much to me once. The climate catastrophe is probably the biggest news story ever, but it isn't being told. While we were in Hungary we found out the total world temperature increase since Industrial Revolution levels has reached two point eight degrees. We see the effects of that all around us, even here, but all we do is suffer it, not remark on it. That's what news gathering has become: we choose what we remark on, and other people choose not to let us.'

'Hasn't it been like that since we were born?' Chad said. 'All the warnings we were given were distant or general. We glimpsed terrible events in other places. I grew up thinking that the world was about to end, but we carried on at school, travelled around, found girlfriends, went to movies, bought things, drove non-electric cars, flew everywhere, but kept worrying.'

'The time for worrying has gone. It's coming to the point of no return. It's happening here and now, not at some point in the future. You and Ingrid don't have kids. But Ellie and I see everything in terms of Ken and Sadie – what all this is going to mean for their lives.'

Chad could see Gregory turning away from his webcam as he spoke, as if wanting to avoid the truth of he was saying.

'So what's to be done? You're not going to quit your job?'

'No, that's not an option – I need the money. Ellie wants me to quit, but when we talked about it most of what she wants me to do is cut out the foreign trips.'

'How do you feel about that?'

'I see her point of view. In some ways, the worst part of the jaunt I've just finished was the long trek across Europe by train. Uncomfortable, big delays. We were never in actual danger, but maybe we were lucky and didn't know it. Ellie seems to think so.'

Here they paused. Gregory looked momentarily distraught. He moved briefly away from the screen, and Chad saw the lighting change as the camera adjusted – the rest of the room behind him was better lit. He saw a low table, chairs, the corner of a TV screen, a pile of books, a scattering of toys, a door open to the rest of the house. Familiar pictures on the wall.

Then Greg returned, holding a small glass in his hand – the image of the rest of the room darkened again. Greg swigged whatever was in the glass. He changed the subject abruptly. He said he had noticed that the firth they lived close to had risen even further while he was travelling, or looked that way. Because it was tidal it was difficult to be sure. Whatever it looked like, of course it was rising. But their house was on a mound of raised land, in distant sight of the water, not directly threatened by it.

'We have to think about the children,' he said. 'Kenny should be going to college next year, and Sadie two years after. We could stay on here for a few more years, but things are so uncertain now. Where will the kids live in a few years' time?'

Chad said nothing for a moment. Gregory was voicing his own fears: the house he and Ingrid lived in was old, but still functioning, still habitable, but keeping it cool was a constant problem in summer, water supplies were intermittent, the solar panels were old technology and needed updating. He knew of other houses in his area where people had simply given up and moved out, unable to keep their places going. He could sink a lot of his redundancy pay-off into a series of repairs and improvements, but now his job was gone maybe it would be better just to move somewhere else?

Chad said, 'You mentioned Great-Uncle Adolf again. Why are you suddenly so interested? Can't you find out whatever it is through your own sources?'

'I've done some of that, but I hit a wall. Do you still have access to police archives?'

'Not officially, but unless they've changed the security protocols I can probably still get in.'

'What about court records and prison tallies?'

'Greg, this is a waste of time. I did a search years ago, in Oslo. You know that.'

'I've been told Uncle Adolf came to London during the 1860s. If he did, it would probably mean he was prosecuted here, not at home in Norway. You must be able to access British court records. You told me once that most of them had been made available on the net. I couldn't find any reference to him when I looked.'

'It depends on the outcome at the time. Each court was required to maintain archives for a minimum of twelve years, but after that it was a matter of available space, or lack of it. And a lot of paper files were destroyed during the Blitz, so it also depends on which court he was in. Anyway, what is this? I thought you were just curious about old Adolf, like everyone in the family.'

'It's more than that now,' said Gregory. 'I'm facing reappraisal later this year, and I have to apply again for the job I'm doing. The BNN management have introduced new standards for freelance contractors. It's a pain, and it's also ridiculous, but they've now extended the security check to include possible criminal activity in the family. In particular, parents, grandparents, and more or less anyone else since roughly the beginning of the twentieth century. They're using DNA sampling to trace and identify ancestors.'

'They surely wouldn't be interested in whatever it was Adolf was up to, a century and a half ago?'

'I thought the same. They say they screen out minor offences automatically, and anything that is no longer illegal by modern standards, or can't be thought of as serious now. But they still need to know. I went through a security check when I started working for BNN, and received full clearance. I never gave it another thought. But apparently they've dug into the family history and identified our great-great-whatever Uncle Adolf as someone with a prison record.'

Chad said, 'Adolf is a sort of family joke. It's all rumours, at least as far as we ever knew. And a scandal – what could that possibly mean these days? Something involving loose women? What shocked people a hundred and fifty years ago isn't going to seem much now. Anyway, all we know for certain about Adolf is that he ran away to sea and never came back.'

'Apparently he did come back. He went to sea when he was a young man. It turns out that years later, towards the end of the nineteenth century, he was living in London. He was in prison for some of that time. In fact, they say he served at least two long prison sentences, possibly three. That's in Britain, not Norway. He never went back to Norway, except for short visits before he was arrested.'

'Do they say what he did? Or what they think he did?'

'They say it was likely it was fraud involving vulnerable women. That's what creates a problem for me. Fraud is an offence of dishonesty. If he had just been misbehaving they probably wouldn't care. But in their eyes fraud is more serious.'

'What can I do to help?' Chad said.

'Turn up whatever facts you can. What he was charged with, when it was, how he was caught, that sort of thing. They also want to know if he pleaded guilty, or if he went to trial and was convicted on evidence. If it was fraud, see if you can find out who the victims were, and how much money was involved. Maybe they made a mistake and got the wrong guy – in fact for my purposes that would be best all round. But if he really was banged up two or three times it looks as if he did whatever they say he did.'

'You said they traced him through a DNA sample? Can I get hold of a copy of the report? If all this happened at the beginning of the last century that's a lot of time for DNA to be contaminated. I've known several cases like that. The police re-open a file because a DNA trace has come to light, but when it's forensically examined the sample is too small or too vague. Or it's been corrupted in some way.'

79

Gregory said, 'Not this time. The DNA is apparently sound. The case our uncle was involved in was notorious and the police took an interest in the outcome. When he was finally released, some of the clothes he had worn in prison were taken in by Scotland Yard. They have, or at least used to have, a sort of black museum of criminals' property and clothes. The DNA traces were taken from his shirt and pants, which were kept in separate storage. No risk of contamination. I already have a copy of the report. I'll email it to you. Could you get on to this soon?'

'How much time do I have?'

'I need it as soon as possible,' Gregory said. 'The actual date of the appraisal is about three months away, but if I could have it before then I'd have time to prepare.'

'I'll try. I can't go back into the office. There are definite limits to what I can do.'

Gregory said he understood. He clearly wanted to sign off, so they closed the connection. Instantly, Chad felt as if an eerie silence was hanging around him. He disconnected his new headset. The feeling of faint nausea from using the equipment swept over him. He stood up, breathed deeply a couple of times, drank a sip of water. The reflux gradually faded.

A few minutes later the air conditioning stopped working. Chad went down to the basement to try to find out what was wrong with it this time.

v

It had been more than a job for Chad, more than a career. A vocation, perhaps even a calling. It had suited him and he was good at it. At the beginning he had little idea what the work would come to mean to him but he grew into it quickly.

Not long after his return from holiday in Norway, while he and Ingrid were newly married and still looking for somewhere permanent to live, Chad was trying to find a job. He happened across an online advertisement for a psychological profiler, and applied for it as one of several jobs being advertised at the same time. The wording of the job description was vague, almost cagey. He did not know what the work might involve, but his degree from Bristol University was in cognitive psychology, so he assumed he would be at least an appropriate candidate for whatever it was.

A few weeks went by, during which he was interviewed for two other jobs, neither of which took him anywhere.

He had more or less forgotten the profiler job when he received an email asking him to present himself for an 'evaluative interview'. Three weeks later he spent two days in London being assessed by an employment panel.

He was interviewed in an anonymous modern office block in west London: while waiting for the meeting to start Chad could not imagine who he might end up working for. The roles of the people interviewing him were also unclear, although they all wore name badges. They described themselves as an advisory committee set up by the Home Affairs Office. The name badges all carried the HAO logo, as did the badge he was given to wear, which was marked *Mr Charles Ramsey, Applicant*. This electronically encoded badge enabled him to enter and leave the building during the course of the evaluation, and also to claim a free lunch on both days. Most of the panel were introduced to him by their position (civil servants), by rank and commission (senior police officers), and in two cases by name (MPs, at least one of them a junior government minister in the HAO). The work he would be doing was described in outline by one of the civil servants and on the second day he was given two example crime files to work on.

At the end of the process he was told that if appointed he would be awarded an honorary police rank, and that he would be working in a civilian capacity with East Sussex Police in Hastings. He should think of East Sussex only as a physical location. He would be employed directly by the Home Affairs Office, not by East Sussex or by any other of the individual police authorities. He was to be independent of the police officers he worked alongside. From time to time he might of course be consulted by officers from East Sussex, but only in the same way as any other police area. He would be answerable to all of the thirty-eight police commissions throughout England, and would on occasion be seconded to work with Scottish and Welsh police forces. Case files would be passed to him for interpretation only by senior officers.

Two weeks later he received a written offer for the job, and a contract of employment.

That was how he and Ingrid ended up moving to Hastings. She almost immediately found work as an interpreter at the international convention centre in town – it was intermittent employment, but well paid. Between conferences she took on translation work for businesses and a couple of academic publishers. Her languages were German, French, Swedish, Norwegian and English.

They found and bought a house on one of the hilly streets of the upper town, a place built at the end of the nineteenth century and in need of remedial repairs. Chad was paid according to a graded civil service pay scale, so the necessary costs were relatively easy to meet. In addition to general repairs, they arranged for solar panels to be fitted to the roof, and an extra set mounted in the rear garden. Air conditioning was installed throughout the house, and an emergency backup generator went into an outhouse against the rear wall. This was in the mid-2020s, a time when the signs of a coming climate emergency were unarguable.

When the first major storm surge occurred in the winter of 2029, Chad and Ingrid realized that because the house was positioned well above sea level, they had made a fortunate choice.

Hastings now had a hot, cloudy and humid climate which continued for all but a few weeks in December, January and February, when it sometimes became very cold indeed and the danger from storms increased. Snowfall was rare, but a blizzard had brought most of the south coast of England to a halt in January 2036. Every year's weather was different in detail, but from about March onwards each year the full weight of anthropogenic climate warming set in — until the end of April a dirty, sand-filled rain poured almost every day. The meteorologists said large areas of southern Europe had become a dust bowl, and the grit was being picked up by the prevailing winds. Then it was full summer: daytime temperatures regularly achieved the high thirties and low forties Celsius, a breathless, killing heat, which receded only slightly at night. The insistent sea ate away at the shoreline, and along the wilder cliffs to the east of the town there were many landslips and collapses.

Most of the town was built on a long spur of shale and greensand downs, which meant the upper areas would probably continue to survive the regular flooding from the sea. What the social and economic cost of that would be was difficult to estimate, but the higher parts of the town would almost certainly become an island within the next few decades.

Hastings was surrounded by low-lying land to the north and west: beyond Hastings was the Weald, open countryside, formerly agricultural land and woodland, but here the ground was already inundated by high tides filling the valley of the Rother, and most of the farmland had become unusable. The Weald was threatened by extra flooding whenever there was heavy rain.

This was not unlike the situation along the North Sea coast on the eastern side of the country, where years of erosion had long ago caused cliffs, dunes and other natural barriers to break down. In East Anglia, Lincolnshire and a huge part of Yorkshire around the Humber estuary, large areas of land, always prone to subsidence, had been regularly flooded for years.

Life in Hastings, and other areas of Britain surviving the changes, went on with a sense of consensual normality. In fact it was a form of collective cognitive dissonance. The rest of the world was in a bad shape – no one could avoid knowing about it. The litany of fresh disasters was listed every day, every week. Countries on the Bay of Bengal were inundated, and much of Kolkata had been evacuated. Jakarta, the Pacific Islands, the Netherlands, the massively industrialized Pearl river delta, the shallow Venetian lagoon, the eastern seaboard of the USA – all were flooded or unlivable. Hundreds of other lesser known areas, each with its own calamity, deaths in the hundreds of thousands and millions, migrants and refugees spreading out across the world. Wars in a score of places, or at least an extreme form of military suppression used against the helpless but desperate population. Famine and drought were suffered in almost every part of the world; everywhere was hot. Viral diseases spread across the world. There were shortages of some kinds of food, but not always the same in every place. Governments all over Europe, the Far East and the Americas had become increasingly authoritarian, but also ineffective because of innate corruption.

But Chad had a liveable home, and he and his wife both pursued active professional careers. Ingrid had become a distinguished and prizewinning translator of books and scientific papers. Chad was absorbed by his work as a psychological profiler.

From his first day in post Chad had to learn profiling by doing it. He knew of no other profilers working for the British police, although in the USA many city-based police forces used them. The FBI in particular had pioneered the technique.

Some of the FBI profilers performed seeming miracles of forensic deduction, working behind the scenes, but others had made themselves into media personalities and pundits, their self-aware appearances on TV reality shows and advertising campaigns removing their anonymity and undermining their independence. They uploaded videos and published books on the technique, which Chad of course consumed with interest. These celebrity profilers naturally recorded only successes: strokes of deductive genius, special insights, hours of paperwork research, possible psychic intuition, hard experience, sheer good luck. Failures were recorded only as partial, or as the result of poor police work. It was more of an art than a technique. Sometimes it was showbiz.

Chad had retained the two sample cases he was handed to examine during his evaluation. At the time of his interview his degree course had receded to a vague memory, and he had no experience at all of forensics. Common sense and intuition were most of what he had to work with. He studied both files again, this time with renewed interest.

Both were real murder cases. Both had defied conventional police methods of detection, with no clues in either case as to the identity of the killer. Because in the end the names had been established it was possible in each case to reverse-engineer the known facts, the evidence, the interviews, pick up the tiny hints or lies or mistakes or gaps that had in the end led to successful prosecutions.

Once he started work in earnest Chad realized successful profiling relied mainly on expertise and experience. It consisted of detailed re-examination of the evidence collected by the police, sifting what might be relevant from the flood of eyewitness claims, time-wasters, overzealous citizens. For the first few weeks he was learning as he went along. Several unfinished files had accumulated in his new department, cases a long time in limbo, sent in from across England, while waiting for someone to be appointed.

The self-publicizing behaviour of so many profilers in the USA had created a negative image of the work in the minds of many police officers. Chad soon detected an attitude towards him, somewhere between polite but grudging admiration of his position, and resentment of him as an intellectual who appeared to think he could magic a solution out of a mystery that had left them baffled. Chad felt from the outset he was not being taken seriously, or at least would not be until he came up with plausible results. He soon became used to, and tired of, the same old jokes about crystal balls, palm reading and tea leaves.

For most of his years of police work Chad operated from a cramped suite of three small offices on the top floor of Hastings Police HQ. The building was one of the largest in use by the East Sussex force, but the staff had had to make room for him, an early source of office resentment. He was allocated a Home Affairs Office budget to employ assistants, and after a few weeks on his own he was in charge of a team of five, two of whom were full-time, and the others who came in on various days of the week. Theodore, one of the people from the town, was a mathematician, a young guy from the Netherlands called Taïs was an AI specialist, one of the part-time workers had a degree in social history, and so on.

The real work of a criminal psychological profiler was deep research based on physical evidence, documents and witness statements. Once things settled down to a routine the normal workload ranged between five and ten ongoing police investigations at any one time, some more complex and intractable than others. Chad's function was to read and understand the evidence the police had turned up, listen to or read or watch videos of witness accounts, and to exercise judgements based on what could then be learned, using past cases as precedents.

His team made continual use of computers, as most of the investigative files that came to their office were already digitized. But Taïs additionally used AI engines to make connections, show trends and directions, eliminate the unlikely. He and Chad sometimes worked with Patrick O'Connell, who ran an independent software consultancy from a site on an industrial park in St Leonards.

Pat was a regular visitor to the building for routine software maintenance, and often called in informally to see Chad and the others. He was fascinated by the general idea of creating a psychological profile, and sometimes would offer ideas for approaches to certain problems concerning the weighting of some kinds of data against others.

Profiling required practical input. Chad and his team worked from historical principles, demographics of population intensity, ethnic breakdown, unemployment figures, crime statistics, the incidence of use of illegal substances, children known to be at risk, standards of housing, the presence of domestic violence offenders. The place or location was relevant, the pattern of criminal activity in the town or district, the activities of gangs or organized crime groups. These and many other social vectors ultimately had an impact on crime, and who was likely to commit it.

Above all, a profile was compiled with common sense. It did not take an expert to realize this, but it did require experience and aptitude to move from the general to the specific.

Intuition was a part of it, but a small part. Chad learned the art of knowing when to follow a hunch, or respond to a sudden idea. A profiler would rarely reveal their method to an operational police officer. Most cops see themselves as uncomplicated hands-on officers, dealing daily with rough physical reality. For them, intelligence and contemplation, not to mention insight, are alien and unnecessary when chasing after or catching an offender.

At the end of the profiling process, Chad or his team gave an opinion on who the perpetrator might be, either by name, if the police detectives had been working with a list of suspects, or by general psychological profile, or sometimes by location. Sometimes they were asked to confirm or establish a motive. In other cases, where an offender was on the run, they would suggest likely hiding places or the identities of other people who might be aiding them. In certain cases they might be requested to give an opinion on what the perpetrator looked like, or the nature of their work, or if they had a prison record, and so on.

Chad and the staff completed about one profile every week. They were not infallible. They accurately predicted the identity of the alleged criminal, or sometimes the *modus operandi*, in about two thirds of the cases that came into the office and which were eventually supported by the courts and juries. They had near misses too, and they also made mistakes.

Out of the office, when asked what he did for a living, Chad was likely to prevaricate. He was reluctant to say to people he met socially that he worked for the police, because it usually raised an agenda of opinions into which he disliked being drawn. He saw his work in the abstract.

He rarely met the officers who submitted the cases to him from other parts of Britain, and he had no contact at all with anyone involved in the cases. They were just names to him.

Sometimes he would see mention in the media of the conclusion of a particular matter: an arrest, a court case, a conviction, and then he would realize he had played a part in the process. One particular case was memorably complex and involved multiple incidents. He and the others wrestled with it for nearly two years – eventually it reached a conclusion, and the file was closed. He remembered that one.

vii

The first sign that Chad's career as a civilian profiler was about to come to an end was the appointment of a new senior officer, Superintendent Thomas Amos. Officers constantly came and went in the office building, but because he was directly employed by the Home Affairs Office and therefore independent of routine police matters, Chad took little interest in who they were or why they were there.

Supt Amos turned out to be different. His arrival coincided with a message from the HAO to Chad, requesting him to work alongside Supt Amos as part of a new management initiative intended to engage operational officers with ancillary and backup functionaries. The news that he was considered a functionary should have been warning enough.

Amos walked into Chad's office the day after his arrival, and cheerily introduced himself. He said he was pleased to meet Chad and assured him of his total commitment to profiling. Chad should understand that the chain of command had been altered, so that from now on he would be reporting directly to him, Amos. Chad was to address him as Tom.

Chad bit back his feelings and politely introduced him to the members of his team who happened to be in the office at the time.

Amos returned the following day. He asked to be shown the papers Chad and his team were currently working on. Much of it was online, or in computer documents. The case had come into Chad's department only the day before. Chad led his new superior through the progress of the original investigation as they had so far analysed it, the difficulty the detectives had experienced with one of the witnesses, a long interview with a man originally accused of aggressive wounding, later released without charge, the evidence that appeared to incriminate someone else but was later found to be untrue. The aggrieved person, victim of the wounding, had moved abroad, but recently returned and was believed to be known to the attacker. He now claimed there were three attackers, not one. A certain name kept being mentioned by two of the witnesses, but the police had not been able to trace that person. It was neither a particularly difficult nor complex case, but no one had yet been charged with the offence.

Amos listened in silence, then said he would consider the matter himself. He scooped up what papers there were, and insisted that Chad should forward the digitized material straight away.

The following week Amos strode into Chad's office and laid the file folder on his desk. He said he had already transmitted back the data files. He pulled up an office chair so he could sit alongside him. Chad opened the file folder, saw a sheet of paper with handwriting on it, and beneath it a page of his own preliminary notes, apparently printed out from the computer. He could see straight away that some of his notes had large 'X's beside them, and others had red highlighter over certain phrases and sentences. Several had lines through them.

'This is a confidential investigation in progress,' Chad said. 'You shouldn't have marked my notes.'

'They are there to help me go through them with you now. I want to learn the way you're thinking, what it is about your approach you think a well-trained cop wouldn't be able to understand.'

'I can't discuss it with you,' Chad said. 'The case has come from another force, and it's a confidential matter between me and them.'

'That system is changing, Inspector Ramsey. Now, show me how you have applied your special methods to what looks to me like an open and shut case.'

That was unlikely to be true, as the investigation in Manchester had already run for several months and the case had come to him from the highest level: the Assistant Chief Constable. Chad outlined the salient facts of the case they had identified so far. There was not in fact much to say – they had barely had a chance to get started on it.

Amos appeared to listen closely, but then seemed to lose interest.

'I'm ahead of you on this, Chad,' he said. He pushed back his chair and stood up. 'You talk a lot of jargon, and they're paying you money for that.'

Chad said nothing. He had heard this sort of thing many times in the past, and usually found it best not to argue.

Amos pointed at the bulky apparatus that had been placed on top of one of the storage cabinets behind Chad's desk.

'I see you've been talking to O'Connell and his people,' he said. 'I was told about this when I came in last week.'

'I don't know much about it,' Chad said. 'Pat brought it in two or three weeks ago and said he wanted to do more updates.'

'Mr O'Connell told me it was in full order.'

'Then Pat would have also told you he and his company are still working on an upgrade. He described some of its features when he brought in the hardware, but I'm waiting for him to come back and go through it with me. I'm expecting him later this week.'

'You know what it does, then?'

'I know what it's supposed to do. It hasn't been tested yet.'

'O'Connell told me it's probably going to put you out of a job. How does that make you feel?'

'Pat said that?' Chad was surprised, as Pat was usually taciturn about the technology he developed, and especially cautious about making claims for a prototype. 'It can't be used for psychological profiling, Tom.'

'But it sounds to me as if it will make your kind of profiling a thing of the past. We have to move with the times. Most of these cases produce a mountain of paperwork.'

As if that was a clinching argument, Amos left the room. No more was said that day.

Chad had grown to trust Pat O'Connell's knowledge of computer technology, and his general software engineering skills. From time to time Pat had given Chad small improvements or upgrades to the software he routinely used. What Pat and his team had been developing, and this was the prototype presently occupying the top of the cabinet, was something that still did not have a name or a descriptor but which Pat summed up as a digital visualizer of forensic traces, including DNA. It was not a new idea as such, but an experimental way of linking various strands of recent AI developments into a formalized process.

Development of the system was currently on hold, Pat had told him, because the police were introducing a new electronic tracking and communications system. It was called an IMC, not his baby and not the same thing – the hardware and the IT were being bought in expensively from the USA. The HAO was being secretive about the IMC, but Pat said he had a good idea what it might be. It was a system that had been discussed in gaming and tech circles for some time.

Pat had already run a brief demo of the visualizer for Chad, using some of the data from one of the profiler files he was then working on. It seemed to have some potential but for now, until he heard more from Pat, it was an unknown quantity. Chad wondered why Amos had shown an interest in it.

viii

Chad sometimes thought the world was becoming obsessed with gadgets. Maybe that was an impression created by the police he worked with and the Home Affairs bureaucrats he worked for, who all seemed easily impressed by electronic novelty. Digital timers, voice identifiers, position locators, vehicle trackers, electronic nightsticks — all of these and many more crossed Chad's desk, trial versions lobbed into police stations by hopeful tech developers, none of the things of any interest to him except as momentary novelties. Most of them were routinely passed over by the police authorities because of funding restrictions. But every now and then one of them, often the most unpromising, would be taken up and authorized and bought in bulk, budget limitations suddenly no longer a problem, and handed out to every operational copper. They were rarely used and usually forgotten, except as one more piece of tech the officers had to put up with swinging heavily from their belts, until replaced by some other piece of experimental gadgetry.

There were two gadgets, though, which were about to change Chad's life. One was the prototype forensic visualizer, not yet in workable condition, that Patrick O'Connell had brought to his office. Chad exempted Pat from the category he privately called the crime-stopping wizards. He knew that a fast-responding identity checker, simple and effective to use and developed by Pat's firm a few years earlier, was still in regular use across the country.

But a second gadget was about to land in Chad's life, unexpected and unwanted.

An official communication arrived in his inbox from the HAO. He was informed that he had been selected to take part in a residential training course at a convention centre somewhere in the east of England. It would run for two weeks and would provide foundation training for a nationwide launch of a new generation of police communications.

Chad wanted to refuse it. Those were two weeks he did not wish to waste doing the kind of training he knew he would almost certainly never need. He sought more details, asking the HAO in particular why a civilian worker in forensic investigation needed that kind of training.

The response came not from them, but through another visit from Superintendent Amos.

'It's mandatory training,' Amos said. 'You'll be sent an email with all the details.'

'I've received an email.'

'You'll be sent another. This is a new initiative, adopted throughout the country. You have to be involved because much of the training includes increasing officer awareness of the work of specialist experts like you.'

'So is it a course in psychological profiling?' Chad asked.

'No – it's about improved communications. You'll find out when you get there.'

ix

Long past its great years as a country residence, the rambling old building where the course was held was set on a shallow hill surrounded by unremarkable countryside, a few miles to the west of King's Lynn. It was now used for business seminars, conferences, workshops, conventions and training courses. The extensive grounds were intact but overgrown. This was February and a bitterly cold wind from the east blustered throughout the early days of the first week. Away from the function areas the rooms were poorly heated. Because of the long summer heatwaves and the uncertainty around winter temperatures, the heating had been disconnected from the corridors and stairwells, and worked only intermittently in the guest rooms. The fen visible from the house had been inundated by the sea, and had rims of ice at its edges. The brackish water was often shrouded in mist and its briny smell could be sensed in most parts of the house. The floors in the old building creaked, doors would not close properly and there was a general sense of dampness.

Chad arrived late after a complicated train journey with several station interchanges. Most of the other delegates were already present. He felt distanced from the event, seeing himself, at least at first, as an observer rather than as a participating trainee. Everyone except him was a serving police officer. There was a cross-section of ranks: a few detective constables, some sergeants, and the rest were at inspector level or higher. They came from forces all over the country. In total there were about thirty course members, with an approximately even spread of genders, the women slightly outnumbering the men.

As with other training sessions he had been required to attend in the past, the first evening was set up as an ice-breaking social gathering in the bar. Chad moved around, hovered, drank a few glasses of wine, introduced himself, did not have much to say. He had never found off-duty cops good company.

Everyone had been given an identity badge, each of which gave the officer's rank and name, beneath that the single name by which they would like to be addressed. Chad's identified him as an inspector who should be called Charles. The course leaders encouraged everyone to circulate and to learn the names of as many people as possible.

The five instructors were also police officers, three men, two women: Ali, Toni, Jacek, Imaya and Helmut. Jacek appeared to be the spokesperson or coordinator for them all. They carefully addressed everyone as Sir or Madam.

No one asked Chad what his role was within the police, and the subject of profiling did not come up.

When he was in his room at the end of the evening he peeled off the plastic cover of his badge. He crossed out the 'Charles' and replaced it with 'Chad'.

The next morning, after breakfast, the course leaders shaved his head, everyone else's too, women as well as men. Chad protested, as he believed his role as an observer meant he should merely observe.

'You signed the consent form, sir,' said Ali, one of the five young trainers, now wielding the electric clippers.

'I was not expecting this,' Chad said, squirming on his seat while another course instructor attended to the woman officer in the place next to his.

'I think you'll find it was on the consent form, sir.'

Ali and his clippers went to work. Chad's hair naturally grew thickly, and neither his father nor his grandfather had been subject to male-pattern baldness. Chad was expecting to keep his hair for as many years as they had. The clippers left a faint shadow of uneven fuzz.

Apart from five of the male officers, who had already shaved their heads by choice or were naturally bald, the course participants mostly reacted uncomfortably. The women officers seemed more phlegmatic about it. One of the younger men briefly started wearing a cap. But the shaving brought an unexpected uniformity, a levelling of the ranks. They had become a meeting of domed heads.

Chad could not stop running his fingers over his brow: the novelty of a smooth bony cranium, the feeling of the lightness of the remaining bristles, surprisingly soft. He felt unprotected and chilled when he moved through the building's unheated corridors.

In the evening of the same day, after dinner, they were shaved a second time, now with care and precision. Afterwards, Chad's head was completely smooth with not a trace of stubble. The trainers advised them to shower every day, washing the tops of their heads night and morning. They handed out a thin, odourless cream to rub into the skin. It would help the hair to grow back more quickly, they said, and meanwhile would keep the exposed skin soft and pliant.

Alone in his room Chad stared at himself in the mirror in the bathroom, reacting to the novelty of seeing the naked shape of his head for the first time. He kept touching it with his fingers, fascinated by the sensation. When he went to bed he was aware of the feeling of the pillow beneath his head.

x

There followed lectures and demonstrations by the instructors, and role-playing exercises, and through these they were introduced to the world of instant mental communication, or IMC as it was known. This involved the implantation of not only a microscopically thin graphene shield, fitted snugly and permanently to the freshly bared cranium, but also the drilling of two holes, small in diameter but painfully deep, in the part of the temporal bone called the mastoid process. Two police surgeons arrived at the conference centre specifically to carry out this work. The delegates were assured that the nanoshield would not prevent their hair from growing back naturally.

The officers Chad was training with had been selected to trial IMC, and later to field-test and evaluate its functionality in live operations. He was included. No one appeared pleased to be there. Many were given plasters for grazes from the clippers, or to help heal the piercings in the sides of their heads. Conversation became subdued. The bar was almost empty in the evening – three of the male officers who had already shaved their heads were drinking together.

Towards the end of the first week the weather suddenly changed and warm sunshine began to play on the grounds outside the building. For the first time since he had arrived at the conference centre Chad was not uncomfortably chilled, and by midday everyone had their jackets off and the function room felt stuffy. The sun blazed down. There was a light breeze moving through the trees and the salty smell from the fens increased. The weather channel on Chad's laptop said that an area of high pressure was stationed temporarily over the north of Europe. This meant the days would be warm, the nights cool. Everyone was nervous about the hot weather arriving so early in the year, as it frequently led to sudden and violent storms.

Moved to the outside patio in the afternoon, the delegates were made to rehearse their familiar police jargon, which they were told would soon be made redundant by the IMC. It was treated as a game – forces in different parts of the country had their own shorthand and code. Most of the cops found the contrasts amusing. Soon, they were told, all contact between national forces would be uniform, initiated by gestures and head movements, the officer's identification and location being factored automatically into every order, request, message or report.

The next morning the countryside was windless under a hot sun. They heard no birdsong. Seagulls wheeled above the fen, whose glittering surface could sometimes be glimpsed in the near distance through the leafless trees. After half an hour the session moved back indoors – two or three of the attendees reported that their unprotected heads were feeling the burning effect of the sun. Chad's own head had started to itch.

Jacek led the next session. He began by informing them that the graphene nanoshield was permanent. It could never be removed except by an expensive and possibly hazardous surgical operation. But there would be no need to take it off: it was inert and harmless and within a week they would forget it was there. Within three weeks their hair would have grown back enough to hide all trace of it. The shield could be left in place indefinitely.

'One day you will die in this cap,' he said morbidly, and they reacted with the sort of thin half-laugh given when you realize someone has made a joke but you don't find it amusing. 'It is properly described by its initials: IMC. That stands for both the process and the hardware. It works by channelling electronic activity within the stress fields of the graphene nanoshield. It is effectively invisible, and its presence will certainly be undetectable by the sort of people you have to deal with. They can't grab it or disconnect it, and in most cases they won't even realize it's there. It is self-cleaning, self-adjusting and upgrades are transmitted to it automatically. We will activate the IMC soon and you will immediately understand its potential, the way it will revolutionize police work. It is already being trialled by the Hampshire force, and you will be joining them. IMC will soon be standard police equipment throughout Britain.'

Later, tiny graphene batteries were inserted into one of their two newly drilled sockets behind the ears, a connection was made to some other metal object that was slipped inside the other, and the nanoshields were ready. The course instructors made sure everyone was seated, then Jacek told them he was about to activate everyone's IMC at the same time.

'After you leave this place at the end of the course,' Jacek said, 'you will be required to be inline whenever you are on duty. You are not supposed to use the shield out of hours. When I activate the IMC it will be for only a couple of minutes. After we deactivate, you will have a chance to discuss with me and the other instructors what you experienced and how you feel about it.'

He gave no warning about what then immediately followed.

There was a brief sensation of false silence, like a radio tuned away from a station but emitting carrier hiss. Steady, almost silent. After about five seconds it was broken. A word, a shout, a rasping noise. The world Chad had believed was his alone, known only to his inner thoughts and self identity, came to an end. His head, his entire being, filled with sounds, voices, shouts, grunts, sharp intakes of breath, inexplicable jabbing noises, loud fearful moans. A turmoil of conflict, seeming to come from behind him, beside him, but mostly arising from within.

He lost all sense of balance, of being able to hold his mind on a single thought. He reacted helplessly, swinging back against the chair he was sitting on, then jerking sharply forward, doubling up at his waist. He fell off the chair. He rolled on the floor. His limbs would not respond – he no longer knew how to control them. The woman in the seat immediately in front of him pressed her hands hard against the sides of her face, her upper body tipping to one side. Most of the others within Chad's suddenly restricted view were shouting or exclaiming. One man stood up, fell to his knees, then lay prostrate on the floor. Everyone else reacted in similar ways. Most were bent double on their chairs, pressing their hands to their heads. In a few seconds they had become a mob paralysed by the intrusive, uncontrollable sensation, thrashing about on the floor but unable to move away, or to stop the reactions, thirty adults with all rational thought demolished.

Chad managed to keep his eyes open, although he could not properly direct or focus them. He tried to close his mind to the exultation of thoughts and emotions crashing in on him. A cacophony of voices rang through his mind. His own was among them. Voices? Thoughts? Gasps? Screams of pain? It was impossible to tell, impossible to know them apart.

The assault was mental, not physical. Chad's leg and arm muscles were unaffected, but temporarily beyond control. By concentrating on his limbs he climbed at last shakily to his knees then managed to half-turn, lean over, crawl back to an upright position on his chair again, steadying himself by pressing both feet firmly against the floor. He looked around the room. Although the maddening intrusion into his thoughts was unabated he saw that a few of the others were recovering, managing to sit upright on the floor, crouch, lean back against the nearest chair. No one met anyone else's eyes.

The screeching voices suddenly ceased. The silence was like the abrupt and total abolition of crippling pain.

The return to normality was a shock.

Chad focused on himself. He felt like throwing up. A man on the far side of the room had done so – one of the instructors was ready with water and cloths to clean up. Looking around at the others Chad realized they were all experiencing the same thing. The feeling of reflux slowly ebbed away. There was again the faint, almost inaudible background sense of the equipment being alive, ready to be used. The artificial silence, the trace of white noise, was itself unnerving, a threat that the madness could be turned on again without warning.

Jacek and the other instructors were standing together,

spaced loosely behind the lectern. They were watching closely. Jacek held up both his hands with the palms towards everyone, calmingly, as if to establish the trust that he would not make it happen again.

'Everyone OK?' he said. 'Anyone hurt? Any injuries?'

Nobody said much, but there was a stirring in the room as people looked around at each other. Jacek stayed by the lectern as the other four instructors moved swiftly through the room, looking down at everyone as they passed. They kept smiling as they checked each person.

'Did anyone faint, pass out briefly?' There were general sounds of denial to that. 'I think that's a first,' Jacek said. 'We must be getting better at this. We normally have a few people pass out for a few seconds. No one's actually died yet, but we keep trying.'

Someone said, 'What the hell did you do, Jacek?'

'It was a demonstration of what this kit does, sir.' His voice was quiet, but it felt intimately close. 'Every sound you heard, every noise or shout, came from you, the people in this room. You were instantly connected directly into each others' thoughts. Not your inner thoughts, but subvocalizations, the rational level of thinking. Every word you say is accompanied by an organized thought. It was instantly transmitted wide-beam to all users on the network. Everything I am saying to you now is coming to you through the IMC. You found it tough going, I suspect.'

There were sounds of concurrence from all around. Not this time from within, but from their voices.

Chad was staring down at the floor, trying to recover his feeling of self. Jacek's voice was central, internal. The others in the room who spoke sounded normal, old-normal. Jacek was interior, they were exterior. What was going on? Thought connections? Not possible – perhaps a form of radio transmission?

Jacek said, looking straight at him, 'Not radio, Inspector Ramsey. Similar, but not that.' He then spoke generally to the whole room. 'This is a new kind of communication. What you experienced was a sharing of responses, your instant reactions. Because you had no idea what was coming at you, everything was a response from all the people here today. But the prime use of the IMC is to send, not receive. It's an unchannelled network so in use it has to be controlled by a rigid structure. That structure is what we will be concentrating on during the rest of the course. You have to learn the way it is organized, and how to work with it. Your thoughts and words have to be made specific, focused. Any questions?'

Silence. Everyone looked around at each other. Chad was hoping someone else would speak first. He was dumbfounded, irrationally terrified that if he were to utter a single word it would unleash the mental chaos again. The faint hissing noise in his head continued. The silence persisted. Everyone must be feeling the same. One careless thought might set it off again.

Jacek was waiting.

Finally, someone in the room said something and Chad tensed up against the expected mental onslaught. But the words were spoken conventionally, not through the IMC. Chad in fact was so preoccupied with his thoughts that he missed what was said. Jacek typed something at his keyboard, but made no reply. The tension in the room was almost palpable.

Gradually, a few questions were asked, to which Jacek sometimes replied himself, or delegated to one of the other trainers. One question had the clear approval of everyone present: was that going to happen again?

'No,' said Jacek immediately. 'Tomorrow we will make a start on establishing the correct protocols for working within a safe format. We'll take it one step at a time. The IMC nanoshield is a sophisticated piece of kit and it has to be used properly.'

He moved on to a more formal lecture, speaking from notes and with an overhead projector.

That evening the bar was busy.

xi

The final days of the course involved intensive learning and practical tests. The IMC was not easy to use or control.

They opened up lines of contact. They sent signals. They silenced each other by blocking, ignoring, paralleling, muting. They were shown how to recognize levels of instantaneity – in the real world of policing the officers would require a clear hierarchy of response urgencies, such as having to deal with mob violence or a hostage situation or an officer down. They were shown the new and improved procedures for calling in emergency backup, how to deploy firearms-capable officers or dog handlers, when and how to bring in explosives experts, crowd and riot repellers.

It was all about operational policing, which undoubtedly had some, but not compelling, interest for Chad. He drifted back into the feeling of being more of an observer than a participant. His mind often wandered. When he did focus he sometimes speculated how this new gadget might affect his future case work, the problems sent to him for analysis and profiling. Would it be in any way useful?

Before the end of the week everyone present could speak directly, silently, with anyone else on the course, including all five of the course leaders. They exchanged solo and double contacts, archived and encrypted each other's IMC addresses, made two-way exchanges, shared group calls, they stacked calls, had periods of silence. They learned how to be anonymous, how to randomize texts and scramble voice/thought calls.

At the end of each day they normally powered down – at first because the instructors had control of the network, but towards the end everyone had the freedom to enter or leave the connection by choice. Powering down left the IMC nanoshield on, but the distracting hiss of carrier wave was absent. Some people left it on full. Chad realized that some of them were becoming addicted to it. Conversations continued after the course sessions, into the evenings. A number of the course attendees were still in contact late into the night.

Chad stopped listening in, feeling like a prude but genuinely not wanting to know what they were up to.

xii

As the final days slipped by, Chad felt a growing distance between himself and the other members of the course. He was interested in the novelty of the technology, with reservations, but the challenge of interfacing with a new system was not something he responded to. The device was obviously intended for operational work.

His main reservation about the technology was that it, or at least the nanoshield he had been fitted with, seemed to have a fault. The shock of the first moments of use, and the feeling of nausea whenever powering down, were clearly a regular occurrence. The others complained of it too. And whenever he had the thing in use, there were occasional and unpredictable bursts of interference – a sudden whiting out, a flash, a loud noise that came with it. The effect was over in a second or two, but it was always surprising and disconcerting, and sometimes so extreme it momentarily stunned him. It did not appear to affect the communication that was going on at that moment.

He spoke to Jacek about it the next day.

'We're aware of the problem,' Jacek said. 'We're all experiencing the same. There's no danger in it, and you'll get used to it. Anyway, an upgrade is due soon, and that'll be transmitted automatically to your shield. There's an online troubleshooting service if you continue to have problems.'

That evening in the bar, Chad sat by himself in a corner and leafed through some of the printed literature that had been handed out. Everyone had a copy of it, but they had been told the course notes would provide them with the most important information they needed. He noticed a section on the life of the battery, and how often it should be replaced.

Experimentally, he reached behind his ear and released the battery from its mount. It popped out as if a spring was behind it, just as the text described. As the battery left his ear bone a feeling of dead neutrality instantly swept over him. It was the removal, the disconnection, of a sensation he had already been taking for granted. The nanoshield had turned him into a sort of cyber gadget – now he was a cyber gadget with the power supply off.

The battery was like none other he had ever seen: it was a thin and shining metal spike, about three centimetres long, slim as a darning needle and with a tiny globe at each end. There were no markings on it, not even indicators of polarity. He had not moved it around in his fingers, so he pushed it back into his skull in the same way it had come out. There was at once a feeling of contact being made, and a second or two later the now familiar sense of general alertness returned. There was no background hiss, just a sense of personal enlightenment returning. It was not at all an unpleasant feeling.

There were pages in the documentation listing 'other uses' for the IMC. From these he learned it was possible to link the device to his phone, and to any computer, that it could pick up all available TV, radio and streaming channels. The internet was constantly online at a speed much higher than any of the advertised commercial packages, and the IMC was its own cloud and browser.

Later, when he was alone in his room, Chad powered up, following the instructions. He was immediately connected to BNN's audio classical music channel. An orchestral piece he recognized as the Sibelius violin concerto was being broadcast: a recording from a live concert. When the music came to an end, and the audience was clapping appreciatively, an announcer said the concert had been recorded in the Usher Hall in Edinburgh. The audience's applause seemed to fill Chad's world, as had the music itself. He was astonished by the clarity and subtlety of the transmission: it was a sensual surrounding that made it feel as if he was close up to the soloist or even seated somewhere within the orchestra. Throughout, he had been subliminally aware of the ambience of an audience invisibly around him.

He had tuned in during the final movement – at one point it was briefly interrupted by the white flash and the cracking sound, but as Jacek had said he was already getting used to that and it did not destroy the experience, except momentarily.

Then he found the video channels: a choice of approximately forty-five online streaming channels, all the familiar British broadcasters, as well as American, European and other international channels, plus links to numerous incremental stations. He paged through them, fascinated not only by the range of subjects and languages, but the astonishing high-definition imagery. He could not see the pictures in a conventional sense – he was somehow *in* them, generating them in a way he found absorbing and inexplicable. He soon felt vertiginous with the feeling of sensual indulgence, switching from one to the next.

The audio stations were regularly interrupted by the sudden white-outs. The visual stations less so, but because of the feeling of being sourced from himself, the intrusions were more disturbing. They were something he felt he would have difficulty getting used to.

There were about a dozen movie channels. There was a vast library of recorded music, from early jazz recordings of more than a century before, through the endless diversity of popular and dance music that followed. Every major composer of classical music was available from the library, as well as a host of lesser-known ones. Where was it all coming from? Chad ceased to question it, but went on marvelling. He sampled and sampled.

xiii

There was one more day before the end of the course. It went slowly by with the cops rehearsing their codes and gestures and mnemonics to communicate with each other. Chad played along with it all.

In the evening he escaped again to his room. There was a film he was keen to watch, and of course the day's news to catch up with. For once his room was neither too cold nor stifling hot, so he sat in relative comfort in the old-fashioned easy chair and connected with the world outside. He had brought a couple of bottles with him from the bar.

The film suddenly cut out. No warning, just a sudden cessation. Chad popped in a new battery and the film resumed from the point of interruption. It was already the fourth battery he had used.

At the end of the film he disconnected the IMC and used his laptop to make contact with Ingrid. Almost as soon as she came online he realized he could have used the IMC as the medium for connection.

She looked sleepy and said she was surprised to hear from him so late in the evening. Chad could see she was still at her desk, so presumably had been working until he called. He told her about watching the film, one he knew she had already seen, but spared her what amounted to uninteresting details about his experiments with the graphene nanoshield and its software. She said she was tired, and was still ploughing slowly through the German translation. The book was a long professorial response to a linguistic theory, as dry as dust, but a demanding work to translate because of the specialist language involved. She said she could only complete about ten pages a day before fatigue set in. Fortunately there was a long delivery deadline; less fortunately she was not being paid by the hour.

The familiar image of her on his screen, and the sound of her voice, made him wish he could leave for home straight away, but he had to take part in a short plenary session in the morning.

They spoke for about fifteen minutes, both of them yawning from time to time. She said she was still amused to see him with a bald head, although she had seen it several times since he was shaved. Now she half-heartedly teased him about keeping it that way.

After the call, he wished he had thought of trying to connect with her through the IMC, but she had obviously not wanted to speak for too long, and it would have taken him a while to search the documentation to see how it was done. Plenty of time for that, another day.

xiv

It was at last the Saturday morning, and the course was brought to its plenum.

The five instructors ran through a series of bullet points for use of the IMC when on duty. Chad listened politely. After that, they were given some spare graphene batteries to take with them. Old ones could not be recharged when they became expended. They were instructed in exactly when and how a battery might be removed, and a new one inserted. Replacements, they were told, could only be obtained through their police division. They were not available commercially. A recycling procedure was outlined.

Alone in his room for the last time, packing up his stuff and bracing himself for the complicated, multi-connection train journeys home, Chad saw in the mirror that his hair was growing back. The tiny hairs were slightly darker than his skin, and hinted at the outline of the graphene shield. He ran his fingers round the margin of the shield, still all but undetectable, where it met his bare skin.

It was difficult to believe it would still be there forever, until he died. What if it stopped working, grew brittle, or developed cracks?

He travelled home. The weather had changed yet again, and now the heat was smothering, almost impossible to hide from. He was happy to be back with Ingrid. He returned to his office on the Monday morning.

The moment he arrived he sensed change. The two outer offices were both unoccupied, with the desks tidied. Chad looked at the roster: both Taïs and Theo were listed to be in that day. His own office was much as he had left it, but there was no sign of the expected heap of files and other documents that normally accumulated whenever he was away for a few days. His mail inbox was full as usual, so he sat at the terminal for an hour or so and dealt with the most pressing enquiries. When he had finished these, there was still no sign of his two assistants.

He spent the rest of the morning partly browsing through a case he had had to leave unresolved when he went to the course, but also experimenting with the IMC. Nothing was coming through the comms channel. He had imagined his fellow trainees leaping into action now it was their first day back on normal duties.

That evening he tried to explain to Ingrid what installing the graphene nanoshield had been like, and what it was supposed to do. There was no physical sign of it on his head, just the tiny incisions made behind his left ear. Nor could he demonstrate it working in any way – there was no one making contact with him. He found it impossible to describe except as a sort of undetectable radio headset he couldn't take off.

'What do you mean, you can't remove it?' Ingrid said. 'Let me see.'

'It's completely hidden.'

But he bowed the top of his head towards her, and she ran her fingers over his scalp, feeling, checking. 'It looks red and blotchy. Are you sure they haven't hurt you?'

'It's OK, really. They gave me something to soothe it.'

'If the police put this on you, are they monitoring it? Are they listening to us now?'

'I don't think so.' He hadn't thought of that. Perhaps he should have done. 'It only works when the battery is in and I switch it on,' he said.

Later, he settled down in his workroom at home and selected a film he thought he would watch. It came through loud and clear, but within the first few minutes there were three separate white-out interruptions, each slightly more disruptive than the last. He closed it down. As the nausea wore off the battery he had been using died. He slipped in a replacement.

That night Ingrid rubbed the ointment on his head, and he liked that.

Chad went to work the next day, passing through the office building with an unpleasant sense that people were looking covertly at him as he went by. A complicit silence surrounded and followed him. He passed his two outer offices, which remained empty. In his own office a large carton had been placed on his desk. His personal belongings were already inside it. All case files and correspondence had disappeared from his desk. His filing drawers were empty. The computer terminal he had been using was gone, and with it the printer, the connections, and so on.

A sealed envelope contained a letter on HAO headed paper. It was a notice of constructive redundancy, effective immediately. It mentioned the compensation sum he would receive. The money would be paid together with his final month's salary on the usual date. He was to sign the copy of the letter, vacate his office and leave the building permanently before 10:00 a.m.

Patrick O'Connell's unused visualizer, left on the cabinet behind his desk, was still there. Chad assumed it was no longer required. He had to use both hands to lift it, but he placed it inside the carton, having first moved out the pens, the clock, the small ornaments, the framed photograph of Ingrid, which someone had already put inside. He did not want to crush any of them beneath the weight of the visualizer. He placed them back in the carton on top of the bulky device, and pushed down the snugly fitting lid.

He left the building for the last time. For some time afterwards he would feel embarrassed by the way they had dismissed him, later resorting to a futile anger that they should set out deliberately to humiliate him. After that he would simply feel numbed. He did not mind in the least leaving the police, but he did greatly dislike having to give up a job he believed he did well, and had come to love.

On that day he stood outside the police station, the carton at his feet, waiting for the coolcab he had ordered on his mobile. The sun was beating down on his head, and he felt, or imagined he felt, a magnifying effect of the sun's rays from the graphene shield. He had never known heat like it. When he looked at his cellphone, he saw that the temperature was forty-one degrees Celsius. He was standing as far back as possible into the shadow of the building, but windows on an adjacent building were reflecting the sun and unbreathably hot air pooled around him. He knew that it was possible to die in such heat if unprotected from it for more than a few minutes.

Then the coolcab arrived.

4

John Smith (1881-1895)

John Smith, convicted in 1877 of multiple fraudulent deceptions against vulnerable women, served his time. He had been given a five-year prison sentence until May 1882, but his term was reduced for good behaviour and he was released on licence on April 14th 1881.

An early release for good behaviour has a particular meaning in the context of penal servitude in Britain. It does not mean that the prisoner acted politely, or was obedient to orders, or that he offered to help with menial chores. Credit for good behaviour cannot be gained or accrued by a serving prisoner. It is assumed and expected from the start. Simply staying out of trouble constitutes good behaviour, while misbehaviour will forfeit the remission that would otherwise be available.

Misbehaviour would be defined as an attempt at escaping, involvement in riotous actions, physical or verbal abuse of prison warders and committing further crimes while behind bars. John Smith apparently did none of those things and therefore won a certain amount of remission.

A release on licence is a form of parole. It is considered by the authorities that a prisoner on licence is still serving the whole of the original sentence, but is serving it in the community rather than behind prison walls. The released person is expected to acknowledge that and use the time to reflect on the punishment and at best make an attempt to rehabilitate to full society. Authorities are not naïve – it is realized that most released prisoners almost immediately find themselves in unstable or chaotic circumstances, without money, a job, or in most cases anywhere to live or a partner to rejoin. Many of them return naturally to the circle of wrongdoers from which they came. Between twenty-eight and thirty per cent of all released prisoners re-offend.

In an attempt to discourage this, prisoners on licence are informed that should there be a conviction for a further offence during the period of licence, they would not only receive a sentence for that new crime, but would be automatically returned to prison to serve out the remainder of the original.

The parole for good behaviour has in modern times been discontinued in Britain. In the present day all prisoners are released from custody halfway through their sentence, irrespective of behaviour. A deliberate breach of the rules, or committing a crime in prison, will extend the original sentence, but not affect the half-time release, except by the extra time, of course halved. The conditions of licence on early release are unchanged.

While he was in prison Smith was issued with an identifying serial number: W523. The 'W' was code for 'convicted in 1877'. This was a fact that was to gain importance later.

His period of incarceration was notable for two events only.

Two years into his sentence, at the beginning of 1879, Smith, who had declared to the court that he was a Christian, applied to the prison authorities for leave to change his religion and be entered as a Jew. Among other enquiries he was examined by the Medical Officer of Portsmouth Prison, who confirmed to the Home Office that Smith had been circumcised in accordance with the customs of his faith. The application was granted and his records were changed.

In the summer of the same year, John Smith petitioned the Home Secretary for remission of his sentence on the grounds that it was too severe. The relevant fact of this petition was that John Smith did not claim to have been wrongly convicted. He accepted his guilt. This was a formal petition against sentence, the sort made by many prisoners or by their lawyers, in which guilt is tacitly acknowledged. Smith's petition was refused.

When he finally walked free, Smith had about thirteen more months to serve on licence. He either returned to the straight and narrow after release, or he managed to escape arrest, because there is no record of him being sent back to prison during his release on licence.

ii

What Smith actually did, or where he went, or which name he was using, is uncertain. There is little known about him for most of the fourteen years between 1881 and 1895.

The definitive information for this period confirms that in April 1894 Smith was living in London. His time on licence had long expired by then. He was arrested and taken into police custody once more, and spent a few weeks there waiting for a court hearing, but the charge was dropped as the trial began and Smith was released.

His past life, not to mention the rest of that fourteen-year period, is full of doubt. The little that is known comes from statements he made to the police at a later date. John Smith was a known liar, and at best he might be considered a florid self-fantasist, so much of what follows is unlikely to be true.

He was born in or around 1839, probably in Vienna. He once claimed to have been born in Great Sturton, near Horncastle in Leicestershire (in reality, it is in Lincolnshire), was taken by his Jewish parents to St Petersburg in Russia, then after his parents' deaths he went to Vienna. These versions converge when he said he went on to study at the University of Vienna. Here the unreliability begins, or perhaps deepens. He frequently changed his name.

He claimed to have gained degrees as both MD and MC (whatever the latter might mean; in any case there is no trace of him in the university archives), then volunteered as a surgeon in the Austro-Prussian war of 1866 (there is no trace of him in Austrian military or medical records either). He later studied leprosy under Father Damien in the Sandwich Islands (later: the Hawaiian islands). He became Surgeon-General in the court of the King of Hawaii. He owned a coffee plantation near Honolulu, on the island of Oahu. He went to the USA, where he said he worked as an oculist, travelling from one state to another. He also claimed he went to Adelaide in South Australia, where he set up a prosperous practice as a physician. He said he had travelled around the world. Other places he claimed to have visited or lived and worked in included Switzerland, India, Berlin, Naples and Munich. In June 1892, he said he became Chief Medical Officer on the mail steamer *Clan MacArthur*, sailing between Calcutta and Malta.

By 1894 he was definitely in London, because this was when he was arrested and charged with forgery against a certain Hoseof Margossian. It was a minor matter, of no interest to the wider public. His earlier trial in 1877 had attracted the attention of sections of the press, evoking not only public outrage about his abhorrent crimes, but also social concern for the plight of the unfortunate women who fell foul of him. John Smith was briefly infamous, then disappeared from sight.

More than a decade and a half later he had been forgotten, perhaps lost inside the commonplace name by which he called himself. The new trial began, but it became clear the evidence against him was incomplete. Mr Hoseof Margossian received no remedy from the court.

Shortly after his release from this trial, John Smith, once again a free man, resumed his criminal activities of false representation and petty fraud against vulnerable women.

5

Adolf and Adler Beck (1883-1884)

i

Teatro Municipal
Jirón Huancavelica
Lima
Peru
August 27th 1883

My dearest brother Adler,

I still hope that one day I shall see you striding
enthusiastically into the front row of the stalls, surrounded by the hundreds of aficionados who pour in every
night to our performances to see me in my glory, celebrated by critics high and low all over South America.
Because you are not here to share it with me I can only
boast about what I am doing, while I wish fervently that
you would come to discover the reality for yourself.

Last night, for example, I took three curtain calls, was
showered with carnations and roses, and another aria
was demanded of me as an encore. A week ago, I was
persuaded to sing two encores, one of them a duet with
the leading soprano.

At present I am singing the role of Figaro in an 'opera

buffa' by Rossini called *Il barbiere di Siviglia*. It is a large and important role for me – I share it with another tenor, performing on alternate evenings. I am on stage three or four nights every week. I sing Figaro in Italian, of course, which I can sing phonetically but not speak. I am often commended by other cast members for my mastery of this difficult task, but most of them are in the same predicament, being Spanish speakers. I am the only English-speaking Norwegian in the company. The operas of Weber would be easier for me, although many of the singers I work with say that singing in the German language is unnatural. Some of the company still insist on thinking I am a German, probably because our surname is shared by many Germans. I am often tempted to make up another name for myself, one more commonplace, at least in either Britain or Peru. (Can you imagine me as a 'Pedro' or 'Rodrigo' or 'John'?)

I earnestly wish you to make the long journey to Peru so that we might be together again, and so that I can show you what I have become. However, I acknowledge that now you have a wife and two small children it must be difficult for you to tear yourself away. Surely, though, you could arrange with your employers that your important scientific experiments (whatever they might be) could be conducted while in this beautiful city? I am told there are immense glaciers in the mountains to the east, and of course we are against the shore of the mighty Pacific Ocean.

You write and tell me you are now gaining an interest in ocean currents. You should be in Lima! Everyone here says that the weather of the entire country and beyond is controlled by a warm deepwater current that flows from time to time from the western depths of the ocean in the far distance. We are close to the Equator, but in normal times the Peruvian climate is temperate – this is because all weather extremes are moderated by the closeness of the sea, and the huge mountains.

But then there is El Niño, The Child (the name of this mysterious current). When that strikes they say the weather becomes unpredictable. The Child is not ex-pected this year, so the newspapers say, but if it were then Lima would probably suffer torrential rain for several weeks, starting about a month from now. In the past these monsoons have brought floods to the towns and destruction to crops. Everyone fears it. At other times The Child brings intolerable heat. Even beyond Lima and Peru, the arrival of The Child has such an impact that it indirectly causes hurricanes in the Atlantic Ocean, drought in places as far away as Japan and Australia, famines in Europe and China, forest fires in the western areas of the United States, and sometimes a period of bitterly cold weather at the end of summer in the Andean mountains.

Your wintry theories would be challenged by a visit here, Adler.

For now, we are at the end of the winter months, but as a European most days here feel to me like the gentlest of summer. When we were children in Christianssund you and I used to hide away in winter, like everyone else. The cold sometimes seeped horribly into me while we were in London, but in Lima every day is a new blessing. Even now, in winter, we sit in cafes by the sides of the streets, stroll the avenidas. I often think of your terrifying theories, but I do not talk about them here. I believe people would take me less seriously if I told them what obsesses my own brother. They do not worry much about rivers of ice, or blizzards, or mountains whose height is increased by the crust of ice, or air so cold it cannot be comfortably breathed.

I write with news, though, my dear brother. I know that in spite of your invariably kind words you have always thought of me as a spendthrift and a wastrel, and that I have traditionally denied it. It is true I have never enjoyed the stability of a formal profession or employment, so throughout most of my adult years I have survived financially from one day to the next, with the occasional difficulties and shortages that implies. I cannot say enough how grateful I have been in the past to you, dear Adler, for the help you have given me from time to time.

I can now tell you that for the last three years I have been permanently employed by the opera company and that they have paid me very well for my singing. Although I am not complacent about it I believe I am at last financially secure. I should remain so for the next few years at least. Perhaps you will regard this as a welcome surprise, but it has become a fact of my life. I have earned it honestly and saved it conscientiously.

However, you are in the same position as me. We have now reached early middle age. The number of roles I might win as a tenor are becoming increasingly competed for by younger men of real talent. I love my work but I have now sung all the roles I can reasonably aspire to, and have played in every major opera house in this vast and interesting continent. I am beginning to think of making a return to Europe to pursue other opportunities, perhaps by way of the United States. I should love to visit Australia, India, and many other places around the world.

Finally, you asked me again if I have experienced any more of those voices in my head. Yes, I have, and what about you? Have you been hearing them too? They are less of an intrusion now because they have lost the capacity to surprise me, but they are still something I worry about.

For several weeks I was convinced a peculiar and disturbing kind of derangement was attacking me. Madness is in fact what I believed it was. One of my fellow singers in this company, trained as a physician, told me that the sensitive treatment of lunatics is being pioneered as a science in the United States, in Britain and especially in Vienna. Imaginary voices in the head are increasingly being interpreted as an early sign of dementia.

So that frightened me and for a while preoccupied me, but then I took a careful stock of my own experiences. Although the sudden intrusion of a voice, apparently emerging from my own mind, is an exceptional event, it is not a regular or normal one. I go about my days feeling sane and settled and entirely equal to the challenges of the world. My periods of such normality extend into weeks and months.

While I was with the Felipe touring company in Argentina in '78 and '79 I heard nothing at all, and the silence blessedly continued for several months after I had returned here to Lima.

Then it started again. At that time I thought it might be connected with my being in Lima, that it was emanating from somewhere around here, but when I collected my thoughts I recalled the several other places where it had also beset me. It is clearly nothing to do with where I am, as it can strike anywhere.

How does the intrusive voice sound to you, Adler?

We often refer to what happens in the plural, but I think it is a single voice that speaks at different times. It has now ranged over many years. I remember one or two puzzling incidents when I was a child, and some while I was shipboard, which I think with hindsight might have been the same thing. Who could be doing this to us for such a long period? I assume it is a male voice, because that is how I perceive it. But I cannot be sure.

And does it seem to you that the voice has a strange accent? It is so long since I have lived in an English-speaking country that I have lost whatever ability I once had to distinguish between accents. So maybe it is a Yankee person? Some of the words I have briefly heard have baffled me. Because you lived and worked in the United States, perhaps you know better?

This is another matter we must discuss face to face. When I finally return to England we must reunite as a matter of priority so that we might share and compare our experiences.

In the meantime have no fears for my madness. It is non-existent. I am able to sustain this bizarre experience, as I am confident you are also.

I shall not be departing Lima immediately. There is at least one more role coming up for me, and even if that should not materialize it will take me some time to make arrangements for travel. This address will be good to find me for the foreseeable future, and as usual if I move on I will leave behind me a trail of forwarding addresses.

From your dear and absent brother, but the same is still your only brother,

Dolf Beck

It was a warm evening in early September and I had been working later than normal. I invariably made my way home by walking across Blackheath, the wide open parkland only a short distance from where I worked. The road in which I and my family lived was called Eliot Hill, and it ran along the southern edge of the park. My day until this point had been an entirely routine one: a lecture in the morning, two tutorials in the afternoon, all followed by a couple of peaceful hours of research and reflection in the library. As I walked home, looking forward to supper with Meredith, eager to see my children again, I was expecting nothing out of the ordinary to happen.

I usually walked so that I stared at the ground a short distance before me. It was only a habit, because my early days spent stumbling and slipping around the crevasses and icefalls of glaciers had given me a lifelong aversion to falling over. But it made me look as if I were deep in thought, as one or two of the more self-assured students have said to me. Most of the time that was not the case, but I was content to let them think so. On this particular evening I was in fact pondering a catastrophic event that had happened on the other side of the world, so for once my aura of preoccupation was probably real.

The telegraphic instrument at the Royal Naval College, where I was employed as a lecturer in marine science, had been receiving a series of startling and shocking messages from Batavia in the Dutch East Indies. A volcano had erupted somewhere in the region of that city. The location was a small island in a narrow stretch of sea called the Strait of Sunda, of which I had never previously heard. I was planning to look it up as soon as I was in my study at home.

The volcano had erupted with unusual violence, causing a huge amount of local damage and disruption. A great number of people had been killed, but the despatches from Batavia said that it was still impossible to count the casualties. Many were known to be missing, many more had been badly injured.

I had recently been taking a serious interest in the effects on the climate of large volcanic eruptions. A few weeks earlier, pursuing that interest, I spent the early part of the summer on an extended tour of Italy.

Italy is one of the most volcanic regions in Europe, and perhaps in the world. There are nearly fifty Italian volcanoes along the narrow peninsula and on its islands, most of them now extinct or at least dormant. I had visited the three currently most active: Vesuvius, Etna and Stromboli. Of those three I had ascended to the icy summit of Mount Etna and peered into its steam-filled crater.

Later, in the city of Catania on the coastal plain of Sicily below, at what one might reasonably assume was a safe distance from the mountain, I inspected the solidified remains of a huge lava flow. In 1693 it had penetrated as far as the moat of the Castello Ursino. The castle survived, but it had been built on a rocky promontory overlooking the sea — as a result of the eruption and earthquakes the castle is now about one kilometre from the sea and in the centre of the town. Where the lava finally came to halt there is a wall of solid rock, maybe ten metres high.

It was a reminder of the almost unstoppable power of volcanic outflow.

When earlier that day I had heard about the eruption in the East Indies I immediately tried to find out as much about it as I could. The main eruption had occurred a few days before, but such was the disruption that all lines of travel and communication were unreliable.

I had already established that there was a direct connection between the explosion of Mount Tambora, also in the Dutch

East Indies, and the intensely cold summer that followed in 1816. It also had a marked cooling effect on subsequent years. From the minimal information in the telegraph messages from Batavia I suspected that the new eruption of the island called Krakatoa would turn out to be on nothing like the scale of Tambora, but all volcanoes were presently of interest to me.

Walking slowly home, looking as usual at the ground before me, I became aware that a sort of roseate glow was illumining the well-tended grass of the park. I looked up.

I was stopped in my tracks, suddenly overcome with awe: a sunset of deep and wonderful colours had quickly developed. Looking to the west from Blackheath, which is on the top of a shallow hill, the view is normally of the roofs and houses and church spires of south London. That familiar sight was made irrelevant by a shocking, lurid and astonishing display of sunset colours. The sun itself was not visible, but it was still just above the horizon, low and already hidden behind evening clouds. It was brilliantly lighting up the sky with a blaze of blood-red and yellow and orange, great streaks and smudges of light and colour. The glow was immense, extending from the area of the sunset clouds across most of the sky: there were many bright streaks of yellow and orange light immediately above me.

I was not alone in reacting to this – around me, many other people had also stopped walking and were standing to stare up at the awesome sight. I heard them exclaim to each other, marvel at it, wondering what it might portend. The brilliance was gradually increasing: the colours were slowly moving across the sky in streaks as if propelled by the heat of the sun.

I had been living in London a long time. I had never before seen anything to equal it. While I lived and worked in Norway I had often witnessed the northern lights, the aurora borealis, but that display was a still and almost calming light, a series of radiant curtains slowly shifting and glowing with beautiful pastel shades of sapphire blue, shining green and, occasionally, a gentle red. London was too far in the south for even a glimpse of the aurora. What I was seeing was a tremendous but angry sky, the luridness of the colours seeming to presage a tempest, a violent storm.

I was stirred by it, thrilled by it, but I also felt a deep and indefinable concern. It must have been a result of the eruption on the other side of the world.

I stood there for many minutes, exalted by the fiery sight. Gradually the colours faded as the sun, still unseen, dropped below the horizon, but they were slow to disappear entirely. Other people drifted away, back to their lives. I remained, determined to see the final act. One by one the streaks of colour paled, became wisps of cloud or haze, and as darkness took the sky they became unseeable.

iii

The next day Meredith was rostered to be working in the afternoon and evening at the observatory, while I stayed at home. I left early in the morning and went into the college to deliver a lecture. I was home by midday in time to join her for a light lunch before she left, played with little Agathe until it was time for her afternoon sleep, had tea with Harald when he was brought home from infant school, then while both children were upstairs being looked after by Lellie, their paid companion, I was able to extend my reading.

The scientific literature of volcanology was not extensive, but it was an area attracting the interest of an increasing number of specialists. As far as I could see in the books I had in the house, and one I had brought home from the college library, the island of Krakatoa was not mentioned in detail anywhere.

In a chapter on the Semangko Fault, which runs through Sumatra and part of Java, as well as much of the western part of the Dutch East Indies, I came across a brief reference to the island, which was part of the Krakatau Archipelago. This was the site of a medium-size volcano, part-dormant for many years. According to the books, all published a few years earlier, the activity observed from the volcano was an unthreatening emission of smoke and steam, which had increased slightly over earlier observations.

My impression remained for the moment that the current eruption had been a relatively minor one.

When evening came and Meredith was still at her job I walked out on the heath and watched as the sunset again lit up most of the sky. It was, if anything, a more thrilling and lurid display of colours than I had seen the day before. I knew, though, that what this meant was that the upper atmosphere had received a vast quantity of pyroclasts: airborne dust, ash and other forms of ejecta. Whatever had happened to Krakatoa in the Sunda Strait, half the world away, it was certainly not minor.

The next day the weather changed dramatically. I went early to the college, trudging through a downpour of heavy rain. Although it was the beginning of September, still a summer month, in Britain weather can rarely be accurately predicted on a seasonal basis. Some September days are magically warm, others are not. This first week in September 1883 was one that was not.

A cold wind came in from the east, propelled by a strong high-pressure system over Scandinavia. The rain was insistent, with an acidic, gritty quality should some of it find its way past the lips, and I was not the only person who remarked that there was hint of sulphur in the air. London air was routinely dirty, but in a familiar way. This was different. As a climatologist it greatly interested me. I started to keep notes again of the weather I was experiencing, the readings taken from the college instruments of wind speed and direction, barometric pressure and air temperature.

In my study at the college I read the transcripts of all the messages telegraphed from Batavia. There were at least a dozen of them, telling in terse but vivid language a story of almost unprecedented disaster.

I learned that the island of Krakatoa was uninhabited, but was surrounded by many fishing villages and coastal settlements in fairly close proximity on the larger islands to the north and south of it. For centuries it had been regarded simply as a volcano in the sea, not attracting much attention, except locally. It was thought to have been dormant for about two hundred years, but in May it began a large eruption, emitting a solid plume of ashes, gas, pumice and so on, with several long streams of lava venting not only from the crater but from several fumaroles. Although it was a big eruption it was not at that stage thought to present a real danger. The ash drifting with the winds was an unpleasant nuisance but not a threat to life. The eruption continued for several weeks, with short periods of quietude followed by renewed activity.

On Sunday August 26th, a huge explosion threw a vast column of pyroclasts into the sky, a toxic mixture of superheated ash, pumice, sulphur dioxide and magma. A series of tsunamis was created, of increasing power and size. Ejected pieces of rock and lava fell from above, overweighting and sinking boats in the Strait and killing many people who were unfortunate enough to be out in the open.

Instead of being depleted by the explosion, the eruption quickly gained in strength. Finally, on August 27th, a series of four catastrophic explosions, each mightier than the one before, caused devastation. The final, climactic explosion destroyed almost everything that was left of the original island.

One of the telegraph messages reported that the culminating explosion was so powerful that buildings in Batavia itself, more than a hundred kilometres away, had suffered blast damage and hundreds of broken windows. Casualties in Batavia were grievous, but many thousands more, who lived closer to the area of the explosion, were expected to have simply been vaporized in the blast. No major relief efforts had yet been possible, although ships of the Dutch and British navies were approaching.

The day I read this was on the Thursday following the terrible event: August 30th. That evening, after a long and miserable day of grey skies and driving wind, the clouds cleared long enough to reveal another brightly coloured sunset. Because of the cloud coverage it was over more quickly than the earlier ones, but again the distressing blood-red light glared down across the city.

Meredith returned from the observatory and told me that barographs all around the world had registered a shockwave emanating from the area of the explosion. She said it circumnavigated the globe at least six or seven times, gradually decreasing.

She also told me that reports of the loud explosions had been coming in from as far away as Perth in Australia, and islands in the Indian Ocean. Many people on the islands of Java and Sumatra, and other East Indies islands, had suffered blast effects and extensive injuries, as well as critical deafness from damage to their ears. She and other astronomers were recording it as an epochal event, a unique catastrophe of historical proportions.

For a few days she and I were entirely consumed by our work on this horrific event. We could barely imagine what the damage in the area of the destroyed island must now look like. The later telegraph reports all described the aftermath: the tsunamis that had overwhelmed coastal towns and smaller settlements, the sinking of ships, the destruction of an important lighthouse, and above all the dreadful loss of life.

I suddenly thought of my brother Dolf, living in Lima on the western side of the South American continent, on the edge of the Pacific. Practically nothing but the ocean and the curvature of the Earth lay between him and this volcano. Had he heard the explosions from Krakatoa, had he been swept away and drowned by tsunamis? I fretted silently about this, not wanting to discuss my fears with Meredith. Then, at the end of the following week, a letter from Dolf arrived from Lima. It was dated August 27th, the day of the final explosion. He made no mention of the eruption that now was dominating my thoughts.

Most of my life I had suffered chronic worries about my wayward brother, but at least I knew he had not been directly affected by Krakatoa's violent end.

iv

Sumatra was no stranger to volcanic eruptions, nor were many of the islands of the East Indies archipelago.

On Sumatra was Lake Toba, the caldera created by a massive volcanic explosion in prehistoric times, some seventy-five thousand years ago. I had seen papers written by researchers who had discovered ash samples as far away as Africa, which were similar in composition to known debris from the volcano. There was a body of responsible theory that asserted that the heat and light of the sun had been blocked for many years by the pyroclasts discharged into the upper atmosphere. This coincided with, and therefore in all probability had actually precipitated, an ice age that lasted more than a thousand years. This theory accorded exactly with my own researches.

As I read the graphic reports about Krakatoa from Batavia,

followed up by vivid accounts written by journalists, I was able to compare them with what was known about the cold after-effects of Tambora. It seemed increasingly likely that the Krakatoa eruption was at least of the same immensity, possibly greater.

As the days went by, Meredith and her colleagues at Greenwich Observatory were reporting that the seeing was poor, and continuing to deteriorate. The weather remained chill, with all the signs of an early autumn. During the days the sky was intermittently both clouded and unclouded, but of course the clouds we are most aware of are at a low level. It was now obvious that the light from the sun was being filtered by haze at high level. The poor seeing at nights, which was naturally when most professional observing took place, was making the astronomers' work difficult.

Whenever I was outside the college buildings and took a look at the sun through smoked glass I could see a definite halation, a sense of mistiness in the sky.

Every evening on my way home from work I made sure I gained a good observation point on Blackheath so that I could watch the sunset from beginning to end. On days when I was not working I went out specially to watch. If anything, the colours were more sensational and dramatic than ever.

One evening as I stood, observing and marvelling, I felt a sudden paralysis. It was as if a flash of light surrounded me, shockingly. I caught my breath.

An inner voice said, 'Why is the – sky coloured like that? What – do you know about it, Adolf? Where are you? What year is it? What is happening?'

Paralysis is pain – to try to move against it is agony. The tiny intakes of breath I could manage slashed my chest like a knife. I could not turn my eyes away from the shocking display in the sky. I was trapped, immobilized. I stood on my shallow rise of parkland, locked against the sky, while a London evening went on around me.

The voice did not speak again, but the paralysis continued a while longer and I could not look away. At the end there was another moment of flashing white light, and I was released.

v

Because of the difficulties of communication over such a great distance, further responsible information about the Krakatoa eruption was frustratingly slow to arrive. HMS *Hermes*, a Royal Navy cruiser, was now in the area and was mounting a survey of the damage. The crew were bringing relief to injured civilians wherever possible. Her presence as a powerful gunboat was a symbolic way of maintaining law and order in the region. This we knew, because the Dutch had initially protested at her arrival, but now the two navies were co-operating in the aftermath of the crisis.

More importantly, I knew there was a scientific officer on board, a Lieutenant Derrick Cowley RN, who had sailed with *Hermes* as a representative of the naval college where I taught. In the end I knew he would report back, but of course that was going to be several weeks away.

In the meantime I wrote to volcanologists in the USA, in Japan, and in Britain, all of whom I knew personally. I asked them to be sure to pass on to me whatever new facts came to light that would be relevant to the understanding of the formation of airborne clouds of microscopic particles of volcanic rock. Their first replies revealed they too were starved of reliable information. Short of mounting a special expedition to the East Indies for an inspection on the spot there was little any of us could do except wait.

One matter was becoming clear, though. Although the Krakatoa event was a major eruption, almost unbelievably destructive and dangerous, it was not in fact what volcanologists were describing as a super-volcanic, or sometimes extra-volcanic, eruption. The terminology was as yet inexact but described the same area of interest: massively violent eruptions, known to have occurred in prehistoric times on a scale barely imaginable, never witnessed or recorded in the modern age.

Some of the biggest eruptions occurred in a part of North America known as Yellowstone Valley. In the present day the valley is one gigantic caldera, long smoothed by subsequent glaciation, by the erosion of winds and rain, grown over by forests and grassland. It is still volcanically active, with areas of boiling mud and water, and geysers venting steam and water, but it has been stable for thousands of years. Volcanologists who have examined the caldera and researched the outfall have discovered tephra traceable to Yellowstone in many different parts of North America, some of it hundreds or thousands of miles away.

Intriguingly, there are several volcanic regions at present stable, but which several volcanologists believe have the potential at any time to become super-volcanoes. One of these is of particular interest to me, following my research into the Gulf Stream.

Combre Vieja is a steep volcanic ridge on the Spanish island of La Palma. It is actively volcanic, although presently dormant. Recorded past eruptions have established the propensity of the slopes of the mountain, during an eruption, to slide disastrously down towards the deep Atlantic Ocean. The danger the mountain represents is therefore geological rather than volcanic, because it has been extensively surveyed and geologists warn that it shows every sign of having faults deep within its complex strata.

If a major eruption were to occur, and the bulk of the mountainous ridge separated along these fault lines, shedding its mass into the sea, a tsunami of horrific proportions would result. This alone would have an almost unimaginably destructive impact, flooding the western coasts of Africa and Portugal, reaching as far north as the British Isles, and as far west as the seaboard of the United States. Major cities like Washington, Boston and New York would be inundated by immense waves flooding unstoppably in.

From my own specialist point of view there would be secondary and tertiary disasters, both of them eventually of greater destructive impact than the floods. The pyroclastic plume would shade the sun for many years, bringing a marked lowering of global temperatures. But the real long-term danger would emerge less obviously. La Palma lies close to the movement of the North Atlantic Drift. The Gulf Stream's delicate balance would be fatally disrupted by the massive influx of the mountain sliding into the sea. The cyclical process which disposes of the freezing cold fresh meltwater flooding in from the Greenland icecap would no longer flow. Bitterly cold winters would follow, and chill summers, and within a very few years the glaciers would be advancing unstoppably.

vi

I was asleep, but then I was suddenly awake. The house was silent and in darkness, but something had woken me.

I listened for sounds from the children, whose room was next to ours. We had no connecting door, but every night we left both doors open into the upper hallway. Lellie, the children's companion, slept in her own room next to theirs, with her connecting door ajar. She was always quick to respond if the children needed her during the night, but when they roused they usually woke Meredith or me too, sometimes both of us.

I was already in denial. I knew what had woken me, but dreaded that it was so.

I listened to Meredith's calm breathing in her bed a short distance from mine. The innocence of my sleeping wife should have reassured me, but I was tense. Our night-time hours differed and we tried not to disturb each other. Meredith usually worked at the observatory through the evening and into the small hours, while I was often awake early, because I enjoyed a morning walk followed by a reflective period of quiet in my college study, before lectures or tutorials.

I turned over, lay still, tried to return to sleep.

Then came a repeat of what I dreaded: the quiet, sinister hiss of mental intrusion. I knew that was what had woken me a minute or two before, which I had not wanted to accept. I braced myself against it, wishing it away, trying to repel it. I knew it was hopeless. I was powerless against it.

Then came the sudden flash of white, with a simultaneous sound sensed rather than heard: like a door being slammed somewhere around me.

Paralysis gripped me. Paralysis was pain. I struggled once again with my breathing.

The voice said inside me, 'Your eyes are closed. Were you – asleep? I did not mean to wake you. I cannot control when – I speak to you. The room is in darkness. What is the time there? Can you confirm the date?'

I forced my eyes open, and focused them towards the long, heavy curtains that covered our bedchamber windows. I had little choice in the direction I looked, but that was where I was facing with my head on the pillow. It was obvious why it was dark, and where I was. Why should the voice demand to know? I knew the date, but in the darkness I could not read the time. I was held rigid whenever the voice broke into my life, and was unable to move or speak until release.

It was still the dead of night, but outside the house, on the other side of the street, there happened to be a lamp that stayed alight every night. It did not intrude on us when the curtains were closed, but it did mean that a vague outline of the windows was dimly visible all night through the fabric.

'You are lying horizontally – on your side. I assume you are in bed. I have no control over this and I am sorry to disturb you. If – you are able, can you indicate which part of South America you are in?'

I was not able. I was in London, close to Blackheath, and the date was November 29th 1883, or now because it was the small hours, perhaps the 30th. I was nowhere near South America. Did he think I was my brother Dolf?

I struggled to find some way of conveying this, but then the carrier wave abruptly died, and silence was in my head once more. Such a brutal incursion, brutally concluded.

I gasped with relief. I was freed. I stretched in my bed, then turned over again, away from the windows. I tried to slow and control my breathing, fighting the surge of panic I felt, awakened in the dark, unable to breathe. It was over. I lay on my back.

'Adler, have you woken again?' Meredith's voice was quiet.

'Yes.' I spoke softly too.

'Are the children all right?'

'I think so. Go back to sleep, my dear.'

'You sound as if you're wide awake. What's the matter?'

'Just a vivid dream,' I said. It was not the first time I had offered her this explanation when the intrusive voice came inconveniently in the night. It had woken us at other times – Meredith was sensitive to almost every movement I made in bed.

Meredith made a sort of mild throat-clearing noise and I heard the rustle of her bed sheets. She climbed out of her bed, then went to the door that led to the hallway and gently closed it. She went back into her bed and I heard her moving the lamp that stood beside her. In a moment there was a click and the electrical light came on. Our lights at home were a matter of need for us both – with the financial help of both the observatory and the college our house had been connected the year before to the new Edison service. With our erratic hours and the amount of close writing and reading work we both did at home, and since electricity had been made available to us by our supportive employers, we had benefited from the clearer and brighter lights, both for living and for working.

I sat up and turned to face her, for the moment mildly dazzled by the light.

'These dreams that wake you,' she said. 'Why will you never talk about them to me?'

I kept still, staring at her familiar and lovely face. Her hair was pinned up for the night. I recognized a look of determination. She knew me better than anyone.

'I don't know how to describe them to you,' I said. 'I can't control them and I sometimes feel ashamed of them.'

'If they are just dreams there is nothing to feel shame about. Dreams are involuntary. Or are you suffering nightmares? This sudden waking in the night has happened several times. I wish you would tell me what it is you experience.'

'I believe I am losing my mind,' I said abruptly, then immediately wished I had not. I had been silent to Meredith about this for so long. 'They are not nightmares – not really dreams, either. I don't know how to describe what happens. It's beyond rational mental activity.'

I was describing my darkest fear. My brother and I had hesitantly confided similar thoughts in letters to each other, with the presumption that it was a private terror, something unique to us that no one else would understand. Something to do with our heritage, perhaps our personalities, perhaps even the fact we were twins.

I had never told Meredith about the full nature of this connection with Dolf, and I knew she had never read his letters. He often described similar incursions to mine. I had once tried to explain about Dolf's footloose nature, and some of the past and continuing concerns I had about him, thinking perhaps there might be a clue there. At the time of this I remember she had been absorbed in some problem with her work, and she had brushed my fears aside. Many identical twins were known to have a rapport that could not be rationally explained, she said then.

I trusted her more than anyone I had ever known, apart from Dolf. Of course the reasons were entirely different. I valued her love and high regard for me and I did not want to squander them. She had an incomparable mind, and a deep well of affection within her. Although Dolf and I often described the events to each other, we had learned nothing about what they were. All we knew was that we were both experiencing much the same thing. He understood it no better than I did.

'Your mind is not at risk of being lost,' Meredith said. 'Your brain is admirable. I revered you for it from the moment we met.'

'No, I am fallible. I suffer delusions, so my sanity can no longer be trusted. I fear mental decline, the loss of reason. I hear voices.'

'Then you are working too hard. You are over-tired.'

'No more than you,' I said. 'We are both absorbed in our work, and by our lives with Harald and Agathe. Like you I am content with life, and any tiredness I suffer is caused by the energy of our time together. But I hear voices. I cannot stop hearing them. They are not continuous, and there are long periods without them. But when they come I hear them whatever I am doing, when I am wide awake in the daytime, sometimes when I am at work in the mornings, sometimes in the afternoons. And once or twice they have come at night while I am asleep. I am convinced I am losing my sanity. It has to stop.'

'What do the voices say?'

We were both sitting up in our separate beds. The room was unheated and therefore night-cold, and my mood was also chill. Winter was early in London that year because of Krakatoa's dimming of the sun. Outside, we could hear a sharp wind blustering down the dark street, with squalls of rain spattering against the glass. The house had been built many years earlier, and although it was a venerable and beautiful building the elderly window frames were faulty, rattling in the wind and admitting draughts. Commissioning a builder to come in and repair them was a job I had put off thinking about while my work engaged me so. Maybe now I should attend to them, in this new and exceptionally cold winter of furious sunsets, shaded skies and bitter winds?

I briefly left my bed and took two spare blankets from the trunk beside the chest of drawers. I wrapped the larger of them around Meredith's shoulders, and she acknowledged it with a smile. I took the other to my own bed.

'Go on, Adler. Please tell me what you have to.'

'I fear madness, and I fear it because it is the only explanation for what I am experiencing. This has been going on for several years, most of my life. The first time it happened I was almost killed by the shock of it, because I was climbing across a glacier. I was still only a boy. I didn't know then what it could be. I still don't know. The quality of the intrusions, the nature of them, has not changed in all the years since. It is neither better nor worse now than it ever was. Sometimes I go for several weeks, sometimes months, without any awareness of it happening. Then it comes again.'

'Is it one voice or many?'

'I often think it is many, but I have come to believe it is just one. It has happened many times—'

'What does the voice say?'

'It tells me nothing, but from the start it has asked questions. Always where I am, what I am doing, what the date is. How can I begin to answer? The experience is so radical that I am paralysed by it. I cannot move − I can barely breathe. I have no idea how to respond. It is imaginary! I can't speak to an impossible voice. And it believes I am my brother, although it always calls him Adolf. That's a mistake − Dolf never calls himself that.'

'For me, your brother is another imaginary being,' Meredith said quietly. She had never met Dolf, knew about him only what I had told her.

'One day you will meet Dolf,' I said. 'He is returning from his travels soon.'

'Tell me more about the voice.'

'It seems to know me in some way. The voice sometimes uses the word "reading", as if plucking information out of my mind. I'm not sure what he wants to know, what he finds out, if anything.'

Meredith was no longer looking towards me. Her face was tilted down. I knew that was a sign either that she disagreed with what I was saying, or that she was thinking.

'Is the owner of the voice listening to you now?'

'I don't think so − I always have a weird sense of awareness when he is present.'

'You say "he". Are you sure it is a man's voice?'

'Yes. Every time.'

'And the same one?'

'That's more difficult,' I said. 'It always feels to me as if I am the one generating the voice. It seems to come from inside. I worry that I am talking to myself. Maybe it is my own voice after all.'

'You know that until about a hundred years ago voices in the head were thought to be symptoms of mania? Women victims were treated as witches. Some of them were tortured in the belief that would cure them. Many were cruelly murdered. Men were locked away in dungeons where they could do no harm to other people.'

'The world has become more civilized,' I said. 'But that is what frightens me. Yes – I constantly fear mania, the loss of a reasoning mind.'

'There are specialists now who call the phenomenon auditory hallucination, something to be analysed and treated.'

'Isn't that just another way of saying the same thing? I'm not imagining the voices. They aren't hallucinations. They are real.'

Meredith was sitting completely upright, facing me, hugging the blanket around her body.

I was suddenly able to see beyond her face – that of my lover, my wife, the mother of my children. I saw back to the intelligent young woman I had met in the observatory near Chicago. Her seriousness then had impressed and slightly intimidated me, although I quickly learned first to respect it, then later to understand it, then later still to see it as a fundamental part of her personality and abilities. The longer I knew her the greater the complexity of her attractiveness became. At this stage of my life I found it impossible to imagine how I might ever survive without her.

She said, 'If the voices are real, and it sounds as if they are, they can only arise from one of three sources. That is what we need to decide, so that we can understand what's going on, and perhaps make it discontinue. The three alternatives are these. Firstly, they are occult or supernatural, such as the result of witchery, and are being used against you by some magical means to arouse in you supernatural fears.'

I started to interrupt. She shook her head to silence me, and went on, 'No, listen to what I have to say. If the voices are not the stuff of witchery then they are the product of dementia, a disturbed or distracted or failing mind. That is what you say you fear. But if it is not either of these, then they are the product of science. I assume you dismiss the supernatural. We are left with the only alternative: that what you are experiencing is the result of scientific method.'

She threw aside the blanket I had placed around her, and leaned forward and up, reaching for the switch that we used for the electrical light.

'Here's a miracle, for example,' she said. 'Even a few months ago what I am about to do would seem to be a marvel to many people. This is science, electrical science, rationally and deliberately researched. But one day soon the magic will be an everyday action familiar to everyone. Even to those who understand the science behind it.' There was a click and the lightbulb went out. 'Goodnight, my dear,' Meredith said. 'I need my sleep. Perhaps you should consider there might be another science beyond your present knowledge. One just as rationally explained as electrical light.'

I mumbled something in return.

In the sudden darkness of the room I listened to Meredith shifting and settling down again beneath her bedclothes.

Sleep was far away from me. I was still sitting up on my bed, swaddled in the blanket. I lay back, trying to stay warm and pressing my head down against the pillow.

The cold wind outside shook the windows. I was calm, but

wide awake. The familiar thoughts of the exactness of science were soothing to me. Also to Meredith. Both of us.

Trying not to disturb Meredith again I reached across to the electrical lamp that stood between us. The small glass bulb, inside which the light-giving wire filament was sealed, was still hot to the touch. I am not a physicist – the wonder of electrical light could still seem close to miraculous to me, even though I had read the theories, attended the public demonstrations, and knew full well that there was practical science behind it. Not far away, on Holborn Viaduct in the centre of London, the Edison Company's coal-fired turbine was turning to generate the electricity, reaching us, reaching many others, spreading itself unseen and undetected across the sleeping city through the cables concealed in gulleys and culverts alongside the streets, ready at an instant to bring warmth and light in our wintry time. It was an extraordinary, almost alchemical joining of ingenious science and robust engineering. And like the best of science, an electrical light was something that could be used by anybody, even someone who did not begin to understand how it worked.

Was that my role now, to have my innocent mind invaded and my body paralysed by some development of science of which I knew nothing and understood even less? This was what Meredith seemed to be telling me. Was I subject to some experiment going on somewhere?

The rapidly cooling lightbulb in the lamp beside me knew nothing of the coal that had to be mined, then transported, then burned to turn the turbine, nor knew anything of the cables that carried the electricity to activate it. It knew only of the small switch used by myself or my wife, that which turned it on and off.

What did I know of the process behind the voice in my head? And what was expected of me whenever it was switched on?

Meredith stirred, turned herself over. I heard her sweet, steady breathing. Now I sensed she was facing towards me.

Sleep fell on me at last. The fierce wind blustered noisily along our street. I was warm and dry. A wondrous dream came to me later.

vii

Chelsea Hotel

222 W 23 Street

New York City

May 29th 1884

My dear brother Adler,

I write to you from the splendour of what is probably the newest hotel in New York City, a treasury of delights. I have been travelling in the United States for several months, and I have lived as cheaply as possible. Although travel-weary I have for once some money in my pocket, and even better I have a brilliant plan for making good use of it. I have never before felt so well off, and for all the temptations of this young and amazing country I have been careful with my funds, because of my greater scheme.

Now that I am coming to the end of my American days I have decided to relax and indulge myself a little, while waiting for a passage back to Britain. This wonderful hotel is pampering me for the next few days. Furthermore, my residence here imparts to me an outward impression of wealth and influence. I am wearing a new suit of clothes, my hair has recently been trimmed, my collar is stiff and white, and I have a tie-pin with a small embedded pearl. I have business to conduct.

Dolf Beck in New York, 1884

Yes, I am coming home at last, dear brother. Naturally, we must see each other when I am back in London, to reassure ourselves we are well and happy. I yearn to meet your beautiful wife and children. I should also like you in return to take stock of me, now that I am a mature and confident entrepreneur.

Tomorrow, in this hotel, I have an appointment to meet a Mr Karl Pedersen, a Norwegian businessman with many interests in our country of birth. He has agreed to sell to me all mineral rights in a newly discovered mine in a small town called Dalen, in the region of Telemark. The mine has been fully surveyed. I am reliably informed there are several rich seams of copper ore, there to be extracted.

What, you will instantly ask yourself, does your operatic brother know of mining copper?

The answer is of course that I know little or nothing, but I have become an investor and capital venturer. Mr Pedersen, who has worked all his life in the mining industry, wishes merely to release some of his capital – he has promised he will stay on as a salaried manager of the mine, using his experience and knowledge to make the most of my investment. We have corresponded over the last few weeks, and tomorrow we are to meet for the first time, to shake hands and seal the deal.

I suspect my past history of making impulsive decisions is already concerning you. Let me assure you that I have discussed my plans in detail with a firm of independent financial experts here in New York. They advise me that I should proceed with confidence, but continue to use common sense to be wary of mistakes. I trust this reassures you, Adler, as it reassured me. I am more wary than you would ever believe.

I have more news, even better.

New York is buzzing with excitement about a great gift that is about to be made to the United States by the French nation, a celebration of this country's independence and its openness in welcoming migrants from less successful countries. It is to be a vast statue nearly one hundred metres in height, which will be erected at the entrance to New York Harbor. The statue is to be known as *La Liberté éclairant le monde* – the freedom that lights the world. By the torch held aloft she, for it is in the form of a woman, will welcome all visitors and newcomers and migrants to America.

She is already partly built: her great head and the arm that bears the torch have already been transported from France and exhibited here in New York, to acclaim and enthusiasm. I myself visited the exhibit yesterday, and the power of it made me exult silently. But work on the major part of her body has come almost to a halt, because of the need to raise the necessary money – that has already been partly resolved by an extra grant from the French government. Much more interestingly, from my point of view, there is a delay because of a lack of the suitable metal with which she is built.

She is, you see, made of copper. A common enough metal as we know, but because of the symbolic importance of this monument she has to be constructed with only the finest and purest form of copper. That precious ore, I tell you with excitement, is found in the Dalen region of Telemark. Mr Pedersen has shown me the tenders he has already put in for the supply of this metal, and when I take over the mine that copper will be mined and processed and shipped to Paris by myself. The statue will be my silent but permanent memorial. (I shall also make a profit counted in the hundreds of thousands of US dollars, but to me that is secondary.)

Returning to the other matter that concerns us both – yes, because you have asked me again, the mysterious voice continues to intrude from time to time. But it is the least of my worries. I find its regularity comforting in a way, but it is still odd. It asks me questions, sometimes about opera. How does this bodyless voice know of my singing? I can't answer it anyway, because speaking is impossible. Once, by some means that completely baffled me, the voice played music that filled my head. I was on a train somewhere in America. It was just a few bars – not a solo instrument or a singing voice. It sounded to me like a full orchestra, marvellously loud. It lasted only a few seconds, but I recognized the overture to Verdi's *Rigoletto*! How that was done I do not know. It seduced me. I could have listened to it for hours.

But at other times, more often than I like, the voice asks insistent and impertinent questions. It asks about crime, about what it is like to be locked up in prison, how I feel about stealing from or exploiting other people. Why should it do that? Why should it ask me? I have no knowledge of such matters. Anyway, I am always unable to reply.

I shall telegraph to you when I know my departure date, the shipping line, the name of the vessel and so on. I can hardly wait to see you again after all these years.

From your prodigal brother, soon to return a new man,

Dolf Beck

6

Chad Ramsey (2050)

i

Chad travelled to his house in Hastings from Heathrow Airport. Because of line closures by the rail operators, who as usual ascribed damage to the tracks because of the intense heat, the only route back involved having to take a bus from the airport into central London, then a train from Charing Cross towards the south coast. Another change of train had to be made at Tunbridge Wells, because of flooded countryside south of the town – it involved a long wait of nearly three hours. This train terminated at Robertsbridge, and the final stage was by another bus, following an indirect route to drop off other passengers on the way. The journey took all day.

He and Ingrid had gone to Heathrow the previous day. They knew they would face similar delays, so had travelled up in advance of Ingrid's departure and stayed overnight in an airport hotel.

Ingrid was on her way to Oslo to see her parents. Disturbing messages from her mother about her father's declining health had made the trip a priority. She and Chad suspected that this visit might be the last.

The decision that she should travel to Oslo had been made

in haste. There was only one available flight that week, and it involved a four-hour wait for a connecting flight in Frankfurt. Ingrid immediately bought one of the few remaining seats. It was expensive.

When Chad finally reached Hastings on the Sunday night, he was concerned about Ingrid and her family, but also exhausted after two days of difficult travel in debilitatingly hot weather. Ingrid had texted him from Oslo's Gardermoen Airport to say the flight from Frankfurt had landed safely and that her mother was there to meet her, so that at least was one less thing to worry about.

When the bus from Robertsbridge pulled into the station yard in Hastings it was late, after midnight. He took the first coolcab in the rank. The house was hot and the air was stuffy because the aircon had been off for two days. He turned it on for a few minutes, but he was ravenous and that was what he was thinking about most of all. The only food in the house was a bag of frozen slabtofu chops. They had been there at least a month, the sort of food standby a lot of people set aside for when one of the occasional national food supply emergencies struck. He would have to defrost the chops before they could be cooked. It was too late at night for that. And he wanted something better than slabtofu.

He turned on a few room lights and put on a kettle to make tea, but then changed his mind.

He went out again and walked quickly to the local twenty-four-hour convenience store. The night air was humid, and a heavy smell of road tar drifted around. The houses he passed were nearly all in darkness. He had not eaten more than vending machine snacks since breakfast at the airport hotel that morning. Most of what the shop had on the shelves were cans of beer and cider. The food section was almost bare. He picked up a small sliced loaf with an expired sell-by date, some delipink processed meat substitute in a paper wrapper, a generic margherita pizza, half a dozen small cakelets. There was no milk or cream – only a seaweed-based coffee whitener in a huge can. Chad decided against it. There were no vegetables or fresh fruit. The guy in the armoured booth at the till said there would probably be deliveries the next day.

Chad was hungry, but repelled by the prospect of what he had just bought. On the way back to the house he saw the pisca and chips shop was still open. He went inside gladly. He started eating straight out of the cardboard wrapper as he walked back up the hill.

It was now after one in the morning. He felt too worn out to do anything more than slump, so he made tea without whitener and squatted in front of the TV. He finished the pisca and watched a late-night BNN bulletin. For the moment he forgot that he was carrying in his head an all-station instant TV receiver. By the time he remembered the IMC nanoshield the news had begun, and he would have to look up the protocols to switch into that channel. The printed instructions he had brought home from the course were in the house somewhere, but he was too tired to look for them.

He slept late the next morning and still felt listless even once he was up and dressed. He and Ingrid communicated briefly by internet – she too had slept late. Before lunch he called a coolcab and went down to the one large supermarket still trading in the town. He stocked up with real food to replace the emergency stuff. This was the day of the week he and Ingrid normally went shopping, sometimes together, sometimes one of them alone. Carrying the provisions back into the house and stacking them in the fridge-freezer gave a brief feeling of familiarity and routine to the day. He threw away the junk food he had impulsively bought the night before.

He showered, ate lunch, and at last began to sense that he

was returning to normal. The house remained liveable while the aircon was on, but it was a central unit and sucked up a lot of power. He went around the house and opened most of the windows, for fresh air not coolness, then closed the aircon ducts everywhere except in his workroom. The temperature on his outside thermometer read forty degrees Celsius. The sun was high in a hazy sky. A hot wind was blowing from the south – when he was outside, Chad had felt tiny pieces of grit on his lips and between his teeth.

The BNN news at lunchtime reported that an extensive forest fire had taken hold around Winchester, but local water resources were low and the firefighters were having to wait for a waterbomber. Convection winds caused by the conflagration were feeding the flames, which were racing towards the outer limits of the city. Another immense fire, dwarfing anything ever experienced in Britain, was still blazing uncontrollably in the Siberian forests. An area roughly the combined size of Spain and France had already been devastated. New fires had been detected in what was left of the Amazonian rainforest. In the American Midwest many farmers reported crop failures after recent storms. A major sandstorm, arising from the Sahara, had moved north and was overwhelming ports and shipping along the African Mediterranean coast. The Indian subcontinent was afflicted with an epidemic of cholera. International relief had been requested. Thousands more human bodies had been discovered on the migrant trail towards Europe. Many of them had bullet wounds. More such bulletins of bad news, from everywhere. The world was being incinerated.

At home the scale was smaller, but the underlying reasons were similar. The London Underground system was immobilized for the third time in a month: warped tracks in the overground sections, and a power supply failure. Repair teams were on the scene, but the workers were currently on strike because of intolerable working conditions in the unrelenting heat. Sixteen people had been killed and another twenty-seven injured when a fast-moving truck ploughed into a street market in Doncaster – the driver had been arrested, then the next day was found mysteriously dead in a police cell. Migrant organizations were protesting about the driver's treatment while in custody. During the night more than three hundred illegal immigrants had been put on a deportation flight from Britain to Libya, but were being held aboard the aircraft because a Saharan sandstorm would make landing impossible. Eleven more such flights would leave for the Sahel in the next few days. Britain remained a small island filled to capacity, so they said. This was the official solution. It convinced no one.

Chad switched off the TV, feeling depressed.

He booted his computer, briefly checked his emails and the social media pages he routinely visited, then sent a message to Ingrid.

After that he looked for the printed instruction sheets for the use of the nanoshield, knowing he had only ever skimmed through them. He found that most of the details were already familiar from demonstrations during the course. The instructors appeared to have done a comprehensive job.

On the back of the final page, in a grid printed for the purpose, Chad saw the protocol tags for the other course members. He had written them down himself, as had all the others making their own lists. They swapped contact details as if they were social acquaintances planning to meet up again. Their ranks went down the first column: Det.-Sgt, Insp., Chief-Supt, and so on. Then their names, their IMC tags, the force they were attached to and the coded entry protocol for connecting with them.

He reached behind his ear and depressed the area of his mastoid process where the switch was. He heard the slight hissing of the carrier signal. For a few minutes he roamed between the various media channels the nanoshield was capable of receiving. All responded normally, but for the first few moments he was once again taken aback by the sudden immediacy and clarity of the reception, the perfect signal, the sense that it was emerging from within him, not merely being received by him.

Every couple of minutes the transmission was briefly interrupted by the white flash of a lost signal, a disturbing sudden sound. It was harmless, so he supposed, but it gave him a transitory feeling of nausea. He wished it could be eliminated.

He stared down at the list of names and connections. He remembered the long days of the course without much pleasure, resentful that he had been dragged into something so intrusive, while at the same time feeling a sense of detachment because he lacked an operational police role. And then there was the exclusive close company of some thirty cops – not an ideal way to spend a couple of weeks effectively locked in a remote country house. He had not forgotten the rough and often objectionable humour in the bar in the evenings, the unguarded and prejudiced remarks based on an assumed consensus of outlook by all present, the attitudes, the culture. That none of this had changed in the two decades since he started working in the police building was dispiriting to realize. He had become used to feeling like a prig in his office, also many times a target for ribald comments, but he had learned from the first few days to keep his thoughts to himself.

He was beginning to see that his removal from the job was in some ways a relief. He was free of all that forever. It still rankled with him, his career ended because one senior officer appeared to take against him, but Chad was starting to realize that in reality the order to kick him out had probably come down from the HAO in London. Was it because of the expense of maintaining his office? A perceived shortage of cases need-ing his forensic input?

That was the most likely – Chad was aware of a long-term change in the nature of policing, which in these days of up-heaval was more about controlling social order and migrant issues than solving crime.

He picked a name more or less at random: a Detective Sergeant he had spoken to a few times outside the hours of the course, attached to the Somerset and Avon force. Nick Tomblay: his IMC tag was Nic0789. Chad entered the comms code, suddenly interested to know what was happening to him now he was presumably back on duty again. The con-nection was almost instant, but all Chad could hear (which meant he experienced it, felt it, transmitted it to himself) was the faint hiss of the carrier signal. He kept the comms open for about another minute but then there was the familiar, un-welcome sensation of an intrusive flash of light, and a feeling that somewhere around him there was a crashing noise. Chad disconnected immediately.

He tried another code: Jan4522, a woman Detective Inspect-or on the West Midlands force. Carrier hiss, then the abrupt break in signal.

He went through several other tags on the list with the same result. With the next attempts he avoided waiting for the in-trusive break and cut the contact when he heard no change in the carrier signal. Then he tried no more.

Finally, on an impulse, he entered the connect protocol for Jacek, the officer who had led the training team. This time the response was again instant but with a difference. Chad heard or felt the carrier hiss die away. The clarity, the silence, seemed to empty his mind.

Chad recoiled. It was like the common experience when flying: a sudden change in the aircraft's altitude which makes the eardrums pop. This time there was a voice, so loud and clear it was as if the speaker was in the same room.

'Detective Inspector Kaminski. I don't recognize your incoming protocol, officer. Cha1010 – who are you, what is your rank?'

'Jacek, this is Chad Ramsey. I was recently on a training course run by you. I—'

'I don't recognize your name, Ramsey. What is your serial number?'

'I held the nominal rank of inspector, but I wasn't on the force. I'm a civilian worker, or was—'

'How did you gain access to this equipment, Mr Ramsey? This is a closed police network, prohibited for use by unaccredited persons.'

'I was sent on your course. It ran for two weeks, during which a graphene nanoshield was connected to my head. I'm trying to find out why the nanoshield appears not to be working.'

'It is working. I see on your file that you have left the police service, Mr Ramsey.'

'No one is using the network.'

'The equipment you have is police property. You have been discharged from the force and have no right of access to it. You lack authority. I'll need to have your permanent home address.'

'Jacek – I only know you by your first name. You were the main instructor on the course. I was sent on the course by the HAO, which was then directly employing me. I was attached to the police through that. I was the only non-operational officer on the course.'

'You will need to have the equipment removed. You have no right to use it.'

'Why is the network not working? You must be aware of that.'

'That is classified information.'

There was a white flash, and the inner sound of the carrier hiss. Chad recoiled, a sick feeling in him. There had been too many of those. A silence endured.

'My hair is growing back,' Chad said, into the silence. The room felt hot and airless.

ii

Chad's parents and ancestors:

His father was called Max Edward Ramsey, who was married to Marianne, born and brought up in Leeds. Her parents had died shortly after she was married. Max and Marianne had given birth to Chad and Gregory in 2002. There were no other brothers or sisters. Of this Chad was of course certain.

Max Ramsey was born in 1974, and had two sisters, Anne and Daisy, Chad's aunts. One was older than Chad's father, the other was younger. Their father was called Connor Ramsey, born in 1948, Chad's paternal grandfather. This was the only part of his family tree that Chad knew with any accuracy, could put names and faces together. As a small child he and Gregory had often been taken to stay with their grandparents, Connor and his wife Helen, who were then living in semi-retirement in Brighton – he never knew his grandparents on Marianne's side because of their early deaths. When they were small children he and Gregory had often seen the aunts Anne and Daisy, but since growing up he had heard almost nothing from either of them. They were the source of most of the speculative gossip he had overheard about Adolf. There were relatives on his mother's side too, but they were less frequent visitors. Many years had passed. He knew Daisy moved to live in New Zealand, while Anne had married someone in the finance world, lived for a while in the north-west of England but moved away, possibly to London or even somewhere abroad. He assumed they were still alive, but had no idea what they were doing or where they lived.

So as far as Chad was personally aware the entire known paternal family of Ramseys consisted of grandfather Connor and father Max. Until recently, he and Gregory had never felt any real curiosity about their more remote ancestors. Uncle Adolf with his dubious reputation was the only exception, but in fact they knew nothing about him at all. They never asked about other relatives and consequently were told little about them. His father had sometimes referred to his own grand-parents, but always in a vague and abstract way, so they had never become memorable personalities in Chad's mind.

Chad's parents, Max and Marianne, had both passed away a few years ago, meaning practical lines of enquiry within the family had become more or less closed to him. To find out more about Adolf, as Gregory wanted, he would have to follow objective research routes.

The name was something of a dark joke. Adolf was a name rarely given to children in the present day, and so was archaic and unusual. Perhaps it was more common in Germany? Or Norway? The name alone made him at least memorable to the two boys. When they heard the family gossip about him they were too young to have lurid imaginings. They had simply grown up with the idea that somewhere in the past there was a black sheep on their father's side called Adolf. For that he was interesting, but no more than that.

Chad felt tied to the promise he had made to Gregory, that he would search whatever police records existed which he might yet be able to access. That now felt less than certain, after his recent brief contact with Jacek. The police personnel records apparently already showed he was an ex-employee.

On the other hand, he had been accessing the police databases for years and knew his way around them, including ways of working around outmoded forms of password security. These still presented a barrier to casual users.

Using his own computer he logged on and was mildly surprised, and relieved, that his old password and identity code still allowed him to enter the database. As often in the past, Chad felt glad of the generally slapdash attitude most police workers had to past cases, and the documentation relating to them.

The overall amalgamated police records went back about thirty years to 2020, which was when a major rationalization had taken place. These records were of course irrelevant for a search that would need to go back to the end of the nineteenth century, or the early years of the twentieth.

Records before 2020 were still accessible and mostly reliable, but at the time of the data rationalization the older files had been sorted into numerous archives. Some of these were based on geographical zones (counties and metropolitan areas), while others, depending on which police force was responsible, were based on court records. Assize areas administered by circuit judges were used as the basis for many of the files until the late twentieth century, and they then became subject to the occasional quirk or whim of individual judges. Extra complications were created if the judge decided not to sit on a particular trial that was listed, or for some other reason sent the case to another area. From the point of view of an archivist, the arbitrary decisions and choices made by judges were a constant problem. Chad knew from long experience that cases allocated to another justice were sometimes still filed under the name of the original judge. One database listed only the cases which had led to convictions. The further back in time you went, the more the erratic methods of the judiciary became problematic.

There were many more sub-archives and cross-referenced newspaper files, some less rigorously organized than others. The older records, before 1918, were mostly in microfiche reproduction, and were of course nearly all hand-written.

However, this sort of exploration had been in his daily routine for years and Chad felt at home with it. Complications always arose – knowing how to detour around them, or make the most of them, was the key to a successful data search.

He spent about an hour trawling through the past, searching for Adolf Ramsey, including the entire London police database, as well as the case files from the Central Criminal Court, and the various assize areas within London. He focused on a period between 1880 and 1910. He found nothing, although a search of prosecutions for fraud produced dozens of possibilities, none of them involving anyone named Ramsey. He widened the search years without any more success.

In the evening he started another search, this time using the more conventional family history websites. It did not take him long to track down his ancestors, all previously unknown to him.

His great-grandfather, Jack Ramsey, was born in 1925 and had two children, one of whom was Connor Ramsey, Chad's grandfather. Jack Ramsey's father was Edmund Ramsey, born in 1901. His father was Harald Ramsey, born in 1877. Harald had a younger sister, Agathe, but no brothers called Adolf, who might otherwise have been, or might have become, Uncle Adolf.

In fact, none of the Ramsey families through the decades had a child or a parent or a sibling called anything remotely like Adolf, or Adolph, and from a search through marriages, sisters, cousins, and so on, there were no Adolfs in the extended families.

Harald Ramsey appeared to have sprung from nowhere.

Chad found both a marriage certificate for him in 1899, when he married a young woman called Laura Shelton, and a birth certificate in 1901 for their only child Edmund, but none of the search engines revealed Harald's parentage.

A help screen in one of the ancestry websites suggested that in the case of uncertain parentage a search of English parish records might provide a source of further information, but only if the birth location were known. Here Chad's search came to an end, partly because the advice was general, not related to the Ramsey family tree, but mostly because he had no idea where Harald Ramsey or anyone related to him had been living.

Ingrid called him later in the evening. He took the call through the nanoshield, wanting to try it again. Her voice sounded close and familiar, almost intimate. He was still unnerved at the beginning of a contact of this sort by its immediacy, but because it was Ingrid it gave him a feeling of gratifying nearness to her.

Her news was bleak, but moderately hopeful.

'I talked with Pappa's physician today,' she said. 'He is not in imminent danger of dying, and she said they have been able to relieve his pain a little. She said it was also likely to extend his life expectancy by a few weeks.'

'How do you feel about that?'

'Life is hope, of course. But Pappa is still in a lot of pain, and his whole body has been so damaged by the cancer that Mamma and I are wondering if this is the best kind of treatment. I've so far only managed a few minutes with him, and he was half-asleep. I want to talk to him honestly, with no doctors around, so that I can find out what he wants. I expect he'll be better tomorrow.'

After the call, feeling subdued, and already missing the temporary intimacy of talking to her this way, Chad remembered the earlier attempt to find Adolf, the archive search in Oslo. That had later led indirectly to meeting Ingrid for the first time, a much more interesting and memorable life event.

Thinking back it had probably been hopeless attempting to search a Norwegian archive for someone called Ramsey. For a while, as he stood in the dusty archive hall, scrolling conscientiously through the old records, all those endless Larsens, Olsens, Pedersens and Andersens, he had in fact thought that if the name was there he would notice it easily. It was not. Ramsey was not a Norwegian name, common or otherwise.

This had given him a defeating thought: if Adolf had married into the Ramsey family, so was not in direct parental line of descent, then the search was hopeless. His surname at birth could have been anything.

Chad returned to the ancestry software, searched for and found Harald's younger sister, Agathe. Chad quickly discovered that in 1903 she had married a man with the solidly English name Foster. She and Mr Foster, a lawyer, had had two children, both girls. Unsurprisingly, neither of them was called Adolf.

iii

'They said you stole my visualizer,' the voice said on the door intercom.

It was the next morning. Patrick O'Connell was at his doorway, glimpsed first through the intruder screen. He was grinning, but had taken up a mock-aggressive stance. Chad swept the door open – Patrick shadow-boxed his clenched fists around.

'Come on in,' Chad said. He could see Pat's car parked crookedly in the road. Pat stepped inside, and Chad swiftly closed the door against the heat. At just before 9.00 a.m. the temperature was already in the high 20s, where it had probably been all night. 'Your thing is still here – do you want it back?'

'I need to see it, check it out. Why did you take it?'

'I was fired by the cops. I thought you knew that. I had about ten minutes to clear my desk. The choice was to leave it there on the top of the filing cabinet, or take it with me. I didn't want it to fall into the wrong hands.'

'The wrong hands being?'

'A building full of cops who suddenly wanted me out. Or at least, one of them did.'

'Namely Tom Amos.'

'Yes. Him.'

'It was none of his business,' Pat said. 'He knows nothing about profiling.'

'Then I did the right thing.'

They went into Chad's workroom at the back of the house. Chad retrieved the visualizer from the storage cabinet where he had put it for safekeeping, and set it on the far side of his own desk. He moved his computer forward to make space for it. Pat watched approvingly then pulled up a spare chair and sat down. Because of the drawer tower at the back of the desk he had to spread his knees to get close enough to work with the device. He opened his leather shoulder bag, pulled out an earthing mat and bracelet, and a selection of inert plastic tools.

Chad said, 'There's a mains socket in the wall by the desk.'

Pat leaned down and pushed in the plug. The visualizer groaned quietly, then went quiet. Nothing whirred, no lights came on.

'What do you have to do?'

'Among other things it needs a software upgrade, and I want to run some diagnostics. Have you tried using it?'

'You said not to. The last time I saw you in the office.'

'That was, what, three weeks ago? These things often go out of date as soon as you think you've finished them. We've been recoding for about a month, and the program now runs OK on the beta version at the lab. I thought as I hadn't seen you for a while it was time I brought this one up to speed.'

'You said it was bulletproof before.'

'Yes, that too,' said Pat. 'We always think that, then something else comes along.'

He was lifting away the metal case. There wasn't much to see inside: the usual tangle of fine cables, circuit boards, expansion slots, a power supply. There was a lot of unused space. Most of the weight obviously came from the case itself, which from its size had presumably been cannibalized from something no longer being used. Pat pushed the earthing mat beneath the chassis.

'I'll make some drinks,' Chad said. He went out of the workroom and put the kettle on. It was still early for him – he had not had any breakfast. Pat called out that if he was offering a drink he would prefer an iced tea or a can of cola, if that was OK and if there was one in the fridge. Chad obliged and took out two cans and a couple of glasses. He forgot about making tea. It was stiflingly hot in the small kitchen. He looked through the triple-glazed window. The garden was dry and withered. He and Ingrid had given up trying to grow things two years before. The intense weather would probably continue for several more months, but what would come after? Last year there had been gales at the end of summer. Today there was no perceptible wind.

While Pat was leaning intently over what he was doing Chad updated him on his abrupt departure from the force, and the couple of weeks before that, when he was away on the course.

'You've been given an IMC,' Pat said. 'I noticed your hair when I came in. I guess that means they installed a nanoshield. Have you tried it?'

'I tried it, yes. Or they tried it out on me.'

'Some people throw up the first time it's switched on.'

'I didn't – but it came as a hell of a shock. Everyone I was on the course with was affected by it. One of the guys threw up.'

'Did anyone pass out?'

'No – I think the course instructors were expecting that, but everyone looked a bit shaken without being ill.'

'When you were over that – what did you think of the system?'

'I never really got used to it. I realized early on it was for the cops, so I didn't pay much attention. The technology didn't apply to the sort of work I did. And I couldn't see how it was going to function in the real world, even operationally. The shield was supposed to make things easier, but I kept thinking about what I know of the actual physical requirements of police work. Apprehending suspects, and all that. They have to move fast sometimes. The technology was impressive, though.'

'Did you experience any signal breaks?'

'If you mean the sudden sense of being struck by lightning, yes I did.'

Pat said, 'The word is that the IMC is not much in use across the various forces, although hundreds of cops have been trained to use it. Like you. There were a lot of complaints about white-outs.'

'I recently tried getting through to some of the people I met on the course. All channels were silent.'

'That's what I've been hearing. It's not exactly catching on, even with the senior officers who have been made responsible for implementing it. The government is still trying to push it through, I gather. But I was in the HAO recently and I sensed they were starting to rethink it. Government departments are advised by the wrong people when they invest in new hardware.

The nanoshield – that was originally developed as a superfast gaming console. An outfit in Ukraine, most people in the business think. The software for it is still available on the dark net – it's unsupported, and you have to have the nanoshield fitted by a third party. There are some who will go to that length – high-end gamers in Russia and the Far East. It still has tech problems. The sensation of being struck by lightning you've experienced – it makes most people feel nauseated after it's happened a few times. But some of the gameplay templates incorporate it as a random hazard. That's gamers. They live for that sort of thing.'

'So how did the Home Affairs Office get hold of it?'

'A group of hackers in New China rejigged it, stripped out most of the gaming architecture, worked on the communications and streaming features, rebranded it, called it IMC, went in for a bit of clever marketing. Sold it not just in Britain, but all over South America and northern Europe. Now they are probably relaxing in their penthouses somewhere. But it's essentially still a games package, with big flaws. I assume you intend to keep the shield?'

'The cop I spoke to said they wanted me to give it back.'

'If you take my advice, don't let them near you. Once a graphene nanoshield is in place there's no safe way of removing it. Perhaps by cutting off your head, if you're willing to go along with that?'

Pat had already removed three of the tiny circuit boards and replaced them with others that looked identical, which he had brought with him. He added an extra one. Some of the tangle of thin cables had connectors, and these he pressed into the new board. He worked quickly and cleanly, his hands moving with precision. He had laid his tools in a neat line by the side of the chassis. Chad took some of his own papers away from the desk to make extra room for him.

Pat worked in silence for a little longer, then began re-assembling. Chad watched, fascinated by the deft movements of his hands and fingers, the ease and familiarity he had with the technology.

When it was complete, with the case screwed down tightly, Pat said, 'I need to upgrade this now.'

'Through the internet?'

'We could do it that way, if you don't mind the risk of errors, and a lot of setting up. But why don't we use your IMC? That's one of the few things it's good for.'

'We can connect to it through the nanoshield?'

'It's already connected. All I need is your permission.'

'All right.'

'Is that a yes you understand, or a yes go ahead?'

'I meant yes, go ahead,' Chad said.

There was a sudden sensation of intense clarity, a sweeping away of mental clutter, then the already familiar feeling of connection. It ceased as abruptly as it had begun. The whole thing took less than ten seconds.

'Good,' said Pat. 'You're up to date. I patched your shield into the visualizer, and I ran an upgrade on the IMC as well. They'll talk to each other now.'

iv

Chad and Pat sat opposite each other by the table under the window. They were in the false chill of the aircon, looking out across the arid desolation of summer. A pall of smoke was passing overhead – Chad felt the automatic sense of alertness to fire risk. How close was the fire, how large? Not yet covered by the smoke, the sun blazed down insistently. The sky was as ever hazy. He and Pat both wore light shirts, feeling the cool breeze from the vents in the wall above the window. Empty drink cans stood on the table between them.

Eventually, Pat asked him what plans he was making for the future.

'Now I'm no longer tied to Hastings, you mean?'

'Your brother lives in Scotland, doesn't he? You could move there – life is a bit more stable north of the border. And there's high ground.'

'Property is expensive in Scotland, and it's almost impossible to find somewhere affordable,' Chad said. 'The Scots have a strict quota for people moving in from England. I don't think Ingrid and I would qualify any more. You have to be able to take in capital, beyond whatever you pay for a house. And we're both too old – me jobless, Ingrid freelance and working for publishers in Europe. I don't think we're ideal immigrants.'

'You've presumably had a redundancy pay-off.'

'We'll be living off that for a while. It wouldn't be enough to buy somewhere to live, not without selling this place. And you know what's happened to the property market here on the south coast. Ingrid has already started talking about moving back to Norway. She has family there.'

'How would you feel about that?'

'It's an attractive place,' said Chad, pulling open another can. 'I'm one-sixteenth Norwegian. Or something like that. But it's never easy changing country these days. You know that. What about you? When did your family leave Ireland?'

'I was just a kid. It was different then. What would be the prospects for another job?'

'Slim to zero. There's not much call for profilers outside the police service. And even that's changed. They don't detect crime any more – they muscle in, lean on it and suppress it.'

'You could try one of the big companies. They've started using psychological profilers.' He indicated the visualizer resting on the rear of Chad's desk. 'I didn't build that just for you. We actually designed and built it with funding from one of the multinationals. Their consultants told them it could help them target their markets.'

'You once told me you only ever looked for backing from universities.'

'Them too. Things have changed. These days, needs must.'

'Working in a corporate is not for me,' Chad said. He felt an inner resistance to joining the job-application scramble again. He had been away from that for years. 'Not yet, anyway,' he added. 'Maybe if things get worse. The companies want to profile what, and how? Customer perceptions, product suitability? And your DNA visualizer wouldn't be much use in a corporate setting. Or I assume not.'

'I patched in the DNA analyser for you, Chad. Now that's done, are you likely to make use of it? I'd appreciate feedback.'

'I've nothing to run it against.'

'You must have some old cases you still have access to. Wouldn't there be DNA evidence in most of them? All DNA results have a sequence number – you input that through the keypad in the normal way. In your case, you don't even need a monitor hooked up. The results will come to you through the IMC. I'd be interested to know what you find. When we were developing the software we tested it with DNA samples taken from me and a couple of people on the staff, but most sample traces have differences. There are certain to be anomalies. No case is ever the same. Anything you can pass on would be helpful.'

'Do you want me to try now? I don't have any old case files to hand, but I know how to get some.'

'Whenever you're ready,' Pat said. 'Later this week would be OK.'

Refreshed, Chad woke up the next morning with the knowledge that he had thought of something important during a waking moment in the night. He went to his workroom, and suddenly it came back to him. Greg had said he would email him a copy of a DNA sequencing report, one which could allegedly be traced to Uncle Adolf through the clothes of his that were kept in the black museum by the Metropolitan Police. Included was a garment Gregory described as his pants: if he meant Adolf's underpants, and the garments had been isolated from possible contamination, then the trace would be strong and reliable.

Why the police a century and a half ago thought Uncle Adolf's underpants were worth keeping was a mystery. There was no DNA technology of any kind back then, and of course not even any awareness of a future science which would gain something from it.

Had Adolf been special in some way, his case sufficiently unusual or horrible that they thought the evidence was worth preserving for posterity? Well, Adolf's moment seemed to have arrived.

While Chad was away on the police course, and in the days since, Greg had sent him several emails. He had opened them as they came in, but because of other preoccupations Chad had so far only glanced at most of them. He now made himself some breakfast, then sat down at his computer with a first mug of coffee beside him on the desk. He looked through Greg's emails, then opened the one which had a file attachment. As soon as it came up Chad saw it was what he was looking for.

Written at the top was the name: *ADOLF BECK (alias John Smith, a.k.a. Ramsey), b. January 14th 1841, Christianssund, Norway. DW523.*

He went to Pat's visualizer and began tapping in the long DNA sequence on the keypad.

vi

There was a sense of being in a half-lit area, a high space above without a ceiling, some ropes, a wall, a tired-looking sign with red lettering, but it was to one side and he could not turn his head to read it. The place had an echo, a reverberation, as if he was listening from one end of a long corridor. There was music, but only a snatch of it. He could see nothing else around him. There was a flash of sheet lightning, and the connection failed.

Chad tried again. This time, no response.

A third try. He was on a ship of some kind. It was dark, but there were coloured lights somewhere above him. They were all he could see, and only peripherally. There was movement beneath him, but he was seated and braced against it. A chill wind. He was not wearing enough clothes to repel the wind. The place where he was sitting was vibrating, as if a huge engine was turning beneath. He was sitting on something wooden. A bench? A chair? He could see nothing. Then he heard the sea, a rushing sound. The connection suddenly failed.

The nausea was worse than he had experienced before. He rushed to his bathroom, but after a few dry retches he felt better.

He contacted Pat, who was away from his work station and Chad had to wait while the person who took his call went to find him. The few minutes allowed him to calm down, to set aside the bad physical reaction. When Pat came on Chad described what he had just achieved with the visualizer: the echoing of distant music, a ship at night.

Chad was thrilled by these glimpses of something other, a feeling that he was pioneering a new way of communicating digitally. He spoke too quickly and excitedly, repeating himself, correcting what he had just said, trying to describe images he had only seen at an angle, or in darkness, unaccountably. Pat made him slow down and tell him everything again. He interjected with questions, most of which Chad could not answer. The moments had been overwhelming, although minimal, so he had retained only impressions, the sort of half-recollection on waking from a dream.

Pat was not interested in impressions.

'The signal should not keep being dropped like that,' he said. 'And you say the burn-out is still happening. I thought I'd fixed it. Let me have a think. I might send you a patch later today. Meanwhile, replay the files and see if you can find more exact info about time and place.'

'Replay them? How would I do that?'

'They're automatically recorded. Look in the work notes they gave you on the course. There's likely to be a date stamp on the files. They're called v-files.'

Pat rushed away, apologizing – he was in the middle of something else.

Chad later located not only the three short experimental runs of the visualizer, but to his surprise an archive of all his connections. This included everything the IMC had been used for during the police course. He discovered how to delete these recordings, and did so. He appeared to have been carrying the list around in his head, a sort of unwanted memory implant from the nanoshield.

He traced and listened to his conversation with Ingrid, a few evenings earlier. Immediately after hearing the recording he called her again, anxious about her, missing her, depressed about the health of Erik, his father-in-law, aware of many things he had not said to her at the time. The news she had was no better, but her father's condition was stable. She had been able to have two good conversations with him.

She and Chad spoke for a long time.

When he went back to the visualizer an hour or so later, he found out from the work notes how to access and reuse archived files. One of them was blank, but recorded in the archive with a serial number and a suffix: *00.00.0000-0000*. That presumably was the second time he had tried, the one with no result.

The first of the three was designated with another serial number, presumably created by the software. It was what Chad assumed might be the date stamp Pat had mentioned: *xx.xx.1881-0000*.

Chad ran the file, and immediately he saw or experienced in his mind the same sensation from the first time. He was standing in a semi-lit place in what felt like a short corridor, an impression of space above him without a visible roof or a ceiling, some ropes hanging next to him beside a wall. Music was being played at a distance, distorted by the tunnel effect. He was in a theatre or hall. Backstage. He played it again: this time he realized it was orchestral music of some kind. By the sound of it the orchestra was a small one, but he could neither judge how well they were playing nor what the music was. He could hear it for only two or three seconds before it cut out. Therefore, a concert hall, an opera house? The flash of what looked like sheet lightning intervened every time.

The last time he played the recording he noticed a faint aroma in the air: scented, vaguely familiar from somewhere.

The third file on the list was stamped *xx.xx.1868–0000*. This took Chad back to the ship at sea, the sound of the wind, the engine vibrations, the slow rolling of the ship in the sea. He smelled the ocean, or the salty air, whatever it was – he had not noticed that the first time. There was little to see, no hint of where the ship was or on what part of the deck he was seated. He ran the file several times, as if by persevering he could make a visual image appear more clearly. He was frustrated by the crisp acuteness of the sounds, the wash of the seawater, the wind on the ship's superstructure, the creaking of the ship's hull as it laboured through the waves. But he still could not see anything. It was like being blind, or blindfolded. The vibration ran through him for a few seconds, before the lightning flash of shocking finality. Always too few seconds to be sure of anything.

He was feeling sick again, so took a rest.

He tried a new, different search on the DNA trace. The battery for the shield had given out, so he replaced it.

As soon as the image cohered he was totally immersed. He could see, hear, feel! He was on some kind of steep and slippery slope, leaning forward for balance. One of his arms was raised, a rope wound around his wrist, biting into him because his weight was on it. Wind blustered at him, but the sound was against his own ears, not the howling of a gale screeching or whistling around something else. He could feel its bullying pressure pushing against his side. The air was freezing cold – to his unprotected face it felt like a slap. He was looking straight ahead and upwards, following the line of the tautly stretched rope on which he hung. Everything was white. There was nothing but whiteness. Snow and ice, white light, a glimpse of sky above, but so brightly lit by a wintry sun that it too was white. Shards of ice and snow were skidding down around him from above. Some of them bounced off his face and shoulders. He could not look away. He was paralysed, staring up and forwards.

Chad struggled to understand. He knew in a few seconds the connection would fail. He said aloud, 'Ad— Adolf? Where are you?' He tried to breathe in to say it again, but then, almost as a relief, there came the sheeting flash of light, and the connection was broken.

Later he looked at the date stamp: *xx.xx.1855-0000.*

If the four-digit numbers were years, he seemed to be travelling back in time.

He braced himself, then ran the file once more.

vii

That night, lying in his bed, waiting for sleep, Chad was haunted by recurring thoughts. They were so insistent that they felt like memories. A crevasse in a glacier. Clambering unsteadily across the uneven, frozen surface, a bitter wind, a dangerous slope. A lost father – had he been searching? A quiet home life in a small house, built of wood, a view of the sea, or a lake, or a fjord. A brother he never saw – not Greg, someone else, Adolf? Music in a theatre, a scented fragrance. Life aboard a ship, terrifying storms, ports of call, back-breaking labour with cargo hoists and winches, and angry shouts and orders.

Some of these he had seen, imagined, witnessed through the visualizer, but others were memories. How could that be?

He lay awake for a long time, dwelling on experiences he had never had. Unearned memories. Finally, he drifted off to sleep.

viii

It was more than two days before Pat called him back, apologizing again, explaining that he had had to make several trips away from the workshop, but that he had been thinking about the problem in spare moments.

'There's nothing I can do for now about the cut-off period,' he said. He and Chad were communicating through the nano-shield. 'It seems to be some kind of default on the IMC you're using. Maybe it's hardwired in. I think I can come up with an override, but not straight away. What we need is a time stamp on each v-file as well as a date. I assume you've seen dates being displayed?'

'Yes, but just the year, I think. Not the month or day.'

'The year is automatically picked up. I've written a sort of workaround for now that will stamp the time next to the date. It's a bit of a compromise: the year you have selected, but your own local time. I'll use the BeiDou twenty-four hour setting. That might have to be a permanent arrangement. I'm working on month and day stamping now. Once you've put up a few time stamps the program will have something to grip. You will probably start to experience longer connections. Can I send you an update?'

'Yes – I grant you permission,' Chad said, incautiously.

Whatever it was that Pat then did to make the update go into action, Chad was pole axed by what felt like a punch to the back of his head. He slumped to the floor, unconscious.

By the time he recovered many minutes had passed. Pat had closed the line and gone. Chad struggled on the floor to get himself upright, but his head was aching and his right arm was painful.

He reached a sitting position, then used his desk to help himself stand up again. As he had fallen his right elbow must have scuffed against the wooden edge of the desk, and taken much of the impact against the floor. There was a long and painful graze on his elbow and forearm. He was disorientated and dizzy. He felt himself for more bruises. His back was aching. He felt annoyed, embarrassed. The front of his shirt was flecked with yellow liquid and a spray of semi-digested food, smelling of vomit. His head was throbbing, and instinctively he pressed his hands to the sides of his head, as if he could stop the pain by pressing physically on the invisible shield.

He remembered only a powerful sense of exploding light as whatever Pat had done reached him.

Chad called Ingrid that evening, wanting to hear her voice again. This time he used the internet – old technology. He said nothing about what had happened.

He did not try using the visualizer again that day, nor for several more days after that.

7

Adler and Adolf Beck (1888-1895)

i

By the summer of 1888 the change in the weather following the eruption of Krakatoa would barely have been noticed by most people in Britain. Five years had passed. Winters were longer, and the cold spells were sharper; springs came a little late; summers were overall cooler than normal, although periods of hot weather still occurred; the leaves on trees started to turn golden slightly sooner than expected. Unless like me you constantly monitored the weather, and knew the averages from the recent past, you might grumble about the long periods of rain, the occasional heavy snowfall, and so on, think them exceptional without realizing a subtle change was taking place.

There was a similar picture around the world. The drifting clouds of ash, dust and gases in the upper atmosphere were barely perceptible from the ground (although Meredith told me the telescope observations were still partly obscured), and were starting to diminish. Sunsets continued to be spectacular.

Weather stations in the Swiss and Austrian Alps reported heavy snowfall, followed by destructive avalanches. The number of icebergs sighted in the north Atlantic was greater than average. The monsoon season in India and other parts of the

Far East lasted longer and caused widespread flooding. British people complained that their seaside holidays were ruined by the stiff breezes and recurrent rain showers. French farmers reported crop failures – American farmers suffered a major reduction in corn harvest. The price of wheat tripled. From colleagues in Norway I heard that all the land glaciers were growing thicker and longer.

All these weather events and many more like them could be attributed to normal conditions, and were. The British habitually complained about summer weather, farmers had good years as well as bad, avalanches happened. I studied extremes and norms, patterns and trends. The state of the glaciers confirmed my own researches.

In 1888 there was a solar minimum: Solar Cycle 12 had ended four years earlier and SC 13 was about to begin. No sunspots had been visible for several years. I was aware of the effects.

I studied and recorded the meteorological facts, both directly from the instruments in the grounds of the college, and from reports sent to me every week by observers in many parts of the world. My teaching work continued uninterrupted, helping to turn intelligent young students into officers of the Royal Navy, but most of my spare time, as well as at the weekends, was taken up with quantifying the current levels of sunshine, rainfall, air pressure, wind velocity and so on from around the world. I also created a huge comparative table, analysing past weather, or as much as was known. But annoyingly for me meteorology had until now rarely been treated as much of a real science on historical principles.

The Meteorological Office had been set up some years before as part of the British government's Board of Trade, but it was mostly concerned with forecasting the weather. It was preoccupied by the need to warn of storms at sea. The notion of weather having a history, or of creating patterns, or of revealing trends from which the future climate might be anticipated, was of little interest to sailors out at sea, more concerned about the wind getting up and the dark clouds and white-capped waves immediately ahead.

I was aware that the weather was almost invariably measured at ground level, while most of the changes or developments occurred in the atmosphere around and above us. This was a constant background frustration in my work. The drifting haze from Krakatoa was affecting our climate, yet few knew it was there and those of us who were concerned with it had no way of ascending to the stratosphere to measure it.

I heard that the French were experimenting with balloons filled with hydrogen, or lifted by furnaces and hot air. In my more fanciful moments I wondered if the future of climate measurements might be up there in the blue. One day I mentioned this in an offhand manner to Meredith. She promptly vetoed my ever thinking about it again.

ii

I had lost contact with Dolf at this time. His letters, always occasional and arriving unpredictably, were more erratic in tone than ever. He changed his mind about everything. Whole areas of his life were blank to me. Where exactly was he? Who was he with? What was he doing?

He had written to tell me that he was leaving New York in the summer of 1884. I assumed he would travel to London and we would meet again. He did in fact arrive in London, but stayed only one night. He was in a cheap hotel in the Earls Court area. From there he sent me a telegram.

PLEASE EXPECT ME TOMORROW, it said.

The next day came, but Dolf did not appear. After two or

three weeks an envelope arrived with a postmark from Norway. It contained a single scrap of paper, with what appeared to be a hastily scribbled message in pencil:

My dear Adler, I had to travel at short notice to Telemark for business reasons. Tomorrow I am going to Paris to discuss the American statue. I will return to London soon. Expect me then. Yours affectionately, Dolf Beck.

iii

The London we were living in had taken on a troublesome aspect, one that worsened year by year. I certainly did not remember it being like this during those first months after Dolf and I arrived from Norway. The profusion of factories opening up, the building of railways and roads, and above all the hundreds of thousands of houses, all spilling coal smoke into the sky, made London into a place of constant haze and fog.

The summer months were not too bad because few domestic fires were lit, but as soon as autumn came the air was thick with a bitter and sometimes acidic smell, creating a choking pressure on the lungs. Distant views became romantically misty, but the romance was false: the air was full of smoke. It was a real threat to well-being. On the worst days there was a deep fog, yellowish, blinding, hateful to breathe. If you covered your mouth and nose with a kerchief or a scarf a black, sticky sediment soon built up, a horrid reminder of what was also entering your lungs. Many people reported to hospitals with persistent and unpleasant coughs, and one heard of a high mortality rate among infants in the poorer quarters of the city.

Naturally, Meredith and I took all possible precautions to protect Harald and Agathe, but they were now at day school so were away from our care. Lellie, the children's companion, was devoted to them and did her best for them on our behalf.

As a scientist whose sensibility was increasingly about our whole world, I imagined that the London problem was one being duplicated in many other countries. I knew that the industrial heart of Britain lay in the north and that the concentration of heavy industries in Yorkshire, County Durham and parts of Lancashire, combined with the huddled homes of the working people, created a nightmare of dirty air, soot-blackened buildings, polluted rivers and filthy streets. The life expectancy of even apparently healthy young adults was short: the statistics of people suffering from asthma, bronchitis and more serious lung ailments were appalling to read when they were published in scientific and medical journals.

Then I thought of the great industrialized marvel of the United States, a dynamic country as never before, inventing and developing new ideas, building hundreds of miles of railroads and thousands of huge factories, drilling for oil, mining for coal, smelting steel – a country where smoke constantly belched into the air. I began to visualize the whole planet becoming a vast creator of coal smoke and soot, where grimy bodies waded through industrial mire, coughing and spluttering and struggling for breath.

I allowed my imagination to roam too much, but it was clearly not a good thing for our atmosphere to have to absorb so much smoke and bear so many noxious waste gases. I began to wonder: would all this industrial haze act like the ashen output of major volcanoes, a shield around our world, reflecting back the heat of the sun?

I took a closer notice of the papers and essays scientists were publishing on this subject. At first the pickings were thin. This was a time in Britain of peak and prosperous involvement with the Empire, and the dark mills and deep pits were turning out their products to an expanding and lucrative market. Scientists who took a sceptical or enquiring negative interest in the consequences of this booming economy were not encouraged. Being one of them I could find no journal that would publish papers with my thoughts.

Essentially, I continued to believe that the industrial gloom would slowly gather at every level of the atmosphere and form a miasma that would filter and shade the heat of the sun. This would precipitate solar dimming, a cooling of the world. It would open the way to what I had feared for many years: the Holocene would end, with a return of ten thousand years of ice age.

But working as a scientist creates the habit of an open mind.

I was becoming aware of the theories of an English colleague named John Tyndall.

Tyndall claimed that the release into the air of various unbreathable gases, such as methane and carbon dioxide, together with the natural presence of water vapour in the form of clouds, would create an effect similar to the glass panes of a gardener's greenhouse.

Tyndall intrigued me. Like me he had started as a glaciologist. Also like me he had moved on to other areas of interest, all of which connected with each other. He was born about twenty years before me – by the time he reached the age I am now he was an established author of books popularizing science, as well as more than a hundred and fifty papers aimed at the scientific community. He delivered specialist lectures to august bodies, but he also gave popular talks to the general public.

Tyndall was convinced that a gradual concentration of what he called greenhouse gases would dangerously retain the planet's natural heat, leading to an overall rise in temperature. What would seem a modest increase, two or three degrees Celsius around the world, would be enough to precipitate the partial or entire melting of both polar ice caps, with a consequent raising of the sea level.

It was plausible, impressively argued, and worrying – but was it the whole story? Tyndall's theories crucially did not take into account the presence or influence of the oceans, except as recipients of meltwater. My research had established that it was the constant flow of the warm and cold oceanic currents that maintained the climate we knew at present. Those could be disrupted only at great hazard, but the sudden influx of fresh water had had a drastic impact in prehistoric times.

I was especially concerned, of course, with the importance of the Gulf Stream. Tyndall's image of the Arctic ice melting, and the prospect of the immense Greenland ice cap flooding its non-saline meltwater into the north Atlantic, simply mortified me.

Our world's climate was as finely balanced as the delicate mechanism of a chronometer. Any disruption of it either way, cooling or warming, would lead to disaster. Tyndall was describing only the first part of global upheaval.

If the greenhouse gases warmed the whole Earth, that process would not be isolated. Had he considered the effect on the rest of the world should Greenland melt? And what of the great Antarctic continent in the south?

Meredith and I spent long hours discussing this, speculating, arguing, theorizing, consulting as broad a range of scientific opinion as we could find.

'There is one hope,' I said. 'Tyndall could be right, and the gradual warming that starts the ice caps melting might, in the end, be enough to mitigate the worst effects of the freezing.'

'Mitigation is not the same as prevention,' Meredith said. 'We do not want the world to become a hothouse. Nor do we want a permanent winter. Which would be worse?'

'I have always said it is about balance. Tyndall is talking about one extreme, I am predicting and dreading another. Could these two major disasters maintain a balance if they began at the same time?'

'But what if they did not?'

There was an unstated concern at the back of our minds. We did not have to speak openly about it to know it was there. We both feared for the future lives of our children.

We were approaching the end of one century and the opening of another. At this time, the end of 1888, Agathe was still only eight years old. Harald was eleven. Their lives would mostly be lived in the twentieth century. When I was feeling at my most optimistic I foresaw the next century as an era when science and technology would burgeon, introducing marvels of which we could still barely dream, and easing the lives of millions of ordinary working people. I wanted my children to live life to the full in that future world. All would be lost to them if Jostedalsbreen and its hundreds of brethren began their inexorable grinding progress down their valleys, expanding and crushing, destroying everything in their way.

iv

> *Covent Garden Hotel*
> *Floral Street*
> *London WC*
> *September 25th, 1894*

Dear Adler, my one brother,

I have received the letters you sent me. I read them all with interest and enjoyment. Your love and concern have been a great support to me at a time when my life, if only occasionally and for short periods, has been troubled. I know you experience long periods of silence from me, and that they upset and worry you, and so I am writing this letter to try to explain some of what is behind all that.

I am leading a busy and successful business career, which occupies most of my waking hours and often requires me to travel. I am constantly on the move. I can tell you, for instance, that I have been in residence at this small London hotel for more than four years. The letters you have sent me have been received here, and forwarded to me, all through that time. However, I am rarely in the hotel in person. In the last twelve months I have stayed the night in Covent Garden about fifteen times in all, but almost invariably for only one or two days and nights, hardly long enough to think of the hotel as my home.

In recent months I have been on business to New York twice, to Paris, to Panama, to Kristiania, to Amsterdam, as well as several trips to the beloved mountains of Telemark, where I have mineral interests. As you can imagine, these journeys are time-consuming as well as disruptive of what you almost certainly think of as normal life.

I have some news I wish you to understand and act on. For a variety of reasons I am now using a nom de plume while I am in London.

Regrettable though it may seem, while here in England I am often taken for a German because of my name, and to some extent because of my way of speaking English. Occasionally, people do realize I am Scandinavian, but that doesn't change their opinion much. Either way, there is an unpleasant streak of prejudice in some elements of London.

For this reason I have adopted a temporary identity, an extremely English one. I now call myself 'John Smith', and under that familiar and widely used name I am accepted without question.

Please, Adler, from now always address your letters to me as 'John Smith'. The hotel I am staying in has been informed of the harmless deception, and will forward your mail to me as usual. If for any reason I change hotels, I will from the outset register as Smith.

While on this subject, let me assure you that everything in the letters I write you is mine. You ask why 'my' handwriting seems to change so often. It is because I am always nervous of writing English, which you insist I use, and so I delay the next letter to you until I have found a companion I can trust. I need someone who writes English and will take the trouble to draft my letters for me. This letter, for instance, is coming to you by the grace of my good friend Mr G. R. Sims, who is a retired journalist and a fellow resident of the hotel.

When I was living in Lima the same service was provided by a certain Colonel Frederick North, with whom I was companionably involved at the time of the war between Peru and Chile (I will tell you of that adventure one day). After Col. North returned to Britain, my friend Major Hans Lindholm, a senior officer in the Danish Army and later an equerry to the King of Denmark, became my temporary scribe.

Therefore, the handwriting you have seen from time to time has been theirs, but the messages and the imparting of confidences are all mine. I am sorry if this has confused you. I mean no harm. That is the recurrent feature of my life: I mean no harm to anyone, but I am constantly getting into scrapes.

Tomorrow I expect to have to travel once more to attend to my Norwegian mineral interests. I am awaiting receipt of my ticket now. I shall be out of London yet again.

You justifiably ask what happened to me in Paris. To my shock and disappointment I discovered when I arrived in Paris that Pedersen, the mine owner from whom I believed I had bought the rights to the copper mine, had already extracted and delivered. The ore was at the smelting furnace outside Paris and the French government had paid for it. The copper was at that very moment being cast as the outer shell of the mighty New York statue. Pedersen, the cunning rogue, had pocketed the payment I made for extraction rights, as well as the substantial fee for the ore itself, on which I was counting. He then disappeared.

I returned to Telemark as soon as I could and discovered that the mine, still legally my property, had been closed. A mining surveyor I consulted told me that the mine had been assayed and was now deemed to be worked out.

After that I set out for New York City in pursuit of the scoundrel Pedersen. I never found him in spite of great efforts, and reluctantly had to turn my hand to other opportunities.

I was ruined financially by my adventure with the copper mine, but since then I recovered some of the loss. I am now investing with much more care. At present I am negotiating an option on another mine in Telemark, I have an interest in a gold reef in Australia, and I have applied for an international patent on an ingenious new kind of locknut, designed with a friend I met on one of my many sea voyages.

I shall contact you again the moment I return.

For now I close with my usual news of the phenomenon of the inner voice, which has bothered both of us throughout our lives. When we were at school one of the teachers made all pupils keep a daily diary. No doubt you too remember this. I recently came across mine, and discovered that I was only fourteen years old when I recorded what I now know to be the first of many intrusions.

I wouldn't normally mention that again, because it is so far back in my childhood. But recent intrusions have developed a threatening and unpleasant note. There is talk of crime, of punishment, of prison. Your most recent letter to me suggests that you have been experiencing the same. Let me say with my hand on my heart that I have never done anything illegal in my life. All the risks I have taken have been with my own money. I would not dream of taking someone else's. The threat of imprisonment is deeply disagreeable to me, because for all the mistakes I have made in my life I have always been honest.

Your loving brother,
'John Smith'

v

139 Victoria Street
London SW
August 25, 1895

My dear brother Adler,

Observe and note my current address, as here. This is now my permanent residence.

Your last two letters were forwarded by the rogue Eccleshare who runs the decrepit Covent Garden Hotel in Floral Street, but he delayed by several weeks. He claimed he did not know who John Smith was, even though I had explained it to him several times. Do not send anything there again (and there is no need for you to use the Smith name as it appears to be more trouble than it is worth).

I am also informed that you called round in person to the Covent Garden address earlier this year while I was in Switzerland on business. Why should you have done this? It created several problems for me when I returned. For reasons of commercial strategy I have always maintained that I have no kin. I do not know what passed between you and Eccleshare, but when I returned I discovered that all my property and effects, normally stored in my room, had been removed by Eccleshare and hidden away somewhere. He also presented me with a bill in excess of £600 which he claimed was for unpaid rent on my room. I had no alternative but to move to my present lodgings.

I am often visited by my friend Colonel Frederick North, whom I knew in Lima. He is assisting me in various enterprises. Col. North happened to be present one evening when the unwelcome intrusive voice broke in. Again I was accused by the voice of dishonesty, and warned of a life in prison. Col. North saw at first hand the dramatic and debilitating effect the intrusion had on me. He strongly suggested I seek expert advice from a specialist doctor, but I am in reduced circumstances so I cannot afford a medical bill. I am wondering if you too have consulted some such physician for the same symptoms, and if so might I use your good name? I can after all claim with complete truth to be Mr A. Beck. I suspect that most people still cannot tell us apart, so a harmless impersonation would be of tremendous assistance to me. I should be grateful to know how to contact your doctor.

Yours &c,

Dolf Beck

vi

In the year 1896 Dolf's troubles became worse and deepened in an alarming way: in London he had lately been accused of a series of petty crimes which I knew beyond a shadow of a doubt he could not and would not have committed. I heard that he protested his innocence at every opportunity, but he remained under arrest. He refused to see me, even when I applied to the authorities for a permit to visit him.

I assumed that the fairness of the British legal system would sort out the mistake as soon as he was before a judge and jury. That was not to be: to my horror and astonishment he was up against a mountain of incriminating evidence, and the jury found him guilty. He was sent to prison for five years. The court must have made a terrible mistake.

I employed and paid for the best lawyers I could locate, who said they would appeal against both conviction and sentence, but for the time being he had to remain in prison.

One morning, after Dolf had been in prison for several months, I was walking to work at the college, crossing Black-heath. I was brooding again about his situation. I felt helpless to know what to do about the immense problem he presented, but as I walked I was also noticing the light of the morning sky, feeling the chill in the air that never seemed to lift, fearful of the future, planning the lecture I had to deliver in under an hour's time, concerned about the children, notably Harald, now a nineteen-year-old looking for a job and asserting his independence from me in a desolating way – thinking in fact of almost anything but the voice that occasionally intruded into my mind, when the voice itself abruptly intruded.

'Adolf!' was the first, peremptory word, close, intimate, within me somehow. 'Adolf? Are you Adolf – Beck? Prison, when? How? For what?'

The moment these words began I was immobilized by the intrusion. It was worse this time than past experiences. It began with a feeling like a blow on my head, a wrench that was simultaneously forwards and backwards, making it painful to do anything, turn, speak, look around me. Breathing became an effort yet again. I had come to a halt, standing motionless in the middle of the pathway I had been following.

I tried to say, 'Yes, I am listening.' I was not capable of speaking. 'Who are you?' But I was strangled by the shock. 'I am not Adolf.' All I managed was a sort of grating noise in my throat. I uttered sounds without words.

The intrusion lasted a longer time than most. I turned my head slowly, slowly, and saw other people passing by normally. I was starting to fret about not being able to gulp more than a few small mouthfuls of air. Then the ambience, the surrounding sensation of space and intimate intrusion, died away. It was replaced by a low, sinister hissing. After two or three more seconds that too became silent.

I was released. I took a step forward, stumbled slightly, managed to recover. There were people walking behind me, and now the man and the woman caught up with me and passed me. They looked at me with concern.

'Are you all right, sir? We saw you—'

'Thank you. I am fine. I think I must have stubbed my toe.'

The man courteously touched the brim of his hat, to which I responded, and to the lady, and then they walked on ahead of me.

I looked around me at the people who were crossing the park on the same path as me, or on the one that connected with it from the other park gate. Maybe fifteen or twenty people were close enough to have heard the sound of my voice, had I been able to do more than croak. None of them appeared to have noticed me when I was seized, or at least were not now looking or staring in my direction.

I fussed with the handle of my walking cane, as if that was the reason I had come to a sudden halt.

The voice was not a delusion, it was not supernatural. The speaker recognized me, or at least spoke the name of my brother. He somehow knew, or thought he knew, what might have happened to Dolf. And what manner of unimaginable futuristic science surmised by Meredith could achieve any of that?

I walked on, trying to appear carefree in the weak sunlight of a chill early morning in March. Something I could not understand had happened to me. The incursion was no different from others, although it had lasted longer, but this time it had left a residue.

I was aware of startling new information that had appeared, apparently spontaneously, in my thoughts. How could that be?

My mind was churning, trying to make sense of this. I could not continue on to the college, as planned. I knew that as soon as I arrived in the building I would see colleagues, perhaps some of the students even so early in the day: I would be tasked with questions, requests, details of some college matters or meetings I should have to be told about. The routines of my job.

I made a quick decision. I knew of a small tea shop in Park Row, the road which runs alongside the college, so I went in there and sat down at a table with my back to the door. I wanted a period of calm in which to collect my thoughts – it was a familiar phrase, but this time it was apt.

My intruder knew that Dolf was in prison. Did he somehow know more than that? Perhaps the intruder would also know who had really committed the crimes for which Dolf was being held responsible. These thoughts made old suspicions re-emerge. What had Dolf actually been doing in New York? Had that been illegal in some way? Even without details of that undescribed period of his life I knew Dolf was an inveterate maker of financial deals, many of which appeared to end up losing him money. Did that make him a criminal?

But now there were new thoughts, realizations, matters I knew as if remembering them for myself.

Why, for example, should I suddenly think of 'Oslo', the old village name for Kristiania, the capital of my country? The authorities had declared the name change, and no one called it Oslo any more – although I knew there were many people in Norway who wanted it changed back.

I had a memory of suffocating, inescapable, killing heat, while I had not even been warm.

I had an unpleasant, itchy feeling that my skin was being crawled over by insects – flies with a nasty bite, yellow flies. I knew of no such insect. Why should that happen to me?

There was an image, a clear memory, of an attractive young woman standing near a shop, somewhere that had books in the window. She was smiling, happy to see me. I could hear her words, but I could not remember what she said.

And then there was a flower. A fragile little white flower with a burst of yellow stamens in the centre. Why should I think of that?

It was puzzling, but in itself not alarming. I liked the look of the young woman, and wondered what her name was. Why she had been there outside a shop? I sensed the name Ingrid: a popular Norwegian name, but I knew no one called that. Had she spoken in English? Or was it Norwegian? And what was the flower? Was it connected with the painfully biting yellow flying insects?

I was bemused, fascinated, puzzled. It was as if my intruder had left a trace of himself behind. Was that accidental? Or was it some kind of message?

I drank the cup of tea that was brought to my table, then continued on to the college. I went through the day somehow, trying to think and act normally, but these unexpected memories still haunted me.

As soon as I was home that evening I wrote a letter to Dolf at the prison. He had told me through the lawyers I myself was employing that he did not want to hear from me until he had cleared his name, but I did not let this deter me.

I was sensing a tragic breakdown of my family connections. Dolf was Dolf, suffering in prison, still maintaining his innocence, which I continued to believe in spite of everything. Meredith was disgusted by what she had learned about him from the court proceedings, and would not mention him. And Harald, my handsome and clever son, still only nineteen years old, was so appalled by what he had discovered about Dolf that he was considering changing his surname. He was in love with a young woman. The one time he and I spoke about this painful subject he told me that her family had threatened to stand in his way, if he did not dissociate himself from the scandalous affair, the despicable crimes of which Dolf had been found guilty.

So I worded my letter to Dolf with care. I urged him to make contact with me as soon as possible, asking him to tell me the truth, the unvarnished truth, about whatever he knew about those crimes for which he had been convicted. I asked him specifically if he had anything he wished to confide in me. I reminded him of the vow he and I had taken privately together when we were boys, in those sad days following the death of our father: that we would always honour him, never betray his high moral standards. I wrote to Dolf to say that he must abide by that solemn promise.

As ever, a long silence ensued.

8

Adolf Beck a.k.a. 'John Smith' (1896-1901)

i

In 1896, the criminal trial took place in London of Adolf Beck, also known as 'John Smith' and 'Lord Winton de Willoughby'. According to British law and legal practice, the fact that he had received an earlier prison sentence was not mentioned in open court, or in the press, for fear of prejudicing the jury against him – they would only be informed of that later, should they return a verdict of guilty against him. His previous record was known to the judge, as well as to the prosecution and defence teams. Under the name John Smith, Beck had been given a five-year sentence in 1877 for a series of crimes similar in nature to the ones he was now facing.

Nineteen years had passed since that earlier trial. In 1896 Queen Victoria was still on the throne. A man named Arnold was the first person in the world to be fined for exceeding a speed limit (then 2 mph) in a horseless carriage – later in the year a woman named Driscoll was the first person to die in a motor accident. The first edition of the newspaper *Daily Mail* was published. Marconi's wireless telegraph system was demonstrated in public.

ii

The circumstances in which Adolf Beck had been arrested were unusual.

Beck was leaving his lodgings in Victoria Street, dressed as he normally preferred in the formal clothes of a gentleman. On the steps of the house he was accosted by a woman as he walked down to the street. She accused him in a loud voice of having cheated her and stolen money. Beck told her he had never seen her before in his life and tried to walk past her. She pursued him up the street, repeatedly shouting accusations at him. Beck ran across the road to try to escape her. She followed. Beck then noticed a police constable on duty, so he hurried across to plead for help. The woman's accusations continued. Beck insisted that she was a complete stranger to him and demanded that the officer arrest her.

The constable led them to a nearby police station to calm them down and try to sort out what was going on. They each told their story. The woman was believed and Adolf Beck was not, because the police already had on file allegations from several other women of fraud and theft by a man with a Germanic accent pretending to be an aristocrat. Once these complaints were noted, Beck was immediately arrested and charged with fraud.

Many of the other women who had lodged complaints were brought into the police station. Without exception, one by one, they picked out Adolf Beck from a line-up of men of similar age and appearance. They said without doubt or hesitation he was the man who had cheated them. They signed written statements to that effect. Beck was remanded in custody, and a date was set for trial by jury.

During the waiting time before the trial could begin a

member of the public wrote to Scotland Yard, claiming that Adolf Beck was in fact the 'John Smith' who had been convicted of fraud in 1877. The police then retrieved the old file. Two police officers who had retired since that time but were named in the papers were contacted. Eliss Spurrell, the constable who had arrested Smith, and Inspector Redstone, who laid the charges against him, both identified Adolf Beck as John Smith. Eliss Spurrell said in a signed witness statement, 'There is no doubt whatever he is the man. I know what is at stake on my answer, and I may say without doubt he is the same man.'

Because Beck vehemently protested his innocence, the police took samples of the handwriting of both Beck and Smith and sent them to Mr Thomas Gurrin, a handwriting expert. Mr Gurrin closely examined the samples, and came to the conclusion that efforts had been made to disguise the handwriting.

Mr Gurrin's statement to the police said: 'I have examined and compared the exhibits therein with the bills and cheques. In this case I am perfectly satisfied that they are all in the self-same handwriting – the disguise then adopted is the same as that now adopted, and the exhibits in that case must, in my opinion, have been written by the person who has written the bills and cheques in this case.' This created a solid evidential connection to the earlier case.

Mr Gurrin added that he would be prepared to give sworn evidence in court to this effect.

iii

On March 3rd 1896 Adolf Beck was produced from custody at Court No. 1 in the Central Criminal Court, the Old Bailey, in London. He appeared before the Common Serjeant, the second most senior judge in London, Sir Forrest Fulton. Beck's defence was paid for from the public purse, and he was represented by a brief called Mr Charles Gill. The prosecution on behalf of the Crown was led by a barrister named Mr Horace Avory.

A jury of twelve ordinary citizens, all men, were empanelled for the hearing. There were seventeen charges on the indictment sheet, all similar to each other, but the prosecution and defence agreed that only three would be proceeded with. These charges were read out to Beck. He pleaded not guilty to all three.

Before the trial proper began, the Common Serjeant directed that the jury be removed from the court, as well as the defendant. He then summoned the two sides to the bench. The shorthand note-taker recorded the following brief exchange:

Common Serjeant: Mr Gill, I see you have some witnesses prepared to swear that this man was in South America at the time of certain other offences.

Mr Gill: My Lord, that is indeed the defendant's case.

Common Serjeant: Evidence of that kind, should it be heard, would represent an alibi for the offences of 1877, but not for the charges he faces today. For our purposes it is irrelevant. We cannot raise the matter of his previous conviction in the present hearing. That is against every precedent in English law, and it is my duty to ensure a fair trial on the evidence.

Mr Gill: My Lord, it is the defendant's claim that because he can be shown to have been in South America at the time of the earlier offences he cannot possibly have committed them. He states vehemently that he has been wrongly arrested and charged, that he is not the man who was sent to prison, that he has never been convicted of any offence, that the police have made a terrible error, and that it is a case of mistaken identity.

Common Serjeant: Then your defence will be based purely on the question of mistaken identity. Your witnesses from South America may testify to the defendant's character, but not to his alibi. Let us proceed with the trial.
Mr Gill: I am much obliged, My Lord.
Mr Avory: I am greatly obliged, My Lord.

This ban imposed by the judge ensured that Beck could not present what would seem to be a cast-iron alibi. However, the ban did not appear to affect the other side of the case. Many of the witnesses, including the police and the handwriting expert, simply assumed that John Smith and Adolf Beck were one and the same. Beck was even identified in the court papers as *Prisoner DW523*, which number had been assigned to him while he was on remand in prison before the trial began. This was a code decipherable by anyone who worked in the court and prison services: '523' was the number previously assigned to John Smith; the 'W' indicated that he had been convicted in 1877; 'D' revealed that he was a repeat offender.

iv

Mr Avory for the prosecution explained to the jury why they were confining their prosecution action to three representative matters. He outlined the unusual way in which Beck had been apprehended, then called his witnesses.

Starting with Ottilie Meissonier, the woman who had challenged Beck in the street, the three alleged victims told their stories to the jury. The method was always the same.

The victim would experience a chance encounter in a London street with a well-dressed, aristocratic gentleman, who spoke with a trace of a German accent. He would seem to recognize her as a member of his social circle, then after he realized his mistake he introduced himself as Lord Winton, or Lord de Willoughby, and mention that by chance he was in need of someone to join his household staff. After the meeting in the street, and having obtained her address, he would send the woman a note written on the letterhead of an expensive London hotel, suggesting that he might call on her. He usually used the phrase *Please expect me tomorrow* and added a time in the afternoon. During their private meeting in her rooms he would hand her a cheque for a large sum of money, and give her a written introduction to a well-known couturier in London's Mayfair where she might buy expensive clothes on his account. Before he left he would borrow any jewellery she possessed, so that he could replace it with expensive gems, and borrow whatever cash she might have on her, for the taxi fare home. She would never see him again. The cheque was fraudulent, and the gown shop knew nothing of him.

All three of the women who gave this evidence were clearly deeply distressed. All three unequivocally identified Adolf Beck as the swindler, when he stood up in the dock.

The retired police constable, Eliss Spurrell, gave evidence that as the arresting officer of John Smith he remembered him well, indeed he would never forget him. He confirmed that the man in the dock, Adolf Beck, was the same man.

Thomas Gurrin, the handwriting expert, came next. He said on oath that he had closely examined the examples of the admitted handwriting of Smith from 1877 and Beck from the present day. He said that although in both cases there had been some attempt to disguise the handwriting, he was positive that it was characteristic of people from Scandinavian countries, or possibly from Germany. He produced to the court several of the samples he had examined, and stated categorically that they had all been written by the same person.

John Smith's handwriting, 1877

Adolf Beck's admitted handwriting, 1896

Adolf Beck's lawyer, Mr Gill, attempted to challenge this witness, asking for more details about how the handwriting samples had been obtained. He also claimed that both Mr Gurrin and the retired police officer had linked the defendant with the court proceedings of 1877, thereby breaking the judge's own ruling.

Mr Gill went on. He argued passionately that his defence of Adolf Beck was that the man who committed the frauds of 1877 was the same person who had committed the present ones. It was Beck's repeated assertion that that person was not him and could not be him, that he had been mistaken for this other man, and that he was entirely innocent. The judge immediately ruled against the argument, reminding Mr Gill that he must not prejudice the jury.

At this point there was a notable disturbance in the courtroom. A man in the public gallery stood up and shouted that the trial was a charade and that it was unfair and unjust. He demanded to be allowed to give evidence in the prisoner's defence.

Two ushers were moving swiftly across the courtroom towards him. Then the judge spoke, and the ushers stayed put. The shorthand note taker recorded the following exchange:

Common Serjeant: You do not have audience in this court, sir. Kindly be seated and keep quiet.
The man in the public gallery: I can prove that Adolf Beck was in South America at the time of the earlier crimes.
Common Serjeant: Sir, you bear a remarkable physical resemblance to the defendant. Who are you?
The man in the public gallery: My name is Professor Adler Beck. I am the defendant's brother. I know for certain where he was when the other crimes were committed. He was in Lima, Peru.
Common Serjeant: We are not trying the earlier case. Ushers, please remove that man from my court.

As the man continued to stand, and the ushers approached him, the three women who had earlier given evidence were staring in fascination at him. Everyone in the courtroom noticed, as if for the first time, that he and the defendant were identical in appearance. One of the women witnesses shouted something abusive at him, and the other two immediately joined in, yelling at him in an aggressive and threatening way. The ushers then reached the public gallery and firmly removed the man from the court.

The judge called a short recess, to allow tempers to cool.

On resuming, Mr Gill opened his defence case. Adolf Beck would not give evidence in his own defence, as was his right. If he gave evidence in open court he would be cross-examined by the prosecution. By this stage in the proceedings he was sitting in the dock, slumped forward, with his head in his hands.

When called upon to take advantage of the court he

reluctantly made a short statement. He stood up and spoke in clear English, but with a distinct trace of a Germanic or Scandinavian accent: 'From the beginning to end of these horrible charges I have had nothing to do with them. I am completely innocent.'

After calling some witnesses, people Beck had been in contact with in London – a lawyer, a tailor, a worker at a hotel where he had stayed – Mr Gill called the witnesses who had known him in South America, but who were forbidden by the judge from being specific about time and place relating to the offences tried in 1877.

Major Hans Lindholm announced himself as a Gentleman of the Chamber of the King of Denmark. He said he had arrived from Copenhagen only that day. He told the court he had known Beck from 1880 to 1884. He described him as a good friend and an honourable man.

Colonel Harris said that Beck was no friend of his, and that he was only giving evidence because he had been subpoena'd to do so. He said he had seen Beck with the very best class of people.

Frederico Pezet, Consul-General of Peru in Liverpool, said he had heard everyone speak highly of Beck.

John Brailsford said that the English thought well of Beck.

That was the end of the case for the defence.

The jury retired to consider their verdict. On their return, the judge ordered Adolf Beck to stand up, but he was shaking and trembling and needed the support of one of the prison warders to stay upright.

Adolf Beck was found guilty, and sentenced to seven years penal servitude. He was transferred to Pentonville Prison in London, where he began his sentence.

9

Chad Ramsey (2050)

i

All the coolcabs, like most private cars and public transport, now ran on rechargeable graphene batteries, capable of holding a charge for more than twenty-four hours. Someone had recently claimed a long-distance driving record for a car on a single charge. Obviously, those batteries were of a much greater size and capacity than the needle-thin batteries Chad slipped in and out of his mastoid process at least twice a day, but they amounted to different versions of the same technology.

After his violent physical abreaction to Pat's upgrade of the system, Chad was wary of the IMC nanoshield and when he started using it again he did so tentatively. However, he soon discovered that Pat must have amended the code. The shocking interruptions of the lightning-like flash were now thankfully absent. The feeling of nausea at the end of a session did keep reoccurring, but it was now more mild.

He was working through the stock of batteries he had brought home from the course more quickly than he had anticipated, even though he felt he was not overusing the nanoshield. He now used it once or twice a day to check incoming emails, he browsed media for about half an hour, and he thoroughly enjoyed the streaming music channels.

He went online to see if there was a way of ordering more batteries. Only two suppliers advertised them: one was in Finland, the other in Germany. Both declared they were out of stock and did not know when new stock would arrive. (When he tried again later, the batteries had disappeared from the sites.) Substitutes were expensively advertised online from a source in Myanmar, but a warning note on a tech website advised against them: the supply of current was erratic and a surge could cause harm to the user.

Chad counted out the remaining supply of batteries and decided to ration his usage even further. He went back to reading social media on his laptop and handheld, and he kept voice calls through the shield to a minimum. He became more selective of the music and films he logged on to.

In Oslo, Ingrid's father Erik had been discharged from hospital and was now back at home. According to the medical staff the new medication would keep him stabilized for several more months. Ingrid, who had been trying unsuccessfully to keep up with her work commitments, flew back to Britain. Chad was happy to have her home again.

She had work to do, and the day after she returned she disappeared into her study, but Chad had time on his hands.

For a couple of weeks he concerned himself with the physical state of the house, and took on a few simple repair and decorating jobs. He had grown to think of it as a fortress against the worst effects of the weather. It was fully insulated, with selectable atmospheric control throughout every room, but the general fabric of the building itself had become something he worried about. The brick walls needed repointing, and the jointing around the windows was starting to break away. The roof was covered by solar panels, but a storm two winters ago had damaged several of them. Chad had paid the installer to repair them, but a new model, said to be more durable, was now being advertised.

Beneath the cover of the panels the state of the roof itself was unknown, being more or less entirely concealed by the installed solar arrays. There were signs of a leak coming from one of the gable ends. Chad contacted one of the big firms promoting the new panels to come to the house and give him an estimate for a roof overhaul. They said they could not carry out roof work until the cooler weather began – they had a waiting list. The person who was supposed to give him an estimate for the work, and agree a start date, did not come to the house when arranged. Chad made regular calls to try to fix another visit.

A day of relative cool came: the midday temperature was forecast to be in the low to mid-thirties, which by current standards was comfortably liveable. Chad, still feeling idle, went for a stroll.

As he left the house and walked down his road, he made a point of noticing which of the neighbouring houses showed signs of still being occupied. He normally hurried through the familiar environment without taking much notice. Nearly all the houses were in the same, or worse, condition as his – about a quarter of them were boarded up. Almost all the exteriors looked shabby, with unpainted window frames, cracks in the fascias, climbing plants clinging to the walls. The gardens were untended and had grown wild. Three houses had fallen into dereliction, with high metal fences around them, put up by the authorities, warning of danger of collapse.

He remembered how the street had looked two decades earlier, at the time he and Ingrid had been house-hunting. Most of the houses were then in single occupation, an area for families, admittedly families who could afford the extra price for living well above the sea, but a neighbourhood that was stable. The steadily rising sea level had seemed like a problem then, but not the tangibly present danger it had since become.

Chad walked down the hill and past the short parade of small shop units. The pisca shop was still trading, although at this time of day it was closed. Someone was inside behind the counter. At the far end of the parade the convenience store looked as bleak and boarded up as some of the houses he had passed, but there were lights on inside and while he was walking past someone came out with a bag of supplies. All the other units were closed and shuttered. There appeared to be no one else around. No cars or coolcabs went past as he walked.

His intention had been to walk down as close to the seafront as he could, but as he turned into the former main shopping street a woman stepped out from a doorway. She was wearing plastic protective overalls and a huge gauze mask of the sort once used by beekeepers. A name, Ketra, was written in large bright-red capitals just above her eye line. The overalls had an official badge of some kind inscribed on the front, but Chad couldn't make out what it was.

She raised warning hands clad in thick rubber gauntlets and said, 'If you're heading down to the seafront you should be wearing protective gear.'

'What's going on?' Chad said.

'An infestation. There are troops down there trying to deal with them now.'

'An infestation of what?'

'Stinging insects. There are millions of them and they're aggressive. Several people have already been taken to hospital with anaphylactic shock.'

Chad glanced across the street, and saw that two other people, similarly clad in protective overalls, were waiting on that side.

'I haven't seen any of them,' he said.

'For now they're mostly along the shoreline. But they swarm and they're spreading inland fast.' She looked around and behind her, as if expecting to see an approaching dark cloud.

'Where have they come from?'

'They were in the shipment of meat that was washed up along the coast.'

A few nights earlier a ship registered in Panama, out of Miami, was sailing along the English Channel, apparently heading for Rotterdam or Hamburg. The cargo included tonnes of carcasses, supposedly refrigerated. Most of that cargo was dumped overboard by the crew, presumably because of a failure of refrigeration, and although nearly all of it was thought to have sunk, many hundreds of tonnes ended up being washed up on the shoreline from Bexhill to Hastings. Within hours the whole area had become polluted by a disgusting stench of rotting meat.

The street was empty as far ahead as Chad could see. An emergency service vehicle with a flashing blue light was parked close to the turn by the old market building, but that was such a common sight in the town that he had not noticed it.

'OK, I'll go back,' he said. 'Thanks for the warning.'

'If you've got screens or filters where you're living, make sure they're secure.'

'I will.'

He headed back up the hill towards his house. The air temperature was rising quickly.

ii

Two days later Chad received on his laptop an encrypted file, sent from an office with a name he did not recognize:

'PoconData'. Wary of it, Chad was wondering whether or not to delete it unseen, when he noticed a second message had come in from Patrick O'Connell.

I've been trying to reach you. Your IMC seems permanently off. Call me online or through the IMC when you've read the file I just sent. As soon as possible. This address is a secure one.

There was a link to follow.

Pat had used the same security protocols familiar from his days in the police, so opening the file was not a problem. The material was from a Swiss-based pharmaceutical corporation called Schmiederhahn AG, head office in Zurich, but with other addresses in major cities around the world. The specification, written in excellent if technical English, had been raised in the Paris office. An outfit in London, PoconData Service, was described as the 'activating associate'.

Chad read the first two pages of the dossier that the file comprised. The word 'profile' was used regularly, but in a context he had never before come across in his work. Every page was stamped *Strictly Confidential*. There was an index on the third page, listing a number of botanical and climatological scientific papers. These were described as presenting contraindicated conclusions. Botany and climate in conflict? Flowers vs global heating?

Chad started skimming. On the final page an unspecified but negotiable fee was proposed for an original profile analysis. Chad stopped skimming. Half would be paid immediately through the activating associates, the second half would become due on submission of a draft or pro forma profile. There was also mention of bonus incentives related to a short response period, and the acceptance of the completed profile, again fully negotiable through the activating associates.

He called Pat straight away.

'I can't take this on,' he said. 'It's not about the fee. I could use that. But I know nothing about pharmaceuticals, botany—'

'Create one of your profiles, Chad. Just read the papers and give them an interpretation. When you've read what they're concerned with, you'll understand. There are complicated arguments on both sides. You'll be working through me, and I can promise you the fee is substantial. You can more or less name your own price. If you won't, I'll name one for you.'

'Pat, you know I'm used to dealing with criminals and detectives. This is outside my ability range. I have no experience of climate science.'

'You're experiencing it every day.'

'Living through it and understanding it are different matters. You're here in Hastings too – you know how every move we make has to be calculated so you don't get trapped outside in the middle of the day, or dehydrated at any time. Just surviving is a daily chore. I don't have time for an overview of what's happening.'

'I left Hastings a couple of weeks ago,' said Pat. 'There are too many issues on the south coast. I've relocated to London. I've been meaning to let you know, but you've been offline. The police did the same thing to me as they did to you. Contract foreclosed, compensation pay-off, out of the building with half an hour's notice. No subtlety, no courtesy there. I later closed the works unit, and moved back here.'

'They did that to you? You were doing good stuff for them.'

'It's what you said – policing has changed. It's now all about brute strength of force, control and intervention. They said I was trimming around the edges of things that no longer concerned them.'

'So where are you now? What about the people who worked with you?'

'Three of them came with me. The other two wanted to go up north, where there's more work. I had been commuting to

214

Hastings from a flat near Tonbridge, and the flooding in the Weald was getting worse every week. Trains and roads were constantly closed. I heard of a large office suite near Borough Old Market, one with living accommodation attached, so I took it. At least there are no biting flies here.'

'You've heard about them?' Chad said.

'Of course. They were on the news for the last two nights. Have they got rid of them yet?'

Chad turned around and glanced at the window behind him. About a score of the deadly little insects were skittering around on the outside pane. They had been quickly identified as yellow flies – *d. ferrugatus*, a species of horsefly, prevalent in swampy parts of Florida and Central America. They attacked humans silently, and the bite was painful and for people with certain allergies life-threatening.

'We're told they'll die off in a week,' he said. 'Meanwhile, everyone is being advised to screen themselves. Ingrid and I are staying indoors until they've gone.'

"This is what I'm talking about. The fucked-up climate is something everyone has to live with. Or the other disaster no one mentions – just being killed by the climate if you're a migrant. It's getting worse. It's not just high temperatures, but a complete upending of the natural world. Today it's a plague of flies coming from rotten meat. What's the next damned thing that's going to happen? The profiling job might be a chance for you to do something about it.'

'I don't really see how. What the cops accused you of, trimming around the edges. They thought the same thing about me. I was just an observer making decisions from the outside. They're not interested in that, not any more.'

'Have you read the file yet?' Pat said.

'I skimmed most of it just before I called you.'

'Read it soon. Stay away from the edges.'

Chad opened the file again. He glanced at the index, read the first of the summaries. Then he looked through the rest, conscientiously paying attention.

Most of the papers, written by a variety of academics, ecologists and environmental consultants, were sourced from science departments in universities in the USA, Switzerland and Germany, but there were others from research agencies or the innovation sections of commercial mining and renewable energy enterprises. There were official endorsements from UNESCO, OECD and the EU. Chad recognized a couple of well-known names, high-up officials who sometimes appeared on TV. Three of the contributors were Nobel laureates in the sciences.

Every page was marked with official corporate or diplomatic stamps declaring deepest secrecy and non-disclosure of content, with lists of the initials of people authorized to read the pages. There were only five in each case: the fourth was PO'C (carefully initialled every time) and CR, his, was the final one. Only a certain marque of encrypting software could be employed to insert his initials: Chad's security rating still somehow extended to documents of highest confidentiality. He had the software to do it.

Schmiederhahn AG was a manufacturer of pharmaceuticals and associated products, a leading name in the industry. Chad had heard of the company without knowing much about it, probably like most people. The introductory pages of the dossier were reproduced from a corporate brochure, listing the drugs they had researched, developed, patented and marketed since the middle of the nineteenth century, when the man who founded the whole enterprise, Helmut Schmiederhahn, worked in a small laboratory with a few assistants. The global company now controlled the patents of several of the best known brand-name products, as well as a host of other more specialized drugs and treatments, identified only by their class names. They were listed by their categories: immunosuppressants, cyto-toxics, beta blockers, corticosteroids, diuretics, antidepressants, and so on.

Another page announced the declared corporate policy: the amortisation of the huge costs of research and development by swift and innovative solutions, the streamlining of tests and trials, a mission to search for remedies and treatments for people exposed to the new and threatening features of extreme cli-mate, and so on. Chad recognized the style, a familiar gloss all big corporations put on their product and marketing policies.

He moved on.

A different style emerged from the next page: the writing was terse, exact, spared few details. Chad became more interested.

Two years earlier the Schmiederhahn laboratories had started to research the medicinal value of the leaves and roots of a woody-stemmed flower called the dryas – *d. octopetala*. The dryas was a hardy alpine-tundra plant thriving in high altitudes and cold temperatures. A tisane made from the dryas was slightly bitter in taste but acted as a mild and harmless stimulant. Until the end of the nineteenth century it was taken as an infusion in certain mountainous parts of the world: the Alps, the Caucasus and the Norwegian mountains.

As a drink it had an extra quality, allegedly curative, a health-giving effect enjoyed at a vernacular level by the people who imbibed the tisane. Some of these people lived to great ages, many becoming centenarians. The tisane was thought to have a resistance to certain bacteria, but until recently it had never been studied in any scientific depth or detail.

The Schmiederhahn researchers believed that the plant had

potential as the source of a powerful new class of antibiotic. They were seeking to cultivate the dryas on an industrial scale, but the plant was now scarce. It required a cold and dry climate, so was found only in the most northern parts of Russia, Canada and Alaska, and on a few remaining high mountain slopes in Europe, the Himalayas and the Andes. The scarcity was blamed on the present climate emergency.

Another paper described the dryas as an 'indicator' plant, in that it actively sought the environment which best suited it. For some years the dryas was believed to be in danger of extinction, but recent discoveries had established that a limited proliferation was occurring. This suggested an undetected degree of atmospheric cooling must be taking place, not only in the remote locations where the dryas still grew but further south and at lower altitudes. No cause for this had yet been identified but there were believed to be anomalies in oceanic drift. The northern Gulf Stream was a particular focus of interest. The downwelling of denser waters in the Arctic Ocean had been decreasing. The Svalbard archipelago was being investigated as a possible site where the dryas might be planted and harvested.

Five palaeontologists at Cambridge University presented a paper concerned with the fossil record of pollen, taken from deep ice cores. The ice cores consistently contained dryas pollen. This revealed that proliferation of the dryas plant had taken place several times in the prehistoric past, and always towards the end of an interstadial: the period before the onset of a stadial, an ice age.

'Younger Dryas' was the name of an abrupt stadial period in prehistory, at around 12,500 BP – a suddenly developing ice age that lasted for about twelve hundred years. The Younger Dryas interrupted and ended a period of global warming, a circumstance uncannily like the present day. The Holocene, a long and warm interstadial period, the only geological epoch known to modern civilization, was approaching its end and the dryas was proliferating. The similarity could not be ignored.

Chad turned to the next paper, which Schmiederhahn had commissioned from the Haddon Ocean Institute, based in New York State.

The oceanologists at the Haddon described their concerns from the perspective of the deep past. The Younger Dryas had been initiated by the sudden draining of Lake Agassiz, a vast inland flood in central North America created from the meltwater of glaciers. It covered a huge territory: the lake extended from what was now Minnesota and North Dakota in the USA, to Manitoba, Ontario and Saskatchewan in Canada. Lake Agassiz bordered on the Laurentide ice sheet, which then covered most of northern Canada. The Laurentide itself poured huge quantities of meltwater into the lake.

When Lake Agassiz finally overflowed, an immense deluge of ice-cold fresh water drained catastrophically into the Atlantic. The Gulf Stream was halted. An ice age descended on the northern hemisphere.

In the present day there was deep concern about the stability of the Greenland ice cap. It had been comprehensively surveyed by satellite since 2000, but since then at least twenty per cent of it had melted. The rate of the melt was accelerating every year. Most of it drained steadily into the sea at the rate of approximately thirty Olympic-sized swimming pools *per minute*. This, together with the Antarctic melting, had contributed to the present high sea level. Beneath the ice cap were vast lakes of meltwater on which it was in effect floating. It was inherently unstable. If only a part of the remaining ice cap were to slide into the ocean, the North Atlantic Drift, the Gulf Stream, would once again come to a halt.

The Haddon had been commissioned by Schmiederhahn to give an estimate of when the ice cap was likely to collapse. Five of their oceanologists gave separate estimates. These ranged between the next two years and the next five years.

Chad stood at the window of his workroom, looking past the insects still clinging to the outer pane and at the desiccated brown wasteland of the garden. He leaned against the inner pane, resting his hands on the frame: the aluminium was hot to the touch. Cooled air drifted down from the aircon vent above. He felt overawed by what he had read, but he was also suspending any kind of opinion.

He went to the kitchen, poured himself a glass of iced water from the condenser, sipped it, returned to his desk. He walked around the room, a space he deliberately left uncluttered because he liked to pace, liked to think while walking to and fro. Overhead, from Ingrid's workroom, he heard the usual and familiar slight noises she made when working on a translation – she tended to move in her chair a lot, fidgeted, took down dictionaries or other reference books from the shelves beside her, typed hard on her keyboard. It was the sound of work going on, and always made Chad feel closer to her.

How much longer could they continue to live here? The impossibility of life in this constant heat, the risk and inconvenience of venturing outside, the sense of disaster about to strike, the feeling of only being able to survive by holing up in a house clearly doomed to become unliveable soon. Britain was a place that was still somehow pulling through, but those who lived there managed that only by closing their minds to the horror of what was happening almost everywhere else.

It was estimated by UNESCO and UN Humanitarian Relief that in the last five years at least two hundred million people had died either directly as a result of the devastating climate, or indirectly while trying to escape it for an imagined better place, somewhere to the north, somewhere like Britain or Norway, somewhere like Oslo or Hastings. That was literally an unthinkable statistic. You had to slam your mind closed. The numbers grew larger every day – what would the next five years bring? While reading the Schmiederhahn dossier Chad had seen that death-rate figure summoned more than once by the academics and engineers and pharmacy innovators who were looking for a solution.

He called Pat, who was waiting to hear from him.

'It's beyond me,' Chad said immediately. 'I'm not the right person to make sense of this. I'm not a scientist, I've no aptitude for it. It's too big, too complex to be grappled with.'

'That's what everyone thinks. Assuming it's too big to solve has always been the essence of the climate problem.'

'Then I can't see a way out of this.'

'It's not what the people at Schmiederhahn believe. They are at least working on a scientifically plausible project.'

'They think the Greenland ice is going to go. Wouldn't that raise the sea level still further?'

'Yes, but only in the short term.'

'So they believe global heating is temporary?' Chad said. 'Or that an ice age would be better?'

'They think the rising temperatures are permanent and unstoppable, as a product of human activity. But they also believe a major planetary adjustment, such as an interruption to the oceanic currents, would be enough to reverse it. Then they argue that modern technology would be able to manage the dangers of a stadial, while the worst effects of the greenhouse problem were reduced or solved. It's all in the dossier.'

Chad stared at the image of Pat on his laptop screen. He felt unequal to what he was being asked to do.

Pat said, 'Read the papers again. Make notes, seize on arguments. Examine the evidence – the answer is always in the evidence. Give an informed opinion.'

'You set me up for this, Pat.'

'Whatever you're saying now, I think you're one of the few people who could manage to present an objective assessment.'

'Seriously, you're obviously much better informed on this than I'll ever be.'

'I'm only repeating what the people at Schmiederhahn have told me. I can't judge it, can't evaluate the relative merits of the arguments. I've seen how you deconstruct a tangle of conflicting evidence. That's what you've been doing for twenty years.'

'Not alone – I was part of a team. And some of our profiles came out wrong. It's an imperfect process.'

'Just read the evidence, Chad. Write the profile.'

v

Chad read the evidence again. Then Ingrid came down from her workroom. They ate a late supper together and watched TV for half an hour before bed.

She said while they were eating, 'I was stung today. One of those insects came in through the aircon vent.' She held up her arm: on the underside of her forearm was a swollen red weal, surrounded by inflamed flesh. 'It hurt like hell, but it's just sore now.'

Chad felt responsible for the insect getting to her. He thought he had checked all the screens. She had already rubbed an anti-histamine cream into the bite wound, but he added some more, holding her arm tenderly.

'Pat wants to commission some more work from me,' he said. 'Another profile. Something special.'

'More murder?'

'I've had to give up murder. This job is corporate. It has "confidential" stamped on every page, so I probably shouldn't even tell you I've seen it. I haven't decided to take it on yet, but once I do I'll tell you what I can about it.'

Last thing at night, just before they switched off the TV, the Schmiederhahn company was mentioned on the news. The report described a research project on the Norwegian island of Spitsbergen, in the Svalbard archipelago, launched by Schmiederhahn. They were making a large financial contribution to the Global Seed Vault. They were developing a huge area of land on the island, experimenting with new strains of a plant designed to withstand the climate.

The reporter contributed a voice-over only, so was not seen, and his voice was distorted by the uneven satellite connection, but Chad suddenly realized it was Gregory! What was he doing in northern Norway?

Chad watched with renewed interest, but then the subject was changed and they moved on to the next item.

Before he fell asleep he sent a brief text to Greg: *Just saw your report from Svalbard. Tell me anything about the Swiss big pharma?*

When he woke the following morning he settled down in front of his desktop computer, opened the files again, and used his laptop to make notes.

The day before he had read the Schmiederhahn research notes closely, but only skimmed the rest. He had noticed that even early on in the huge file a few dissenting notes had been recorded. For instance, immediately following the Schmiederhahn plan was a brief report from the Pharmacological Department of Basel University.

This challenged the alleged analeptic qualities of the dryas. It was a stimulant only, they claimed, and had no medicinal qualities. It was supported by several pages of biochemical investigation of the plant. Even so, their tests revealed a propensity to attack or resist certain bacteria, observed but not analysed, on which their minds remained open.

Another laboratory questioned the dryas proliferation theory, with a huge armoury of investigation reports into all the sites Schmiederhahn was intending to develop. They said that indications from several sites, all small ones, showed a decline. However, they confirmed that one large area of dryas growth in the north of Norway did show an extra spread of the plants, compared with a more general survey two years earlier. This survey had not at the time taken a special interest in the dryas, so again the contraindication was not definitive.

Chad was starting to understand the arguments the report raised. But he was still some way from fully comprehending them, and finding out how to assign weight to one against another. He was missing the team he used to work with, their insights and ideas, their particular specialist backgrounds.

From Greg: *Back to mainland tomorrow. Falling out with BNN. Next story restricted by powers that be. Swiss pharma using weapon-strength security. Heavyweight honchos amok! Russians annoyed as hell. Anything for me yet on Uncle Adolf? Job still on the line.*

Chad: *Getting to Adolf. More later.*

Wanting some music he selected one of the music channels on the IMC receiver. As before he was immediately astonished by the clarity of the sound, the feeling of oneness with it. Then he remembered the problem of the short-lived graphene batteries: fifteen minutes of music would normally use up a whole charge. He disconnected the channel.

The visualizer was on the desk beside him, so he switched it on and keyed in the long DNA sequence for Adolf Beck (alias John Smith, a.k.a. Ramsey). It was the first time he had tried connecting since the day of Pat's memorably upsetting software upgrade. While he was waiting for a connection, or whatever should follow, he heard the tonality of the background hiss changing subtly, as if switching or seeking through various wavelengths.

Without warning or a sense of transition Chad was suddenly standing in the open.

The air was cool in a way he had not experienced for a long time, slightly misty, maybe not long after sunrise on a morning in a late British summer, or an early spring. It was the kind of day he remembered from walking to school, the years when he had been old enough to walk on his own and when it was still safe enough for children to go out by themselves.

Invigorated by the memory, he tried to take a step forward. He was paralysed.

He was standing and staring, looking not straight ahead but to one side. His breath was clouding lightly in front of his face. (How long was it since that had happened?) He could see other people, mostly men, not far away. Unlike him they were moving, walking along a pathway that was at a converging angle to the one where he was standing. Some of them were striding briskly – he was struck by the sense of purpose they evinced. Other people were coming up from behind him on the same path as his, and they walked past, stepping slightly to one side to avoid him. He noticed the clothes they were wearing: long coats, trousers with short rows of small buttons above each ankle, leather shoes or boots, hats – all of them wore hats, mostly high crowned and with brims. The few women he could see were in long coats, their heads covered with bonnets or scarves, gloves on their hands and arms. Many of the men were walking alone, while no woman was by herself.

Everything was in the subdued light of an early morning shrouded by clouds and a standing haze.

Chad wanted to exclaim, to share aloud the welcome feeling of cool air, to sense the misty smell rising from the damp grass and the fallen leaves. But he was strangled by a lack of wind in his lungs.

He croaked in his voice. Tried again. 'Adolf? Are you Adolf – Beck? Prison, when? Why? For what?'

But his breath failed. It took all his effort to recover, to breathe in. The paralysis persisted.

No answer, but he sensed a tensing of the neck muscles as he tried to turn his head. Chad felt constrained and silenced by what had happened, what was still happening. He was tongue-tied, the way he remembered with embarrassment, still, the first awkward minutes after he met Ingrid outside the Oslo bookshop, paralysed by shyness, that happy time of falling in love years ago. How to get past a similar paralysis now?

He knew he should be trying to speak again, to make contact with Adolf, for it must be him, but the sudden clarity of what he could see in the park, the mist softening the trees and the parkland but not blurring them, a gentle breeze in the trees, the greyish light from the clouds, the sounds of people walking with leather soles and heels on the paved path, were all overwhelming his senses.

What he could see around him in his narrow sideways view was familiar, customary, but to Chad totally unexpected. These people were not strolling for pleasure, but were striding purposefully, as if walking to work. Their appearance was archaic, their clothes were from a previous century, but what they were doing was comprehensible, ordinary. He was an intruder. He knew nothing about Adolf, this life he was glimpsing. He was barging in.

He heard footsteps coming up unseen, behind him on the path, two people close up. He backed mentally away from the contact, closing the IMC connection with the method a cop had trained him in, in what already felt like an age ago.

The vision dimmed at once. The hiss of the carrier wave returned, quietly present, in the background.

vii

Chad was back in his workroom, exactly as he had been when he keyed in the DNA code, dressed in lightweight shorts and sandals, a loose shirt around his shoulders, unbuttoned.

He was aware of the bright unyielding sunlight in the burned-dry garden behind him. If he turned in his seat he would see the helplessly dying trees through the slats of his half-closed blinds. The last of the yellow flies might still be there on the glass, but he had heard earlier on his news feed that the swarm was dying off or starting to disperse.

Where had that park been? The image, the imagining, whatever had come to him in his quest for Adolf, was real beyond question. It had a visionary quality, the unexplained starkness of a dream image but one that did not slip from memory on waking. It had sound, movement, smells, feelings. He had been there – it really felt as if he was present. Just a few seconds of another life.

For those few moments he had been in a different world. The people: what were they wearing? Their old-fashioned clothes were what he had noticed most. The sight of them reminded him of some half-recollected television drama set in the nineteenth century, but there was an ordinariness to the way the people had moved and the way they were dressed. They did not look like actors dressed up in period costumes and comical hats, parading for a camera. What he had seen were ordinary people wearing ordinary clothes, the ones they wore every day, or something similar. It was a routine event, the time of morning when people walked to work.

A cool, lovely morning while they crossed the park, in the century before last.

He felt emotionally dwarfed by what he had just done – an apparent leap into a past world, an intrusion into another man's mind? Could it be real?

He looked around at his own present reality. An empty glass tumbler stood on the desk beside his hands. The background rumble of his air-conditioner pumps, always faint but continuous. His familiar room, untidy but liveable, far too warm in spite of the cool draught from the vents. The quiet sounds of Ingrid working in the room above. The photos he had put into frames and which hung on the wall where he could see them: two of Ingrid from the early days, one in jeans and sweatshirt with her hair blowing loose in the wind, the other in a long dress before they left for some long-forgotten party, another of him standing happily beside her, their arms linked. All these occasions were at least ten years in the past.

Another was an enlarged and interestingly composed view of the familiar seafront of Hastings, months before the sea wall and Bottle Alley had caved in and rumbled down into the storm waves. It was a good photo but it was now a period piece, a memory only, a memento of something they had grown used to seeing in their earlier, younger lives. All photos were inevitably of the past, but some carried a more meaningful freight of memories than others. These depicted a world that had a remembered personal continuity with the present, but even so it was a gone and unattainable world. The future no longer bore thinking about.

So, tomorrow? What to expect of tomorrow?

The future had become a sequence of days: they survived this day, worked through it as it came, managed somehow. Tomorrow dawned with the apprehension that something else might have to be survived, worked through, managed. They lived on the edge. How long before they would have to join the general drift away from the increasingly hazardous sea-shore, try to find somewhere to live inland that was higher and safer, perhaps a little cooler and with better facilities, a more tolerable refuge, along with the hundreds of thousands of other people all seeking the same temporary solution to a permanent nightmare?

Chad went to the kitchen, drew off another glassful of iced water, sipped it, carried it back to his desk. His room was humid: condensation formed instantly on the sides of the glass. Simply glimpsing the static glare of the sun through the horizontal slats made him nervous – he closed the blinds a little more.

He had heard talk in the town, and on the daily news feed, that one day, not long from now, Hastings and several other south-coast towns would have to be abandoned, evacuated.

Already the physical symbols of civilization were serving notice. The hospital was taking emergency or casualty cases only, and a handful of private patients. The maternity wing was about to close. The trains still ran, but not all the time and not every day. Food shops maintained supplies for now. The town drains were often clogged, the electricity supply was intermittent, no one drank tap water. It was becoming difficult to find a supplier of fuel for the generator, none of the roads had been repaired in years. The town had a persistent background odour: the smell of sewage, of hot road tar, of diesel generators, of spilled garbage and droppings and the remains of the dead.

They hung on, day after day, expecting nothing of tomorrow.

The central plains of England, away from the coasts, were still protected from the rising sea, but crops no longer grew reliably, trees died or went up in flames. Smoke was often drifting, sometimes only faintly. The hilly parts of the country – the Pennines, Snowdonia, the moors in the south-west, the Lake District, the Yorkshire Dales – were inhabitable only by those with power or influence or excess money, those few who were media celebrities or successful sports people, owners of companies, those who were criminal or corrupt, those with underground shelters or an armoury of guns. Everyone else stayed away, or was kept away. Options were running out. For some years Hastings and a handful of former holiday resorts like it along the coasts had seemed like a refuge from this, still inhabitable so long as the sea could be held back, and with property relatively inexpensive, but on the edge.

Now most of what was left was the edge, the front line. The sea was rising, the sea was taking over. Waves of heat billowed in every day from the prostrate European continent on the other side of the English Channel and the North Sea, and with it the dangerous new epidemics, the mutated viruses, the killing bacteria that invaded the body by way of infected food and water. Also the forlorn refugees, scraping their flimsy boats over the English shingle and falling exhausted in desperation and relief on the beaches. There were fewer migrant arrivals now than in earlier years because of brutally efficient interception at sea. Sea borders had been outsourced to private corporations. How they intercepted and what they did was something few people knew, or ever asked. Some refugees made it through the borders, but they were faced with almost certain arrest, callous imprisonment and eventual forced return to the uninhabitable furnaces they had fled.

To stand and look out to sea, as Chad had done many times in the last few years, less frequently in recent months, was to look towards the next day, what tomorrow would bring, what could be expected from it. What you expected was inevitably laced with hope.

Tomorrow might be better, but that was true no longer. Chances were exhausted.

viii

Chad went to the visualizer and checked the date stamp of the experiment he had just carried out. Following the serial number it said: *04.03.1897-1150.2050*. He stared at it, slowly deciphering it.

The year he had encountered was 1897; that seemed certain, if only from a subjective sense that it was right, it felt right. But '04.03' could be April 3rd or 4th March, depending on the preferred format. If European, then it had been 4th March. How much difference would that make? he wondered. He and Pat were Europeans, working in Europe, so that was probably the answer. '1150' was the BeiDou time – he looked at his wristwatch. Like every wristwatch in the world manufactured in the last quarter-century it was linked to the BeiDou orbital array: it showed 1159 now. It was roughly ten minutes since he had been experimenting.

His earlier entries into the visualizer had been unpredictable, sometimes manifesting in a period earlier than this one, or later. The images and their times were haphazard, usually inexplicable. It was the clarity of this latest one that had startled him. It seemed a new kind of certainty, a genuine witnessing of Adolf's experience. If he could set or pick the date, making a sequence of entries in time order, then he would gain a greater sense of what was happening.

He called Pat to ask him. There was a long delay before someone picked up, then an even longer wait for Pat himself to come on.

'You're connecting with a DNA sequence, not a date,' Pat said, sounding preoccupied with some other matter. 'The existing v-file is date-stamped, so there could be a way of incrementing it. Say by a month or a year. Or even the other way, to an earlier date. I could put in local time stamping too, but only as a target.'

'Is the program date-stamping in European or American format?' Chad asked.

'Euro, of course. I could probably come up with a workaround for those too.'

'I was only asking,' Chad said, but Pat had already closed the line.

That night there was a long and heavy thunderstorm, with an epic display of lightning and a downpour of rain. It created a surging but temporary river in the road that ran down the hill past the house. Chad and Ingrid had just gone to bed when it started, but he left the bed and went in the darkness to the window to watch the lightning. As a child he had been nervous of storms. That was no longer true, but the sound of thunder still had the capacity to break in on whatever he was doing. Ingrid turned over in bed, to face away from the window and the flashes of lightning. She pulled up a blanket to cover her head. Weather had become an obsession for Chad. Childhood nervousness of thunder had been supplanted by adult dread, any extreme change or event making him wonder what new development it might signify for their lives.

He noticed that there were no lights showing from the houses opposite, and when he tried his own he found his power was out too. He went to the stairwell and listened for the sound of the generator. Silence from below. The mains supply was off, and the generator had failed.

In the morning the ground, which during the night drowned in the rush of deep rainwater, had already dried out. The mains electricity was still off. In the basement he discovered that the backup generator had run out of fuel. It took him most of the morning to locate an oil supplier, and the tanker truck did not arrive until the end of the day. He and Ingrid sweltered in the airless heat of the house, unable to work, unable to leave, unable to think. They sat around in their underwear, eating little, drinking water. That too was warm, because the condenser needed electricity.

Chad could not even glance at the Schmiederhahn files. The earnest discussions of arctic flowers and permafrost hydrates of methane seemed like a fantasy while the air was so unbreathably hot and humid.

The power was restored as soon as the generator fuel was pumped in and the aircon whirred into action. But the fuel tank had only been topped up less than halfway – the supplier was having to ration deliveries. Chad booked a second visit while the driver was still there, but two weeks later was the earliest availability of another delivery. Even that could not be guaranteed.

In the evening, after a cold shower, a change of clothes and a supper, Chad made a third attempt to read and understand the various arguments in the Schmiederhahn documents. Were any of these written by the heavyweight honchos Greg said he had encountered? It seemed unlikely – these papers were the reasoned persuasions of scientists, intellectuals, not of muscle and threat, as Greg had implied. At last he began to see a pattern, or rather a number of patterns. That was all he wanted as a starting point: arguments he could shape and try against each other.

Pat had transmitted an upgrade for the visualizer through the IMC – he requested permission properly, saying that this time it would not have a traumatic effect. Even so, Chad made sure he was sitting on a chair before it began. It was done in a matter of seconds, imperceptibly.

'What progress with the Schmiederhahn profile?' Pat said before he hung up.

'I'm getting on with it, but there's a vast amount of reading involved.'

'Probably not a good idea to be wasting time on the visualizer just now. The Schmiederhahn people contacted me twice today, leaning on me for a result.'

'I'm cracking on with it,' Chad said, realizing it probably sounded unconvincing, and wishing it was not Pat, of all people, he was making excuses to. A whole day had been lost to the heat. 'I've read the dossier at least twice but it's a lot to take in, and even harder to isolate which parts of it are relevant. I need to take breaks from it, for thinking time, but I hope to have a result tomorrow, or maybe the next day.'

After Pat closed the call Chad looked at the Schmiederhahn file again, but he found it hard to concentrate. The brief exchange of text messages with Greg had given him a new and unexpected insight into the Swiss company. What were they doing out there, in the northern seas of Norway? Why the obsession with security? Somehow it must be connected with the material he was supposed to be analysing. The knowledge was not a discouragement in itself – the difficulty of the subject was enough for that. Nor was it a spur.

He turned back to the visualizer.

What Pat had said was correct: the date obviously could not

be incorporated into the DNA sequence, but what was now possible felt almost as good. By using and reusing a copy of the last file he had opened, then manually amending the date, he could specify different months and years. He could also target time, adding or deducting hours from the existing v-file. The DNA trace was not affected by that.

His most recent exploration had been the clearest, most memorable yet. He decided to use that as the date baseline.

He thought he might experiment with dates before 1897. One of his earlier, random experiments had taken him to a static close-up glimpse of a snow-covered mountain, or possibly the slope of a glacier. The v-file for this was date-stamped 1855. He had no idea of when Adolf had been born, but it seemed likely the event on the mountain had happened when he was still a young man.

Chad added four years, adjusting the date on the parkland file thirty-three years back to 1864, which he tried twice in different months.

The first took him to what seemed likely to be a shipboard image – a fairly calm night, immense darkness, a cold wind, swaying and pitching, a sense of engine noises deep below.

The second time he was standing at a tall wooden desk in a poorly lit room. There was something written on a printed form resting on the desk, but the eyes through which he was seeing were not focused on the page. Chad felt as if he was daydreaming, without knowing what it might be about. He sensed an image of a woman, a recent involvement.

Two more years forward, to 1866, which again he tried at different monthly intervals. The most lucid of these was also inconclusive: he was among a group of young men standing together on a stage. A theatre? The lights beaming down on them were dazzling, so that he could not see past them to discover if there was an audience or anything else beyond. A small orchestra was playing, but he could not see that either. All the young men were singing enthusiastically: it was evidently a choral work of some kind, but Chad could not identify it.

Afterwards, he thought of Mozart.

Another visitation in the same year was even less informative: initial darkness, then a jump, a light seeming to come on as eyes opened, an unfocused, sleepy view of the open pages of a book lying on a lap, a diagram of a graph of some kind. It was impossible to decipher anything from it. The book slid off the lap, hit the floor.

Chad cut the contact, moved away from it. He felt guilty for having woken up his target. He returned in an instant to the humidity of his home workroom, the droning of the aircon fans, the unliveable, deadly glare from outside.

x

He knew he was losing time on the visualizer, that he had potentially lucrative work to do. In the past he had often worked like this: periods of intense concentration, paced by diversions. Time was pressing on him now. He turned back to the Schmiederhahn analysis, initially with reluctance but then with growing interest.

He was becoming familiar with the jargon used by many of the specialists. Their abbreviations, acronyms, mathematical terms, and so on, were intended not for a lay reader like himself, but obviously as terminology understood by other researchers in adjacent fields of scientific theory, where assumptions were considered to be common.

Chad began by focusing on the plainer arguments. A phrase he noticed occurring several times was 'abrupt climate change', which at first looked counter-intuitive.

Like everyone he knew, Chad had been aware throughout his life that the climate was changing, growing warmer, with no possible end in sight beyond a bad one. But the process was far from 'abrupt'. Because the increases in temperature were slight, with variations from year to year, and were by no means obviously following a steady path, it was difficult to make climate deniers accept what was happening. They could always point to a sudden cold spell, a season of storms, an unusually harsh winter as proof to the contrary, using particular instances to try to declare the larger problem unreal.

So long as it was possible to believe that the final catastrophe was only likely to occur far into the undefined future, the delusion existed that it might never happen. Even now, when there was abundant evidence, with reports of the destruction of unique natural habitats and the loss of species, the extreme weather already wreaking hellish conditions and displacing or bringing death to millions of people, climate deniers still existed, even within many governments. The climate problem would somehow solve itself, they said.

Now Chad discovered there was a scientifically accepted concept of an abrupt event in the context of the climate. The word 'abrupt' recurred frequently.

One of the contributors used it, defining it as a perceptible change of climate within the theoretical lifetime of a single human being. Use of the same phrase in other papers confirmed to Chad that the meaning was a general concept, not the coinage of one specialist.

Some examples of abrupt change came from a volcanologist. She described how extremely large eruptions, inherently unpredictable but always possible, could eject clouds of lava pyroclasts and other kinds of tephra into the upper atmosphere, triggering an abrupt dimming of the heat from the sun. She described several past instances, some of which Chad had heard about, although not in great detail, while many of them were obscure events in prehistory.

Victor Nikolajsen, a Danish glaciologist, conducting research into the vast lakes of trapped meltwater beneath the Greenland ice cap, described two relatively recent events. One was the flushing of part of the ice cap into the Greenland Sea in 1978, and another slightly smaller one into the Labrador Sea in 1997.

According to Nikolajsen both of these had created a huge increase in the number of icebergs calved and drifting in the oceans, but more importantly they caused a slowing of the AMOC: the Atlantic Meridional Overturning Circulation, or the conveyor belt of deepwater and surface currents that maintained a temperate climate in parts of the eastern American seaboard and much of Europe.

Although at first sight insignificant when compared with the present state of global heat, the abrupt and total loss of the Gulf Stream would have a drastic cooling impact. Its mild and benign influence, taken away, would expose a new reality. Harsh and prolonged winters would afflict much of the northern hemisphere.

The earlier abrupt Greenland events, in 1978 and 1997, both relatively minor, had for about ten years cooled global temperatures by a measurable if not serious amount. Most ordinary people would have hardly been aware of the change, except perhaps to grumble about a spoiled summer holiday or an exceptional blizzard in winter. At the time these cooling events were seen by climatologists as brief respites from the generally mounting temperatures caused by anthropogenic greenhouse gases.

The AMOC, already much weakened by the general rise of sea temperature, needed to be stabilized. The downwelling inversion of dense salt water, normally cooled by evaporation from the surface, was faltering.

On the other hand – Chad turned to the next paper.

Two eminent climatologists argued forcefully and plausibly against the entire project. The present global warming was unstoppable, they contended. The density of greenhouse gases was constantly increasing, the process was irreversible and endlessly propagated by human wastage of energy and the continued reckless burning of fossil fuels. The massive release of methane from the disintegrating Russian permafrost constituted the final tipping point for the climate. Many glaciers had already retreated or, in many cases, disappeared entirely. Even if 'abrupt' cooling events took place they would be merely absorbed by the existing global overheating.

These climatologists' arguments were also supported by detailed graphs, and results of computer modelling. They had run various scenarios which included a meltwater collapse from Greenland, and in one case the Antarctic. Every single model showed that the cooling effect would be minor and short-lived, and ultimately negligible.

An abrupt climate event was not going to be enough.

xi

The main paper was the one presented by Schmiederhahn's directorate of research. It concerned the corporation's interest in the dryas wildflower. This had all the appearance of an ongoing practical project, with industrial, commercial and pharmacological aims in view.

Chad's mind was starting to spin after so much theory.

He read again of the global need for a new antibiotic, one which would not lose its efficacy with repeated use. The research directorate had carried out a range of tests on the antibiotic qualities of the dryas, and was convinced that it would provide a medium to long-term answer to the problem. They rated the probability of success at between eighty-seven and ninety-two per cent. They were currently held up partly by the shortage in the availability of the plants, but also by the need to set up a full program of testing and evaluating, ultimately using human volunteers, a process that could take several years.

There was the possibility that the antibiotic quality of the plant could be cloned or synthesized – this was a separate project in need of resources and finance.

Their projections were indicating a proliferation of the flowers in the wild, but the numbers were still insufficient for commercial exploitation. The company was in negotiation with the Norwegian government to create an area within their territory for industrial cultivation. The Russian government was claiming that part of the land was subject to a commercial treaty based on historical mining interests in the area, and they were threatening to delay any further development. Several Russian warships were moored off the shores of Spitsbergen.

Chad now understood better his brother's brief comments about heavy corporate security in the Svalbard islands. Their theories were being turned into practical actions.

He read on. More concerns, pro and con.

Economics, for instance. The analeptic quality of the derivatives was as yet not certain, and the scarcity of the plant would necessitate deep financial investment, at least in the early stages. The entire corporation could be endangered by the venture, if it failed. The principal shareholders in the corporation, and several of its executive officers, were members of the extended Schmiederhahn family, who saw the worldwide success of the company as the result of traditional values and conservative practices.

There were more consultants who had spoken out about the false hopes of an abrupt climate event, saying such an event was mere wish-fulfilment. One of these was a renowned Nobel laureate, an eminent climatologist. Several independent writers said that the evidence was overwhelming that global heating was about to reach its tipping point, if it had not done so already. Climate catastrophe could not now be reversed, much as one might wish it to be.

These at least were arguments that Chad could understand. He was being asked to evaluate them, not agree with them.

xii

He heard Ingrid moving about in the room above: during her work hours she rarely left her desk, having arranged her shelves and workspace so that all the books and files she needed to consult were within reach. The movements he usually heard as she worked were constant, but tiny: the mild drumming of her fingers on the keyboard, the chair shifting as she changed position. Now though she was walking about in her room, pacing. He could hear her going to and fro. Then she came downstairs and into his room, and at once he sensed what had happened.

'I'm going to have to go home again,' she said. 'As soon as possible. Mamma has emailed to say my father has been taken back into hospital. They will be carrying out an emergency operation this evening. He's bleeding internally, and they believe the operation will help. Even so, the short-term prognosis is not good. I've got to be there.'

Her face was flushed, her eyes pink-rimmed. She had tousled her normally tidy hair. He went to her and put his arms around her. He felt the small of her back under his hands: her T-shirt was sticking wetly to her body. Holding her was always a reminder of the physical love he felt for her. The temperature in the house was above even what they had come to think of as normal.

'Will you help find me a flight?' she said. 'I've looked on the usual websites, but most of the planes are fully booked. I wanted to talk to you first, though. See if you can find me a connecting flight. I saw a couple serving the regional airports. I looked for a while, but I couldn't make up my mind what to do.'

She was normally a decisive, organized person.

All the main airlines with direct flights to Oslo were sold out for the next two weeks, but Icelandair had a once-weekly service between London and Bergen, with a connection to Oslo the following day. The next Icelandair flight was in four days' time. They could find nothing earlier than that. Ingrid said it would be all right. Her father would be kept in hospital for a few more days, recovering from the operation. Her mother had said they thought he would be able to return home afterwards.

Then she said, 'Would you come with me this time?'

'To Oslo? To see Erik?'

'Of course. I dread being alone there, but Mamma needs me. It would make a huge difference to me if you were there too.'

He put his arm around her again, pressing her to him. He could feel her trembling. He felt guilty because he had been so wrapped up in his own concerns. Ingrid had barely mentioned her father in recent days, and if she had he realized he had not given her the emotional support she obviously needed.

'I'll reserve the tickets now,' he said. She sat down beside him in front of the computer as he started browsing the agencies' websites.

Chad thought about finishing the profile before committing himself to a trip to Norway, but said nothing to Ingrid – if he tore himself away from the fascination of barging in on Uncle Adolf's life he could complete the Schmiederhahn evaluation before they left. Ingrid stayed beside him, her hand lying gently on his knee as he followed the familiar process of ordering flights online. They paid. The confirmations eventually came through.

xiii

Chad read the Schmiederhahn files again, looked at the notes he had made, then began to type on his laptop. He began by summarizing not the whole of each argument, but the elements of the notes that most impressed themselves on him. What he did not use remained unremarked, without interpretation.

It was not unlike the sort of police case files he had worked with. Schmiederhahn clearly believed that their research would lead them towards the antibiotic they knew or suspected could be derived from the dryas. But the peculiar circumstances of the flower, and the times they were attempting to navigate, had thrown up a multitude of other factors about the climate, none of which could be ignored.

Many of the crimes Chad profiled in the past were linked with what the detectives apparently believed to be an open-and-shut case: a clearly identified culprit, but with other evidence that weakened or sometimes contradicted that case.

Thinking back to the way he had learned to work on crime profiles, he thought of it as a gathering of evidence, isolating what was relevant, setting aside that which was not. Evidence was often in dispute. One witness would say what they had seen or knew, another would flatly contradict it. Where did the truth lie? Distance from disagreement helped, which was one of the reasons he frequently allowed his thoughts to wander to other matters. On returning to the case the weight of evidence would often become clearer. Common sense could also be deployed. He had learned to seek the keys to the arguments, the critical principals.

For about an hour he worked contentedly on the Schmiederhahn material, processing data and facts in a way that again felt familiar to him. This time he had to contend with several mathematical arguments – police work had never involved those. Without being able to check them he took the proofs for granted, singling out the results from the summaries.

The images, charts and graphs presented a similar problem. Each one had been carefully captioned or analysed – he had to assume the data behind each were accurate, but was more selective in his use of those charts where he felt the creator of the report might have set out to fit the facts to the argument.

He read through what he had written, corrected it, rephrased some of the wording. He celebrated with a bottle of icy cold beer, and stared again at the laptop monitor, focusing on the whole subject from beginning to end. At no point had he tried to channel his thoughts into a summary – at this stage he was more concerned with the facts. But facts were not what he was being commissioned to list. Finally, he wrote,

From the evidence it appears that an abrupt reduction in global temperatures is probable and indeed likely to occur in the near future, possibly within the timeframe of the next two or three years. I accept this as hard science, neither speculation nor opinion. The world would then, astonishingly, be heading towards a new ice age. Although this would of course create a major new threat, unlike anthropogenic global heating, caused by greenhouse gases and other factors, a sudden or drastic cooling would in theory be manageable by advanced modern technology, leading eventually to a balanced climate, and—

He paused.

The evidence of an abrupt cooling of the planet was compelling. The key to this was the oceanic currents. While the North Atlantic Drift was known to have slowed measurably in the last ten years, it was for two reasons: the warming of the overheated atmosphere had weakened the downwelling effect in the northern seas, and there had been an increased flow of fresh meltwater from ground-based ice sheets and glaciers in Antarctica. Apart from the worldwide raising of the sea level the lower temperature of the Drift had not been discernible as an influence on the climate of northern Europe and the eastern seaboard of the USA, because of the overwhelming presence of greenhouse gases.

However, should the solidity of the land-based Greenland ice cap be compromised by the increasing temperatures, with trillions of tonnes of ice and fresh meltwater dumped abruptly into the northern oceans, it could prove to be the determining third factor. The northern hemisphere would enter a period of intense cooling.

Then there was the sunspot cycle. Chad had not come across this subject before, but one of the papers, written by a solar astronomer at the Chacaltaya observatory in the Bolivian Andes, stated that the year 2050 marked the end of a regular solar maximum. A greater than usual number of sunspots had been observed in recent years. That cycle was now at an end. The sun was moving into a grand solar minimum, a period of reduced solar heat and light which could last up to ten years. All recent observations indicated the deepest part of the minimum would occur within the next three to five years.

Under normal circumstances this would have had only a marginal impact on the climate, but should it coincide with a rush of cold meltwater into the Gulf Stream, a fourth vital factor would exist. Chad wrote,

A grand solar minimum, coincident with a dramatic release of Greenland meltwater, would represent the final element of change, leading to an era of intense global cooling. If Schmiederhahn AG see a future for antibiotic research and development, the circumstances they are seeking—

He paused again.

Was this the essence of what Schmiederhahn were seeking to know? They wanted to develop a successful antibiotic, but the experts they consulted were engaged with what they saw as the larger issues surrounding the project. Was he in turn being distracted by the disagreement between experts?

Suddenly, his IMC came alive. He had almost forgotten it was there, while he had been ploughing through the more familiar technology of computer files and folders and a text editor.

It was Ingrid, speaking from a few feet away in the room directly above him.

'Can you hear me?' she said. 'Is this thing working?'

'Of course.' He was still surprised by the clarity of the IMC connection, especially in the first couple of seconds as it opened up. Ingrid sounded as close to him as she had when they were sitting side by side searching for a flight.

'I just heard from Mamma – the operation was carried out earlier this evening and they say the signs are good. The bleeding has been halted, and Pappa can probably go home in two or three days.'

'I'm so pleased to hear that,' he said, inadequately. He heard her bumping in the room above, a familiar noise she sometimes made when she sat down suddenly. 'I'll come up and see you.'

'Your voice sounds weird when you use that headset,' she said, her own voice sounding weird, but in an enhanced extra-normal way, very close.

'It was you who made the call!'

He cut the connection, and went upstairs to see her.

While he was there they heard a weather warning on the local news feed: the massive dust or sand storm that had arisen from the North African deserts two days before had encountered an intense low pressure system and changed direction. It was now moving northwards. It had been blowing dramatically across the parched fields of France during the day and was gaining strength. It was likely to cross the English Channel. People in southern England were warned to stay inside, and check the seals on windows and doors.

xiv

When he went back to the Schmiederhahn file the plight of Ingrid's father was still on his mind. Erik was elderly, intelligent and cultured, approaching the end of his life, clinging on, undergoing radical medication and now major surgery, for the gaining of a few more days or weeks of life.

An attempt to profile the climate and the hoped-for antibiotic seemed to Chad a futile thing in the context of the terminal illness of a close, loved and admired member of his family. The dryas project, the concern of a globally renowned company, seemed irrelevant to him and to his life, or indeed to the people he was closest to.

He wished, as he had wished before, that he had not agreed to work on this profile. But he was determined to get through it before the journey to Norway began, so he sat at his desk again, looked through the reports, his notes, the arguments he had highlighted.

He read the sentences he had written, made minor changes to the wording, then added more.

He went to the fridge for a second bottle of beer, rolling it, as was his habit, against his face and neck before opening it.

He reflected for a while, then wrote:

The reality, the unpalatable truth, is contained in what Dr Stenmuir said in her brilliantly argued report. She is probably the world's leading climatologist, and is of course a Nobel laureate. She wrote that to look for an abrupt and unexpected solution at this final stage of climate disaster, a last-minute reprieve, a *deus ex machina*, which many people want and secretly think will magically appear from somewhere, is no answer. The problem of global heating is intractable. To hope that there might be some way of stopping it with the intervention of a period of cooling is mere wish-fulfilment. Even if true, would a barrage of encroaching ice sweeping down from the north be any better?

Chad became aware that a wind had sprung up while he was staring at the reports, fitfully writing what he increasingly saw as his inadequate judgement. He was as usual sitting with his back to the window, but it was now late in the evening and the oppressive daytime effect of the unrelenting sunshine was beginning to subside.

The air remained hot and humid, however, and the aircon was working hard. Chad noticed it was making a new sound, a harsh grinding. It was time to have it overhauled if that was still possible, if the firm who installed it years earlier was still in town, still in business. He was distracted, wasting thinking time. He heard a spattering noise against the window, almost like a handful of pebbles, and without turning he assumed it was a sudden burst of rain, a squall from the sea. He knew he should concentrate.

He carried on, thinking hard about Dr Stenmuir's argument, forcing himself to write the words:

I have determined an overwhelming consensus of doubt about the Schmiederhahn project. I accept what Dr Stenmuir has said. We have left it far too late to restrict or halt the destruction of our environment, to remove somehow the six hundred parts per million of carbon dioxide from the air, to abolish forever the use of fossil fuels, to reverse the global flooding by the sea, to restore to the world of nature the hundreds and thousands of bird, animal and insect species made extinct by our way of life, to clear our seas of toxic levels of waste plastic, to eradicate the endless new strains of mutated viral infection. There is nothing we can do, except wait for the end. To place our hopes of rescue from this self-inflicted plight on glaciers and sunspots is—

He stopped. He was drained. He had run out of words, out of feelings.

It was anyway wrong. It was a denial of the evidence.

Evidence was often contradicted. People tried to undermine it, sometimes it did not make absolute sense, but that did not invalidate it.

There existed in the Schmiederhahn arguments a balance between common sense and evidence. Dr Stenmuir eloquently reflected the common sense of everyone who was alive today. No one could deny the present parlous state of the climate. It was in everyone's experience: from those millions already senselessly killed while trying to escape it, to those further millions who were unwittingly about to die for the same reason, and also to those still surviving, like himself, who were endlessly inconvenienced by it every day, who dreaded a worsening of the disaster, but who even so saw the possibility of life ahead.

The climate catastrophe dominated every moment for everyone in the world. Those who still lived felt despair.

But scientific evidence showed there was an alternative, and this evidence gave rare hope. Not a fulfilment of a wish, a dream, a response to a prayer, a denial of common sense. A rational scientific endeavour, calmly argued, worked out, backed up, tested, reviewed.

The Schmiederhahn project was an antidote to despair, a confident application of the evidence. They had discovered an unexplained proliferation of the dryas, an obscure and humble flower. It was a flower that responded to a cooler climate, an indicator plant. Now, against all common sense and collective experience, it indicated that global cooling was imminent. This was science that was being overlooked, swept away by the assumptions of common sense.

Follow the science. Trust the evidence.

Chad deleted what he had already written, then in a rush of assured belief and an urgent sense of anxiety, to get it written before he lost his nerve, he wrote a completely new profile. He sustained the effort. He did not allow himself to be distracted.

It was short and to the point.

Hope must always triumph, he wrote. He gave his reasons. He accepted the evidence. The heat could be beaten, the global warming would cease. He had become a man of hope.

He was thirsty and sticky with sweat. He read through the wording of his final report, checked it, corrected minor errors. He laid out the profile in the document format Pat had specified when he first sent the Schmiederhahn dossier.

It was a few minutes before midnight. The wind was still blustering noisily against the house. He sent the profile to Pat, to PoconData Service, somewhere in London.

The aircon emitted a short, strangled shriek, then fell silent.

Ingrid came to his workroom. She was preparing for bed and about to take a shower, and was holding a large towel around herself.

'The aircon has gone off,' she said. 'Can we do anything about it?'

Chad was still at his desk, the bright glow of the monitor shining on his face. He had never felt like this at any time in his life. He was trembling, giddy with the exhilaration of what he had realized, what he had written. Perspiration was dripping down his neck.

'Chad?' she said.

He forced himself out of it. He tried to speak, choked, made it into a coughing sound, looked away.

'I'm sorry,' he said. 'I only just finished what I was doing. I completed the profile and I sent it to Pat.'

'What about the air conditioning? Did you hear about the dust storm? The last time we had one of those the intake ducts were blocked.'

Chad stood up, discovering that his knees were shaking. He went to his window, moved the blind aside.

It was mostly dark out there – the few other houses visible were showing no lights. Ingrid stood beside him. There was a thick snake of dust or sand lying on the outer sill, visible in the weak light spilling from the room. The wind was still battering across town, moving some of the sand away from the sill, instantly replacing it.

'Let's leave it until tomorrow,' Chad said. 'I'm exhausted. I don't want to clamber around out there, trying to clear the sand. Anyway, it's still coming down on us.'

'There's something else. I heard on the news that Iceland is grounding all flights to and from Reykjavik. Because of the dust storm.'

Chad tried running the news channel on his laptop, but the internet was down. His IMC media channels were also off. He stood across the room from Ingrid, still distracted by the immensity of his decision, staring at her in a state of inner confusion, part jubilation at what he had written, part the exhaustion of it, the comedown, the satisfaction of having made the decision, but also an irrational feeling of defeat, a sense that by spending so much energy on it he was still somehow failing the woman he loved.

The clogged aircon, the storm of African sand outside, the endless bluster of the hot wind. The potential delay that was for her a terrible new disruption to her plans. The conflict remained between common-sense facts and the spirit of hope that was inherent in the evidence.

They shared a shower, then went to bed. Chad was awake for a long time, lying in the sweltering heat of the room.

xvi

In the morning they viewed the reddish dust and sand that had fallen on the town, blown into deep drifts in many alleyways and narrow passages. Houses and gardens were covered with a thick layer. Miraculously, a mechanical sweeper operated by the town came down their road and cleared a track through the sand, but it only went one way and did not return. More pressing for Ingrid and Chad was to clear the vents of the aircon and try to get it working again. The vents were swiftly dealt with but the filters had to be removed and thoroughly cleaned, and this took time. When they were finally able to switch it on there was a constant grinding noise from at least one of the circulatory fans.

Chad left a message with the service contract company, not really expecting that they would respond. Cool air only trickled through.

It would matter less if they were able to fly to Norway as planned. However, the news they had heard the night before, that Icelandair were suspending all routes, was confirmed. It was not the sand – it had not travelled that far north. Eyjafjallajökull, the volcano buried beneath a glacier in the southwest of the country, was erupting again. On the scale of things it was only a small eruption, but Eyjafjallajökull was notorious for ejecting extremely fine tephra. Some forty years earlier it had thrown a cloud of fine ash nine miles up into the stratosphere, causing most flights in Europe to be grounded for six days. Now, together with the impact of the Saharan sandstorm on several airports, it had again ensured that no flights were possible.

Chad regularly monitored the Icelandair website for their promised updates. Meanwhile, two unexpectedly good things happened. Pat instantly accepted Chad's profile, and credited a fee as huge as promised to his online account – the second half would follow once there was a response from the Schmiederhahn corporation. Chad was stunned by the size of the fee, and contacted Pat at once to register his appreciation.

Pat said, 'What you wrote was exactly what they wanted to hear.'

'It turned out to be exactly what I thought had to be said.'

'Then all is well.'

'The world is still going to hell,' Chad said. 'Most of the information in the consultants' papers was news to me. I knew things were bad, but I found it terrifying.'

'Yet you made an optimistic report.'

'I said what I thought was right. I followed the scientific evidence.'

'Then all is well,' Pat said again.

Later that morning the second welcome surprise turned up at the house: the air-conditioning engineer arrived, spent two hours dismantling the pumps and filters, replaced two of the fans, and assured them the system would be good for another six months. Chad recognized the woman: she was one of the partners in the firm. As she finished the job she warned him that the firm was soon to move away from Hastings and close their depot. She told him that most of their biggest customers – two of the schools, the hospital and the one remaining supermarket – were about to relocate inland.

Icelandair confirmed that all their flights into and out of Reykjavik were grounded. They were constantly monitoring the atmospheric ash cloud, and would resume services as soon as possible. Their flight booking remained confirmed. Chad looked around on the internet to see if they could transfer to other carriers, but all air corridors across Iceland, Scotland, Norway, Sweden, Finland and Russia were closed.

His brother Greg sent several texts. He said he was in Tromsø, and was travelling overland to Bergen.

He had suddenly quit his job with BNN, following a disagreement with the channel about their cancellation, yet again, of one of his reports. He had been shadow-working as a freelance media consultant for Schmiederhahn, but was now on the permanent staff. They were setting up an official neo-diplomatic representation channel with the United Nations, which was soon to complete its relocation to Bergen. As more diplomats and envoys arrived in the Norwegian city and established their positions, the shape and purpose of a revitalized United Nations was cohering. The UN, against the wishes of many sovereign states, was moving rapidly towards the condition of being the world government.

You quit BN News? Chad texted back, when the flow of messages from Greg ended. *You work for Schmiederhahn???*

More freedom, more responsibility, more dough. Yeah.

What about Uncle Adolf? I'm still looking for him.

Not necessary any more, said Greg. *New job. Forget Adolf.*

But Chad suddenly had time on his hands, and the mystery of Adolf Beck (alias John Smith, a.k.a. Ramsey) would not let him go.

xvii

The IMC, which had gone offline during the worst of the sandstorm, started up again as soon as he slipped in a fresh battery. His stock of replacement batteries was running desperately low. He made several attempts with the visualizer to make contact, but with mixed results, mostly negative. He wondered now if he was groping in the dark. All he had to work with was the DNA code and the ability to modify date and time.

He chose a year more or less at random, a guess: 1868. Nothing to see or hear – there was blackness, silence. Did this mean sleep? Unconsciousness? The sensation of helplessness sucked him in. He disliked the feeling, and retreated.

After a few more similar unsatisfactory attempts at 1868 he tried again, nudging the date back by four months. This put him into December 1867. After a moment's pause with various background hissing tones coursing through his mind he suddenly made a vivid contact.

He was in a crowded room, dimly lit, full of loud voices.

The thudding of a huge engine could be heard and felt far below. The room was tipping slowly and steadily from side to side in shallow arcs. They were on a ship. Why were there so many ships in the life of this man? An airless, unventilated room with a mixed bar-room smell of tobacco smoke and perspiration and cheap perfume and liquor. A table with glasses holding several different varieties of drink. The table had a metal border around the rim, to stop the glasses sliding off. A hand rested on the table – Adolf's hand? It was stretching out to pick up one of the glasses, but it had been immobilized by Chad's intrusive arrival.

A woman sat beside him at the table, raising a glass to her lips. She looked dishevelled, drunk. Her hair was loose and wild, and buttons on the front of her tight dress had started coming undone. She was leaning towards Adolf so that her weight was on his arm, but at that moment she was glancing away, laughing. Then she turned back towards Adolf, took a sip of the drink, and peeked suggestively above the rim at him. A man with a round face, watery eyes and a florid complexion was standing next to her and he put his hand on her shoulder, squeezing it. He was jacketless, with a waistcoat undone and his sleeves rolled up. His collar was open. The woman shrugged her shoulder, irritated and dismissive, and the man took his hand away. More people were crowding around and beyond, many of them sitting at other tables, but most of the others were standing and holding drinks, bracing themselves against the slow movement of the ship, speaking excitedly and laughing loudly. Someone beyond the crowd was playing a piano, but it was impossible in the noisy saloon to hear the tune.

Adolf was drunk. His eyes could not hold focus, and Chad recognized a familiar sense of physical detachment, a looseness, a carelessness, a drifting purpose. Adolf was sexually excited by the intimate closeness of the woman's body – Chad experienced that too.

Chad once again found himself inarticulate, strangulated by

the peculiar integrity of the scene he had entered. It happened every time – a side-effect of the visualizer? The figure of Adolf was immobilized by his arrival, while he could barely speak.

But after several seconds he managed to say, 'Adolf Ramsey, is this you?'

There was no answer. The hand which had become immobilized while reaching for the glass began to tense, then jerked forward, fingers extended. The ship rolled more sharply, or Chad's words had disrupted the action and disorientated Adolf, because the ends of his fingers fumbled against the glass and tipped it over. The beer spilled across the tabletop, some of it splashing on the woman close beside him. The glass rolled to and fro in the spilled pool on the polished surface of the table, clinking against the metal protective strip. The woman laughed raucously and brushed with her hand at her dress where it had been splashed, deliberately touching Adolf's leg as she did so.

Chad gave up, and retreated.

Back in his workroom, aware of the sweat under his arms and trickling down his back, his neck and brow damp, his eyes feeling moist, Chad stepped away from his desk and the visualizer. He was uncomfortable with what he had seen, barging in uninvited, no matter what was going on or what Adolf was doing. There seemed to be no subtle or indirect way to do this.

The battery had died again.

He washed in cold water, then put on a clean shirt. He could not shake off the clarity, the exactness, of the scene he had just witnessed. How had it arisen, what in fact was it?

He wondered, not for the first time, if these intrusions were illusory in some way. Was he tapping into memories – someone else's, or even his own? Or a recent dream? Or false memories, cryptamnesia, aggregated from long-forgotten scenes in films or on television? Even a memory made visual, based on some story he had read or an anecdote he had been told?

None of this resonated with him as a plausible explanation. There was instead a feeling of casual, unplanned actuality, inexplicable as fragments of reality might seem when briefly glimpsed or taken out of context. He was there, he lived it.

Some incident on a glacier. Where had that come from, if not from a real experience? People walking to work one morning – a prosaic image of a past era, dull but true. Backstage at a theatre while an orchestra played. A drunken night in a ship's saloon. Fragments of a real life, nothing you would invent.

He slipped in a replacement battery and tried again, this time moving the file date forward to 1875.

He was in a street, the sun baking down. It was the heat he was most aware of at first: a different sort of heat from the muggy, claustrophobic humidity, full of rank smells and silent threat, that he endured every day at home. This was the sort of summery heat that made you want to take off your outer clothes and throw back your head to soak up the warmth – dry, steady, mature sunshine, coming from almost overhead, a day to make you lazy and thirsty, as it routinely did. The sunlight bleached the dusty streets and the white stucco of the walls around him.

He was standing in a group of men, a loose circle, outside a large building with steps up from the sidewalk, then a portico with great pillars. A huge poster draped across one of the pillars was advertising what was clearly an opera – Chad could only glimpse peripherally an image of a woman's face with a rose in her hair, and stylized musical notes, because Adolf, whom he had intruded upon, was not looking directly at it.

The men were all casually, untidily dressed. Working clothes? Or because of the hot weather? They wore broad-brimmed hats, some made of cloth, others fashioned out of straw or raffia. Horses pulling carts and carriages clattered past slowly. There was a smell of spice or flowers on the air. The sun struck down relentlessly, but without harm.

The men were arguing in an animated but companionable way, speaking loudly in a language that Chad did not understand. It sounded to him like Spanish or Portuguese, neither of which he had learned. They smiled and nodded, gestured with their hands. Nearly all of them were holding cigarillos, rolled with brown leaves.

Chad was staring fixedly across the group, directly at the man who had been speaking as he entered, but one of the others responded. The man turned aside to pull on his cigarillo. His fingers were hooked around its glowing end. When he looked back he noticed that Adolf, now intruded upon by Chad and immobilized, was apparently staring at him in silence. His response was immediate and reflexive: he turned full body to confront Adolf, a reaction to the perceived challenge.

The situation quickly changed – two of the other men now stepped away from the group, raising their hands in a brief informal salute, and walked off. Adolf went on staring, locked in place by Chad's intrusion. One of the remaining men noticed Adolf's rigid stance, and made a playful stab at his arm, to stir him. The threatening man stepped towards him.

Chad retreated.

In 1886 he brought Adolf out of his sleep in the night. He lay there, awake but immobilized. Chad, once again feeling repelled by what he was doing, withdrew.

He sensed the graphene battery was again losing power, so he pushed in another fresh one. He ate a snack and watched the BNN news on TV.

The main story was the devastating impact of the sand and dust storm on southern Britain. There was footage of the aftermath revealing scenes similar to the ones he and Ingrid had seen around their house. It was said to be impossible to gauge the total weight of the sand that had landed on the country, but one expert estimated that it would take many weeks to clear. The news broadcast did not mention Hastings or any of the other towns on the south coast but went to parts of England where it was said the heaviest falls had been recorded: the Thames Valley west of London, Heathrow Airport, the Chiltern hills, Salisbury Plain, large parts of Somerset and Devon. Some rivers, including the Thames, would need dredging. The streets of London were clogged, but most of the important thoroughfares had been cleared earlier that morning. There was an argument developing about where the mounds of African sand should now be removed to.

The Icelandic volcano followed this story. There was nothing new here, simply confirmation of what he and Ingrid had already been told about delayed and cancelled flights.

Chad took a long drink of water, then moved the v-file date forward to 1897.

xviii

He was in a small room, one which felt snug, civilized and intimate. It was well lit with electric light bulbs and the furniture was solidly made. The walls were lined with textured dark-coloured wallpaper. Heavy drapes were drawn across a window. Chad could see part of a tall and well-stocked bookcase, and two paintings. He could smell furniture polish. From the moment he arrived Chad sensed old-fashioned values of respectability, with conventional but cultured taste.

He was sitting on a wooden chair facing a large roll-top desk. This was open, with various papers standing in piles or scattered loosely on the top shelf of the desk. A small lamp was balanced on the surface, throwing a strong light across the working area. All but one of the shallow drawers were closed – he could only glimpse the contents from where he was sitting, but he saw some keys, pencils, an eraser, a pen-knife, a loupe, a small tin box with a lid. The array of open compartments above the writing surface were all filled: papers and cards were stuffed into three of them, a child's drawing standing up in another, a sepia-tinted photographic portrait of a smiling young woman posing with two small children, a few notebooks.

Nothing was out of the ordinary or surprising, and on the contrary the desk conveyed a sense of the owner's tidy mind and calm purpose while working.

He was holding a pen. He had been in the process of writing when Chad arrived, and as Chad knew was the invariable case he was now paralysed by his intrusion. Where the pen nib touched the page of the notebook there was most of the word he had been writing: *concentr*. A small flow of ink was running down from the nib and building up as a blot where the letters ended.

Chad again felt the same inhibition in knowing what to say in such a circumstance, but this time he had braced himself before starting.

It was still difficult. He struggled for a moment, then said, 'Sir, I am seeking Adolf Ramsey. Or maybe the – name is John Smith. Is this you?'

Even as he forced the words out he was aware of their brusqueness, their inadequacy, the lack of explanation or context. What must it be like to be going about your normal life, then have someone enter your mind in such a peremptory way, uninvited, inexplicable, demanding information, asking questions?

For a moment he thought his awkward words had not been heard, because the immobility persisted. Nothing was said, or at least nothing came out that he could hear or be aware of as a reply. A pendulum clock ticked slowly and steadily in the same room, somewhere behind. Then he felt and noticed a gradual movement, painfully slow.

The hand that had been holding the pen lifted away from the page of the notebook and released the pen. It landed on the page, made another smaller blot, rolled an inch or two and stopped. The hand reached slowly up towards the row of compartments above the desk's writing surface. It went steadily and directly to the one at the far right-hand end, where a piece of white paper, folded in four, was stacked by itself, leaning to one side.

The hand withdrew the page, opening it and turning it so that the words written on it became visible. When the page was in direct line of sight of his eyes, he held it steady so that the words were before him. Chad then read the following:

Who are you to intrude on my life and what do you want? Why do you intermittently contact me and my brother? What manner of science are you employing? How is this possible?

My name is Adler Beck. My brother is called Dolf Beck. We do not know anyone called Ramsey. The name John Smith is anathema to me. What do you know of that man?

I am a climate scientist, working in London where I teach oceanic and marine science to students at the Royal Naval College.

My brother Dolf, a former leading tenor of the opera, is a traveller and investor. His life is at present in crisis. He is serving a long prison sentence for offences he did not commit. He was wrongly convicted. The real criminal was a man called John Smith. Much of my time and energy is involved with trying to get my brother released. If you have information about Smith, please pass it on as a matter of urgency.

I am eager to communicate with you, and if I know you will return I shall write my replies in this manner. Please do not leave it several months or years before you return.

(Signed): Professor Adler Beck — lecturer in Marine Navigation and Ocean Sciences, Royal Naval College, Greenwich.

Chad stared at the page, reading it twice. The hand holding it remained steady: it was his own hand, Adler Beck's hand. It was final proof that these experiences were real, not in any way illusory. What could he say in reply? The familiar inarticulate feeling was again gripping him, undermining him as ever.

He thought, he planned what to say.

Finally he said, his voice tightening with stress, 'My name is Charles Ramsey. I believe I am your distant descendant – and that of your brother. I was born – in the year 2002. I am now forty-eight years old. I live on the south – coast of England. I am trying to discover – what happened to Adolf, and did not realize he had a brother. The science I am – using is too complicated to explain. I do not fully understand it myself. Please write down whatever you can tell me about yourself and the trouble you say Adolf is in. I will come back in about an hour.'

Adler gave no sign that he had heard or understood, but remained immobilized in his seat. He was looking down at the sheet of paper, which was now lying face-up on the surface of the desk. His hand was moving back. There was a sound in the room, a familiar one. The handle of a door had turned. Adler forced his head around and looked towards the door. Through his eyes Chad saw that a woman was entering the room. Chad immediately knew she was the woman in the photograph, sitting with her two children. She gasped when she saw Adler unmoving.

With a sense of dizzying shock, Chad recognized her.

His strangling hold on Adler Beck was already weakening, and he retreated.

It was now evening.

More than an hour had elapsed since he had made contact with Adler, and he could not escape a nagging feeling that he should honour his promise to return within that time, even though he knew that he could use the visualizer the next week, the next month or the next year, and still turn up in Adler's life an hour after their first meeting.

The actual timing was anyway more or less irrelevant – he was anxious to resume contact.

Ingrid was preparing a meal, so Chad set aside the visualizer and the thoughts it raised, removed the battery from the IMC connector, then spent the next hour or two relaxing with her. She told him she was finding it impossible to concentrate on her work until they knew when they would be able to travel. She had been checking the Icelandair page at regular intervals. The most recent information was that the volcanic eruption was subsiding and the pall of atmospheric ash was slowly dispersing, but that no flights could yet be scheduled.

Still they had to wait. They were packed and ready to go, and could set off to the airport at short notice, but they had to assume from their last experience that the difficult journey to Heathrow might take them more than a day. They were both tense about this, knowing they would miss the flight if they found out about it too late.

The next morning Icelandair posted the news that there would be no flights from Britain that day. Chad went to his workroom and switched on the visualizer.

Overnight he had thought carefully about the possibilities of communication. He adjusted the time of his most recent v-file by one hour forward on the same day, then keyed in the DNA code.

He immediately smelled excrement, sweat, unwashed clothes. He was in an ill-lit place, penned in by walls. The air was stagnant, all but unbreathable. He forced his eyes open. The only source of light was coming through a metal grille above the iron door. He was lying on his back on a hard, uneven frame, the lower part of a double bunk. His eyes focused, as if waking. Chad realized that once again he had burst into Adolf's sleep. The upper bunk was about eighteen inches above him. A muscular, hairy arm dangled over the side. Another double bunk was alongside his: other men slept in awkward positions. The part of the wall he could make out close to him had been painted dark green, but dozens of graffiti had been scraped into the surface. In the near distance, voices were shouting, echoing as if in a confined space, muffled and distorted but full of the disputatious sounds of authority, resentment and anger.

Chad retreated, regretting what he had done.

He altered the time by six hours, but again he returned to the prison cell. Adolf was now half-crouched, half-seated, on the edge of his bunk. Three other men were in close proximity. The smell of human waste was vile. Someone close at hand was weeping loudly.

Chad retreated. He did not want to intrude on Adolf again, but he did not know how to manage that.

He returned the time setting to one hour after his incursion into Adler Beck's study, then added a few minutes, hoping for the best.

He got it right. It was as if Adler Beck had not moved. He was seated at his desk, staring ahead, clearly waiting for this moment.

There were changes, though. The surface of the desk was much tidier, the loose papers from before were now sorted into a neat pile and stacked to one side. All the shallow desk drawers were closed. The photograph of the woman with the children had been moved to a prominent position in his direct line of sight. And a single sheet of paper, with handwriting in ink, sat ready in the centre of the desk's surface.

This time there was someone with him. Chad could feel the weight of a hand on Adler's arm, the light pressure of someone leaning against him. She was so close to him he could hear the gentle, regular sound of her breathing.

Adler was straining against the immobilizing effect of Chad's arrival. He slowly picked up the sheet of paper lying before him, and held it up in front of his eyes.

Chad read:

To Mr Charles Ramsey – I believe what you have told me: that you were born slightly more than a hundred years from now, in the year 2002. That is unimaginable, the stuff of fantasy. However, I am a pragmatist and I have thought about it. Because you say you are now forty-eight years old I assume you are living in the year 2050, or thereabouts.

2050 is a year of scientific interest to me, because as a climate scientist I have predicted there will be a huge upheaval in that year. I have amassed a wealth of scientific data that shows, at least to my own satisfaction, that if a catastrophic cooling of the climate has not taken place by that year, it will unavoidably follow shortly after.

I assume this is why you have been trying to make contact with me. I also assume your scientific interests are close to mine, and that we have common concerns to discuss. Perhaps you are aware of the several scientific papers I published in professional journals?

As for myself, this evening I am here now with my wife Meredith, who has been a great support to me when I suffered

your various exploratory attempts to make contact over so many
years. Meredith is a scientist in her own right, and works as an
investigating astronomer at the Greenwich observatory. She is of
course the mother of our two children: Harald, at present twenty
years old, and Agathe, who will be seventeen in a month's time.
The photograph on my desk was taken several years ago, when
the children were small.

My main concern at present is the fate of my twin brother
Dolf, Adolf as you call him. Dolf is enduring a ghastly sentence
in Pentonville prison in London. He is innocent of every charge
against him. His lawyers and I are fighting to get him released.
There is not, though, much hope of that: the evidence against
him was conclusive. We do not know how that happened. All I
wish is that he should survive his long ordeal, and once he has
earned his release he is able to return to his normal life.

Mr Ramsey, sir – if you have the mysterious ability to see
my life from a future perspective, please will you offer reassuring
information about how my brother's terrible ordeal will end?
(Signed): Adler Beck.

Adler turned his head around slowly so that he faced his wife,
and Chad was able to see her close up for the first time. As
often before during these intrusions he felt tongue-tied, but
the sight of Meredith's face had the same striking effect on
him as before, when she opened the door and entered the
room.

He saw, detected, could not avoid noticing, a true resemblance. She bore a family likeness to his own father, to his
brother Gregory, and therefore presumably also a physical
similarity to himself. It was a shocking, emotional insight.

These people were more than just ancestors, random names
he might come across on the internet. They were his family,
his close relatives.

He wished he could see Adler too.

Adler was turning slowly away from his wife, facing again towards the tidy surface of the desk. Chad tried to think how to speak in response. He had to assemble his thoughts against the constant difficulty of using his voice.

Finally, he said, 'I will try to reassure – you about your brother. I thought he would have our family name, Ramsey. Now you say your names are Beck. You say he is your twin: are you fraternal? Identical? I am also a twin, with – an identical brother. His name is Gregory Ramsey. I am not a climate scientist, but I am intimately involved with the ecological disaster unfolding in our lives. We do have a – lot to discuss. I have not seen your published papers.' He felt his voice faltering. 'I will try to make contact again. Expect me tomorrow at this time.'

Against his own wishes, as his hold weakened, Chad retreated.

He was in his workroom again. He was physically shaking from the mental and emotional extremes he had been undergoing. He sat at his desk, his eyes closed, trying to understand everything that had just happened.

Then Ingrid said, 'Chad, are you all right? What was happening then?'

He opened his eyes. She was by the open door to his workroom. She must have entered while he was in contact with Adler Beck. He had never told her what he was doing with the IMC and the visualizer – it was not a secret and he was not secretive, but in the rush of recent events he had never found the time or the right way to describe what he was able to do. What must he have looked like to her, as he grappled with the sights and explanations of the past? When he spoke to Adler, did she hear his words too?

'They've allocated us a flight,' she said. 'This evening at eight o'clock.'

'What's the time now?' Chad was still disorientated by his contacts with the past.

'Nearly midday. Can we reach the airport in time?'

They rushed to get ready. At the station they were told that the route had reopened but there were two lengthy diversions to other stations on the way, with at least three necessary changes. Rather than risk further delay, Chad found a coolcab driver willing to drive them the whole distance to the airport. It was extremely expensive, but the timing was a matter of urgency and since the Schmiederhahn advance, money was no longer a problem.

The plane was late coming in to Heathrow and later still taking off, and they did not land in Bergen until the small hours of the morning.

IO

Adolf Beck, a.k.a. 'John Smith' (1904)

i

Adolf Beck was re-arrested in early 1904, and charged with five separate offences of obtaining money and goods by false pretences and larceny. In 1896 he had received a seven-year prison sentence, but was released in July 1901 because of good behaviour. He had emerged from prison a broken man, physically weakened and psychologically demoralized, but with the support of a close family member had made something of a recovery. By 1904 he was pursuing his normal life again. This, unfortunately, included a return to his former offending behaviour when he allegedly committed the five crimes for which he was now being charged.

Before the trial began the Director of Public Prosecutions briefed counsel in the usual way, pointing out the significant factors in the case.

Firstly, Beck had been positively identified as the offender by all five of the women who were his alleged victims. Secondly, police officers who recalled the earlier case were certain he was the man they had been looking for. Thirdly, there was hand-writing evidence that linked him to the offences. Finally, Beck himself had indicated that he did not wish to give evidence in his own defence, which was his right, but that he intended to make a statement to the court.

This was the third time Beck had appeared before the courts, having been found guilty at the first two trials. During his first spell in prison, when he called himself 'John Smith', he had accepted the fact of his wrongdoing and made no appeal to the authorities for clemency and release. However, during his second prison sentence, between 1896 and 1901, he and his lawyers had made thirteen separate appeals on the grounds of mistaken identity. Because of the strength of the evidence against him these appeals were all ignored or turned down.

Sir Forrest Fulton, the Recorder of London, had been set down to judge the new trial, but when Beck's legal team discovered this they launched a determined effort to have the judge replaced. They argued that in 1877 Sir Forrest had prosecuted Adolf Beck (as 'John Smith'), and adjudicated his second trial in 1896, and that it was not in the interests of justice for him to sit in judgement on this man again. After a peremptory refusal by the judge to alter his schedule for such a minor reason, he eventually gave way. The application was accepted and Sir Forrest Fulton stood aside.

None of this advance information was announced in court when the trial opened, and none of it was known to the jury.

ii

On June 27th 1904, Adolf Beck was produced from custody at the Central Criminal Court in London, the Old Bailey. He appeared for trial before Mr Justice Grantham (Sir William Grantham KC). The prosecution was led by Mr Mathews and the defence by Mr Leycester. A jury of twelve ordinary citizens, all men, were empanelled for the hearing. Beck had the five charges read out to him, to every one of which he pleaded not guilty.

Throughout the prosecution case, which opened the trial, Beck sat quietly in the dock. He was a diminutive figure, low on his seat, guarded on each side by prison warders. At times he sat so still, staring with unmoving eyes and seeming barely even to breathe, it was as if he were paralysed. For one five-minute period, recorded by the judge in his notes, he stared fixedly at one of the witnesses as she gave evidence. This was behaviour which normally would cause a judge to intercede and put a stop to, but Mr Justice Grantham also noted that Beck's demeanour was in general so tremulous that he did not seem to be trying to intimidate the witness. At other times Beck appeared to slump in despair, shaking his head miserably when he heard these women describing his contemptible behaviour.

The prosecution led the five main witnesses through their stories, which, a few details aside, were more or less identical.

Each of the women had at different times been approached in a London street by a man of gentlemanly appearance. He claimed to be a wealthy aristocrat, looking for a replacement housekeeper. Making an arrangement to meet again he obtained the woman's address and followed up with a letter written on the printed notepaper of an expensive hotel, saying she should expect him the following day when he would call on her. During the visit he would write an introduction to a fashionable gown shop in Bond Street, and draw a cheque on a London bank in the value of two hundred and fifty pounds, which he said she should treat as an advance on her wages. He would ask to borrow whatever small pieces of jewellery the woman happened to possess, and take from her any spare cash – his valet, he said, had that morning neglected to put some in his pocket. He would then leave, never to be seen again. Neither the bank nor the gown shop knew of him, and the jewellery was pawned.

All five of these women had previously identified Adolf Beck to the police as the thief, and during their evidence in court they again pointed to him in the dock. They were in no doubt that Beck was the man who had swindled them.

The women were each cross-examined by Beck's defence advocate. All insisted that they were not mistaken. One pointed out his nose, which she described as 'most peculiar' and which she said she would never forget. On another matter they all agreed: the thief had not worn spectacles, even to write his notes. Beck was wearing glasses the whole time he sat in the dock, but the police, when organizing the identity line-ups, had made Beck remove his glasses.

The handwriting expert, Thomas Gurrin, was called. He testified that he had examined samples of the handwriting and that it compared with the examples he had seen in the earlier trials. He was certain they were written by the same person. He confirmed that all the examples revealed an attempt at disguise, but that he saw what he called 'peculiarities' in them all. These were commonly found in the Scandinavian countries, he said, notably in Norway and Denmark. He described some of the peculiarities he could detect in the letters 't' and 'f', as well as in the capital letter 'P': he said that the 'umbrella' part went through the main, vertical stroke.

Challenged by the defence on the fact that there were several small dissimilarities in the samples, Mr Gurrin said opaquely that they were 'not what I should expect to find in the writing of two different people'.

The defence was opened by a statement from Adolf Beck.

He stood up in the dock. Speaking with an accent several people identified as Scandinavian, he said, 'Before God, my

Maker, I am absolutely innocent of every charge brought against me. I have not spoken to or seen any of these women before they were set against me by the detectives. I can bring many witnesses to prove I have acted honestly in my business in the city from 10 a.m. to 6 p.m. I ask the press to help me get all evidence in my support from my solicitor.'

The prosecution pressed him for more details. He was not under oath so was not obliged to say anything, but Beck was eager to explain. He gave various accounts of his whereabouts on the dates when the offences were said to have taken place. Without independent witnesses these claims could not be corroborated. On the subject of his eyesight he said that he wore eyeglasses constantly, and had two pairs of pince-nez, one for distance and one for reading. He said that the letters sent to the witnesses were not written by him, that he could not write without his eyeglasses, that he could barely write two sentences in English before having to consult a dictionary, and that he frequently asked English-speaking friends and colleagues to write letters for him. He said he was being mistaken for a man named John Smith. He did not know John Smith and had never met him or even seen him, but from the accounts of these women he seemed to be his physical double.

A solicitor named Matthew Williams gave evidence in Beck's defence. He said he had known the defendant for fifteen years. He told the court he was used to reading handwriting in the normal course of his work, and that he had seen many letters written by Adolf Beck. He therefore knew his handwriting well. He said he had now been shown the letters written by the thief in this case.

'They were most decidedly not written by the defendant,' he said on oath. 'I do not trace the slightest resemblance.'

Under cross-examination Williams admitted that unlike Mr Gurrin he would not claim to be an expert in identifying handwriting, but that he could know 'the general contour' of a style.

The prosecution and defence advocates made their final statements to the jury, whereafter the jury retired to consider their verdict. When they returned the jury foreman declared that their verdict was unanimous and that they had found Adolf Beck guilty of all five offences.

Mr Justice Grantham then addressed the open court. He said that the defendant had been convicted by the jury on the evidence before the court, and that the evidence had been overwhelmingly plausible and consistent. Mr Adolf Beck would therefore be returned to prison. However, he added that in spite of the convincing evidence he found the case unsatisfactory, and that he wished to hear more from the Home Office, who had performed an examination of Beck while he was in prison, and from the police. He would adjourn the matter and decide the sentence at a later date.

Adolf Beck was taken down to the cells.

I I

Chad and Greg Ramsey (2050)

i

Chad and Ingrid were still waiting in the baggage hall at Bergen Airport when Chad switched his phone back on and found a message from his brother Greg, sent several hours earlier.

What are you doing in Bergen? I am on my way there now

It was four in the morning, but Chad texted back, *Passing through, going to Oslo to see Ingrid's parents.*

He didn't expect a reply, and none came.

Their original booking with Icelandair had included an overnight stay in a hotel, and that remained open. Unexpectedly, because of the general upheaval their replacement flight from London was in fact a day earlier than the one they first booked. It meant they had an extra day to wait in Bergen, before catching the onward flight the following morning. It seemed like a long time to wait. Ingrid was anxious to see her parents as soon as possible. They tried to find a train, but the only suitable one was fully booked. In the end they cancelled the overnight hotel and transferred their onward tickets to a flight leaving in the late afternoon of the same day they arrived. It meant they would still have time to kill in Bergen, but not as much.

They put their luggage into airport lockers, and took a taxi to the centre of the city. They were unwilling tourists. Ingrid said she had happy memories of Bergen, but they were not in the mood to rekindle them. They had gone through a day and a night without sleep, the stress of last-minute travel, then waiting around, sitting on the plane, and were now in that half alert, half drowsy state of the sleepless. Day was breaking. Ingrid drifted off in the taxi, but Chad was dazzled not only by the fabulous views of the mountains and fjords as they were driven past, but by the cool, breathable air, even the glimpse of snow on some of the higher peaks. As they entered the city itself it began to rain. Because he was used to the warm and sticky drizzle that often drifted across the south coast of England, the clear heavy raindrops in Bergen were a novelty.

They were dropped at the Bryggen, the famous quayside with colourfully painted wooden buildings, where they found a place they could buy breakfast. They were both still sleepy and uncommunicative. The hours of the day loomed ahead. They discussed taking a room in a hotel where they could sleep for a few hours. The rain was constant, so that was a tempting idea. They ate some food, drank some coffee. They began to wake up. They hadn't been together in Bergen for many years.

Then Greg texted, *Stay where you are, I'll be in Bergen from tomorrow*

Chad showed the message to Ingrid, but she simply shrugged.

The rain held off and the clouds started to clear, so they walked the streets, unresponsive to the place, waiting for the afternoon. Everywhere they went there were placards and posters and electronic signs announcing the imminent opening of the United Nations Secretariat in Bergen. Chad picked up an information sheet and read it while they sat under a tree in a small park, waiting out the hours.

He was familiar with the background. Two decades earlier, in a series of major incidents that had shaken the world, the

UN's main complex in New York City had become unviable. Terrorist attacks disabled the main buildings – later, inundation from the rising sea and the general chaos in the city made any prospect of staying on in New York impractical. Since then, the organization had functioned on a decentralized system. For the past ten years a new administrative centre had been under construction in Bergen. Parts of the new complex were already in use by the General Assembly, although for now the Security Council continued to meet in Geneva. There was to be an official opening the following year. To date, the new and refreshed UN's role as a de facto government had been ratified by one hundred and seventy nations. Russia, China, the United States and Britain were among those who had not yet signed, and seemed unlikely ever to do so.

Late in the morning Chad and Ingrid took the Fløibanen train to the top of Mount Fløyen, and sat in the viewing platform looking down across the city, the port and the fjords. The immense new UN campus was clearly visible on the slopes of one of the mountains on the other side of the city. The hundreds of trees planted to screen the site had not yet grown thickly enough to shade it. The campus was built in a series of terraces, following the natural contours of the mountain, the architecture consistent not only with the unique look of the older parts of the city, but employing many modern building techniques and security arrangements.

Ingrid called her mother and they spoke in Norwegian for about fifteen minutes. Chad could hear the tiredness in her voice, but sometimes she laughed thinly at something that was said. At the end of the call she looked sad.

'He came home yesterday,' she said to Chad. 'He's feeling better, and has been moving around in the house. Mamma took him for a short walk this morning.' She put her phone back into her bag. 'I want to be there as soon as possible.'

'Not much longer. We can go back to the airport soon.'

'Let's have lunch in the restaurant here.'

So the afternoon drifted slowly by. Chad still felt numb after a sleepless night, and the sense of unreality that came with it. He knew Ingrid must be going through much the same. They had little to say – they were detached from each other by the travel and the fatigue.

Looking down at Bergen spread below, Chad remembered the first time he had been here. It was a quarter of a century before, when he and Ingrid had just met and were in the thrall of falling in love. They travelled from Oslo by train. They stayed in a cheap hotel with a tiny room at the top of a perilously steep flight of stairs, leaving the room from time to time for meals, long walks, sometimes a film. Bergen had seemed magical and romantic, a warm July. Local people kept warning them it was going to rain, it always rained in Bergen, but while they were there it never did. He and Ingrid were still the same now, long married and middle-aged, but contentedly in love. Although in the years since, Bergen had become a larger city, it felt little different. It was a beautiful place, probably soon to be transformed into the new world capital city. Where better? University city, active port, civilized lifestyle, cool or temperate climate, scenery unique in the world? Today he felt isolated from it though, just passing through while preoccupied with other things, a place he might come back to soon and appreciate as he had once before. For now it was only the background to a long day they had not intended to spend.

Ingrid was sitting with her head drooping forward and her eyes closed. Her hair, now with fine streaks of grey, partly concealed her face. He put his hand gently over hers. She looked up at him.

'I was just thinking,' she said.

'What about?'

'You know – us back then, me and you, when we were here. I still love this place.'

It began to rain again, blowing in suddenly under the protective awning, and they both laughed.

At last they returned to the city by the funicular, walked to a taxi rank, and half an hour later were waiting for their flight to Oslo. They were early and the wait was long. Ingrid fell asleep in the departure lounge, her head resting on Chad's shoulder.

The plane touched down in Oslo before nine in the evening. Ingrid's mother was waiting to collect them.

ii

Two days passed. Her parents' house was full of light, unobtrusively modern, with many windows and a long south-facing balcony. Chad had been there a few times before. It had not become a house of sickness, a place overwhelmed by the feeling of being inhabited by someone with a terminal illness: Erik slept late in the mornings, but once he was out of bed and dressed he seemed determined not to let his condition control the mood. He joined in with conversations, ate meals with everyone else. It was difficult, though, not to be aware of the times when he became breathless with pain, or to notice the amount of medication he needed hourly. He walked slowly, sat at awkward angles, his appetite was small. Kirsten, Ingrid's mother, looked after him with quiet efficiency.

During the second day Chad booted up his laptop and went online. Adler had mentioned he was the author of several published scientific papers, and Chad suddenly wondered if any of them might be available to read online. He spent more than an hour groping through the past in the way familiar to everyone searching the web for something with an identity only vaguely

280

known. He was not at all sure what he was looking for or how it might be archived, if at all.

The only entry he came across was so incidental he almost missed it. He was looking through a personal website, dated some twenty years earlier, which carried a long list of books dealing with climate change. Searching for 'Adler Beck' located nothing; then as usual he tried 'Beck' alone instead, and he went to a listed entry for 'A J Beck'. The book was called *Take Heed!* It had a subtitle: *A Scientist Warns of the Terror to Come.* The publication year was 1905.

Three asterisks were against the title. The footnote said that all books marked with three stars meant they were in the genre of 'independent, unsubstantiated or variant theory'. There were in fact several other books marked out on the list in the same way. One that Chad recognized was a title from a couple of decades ago, by a TV celebrity who had made a reputation with his paranoid conspiracy theories about climate change. He thought it was being caused by thought waves beamed down from the planet Venus. None of the other names with three warning stars meant anything to Chad.

In the past Chad had been in touch with specialist booksellers, searching for out of print titles on the history of forensic detection. He looked up their pages and after a bit of digging through old catalogues he found a 'reading copy only' of Adler's book, for five British dollars. He ordered it, specifying it to be delivered to his address in Britain.

He was intermittently in direct contact with Greg, who was now based in the lobbyists' building of the new UN campus in Bergen. They spoke on the phone several times. Greg told him working for Schmiederhahn would enable him to move Ellie and the children away from Scotland. He and Ellie had found a house in Bergen, and they would be relocating as soon as they had found a buyer for their old home.

Chad asked him exactly what his new job involved.

'I was in contact with them last year, so it wasn't exactly a leap in the dark. They described it as PR work when I was first talking to them about a job, which I thought would mean doing the sort of journalism I've been writing for years. I guessed the angle would have to be different. But I left BNN full-time two years ago, and I've been freelancing since. I've been unofficially connected with Schmiederhahn for a month and a half and it turns out it's more hands-on than that. I'm in effect a lobbyist, essentially putting forward the cause of dryas proliferation to the UN. Have you heard about the dryas?'

'Yes, I have. That's why you were on Spitsbergen, I guess.'

'Also because the Russians were suddenly interested. They got wind of what's going on. They say they own half the islands.'

'As I understand it the Russians have leased the mineral rights, but the islands remain Norwegian sovereign property.'

'That's Norway's version. Russia thinks differently. Old treaties, and all that. And a navy armed to the teeth in the Arctic. One of the things I have to do is monitor the negotiations.'

'So what's going on?'

'Corporate confidentiality. My lips are sealed.'

Chad said, 'Schmiederhahn thinks there's going to be an abrupt change in the climate.'

'Where did you hear that?' Greg said.

'I'm a sort of lobbyist for Schmiederhahn too. I know what they're planning on the Svalbard islands, but I didn't realize it was high-security.'

'It wasn't, until the Russians started trying to muscle in. Before that, the company was acting in the general good, or trying to. At least they saw it that way. They're a conservative old Swiss family business worth a few trillions, harmlessly potting up a few alpine flowers to see what they could make from them. Then look what they discovered about the climate. It's sensational stuff. It will change everything if they're right and the world's weather is in for a big change. At the highest corporate levels the Schmiederhahn people are certain about it. The Russians don't like it – for one thing, there's a historical dislike of ports freezing up in winter.'

'Was that a joke?'

'It's what the Norwegian delegation says.'

'I know about the search for an antibiotic,' said Chad.

'Everyone wanted that. It's become a delicate subject.'

'Everyone wants a solution for the global heating.'

'That's a tricky one too. But Schmiederhahn are on to something here. The two go together.'

'So that's your brief with the UN?' Chad said.

'That's my brief. Look, I know you're with Ingrid's parents, but do you think you could get away for a few days?'

'Where to?'

'Come back to Bergen. I'm about to take a trip into the mountains to the north of here. Something weird has been happening. My boss at Schmiederhahn wants me to find out more about it. I think you'd find it interesting.'

'What is it?'

'It's about the glaciers. Some of the smallest ones have been shrinking for several years, but now the big ones are going too. There have been discoveries in the moraine.'

'All right,' Chad said. 'Yes – I'll come.'

'Better bring some winter clothes.'

iii

Greg had to be out of town on some unexpected work-related task when Chad arrived in Bergen, but he had left a welcoming message and arranged for Chad to be met by a member of the Schmiederhahn staff. He was given dinner and a guest room in the lobbyists' building. The next morning Greg found him while he was drinking a second cup of coffee after breakfast.

It was a long time since the two brothers had met face to face. They gave warm greetings, but they embraced rather stiffly and tentatively. Greg remarked on Chad's hair, which had by this time grown back fully, and Chad teased his brother for the dark grey business suit he was wearing and the fact he looked as if he had put on weight.

There was a car waiting for them outside: a corporate limousine, with two drivers on hand – maybe one driver and a security guard, but Chad did not ask.

They were driven at a moderate speed through the city streets, soon reaching the wide freeway that led across the exhilarating terrain of mountains and fjords to the north of the city. They were still slightly on edge with each other. The family ties were strong, but they had led such different and separate lives for so long that a distance was inevitable, at least at first. Chad had never seen his brother wearing a suit before, or not often – at their parents' funerals, perhaps, but that was different.

Greg indicated that the glass partition was closed and the intercom was off, providing privacy from the two men in the front seats.

He said, but more quietly, 'So what's your connection with the company, Chad?'

'You mean with Schmiederhahn?'

'You said you were lobbying for them.'

'Not exactly. I shouldn't have put it that way. I was approached as a freelance for a profile – the sort of thing I used to do for the cops. I don't really have a connection. It's more a consultancy thing. Just the one job, really.'

'Connected with the dryas.'

'With that, and the whole global heating problem.'

'This was from – which branch of the company? In Zurich?'

'I think it came from the Paris office.'

'*Département Recherche Pharmacologique*. That makes sense. They're central to the thinking of the family. They seem to have found a way out of this mess.'

'Yes.' Chad looked away, suddenly moved, remembering the passion with which he had been swung by their reasoning. Now everything so complex and insoluble and terrifying could be contained in a single affirmative – yes, there's a way out.

He said, 'I simply read the scientific evidence they had commissioned,' he said. 'There I was, in full-on global heating, sitting in my crumbling old house in a town slowly falling into the sea, every day a different sort of challenge, often in temperatures that could kill me. I didn't see at first what an obscure alpine flower could do against that. But in the end I came around to it.'

'That's my brief now,' said Greg. 'Optimism about the climate is official company policy.'

The road had climbed with the mountainous terrain, but clouds were gathering. They could see none of the upper peaks from the car. Steep rocky slopes rose on both sides of the road, giving way occasionally to admit stunning glimpses down to a valley or a fjord.

'Tell me what you found out about Uncle Adolf,' said Greg after a while. 'The need to know has passed, but I'm still interested.'

'Well – the first thing is that he wasn't a Ramsey. There was a change of name in the family at some point. His real name, the one he was born with, was Beck. A traditional Norwegian name. That held me up for a while, because the genealogical websites I was looking at never included him as Ramsey. The earliest Ramsey I found in the family was Harald, who was a nephew of Adolf.

'Once I overcame that snag I discovered the stories we heard about Adolf seem to have been true. He served at least two prison sentences, perhaps even three. He was a bit of a fraud. He picked on lonely women.' Chad described what he had found out about Adolf's crimes. He went on, 'He seems to have been leading a double life, calling himself by another name. When they found him guilty there was overwhelming evidence against him. All the women he had cheated identified him again and again. His handwriting was everywhere. It was definitely him, but he repeatedly insisted he didn't do any of it. He says he was in South America when the first crimes were committed, so it couldn't possibly have been him. I still haven't got to the end of it, but he claimed there must have been another man who looked just like him, a physical double.'

'Like you and me.'

'The weird thing is that Adolf was also a twin, an identical twin.'

'That's the explanation, then. His brother must have done it.'

Chad had never actually thought of that before. It was so elementary and obvious that it had never occurred to him. He recoiled for a moment, thought hard.

'No, it can't be that,' he said. 'His brother, who was called Adler and who was Harald's father, was a respectable climate scientist. A glaciologist. I've been able to make contact with him, and I know he feels responsible for his brother's behaviour. It was always like this, apparently, even when they were kids. Adler was the sensible twin, Adolf was a bit unruly. Their father died when they were still at school, and it seems Dolf went off the rails after that.'

'Adolf Beck. That's interesting. Things are starting to make sense. And you say his brother knows about glaciers?'

'Adler was a leading expert. His father was also a glacier specialist, and Adler followed in his footsteps.'

A silence fell between them. The heads of the two men sitting in the front seats of the car made no movement. They never even appeared to speak to each other.

Greg then said, 'What do you mean, you made contact with his brother? He must have been dead for . . . when was this? The beginning of the last century?'

'He died in 1920, when he was nearly eighty. I looked him up.'

'So how could you have been in contact with him?'

'That's not easy to explain. How long have we got?'

'We won't get to where we're going for more than half an hour. Tell all.'

iv

Once Chad had started on the long story about working for the police, the training course he had been made to go on, the unorthodox use he had been making of the graphene shield, he realized how complicated the whole series of events had become.

Greg said, interrupting the flow, 'This graphene shield – it's called an IMC?'

'That's what the police called it, yes.'

'I know exactly what it is. Are you wearing it now?'

'It's not a question of being worn. The thing is sort of welded to my skull. It'll never come off. How do you know about it?'

'The people who run BNN were thinking about acquiring it last year. They were being offered it as a new method of speed-ing up news reporting. They called in most of the reporters, gave us a demonstration and we talked about it. We came to the conclusion it was unreliable. No one, including the commercial agent who was trying to market it, really knew where it had come from, or who invented it. The software turned out to have been based on a gaming algorithm, adapted by an unnamed outfit, Ukrainian probably. Journalists are always wary of new connectivity, wondering who might be listening on the other end. And we didn't want foreign software being piped anywhere near our heads. We were suspicious of the whole thing. So we voted unanimously against it, and BNN dumped it. But you say the cops bought into it and are using it now?'

'They were for a while, but as far as I know they couldn't make it work for them.'

'And in the process they welded one to your head.'

'Yes.'

'Not a great idea. How did that get you in contact with Uncle Adolf's brother?'

'Through his DNA – remember you sent me the code?' He began telling Greg how he had been working with Pat O'Connell, and the visualizer Pat had created for him, but again Greg interrupted him.

'Patrick O'Connell? The software engineer?'

'You know Pat too?'

'Not personally, but he's worked as a contractor with Schmiederhahn for a long time. They rate him highly.'

'It was through Pat that I was given the dryas material to profile. Before that, Pat set up a comms link between the IMC and a DNA visualizer, which was a unit he developed in the days when I was paid to profile criminal evidence. That originally had restricted access, but after Pat rewrote the software I found I could make brief visual contact with Adolf through his DNA. This was how I discovered there was a twin brother: they of course have the same DNA sequence, which meant sometimes I made contact with Adolf himself, but at other times it was his brother Adler.'

'And Adler was a glaciologist. In another world I would call that a coincidence.'

'A coincidence with what?' Chad said. 'And what other world?'

'At Schmiederhahn they say there is no such thing as co-incidence, only inevitability. They are strong on corporate determinism. Nothing ever happens by chance.'

'Including the discovery that the dryas is going to save the world?'

'The people in Paris say they worked for years for that result,' Greg said. 'You said you were only convinced by it at the end. I found the arguments pretty compelling. What took you so long?'

The car had been descending through a series of bends in the road, and was now about to cross a fjord via a high suspension bridge. Chad turned away from Greg to take in the view. The sun was briefly out from behind the clouds.

'When you're running a profile you try to see all sides of the argument,' he said as the road climbed back towards the mountains on the other side. 'The evidence for what Schmie-derhahn is planning was clear, almost unarguable. But one of the dissenting opinions struck home to me. Hilde Stenmuir wrote that the project depended on a *deus ex machina*, an abrupt upheaval that would tip the climate from warming to cooling. She described it as wish fulfilment. Global heating had gone too far, she said. It was beyond the reach of a miracle rescue. It wasn't going to happen and if it did it would be too little too late. Because of living on the south coast, seeing the effects of the catastrophe almost every day, I thought that was sensible. She convinced me for a while. But then I looked again at the scientific evidence, and I thought differently. She has ultimate authority on the subject, but she was only expressing common sense. Or an opinion.'

Greg said, 'You got it right. Schmiederhahn are working on the belief that the *deus ex machina* already occurred. The cooling started about five years ago.'

'That isn't what the records say. Temperatures have continued to rise.'

'Those are air temperature, sun radiance, humidity. When was the last time you went for a swim in the sea?'

'I can't remember. When we were teenagers, probably. That holiday in Spain.'

'If you went in now you'd get a shock. The temperature of sea and ocean water has fallen by an average of five degrees. Globally.'

'Because of the poles melting?'

'That's only part of it. The Arctic ice was mostly frozen seawater, but the big change has been caused by the melting of the fresh-water ice cap in Antarctica, and the Greenland ice cap. The same is true of meltwater from the glaciers, which at present are shrinking everywhere and flooding into the rivers. Icebergs are non-saline, and the numbers calving are increasing every year. Fresh water is less dense than seawater and the two don't mix well when there are huge quantities. When fresh water pours into the ocean the result is unpredictable. Even more so when it is swept up by one of the currents, which it always is. It's an ongoing process. But we already know it leads to a reduction in overall sea temperature. The impact of the fresh water is occurring all over the world. Oceanologists have always maintained that the oceans are the key to the climate, and that's now clearly what's happening.'

'You sound as if you've become an expert, Greg.'

'I've been working for one of the most environmentally aware corporations in the world. I was originally attracted by the money the job offered – I worry about the kids, we needed to move house soon, that sort of thing. We wanted to be further north. But from day one with the company I discovered I was in a different world. The first two weeks I was being trained in what they know and theorize, and what they predict. It was an enlightening time.'

'What about the greenhouse gases?'

'What about them?' said Greg. 'We'll have to live with them for several more decades. The Earth is a self-regulating system, but it regulates slowly. The gases have created a catastrophe of the man-made kind, but they'll go on melting the ice until the planet finds a new balance on its own terms. Whatever we do will by then be insignificant. The best hope at present is that modern engineering might be able to moderate the impact of an ice age, at least to some extent.' The car had slowed suddenly, while still climbing the gradient, and now turned into a narrower road leading even more steeply upwards. 'The first problem is going to be how we deal with the glaciers.'

'They're retreating, though.'

'For now they're retreating. That's not going to last. They'll be back with a vengeance.'

v

They left the car and walked up a pedestrian track towards a modern building. The pathway was not steep, built for easy access. They were followed at a discreet distance by the man Chad had at first thought might be a second driver. It was bitterly cold on the mountainside, with a brisk wind blowing across the east-facing slope. Much of the ground was bare, but there were tussocks of a long grass, and many small bushes. Chad walked, looking ahead. He saw no alpine flowers. There was a large display sign saying: *Jostedalsbreen Nasjonalpark – Besøkssenter*, with translations of access times and entry fees in a dozen or more languages beneath. Below the sign was a stylized painted image of tall mountains with a river of ice wending its way between them.

The main door to the Visitor Centre was temporarily obstructed by an arrangement of guard barriers covered with black and yellow adhesive tape.

Chad turned, and for the first time noticed the valley below. Because they had been talking in the car, facing forward, and because of the way the car was parked, he had started walking up towards the building without turning back to see what was below them. It was an immense U-shaped valley, with a vast lake of white glacier across the floor. There were other glimpses of smaller glaciers on the way up from Bergen, but this was a magnificent sight, seeming to stretch along its valley from one horizon to the other. It was irregular in shape, with several smaller glaciers feeding into the main one from clefts and smaller valleys in the mountains on each side. The surface was streaked with dark lateral lines of surface moraine, curving and snaking in a sort of zigzag pattern across the width.

'Jostedalsbreen is still the largest glacier in Europe,' Greg said. 'But it's lost about a tenth of its bulk in the last few years. We're here to see what it has left behind.'

While they were staring down at the glacier the man who had been following them went to where the barriers were placed and showed some kind of pass. Immediately, a man and a woman wearing Nasjonalpark windcheaters and caps appeared from inside and moved the barriers to make a gap. Chad and Greg walked inside.

It was not a large building, but it was no longer open to visitors and had been stripped of most of its contents. The walls were still lined with many photographs of Jostedalsbreen, and the varieties of wildlife that were found in its area. Several information panels explained the nature of a glacier like Jostedalsbreen, the size, volume, how long it had been in existence, and so on. The importance of the presence of meltwater, and the concepts of glacial sliding, internal deformation, moraine, compression and extension, were all displayed diagrammatically with explanatory panels in a multitude of languages.

Most of the floor space was bare, but a large part of it was taken up by a heap of tangled metal wreckage. Greg and Chad went to look at it. One of the staff members was standing beside it. Her badge announced that she was an official Jostedalsbreen guide. Her name was Hege.

She said in English, 'I think this is what you have come to see, gentlemen. It was a most extraordinary discovery, revealed to us from the depth of the glacier. We think we have finally identified what it is and how it ended up in Jostedalsbreen.'

The wreckage, Hege said, was part of a huge aircraft, almost certainly flown by the German Luftwaffe during the Second World War. What had been brought up to the building was the only recognizable part that remained: one engine and a fragment of the wing on which it was mounted. They had identified the aircraft as a six-engined heavy transport, a Messerschmitt Me 323, the largest land-based aircraft in use by any air force during the war. No official records survived of German flights in and out of Norwegian airspace during the occupation, but these giants had been flown by the Luftwaffe to supply the German troops. This one had clearly crashed, or crash-landed, on the glacier. No one had witnessed the accident, and no survivors had reported the crash. When the wreckage was found in the moraine as the glacier receded, they conducted a search for human remains, but none were found. There was normally a crew of five or six.

'It was unusual for there to be no trace of the men who were on board,' she went on. 'But not unknown. What a glacier

293

does with material accidentally entering it is a mystery only Jostedalsbreen could explain. We think this crash might have happened in the summer months, when the ice was moving more quickly and changing shape. However, if the plane land-ed on the glacier in winter and the crew were buried in the ice, they would show a remarkable degree of preservation, because of the intense cold.'

It sounded like the well-rehearsed explanation a guide would give to visiting tourists. She indicated an open portion of the casing through which part of the interior could be seen.

Chad and Greg looked closely. The engine was just about recognizable by its rounded, bulbous outline, but much of the metal nacelle was either corroded or broken. All parts visible inside were a scramble of twisted cabling and metal plates. It was sobering to think of this aircraft, smashed up and hidden inside the glacier for more than a century. Everyone involved with the incident, the crew, their loved ones, the colleagues who knew them and had seen them off from the airbase, or the people waiting to greet them, and their families, children and grandchildren at home, were almost certainly all gone.

'But now I am sure you would like to see our prize recovery from the great glacier,' said Hege.

'I think this is what we have actually come to see,' Greg said quietly. Chad looked at him questioningly. Greg added, 'You spoke of Uncle Adolf's name when he was in Norway. As I said, everything is inevitable in Schmiederhahn's determinist world. Coincidences never happen, they are never admitted.'

vi

Hege led them through an unmarked door towards the back of the building. Chad noticed that the company minder who had been in the car with them was still in close attendance. He did not follow them through the door.

The room they were now in was as bare as the main area had been, although here too there were still signs of past use and occupancy. A long table stood in the centre of the room. Lying on it were some clothes, roughly outlining the body form of their past wearer. Although misshapen and in places torn, they had been cleaned and were laid out carefully. There was a thick jacket, sturdy trousers, something that might have been a cap mangled out of recognition, two stout boots, heavily deteriorated.

Chad stared at the human shape adumbrated by the recovered garments. The clothes without the man.

Something resonated within him. He had a feeling he had lived this before, a false memory of being trapped briefly inside a crevasse, but also a powerful sense of aching loss about a dead father, of hearing the shocking news from a tearful aunt, of leaving the house where he had been born. These sensations, channelled from his contacts with Adler and Dolf, were now a part of him. Memories of a life he had not lived.

When he intruded on either of the brothers he was immediately aware of what he saw and heard around him. But the two brothers were not objective cameras recording mere images or sounds. Chad had intruded also into their subconscious identities, their psychological make-up, their experiences, their memories, their hopes, their whole lives.

They became a part of him too, these images of secret knowledge.

'Earlier this year, while the mountain squad were searching for the remains of anyone who might have been on the aircraft, they discovered a body,' Hege was saying. 'Not connected with the plane. The body of the man who was wearing these clothes. The plane was released by the glacier about a year ago. Some

295

of the staff came across the wreckage during a routine survey of the terminal moraine. The wreckage had been lying in the moraine unnoticed for a long time. It was easy to miss: the moraine is a place of chaos, and the aircraft had been shattered by the impact. Its parts were scattered over a wide distance, and many small pieces were buried inside. Most of the wreckage is still out there.

'But because the team was searching they came across this body. It was found two kilometres away in another part of the terminal moraine, and from the appearance of the clothes we knew that whoever it was had been killed on the glacier a long time before the aircraft crashed, many years before. Some parts of the glacier are shrinking more quickly than others. The interior of a big glacier is deformed. You will have seen the streaks of moraine visible across the surface, the way they form patterns. That is a result of the uneven compression within a glacier, and the different speeds at which it travels. We believe this body was exposed only shortly before we found it. It is possible that the dead body and the remains of the aircraft were revealed at roughly the same time, even though the incidents themselves were many years apart.'

Chad was barely listening, his thoughts focusing on the ghostly, absent body of the dead man. He stared down at the tabletop. He could almost visualize the man inside the clothes. He felt he knew him.

'When did he die?' Chad said. His voice suddenly felt tight, difficult to get out, the now familiar experience of being constrained by the entry into other lives.

'We believe the accident happened nearly two centuries ago, in 1853. Papers were found in one of his inside pockets which identified him. They had been preserved by the intense cold. So from those we were able to discover that from about 1849 he worked as a scientific observer of this glacier. We already had in our records a note of staff involved in accidents while on the glacier. Over the years several have been trapped by the ice, or have fallen irretrievably into deep crevasses. The earliest known of these disappeared in that year, in 1853. His body was never found.'

'So you know his name?' said Chad, thinking: it was Beck, *it was Beck.*

'His name was Beck,' Greg said to Chad. 'Joseph Beck.'

The guide smiled to confirm this.

'Joseph Beck was a great man in our history,' Hege said. 'He was a pioneer, for us at Jostedalsbreen a hero. I have some early daguerreotypes of him in the office, which I will show you now. He was legendary for being brave and adventurous, but he always said how scared he was of glaciers, of Jostedalsbreen in particular. He believed the glaciers would start expanding again one day, return down the mountain passes, and ice would cover the world.'

She indicated an inner door, presumably leading to the office. She went ahead of them, opened it.

'So maybe he was not right about everything,' Hege said.

12

Adolf Beck (1904)

i

Adolf Beck, guilty of five offences of obtaining money and goods by false pretences and larceny, had been returned to prison at the end of June 1904. The trial judge suspended the imposing of a fixed sentence because he ordered that some of the background facts in the case should be investigated. Beck therefore had uncertainty hanging over him, not knowing how long the dreadful sentence was going to be.

He was taken to Pentonville Prison, in the north of London. The prison had been built some sixty years earlier, and at the time it was opened it was recognized as modern and progressive, with the enlightened intentions of rehabilitation and education. By the early years of the twentieth century almost everything about Pentonville had deteriorated. The old building was falling into disrepair and the system was understaffed. Prisoners were locked inside their cells for up to twenty-three hours a day. The cells were crowded and verminous. The sanitary arrangements were basic to say the least, and exercise in fresh air was granted only occasionally. Long-term prisoners were housed in Pentonville, and since the closing of Newgate Prison two or three years earlier it was where all the executions took place. Two or three prisoners a week were taken from the condemned cells to be hanged. Many piteous scenes of traumatized relatives and supporters took place in the street outside the prison gate.

What Beck did not then know, as he waited for the inevitably bad news about his new sentence, was that petty frauds against vulnerable women were continuing on the streets of London.

The *modus operandi* was identical: a man posing as a wealthy aristocrat, an offer of a job, the writing of a dud cheque, a theft of small items, a wretched woman left in despair. These mean and shameful crimes were committed between April and July, in other words at the same time as Beck was in custody waiting for the trial to begin. They were still going on even as the trial itself was in progress, and also in the days since June 27th when he had been returned to prison.

In early July, police suspicions were centred on a man recently arrested in a pawnshop, trying to sell cheap jewellery which had been reported stolen. When charged at the police station he gave his name as William Thomas. One of the detectives who had been present during Beck's two trials went to see the prisoner.

William Thomas bore a superficial resemblance to Beck: he was grey-haired, grey-moustached, built slightly more bulkily than Beck and had a scar on his right cheek (which some of the witnesses had mentioned in evidence, no one troubling to point out that Beck had no such scar). He spoke English with a faintly Germanic accent, while Beck's English contained a trace of Norwegian – it was probably easy to mistake one for the other by those who were unfamiliar with the languages.

The police officer looked into the matter, and realized who this man in custody might be.

He arranged for three of the women who had recently

testified against Beck to be brought to the police station where William Thomas was being held. They went to a police line-up. This consisted of eight men, volunteer members of the public, and William Thomas. All three women instantly picked out Thomas as the man who had swindled them. That they had previously identified Adolf Beck for the same offences was not mentioned.

The police started enquiries into William Thomas's life and background, and searched his lodgings. They found many incriminating pieces of evidence against him. Although at first he denied any wrongdoing, Thomas finally confessed. He appeared in court on September 15th and after a plea of guilty, and due process of the court, he was sentenced to five years' penal servitude.

During the course of the hearing the multitude of names he used was revealed. He claimed that he was an Austrian national born in Vienna, and his name was Wilhelm Meyer. Meyer admitted he had worked under a number of names throughout his life: Vilvoir Weisenfells (which might in fact have been the name he was born under, but this was never established for certain), as well as the aliases William Thomas, Dr William Augustus Wyatt, Augustus William Meyers, William Weiss, Dr Marsh, Lord Winton de Willoughby . . . and John Smith.

The story of the unfortunate Adolf Beck, who was now definitively accepted as wholly innocent of all the offences, was also read out in court. Asked if he had anything to say to the court about this, Meyer replied, 'I am exceedingly sorry.'

He was taken down to begin his prison sentence, and thereafter disappeared not only from this story but also from history.

Two months before the Meyer trial began, and shortly after he was arrested, the evidence discovered by the police made it clear that he was responsible for every one of the offences, as far back as 1877. Adolf Beck was immediately released. This was on July 19th. Ten days after his release Beck was granted a King's Pardon for both his convictions, and awarded a sum in compensation of £2,000.

ii

The story did not end there. A Committee of Enquiry was set up, and many officials were summoned to be interviewed. These included Sir Forrest Fulton, who was the prosecutor in the 1877 trial and the judge in the 1896 trial.

Adolf Beck, 1904

John Smith, 1904

Key among the mysteries of this matter was the positive identification of Beck made by so many women. He was picked out almost invariably at identity parades, and they repeated their certain identification in open court. Yet when the true identity of 'John Smith' was known, it was obvious that the visible physical similarities between the two men were only superficial. They were approximately the same age, they were portly in appearance, they both had grey hair and a moustache. Other, more crucial differences existed, but they were not apparent from outward appearances.

The prison authorities confirmed that on arrival at Portland Prison in 1896 Beck was allocated John Smith's identity number: W523, with an extra 'D' to indicate he was a repeat offender. This added to the presumption that Smith and Beck were the same man. The authorities accepted this presumption, and never questioned it.

The prison, through the Home Office, also revealed that during John Smith's sentence between 1877 and 1881 he had declared that he was of the Jewish faith. A physical examination determined that he was circumcised; during Beck's imprisonment between 1896 and 1901 he was also physically examined, and this showed that he was not. The information had been passed at the time to the Home Office: an absolute and unarguable refutation of identity. The Home Office did not reveal this crucial evidence to the court, possibly because it was thought that there was so much other evidence against Beck he would inevitably be convicted. Whatever the erroneous reason, the courts were not informed and no other action was taken. Beck remained imprisoned.

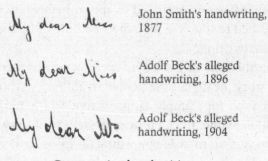

John Smith's handwriting, 1877

Adolf Beck's alleged handwriting, 1896

Adolf Beck's alleged handwriting, 1904

Comparative handwriting

Also deeply suspect was the evidence given by the handwriting expert, Mr Gurrin. In British court procedure an expert witness does not appear for one side or the other. The witness is called to present their expertise to assist the court – that is, the jury. Mr Gurrin was therefore technically neutral, yet the emphasis of the evidence he gave at the trials was partisan: he seemed intent on convicting Smith, or Beck. All the samples he worked on were from John Smith's hand, but one sample was presented as having been 'admitted' by Beck.

As Beck himself had said in open court, he did not like writing in English and found it difficult. Later investigations established that Beck's real handwriting looked nothing like the samples Mr Gurrin had examined. When Mr Gurrin was shown samples of Beck's real handwriting, he admitted he had been in error. He withdrew his earlier evidence and said, 'I can only express my heartfelt regret that his innocence was not discovered in time to spare him his many years of suffering.'

Adolf Beck's handwriting, 1904

Thomas Gurrin continued to appear before courts in future trials, called to testify as an expert because of his forensic skills with handwriting.

From the start of Beck's inadvertent involvement with this sordid story, nearly all the people in authority who came into contact with him simply assumed that Smith and Beck were one and the same. Beck's protests were waved away as attempts by a guilty man to evade punishment. Even Sir Forrest Fulton admitted to the enquiry that he had assumed from the start that Beck was Smith.

Sir Forrest's role in this miscarriage of justice was crucial. At the enquiry, when asked why he had not declared that he had prosecuted John Smith at the earlier trial (and was therefore unfit to sit as judge in the 1896 case), he claimed he could not remember. Barristers maintain a fee book, a record of all the cases they have worked on. Sir Forrest said he was sorry and realized it was inconvenient, but he could not find his at the time.

Sir Forrest maintained that whether or not Smith and Beck

were the same man was irrelevant. He pompously defended his actions and decisions from behind a web of legal niceties and the sort of Latin tags jurists fall back on when cornered. The evidence presented in the trial was overwhelming and convincing, he asserted, and he had directed the jury correctly. Yet only one half of the story was told, and that was full of errors. Beck was found guilty.

Sir Forrest said to the enquiry, 'The jury's verdict is sovereign. It is the duty of a court of law to accept all evidence given in good faith, even if in some respects it seems to be in conflict with common sense. The jury system relies on the jury to give common sense the correct amount of importance while weighing their verdict.'

This would be correct and fair had he allowed the defence to be heard.

As a direct consequence of these three cases, and the miscarriage of justice suffered by Adolf Beck, the Court of Criminal Appeal was set up in the United Kingdom, where it exists into the present day.

If a matter of witness identification comes into a criminal case in Britain, lawyers will still sometimes cite the case of Adolf Beck as a reminder of the dangers. Because of this, if the police or a court are dealing with a witness who claims they saw the defendant with their own eyes and can therefore identify him or her, the rules under which that sort of evidence may be given are stringent, and strictly applied. It is no longer enough to point a finger of accusation.

Juries are invariably warned to treat evidence of eyewitness identification with the greatest care, and should rely more on corroboration from other witnesses. It is now forbidden for a witness to point to a defendant in the dock and declare he or she was the person who committed the crime. Any attempt by a witness to do so results almost invariably in a mistrial.

Sir Forrest Fulton continued with his brilliant and fair-minded juridical career, receiving many awards and honours, culminating with his appointment as Recorder of London. He held this most senior post for nearly a quarter of a century, until his retirement in 1922, aged seventy-six. He died in 1926.

When the facts of the Beck case became known, largely through the campaigning work of a newspaper journalist, George R. Sims, there was a public outcry. The compensation fee was raised to £5,000, but none of the authorities who had contributed to the miscarriage was punished or even reprimanded.

Adolf Beck never recovered from his experiences, and suffered ill-health for the remainder of his life. He died in 1909, aged sixty-eight.

13

Chad Ramsey (2050)

i

Chad flew back to Britain, hired a coolcab at Heathrow Airport, and returned to the house in Hastings. After his brief stay in Norway, his senses had become attuned by the cool atmosphere to the sight of the stark, clean landscape of mountains and fjords. The countryside between London and the south coast looked bedraggled and damaged, with many fallen trees and past and present evidence of flooding. On arrival in Hastings he was shocked by the dilapidated appearance of most of the surviving buildings. His own house was much as he and Ingrid had left it two weeks earlier, but after the clean lines and bright colours of the Norwegian houses and buildings it looked aged and structurally unsound.

Indoors, he started up the aircon, drew the blinds, waited for the steamy heat to disperse. Through the window of his workroom he surveyed the charred stalks and open patches of his garden, and noted that one more of the houses visible beyond had suffered a collapse or partial demolition. Reddish sand was still covering the ground. He booted his desktop computer and checked to see if any emails had arrived while he was travelling – there were a few that he had not already picked up on his phone, but nothing of great interest. Social media sites were full of comments about subjects that no longer concerned him. He sent a message to Ingrid, still at her parents' house in Oslo, to let her know he had arrived home.

There were three pieces of positive news, which had been delivered to the house by mail, or perhaps by courier, while he was away.

First of all he received a written, formal confirmation from his bank that a payment from PoconData Service had been credited to his account. Chad, still disbelieving the amount, stared at the simple document with a sense of awe. At a stroke Schmiederhahn had made him wealthy – for the first time in his life he was in possession of more money than he knew how to spend. When he went online to check his account, the figure glowed back at him. Chad spoke to Pat to let him know he had safely received it. Pat was almost as euphoric – he, of course, had taken his agreed commission.

Chad mentioned he was running low on batteries for the IMC, but Pat said the version sold to the police had been non-standard, and the batteries, customized to the particular kit, were not available commercially.

'They discharge quickly,' Chad said. 'I thought the ones I have would last for months.'

'I'll see if I can find some more for you,' Pat said. 'There might be a dealer who has some. They're designed for a steady release and single use, but because you're connected to the visualizer there is a surge at the beginning and another at the closing down procedure. I can't see any way around that. No one has made rechargeable versions available. Once you're connected they should last several hours.'

Chad said nothing, because his contacts with Adolf and Adler had always been short. His arrival meant slow strangulation for his host. He and Pat agreed to meet up to celebrate in the near future.

A copy of Professor A. J. Beck's ancient book, *Take Heed!*, had been mailed to him by the dealer. Chad fingered it gently while he dipped into it. The boards were scuffed at the corners, the binding at the spine was brittle and it crackled as he leafed through. The pages were brown and brittle. The print was fading but still legible. There were faintly reproduced line illustrations. The book had a musty, dry smell, something only book collectors loved. Chad set it aside to read later.

Finally, there was another house purchase order from the local authority, who were intending to buy and demolish the upper town's existing housing stock, and replace it with modern, climate-proof buildings, to ensure, as they said, the continued occupation of Hastings and St Leonards into the future. This initiative had been going on for some years, with the low and unattractive price on offer gradually increasing with time. Many householders had grudgingly accepted the money and moved out, but Chad and Ingrid always decided to hold on. They were in one of only a few remaining single-occupant houses in the street. What with his new found financial independence, and he and Ingrid already talking about relocating, Chad realized the time might have come at last to take advantage of the offer and sell up.

ii

Chad invariably felt listless after a journey, bored with things, even after he arrived home. He took a shower and changed into fresh clothes. Five minutes later the shirt was damp with sweat. The aircon was already set to max. He ordered some groceries online, agreeing to pay the hefty delivery charge. The food would be with him the next day. Meanwhile, he got by with what they had left in the freezer before they went away.

The next morning he woke to find a message from Ingrid. Erik had had a bad night, and the doctor was being called. Ingrid and her mother were consumed with worry. But she changed the subject suddenly, and added that she had applied to the UN Secretariat for a job as a translator or interpreter. If she was successful it would mean they could move to live in Bergen. She was excited by the prospect. How would he feel about that?

Chad did not know, except he was pleased for her and the thought of living in Norway was attractive. He spoke to her on the phone later, but all they talked about was her father. The doctor had visited, Erik was feeling better but was staying in bed. Ingrid and her mother were taking it in turns to sit with him. It looked bad.

BNN news, which Chad watched on TV as he ate a snack lunch:

A weather station in the Thames Valley reported an air temperature at 10 a.m. of forty-six point seven degrees, a record for the British Isles. Several people had died of heat exhaustion. Water reserves were critical, and rivers were running dry.

A repurposed luxury cruise liner, a huge rusting relic of a past age, had gone aground in the shallow waters off the north Kent coast. It was on fire in one deck area, following an attempted intervention by two armed border patrol ships. There were thought to be at least ten thousand refugees from sub-Saharan Africa on board, all young males – at an earlier interception at sea a French naval vessel had taken off hundreds of women and children. A new strain of infectious mycobacterium ulcerans was believed to be spreading on board.

A tropical storm, level four, had arrived in the Atlantic approaches, and was expected to cross into the south of Ireland or south-west England later that day – residents in low-lying areas were being warned to evacuate their homes.

In the USA it was confirmed that mid-term elections, due in November, were being postponed until next year. President Matt (Mateusz) D. Chester remained in hospital in Toronto under secret service guard, and was said to be responding well to treatment. Vice President Hussain continued to consult with him daily.

The British government had been defeated in a parliamentary vote of confidence for the third time in a month, but emergency powers continued in place.

The United Nations was renewing its regular invitation to the British to ratify the Central Administration Treaty. Since the last reminder the countries of Albania and Azerbaijan had become signatories and were joined to the treaty. New Zealand was expected to be next.

Chad turned off the TV.

He had not used his IMC at any time while he was away, so he switched it on, neglecting for the moment the impact it sometimes had on his mind. He belatedly braced himself, but there was no signal, not even the background carrier hiss. He ejected the battery and pushed in a new one, thinking as he did so he should be eking out his remaining supply. The sensation of easy connectivity was still a novelty, so he left it on a classical music channel while he browsed a website set up by the HAO, which listed court archive files.

Ingrid called him, and because the IMC was connected she came through on that.

'Pappa has collapsed, and is having trouble breathing,' she said, her voice betraying her stress. 'We're waiting for the ambulance now, and we'll be going together to the hospital with him.'

Chad said a few words of consolation, but he felt the vast

distance of sea and miles between them, in spite of the anxious closeness of her voice. Ingrid said she would call back when she could, and hung up quickly.

iii

Erik died that night in hospital, a peaceful passing, relieved of pain, suffering no more. Ingrid phoned Chad while she was still in the hospital. He picked her up on his mobile. She sounded subdued but not tearful. She said she would probably have to stay with her mother for several more days. She described the way Erik had been during his last minutes, half asleep but aware. He had spoken, but they were not able to hear the words.

iv

After Erik's funeral Ingrid stayed on in Oslo with her mother, but she and Chad were in contact every day, attempting to discuss plans, make decisions, all at a distance, by phone and sometimes on the internet. Chad kept the IMC out of use. They discussed the move away from Hastings, finding somewhere to live in Bergen, what they would do if she failed to land the job with the UN, what her mother would wish to do. Kirsten was in her early seventies, and now faced the prospect of living alone in the large Oslo house. Would she move to Bergen to be with them? Would they wish her to? She was proud of her independence. There might be some way they could make it work. It was not a decision any of them wanted to rush into. Ingrid told Chad she would arrange a flight back to Britain as soon as she could.

Later that day she was summoned to the UN Secretariat, and after a hurried journey to Bergen and two interviews she was offered the interpreting job she was seeking. That at least was a firm basis for sorting out the rest of their plans. She returned to Oslo, then booked a flight back to Britain. She would be home in two days.

Chad was still trying to find out what had happened to Adolf. Painfully aware of how quickly his stock of spare batteries was diminishing, Chad used conventional internet access to search whatever court or prison records were available between the approximate years 1870 to 1910.

The prison records were available in online databases, but were stored behind a range of encryption and password barriers. Anyone serving a prison sentence in Britain was considered to be a vulnerable person. Although most convicts and their families seemed to be unaware of this, it entitled prisoners to anonymity from all but high levels of authority. However, the records did exist, and Chad was finally able to access some of them, using connection protocols he had learned while with the police.

There was no record at all of a prisoner with the name Adolf Beck, or anything even remotely like it. The name John Smith elicited a list of more than forty convicted men with that name, tried and imprisoned for a range of offences, serious and relatively minor. One or two were acquitted. Most of them were clearly not the man whom Beck had been mistaken for, but there were two probable cases. In 1877, John Smith was convicted of larceny and deception (five years), and in 1896 was again convicted, this time for three offences of theft and deception (seven years). There was no hint that the latter Smith was in fact Adolf Beck, or that he was not.

After the second period in prison was a comment: *Released.* (There was no date.) There was no other reference to Dolf in court or prison records.

Because he had been able to establish the date of the trial, which had extended across two days in March 1896, Chad used the rough triangulation of the v-file dates to locate it.

His first few attempts were unsuccessful: it was a blunt instrument and he felt he was groping around in the past. For the first time he was seeking a specific event. He made several contacts while Adolf or Adler were sleeping, causing them to wake up. He made no attempt to speak to them. Each time, the battery he was using failed when he tried to use it a second time.

He was finding the whole process of communicating with these two increasingly arduous. He was not yet prepared to accept his new reality in so many words, or even thoughts, but his own life was clearly about to change in stimulating and involving ways. His ability to make contact was anyway limited, defined by the remaining batteries he kept in the little pouch in his desk.

He felt guilty about abandoning the Beck brothers, because in spite of all the difficulties he had a sense of collective consciousness. He was still experiencing false memories: some incident or event that he recalled, sometimes to do with past moments as a star of the opera, an awareness of long sea voyages he had never taken, an interest in cold places. He experienced these memories for a few seconds as if they were his own, before shrugging them away. His curiosity about Adolf was largely satisfied.

He kept looking, though, and the next day he was more successful. At his first attempt he reached Adolf. The close sensation of contact was the most positive result of this, because Adolf was not a welcoming recipient. He was in court, but slumped in his seat. Two burly uniformed men were on each side of him, pressing their bodies against his. He was staring down, past his lap, past his knees, down to where his feet were compressed into a tiny space.

Chad knew he must have entered at some point midway through the trial, because although Adolf was not looking in that direction, a woman somewhere across the courtroom was answering questions. Her voice was faintly heard, her words simply chosen. The advocate questioning her, a man, had a ringing, imperious voice, well educated, but seeming to be pushing the woman to say what he wanted to hear.

Chad said, 'I am here for you, Dolf. I need – to listen to what is being said.'

Adolf gave no sign that he had heard or was aware of what was happening. Chad tried to listen across the courtroom, straining to hear the woman's faint and tremulous words. His hearing had become Adolf's, which was not perfect – age was taking its toll. But Chad could just about make out this exchange:

'. . . he said he was going on a trip to Italy.'

'Did he say where in Italy?'

'No, nothing like that. He would like me to go with him, and that I should want a new outfit.'

'And how did you feel about that?'

'It was a bit sudden, I thought to myself. He'd only just met me in the street. But I'd like a new dress or two, because I would, wouldn't I? So he had this bit of paper, and he said he was going to write down a list of dresses.'

'You saw him write this?'

'Yes, it was right in front of me.'

'My Lord, this piece of paper has been produced as evidence, and is identified as EEM2. This is one of the samples of hand-writing on which our case depends.'

'Thank you, Mr Avory,' the judge said. 'Pray continue.'

'Did you make any promises to secure this offer?'

'No – he just did it.'

And so it went. At no point did Adolf raise his eyes to see the manner in which the woman gave her evidence. Chad, trapped by Adolf's eyes, could only imagine how she appeared, what her posture was like, where she was looking, what she might be doing with her hands. She sounded resentful, frightened. Chad could feel Adolf straining to breathe, and he knew he should withdraw as soon as he could. He wanted to stay on, hear the rest of the case, but the paralysis he was causing Adolf was dangerous.

Reluctantly, he withdrew. He was back in his workroom, the aircon whirring and grinding, the endless sun beating down on his garden, glimpsed through the slats of his blinds. He pulled off his shirt and threw it aside. He walked to the next room, opened a bottle of beer from the fridge.

When he returned to his desk he discovered that the battery he had just used was now discharged, so he slipped in another. He clicked on the same v-file. Moments later he was back in the courtroom, but from an entirely different point of view. He had entered Adler, seated presumably in the public gallery. He felt Adler reacting to his usual incursive arrival.

Adler was sitting on a hard narrow seat, with a railing in front of it. The surface of the seat was shiny and tipping slightly downwards. It was extremely cramped and uncomfortable. He was staring across the courtroom, looking in fact towards the witness box, where the small, slight figure of a woman was visible. Adler was already struggling to breathe as a result of Chad's intrusion, but otherwise remained still. The judge, in full wig and bright scarlet gown, was seated on a large and upholstered chair on a bench about a metre higher than the rest of the room. He looked as if he was on a throne. The judge was not moving – his head was inclined so that his face could not be seen. A lawyer in a black gown and an off-white wig was standing in the well of the court, holding a bundle of papers, looking towards the witness.

Chad said, 'Professor Beck, I apologize – for intruding.'

Adler made an effort to move his head – an acknowledgement? Or because the witness was speaking quietly perhaps he was trying to hear what was being said.

The lawyer was listening to what the woman said, then thanked her for coming to court, and sat down. Another man, similarly garbed in wig and gown, stood up, and after consulting the notes in his hand began to make the woman confirm the evidence she had already given. Chad could hear her only dimly. She did not look well. She was shabbily dressed, extremely thin and her hair was an untidy sprawl. She had several pocks on her face. She appeared frightened of what was happening.

Knowing he could not hold Adler in paralysis for longer than a few more seconds, Chad said, 'This matter will go badly – for Dolf and he will have to be – sent to prison. There is no alternative, nothing you can do to help him. However, he will – be released eventually, and an investigation will establish that he has been mistaken for another man. I think another trial was held, but the – records for that have been deleted. His innocence will – be known.'

Adler was shifting his position on the uncomfortable seat, straining to reply. Chad again felt the helplessness of this constrained manner of communicating – it felt like having to shout against a strong wind, forcing out the words without inflection, or any hope of reply.

He added, 'I will try to make contact with you again soon.'

He could feel the background hiss suddenly sharpen, and the contact was brusquely ended. He was in his workroom, his eyes swimming with the perspiration that had flowed from his brow while trying to speak to Adler. He felt it dripping around his jaw, running off his chin.

He rested, drank the beer, and walked around the house, feeling trapped by the old and familiar rooms. They felt dark to him, worn out by their use. Ingrid's room was tidy, as she always left it. Their bedroom was a mess. His workroom needed cleaning. The kitchen was barely serviceable. He disliked the thought of Ingrid coming home to this in the next day or two, but as so often the unrelenting heat made him sluggish about housework. He washed a few dishes, but took the cleaning no further.

Later, he ran the visualizer again, setting the target a few hours later on that day of the trial, hoping not to find Adolf. His first effort took him to a darkened place, a closed space of rank air and a disgusting smell. Chad withdrew immediately, changed the battery and tried once more. There were only two more batteries remaining after this one. He keyed in the DNA sequence again.

He was in an easy chair, fluffed up with cushions. A fire was burning in an open grate, and Adler was staring at the glowing coals. He responded as soon as Chad arrived, slowly turning his gaze away from the fire to look across the room.

Meredith was in the room, sitting aside from him, in the warmth of the fire. She had a book on her lap, which she closed as Adler's gaze fell on her. She folded her hands across the book.

Chad had prepared what he wanted to say, but to look again at Meredith had the same disconcerting effect as before. He knew everything about her, recognized her, loved her because Adler loved her. She daunted him with her familiar looks, so closely felt.

Finally, he was able to speak against the strain, make another stuttering assertion, shorn of nuances. 'Professor Beck, I have news. The glacier in which – your father died has retreated. A body was discovered. It was identified as Joseph Beck, and I assume – that was your father's name. His remains were given a civilized funeral. I was not there, but I was able to see what they had found of – the clothes he was wearing. He was described to me as a hero.'

Adler responded. Chad could feel his whole body straining against the paralysis, and to his astonishment he felt tears pricking Adler's eyes. Through the sudden veil Chad could see Meredith putting her book aside, leaving her chair. She crossed to him, and knelt beside him, an arm around his shoulders, the other holding his arm gently.

She said, looking up towards him, 'Today Adler saw his only brother disgraced by a cruel and mistaken judgment in the court. Dolf was sent to prison for seven years. It is an outrage, a terrible event. Dolf is not well, we fear for him.'

Chad said, into Adler's mind, 'Dolf will be released early, all will be well. There is nothing I can do except tell you this. There will be another trial after that, but then the truth will be known at last.'

But Adler's chest suddenly heaved, and Chad knew he was struggling for breath. There was so much more he could say! There was so much more he should have said better. He felt the procedure of retreating begin, and the carrier hiss grew louder.

Then he was abruptly back, alone in his workroom. He gasped for clean air.

14

A Postscript (1905, 2050)

i

Ingrid returned from Norway. They began in earnest to make their preparations to leave the house, look for somewhere they could live in Bergen. Their days were filled by the upheaval of the impending move, and the plans for it. They accepted the buy-out offer from the local authority, they scanned the internet for properties as they came on the market in Bergen, they did as much dumping of unwanted clothes, books, utensils, and so on, as they could. They did some preparatory packing of the rest.

After two weeks Ingrid returned to Norway to look at some of the houses they had picked out as possible purchases.

Chad was left to finish off arrangements for shipping their remaining property, and deal with the mountain of formalities.

ii

One book he had not packed away was the one Adler had written. It lay on his desk next to his computer, where it had been from the day it arrived.

The day he finally picked it up began with an unusual patch of cool weather. Rain was falling, blowing in on a wind from the sea. His workroom was so effectively chilled by the aircon that he switched off the system. The BNN weather channel warned that a high-pressure system was forming over the North Sea, which later in the day would pull in more hot winds from the direction of France and Belgium. The usual warnings about heat exhaustion were repeated, the daily routine. Chad stared through his window, looking at the novelty of the shallow puddles forming on the wrecked ground laid bare by the heat.

He started reading Adler's book *Take Heed!* It had the subtitle *A Scientist Warns of the Terror to Come.* To begin with he found the writing style awkward to follow. It was ponderous, circumlocutory, almost self-conscious. The paragraphs were long, so were the sentences. There was a kind of schoolmasterly tone, a few clumsy attempts at levity, an insistence on detail.

The first chapter, a long one, was a history of glacier studies from first efforts until the time Adler was writing, which was presumably in the first year or so of the twentieth century: the book was published in 1905, so Adler would have been writing it a year or two before. This material was clearly autobiographical in some of the anecdotal details, but an ungainly use of the third person made the going heavy.

The rain started falling more intensively. Chad stood up, went to the window and for the first time in ages raised the blind so he could see out without peering through the slats. He took the handle and pushed at it, and after an initial resistance the frame loosened itself and the triple-glazed window opened a short way. He pressed his face to the aperture, feeling a few of the raindrops landing on his cheeks and brow. He could smell the soil of the garden. The rain was cooling the air. It was similar to the rain he and Ingrid had seen and felt that afternoon in Bergen: clean drops falling hard. Chad took several deep breaths.

He left the window open so he could hear the rain spattering on the ground.

He went back to Adler's book and persevered with it. The second chapter was about his father, Joseph. There was a biography, and several accounts of explorations he had made of Jostedalsbreen and other Norwegian glaciers. The upset reactions of Adler and his brother when Joseph was killed were tastefully described. The chapter ended with the news that his body had eventually been released by the glacier, although he did not describe when it was found, or how he knew about it.

This book, published in 1905, described an incident that did not occur until nearly a century and a half later. Adler omitted that detail: how he had discovered it.

In the next chapter the style lightened up. It was possible the publisher had been hoping to find a popular rather than a specialist audience for the book, and made sure the author aimed the rest of his work in that direction. This approach had been subtly indicated by the breezy title, but the style now had taken on more of a colloquial tone. Chad sensed there had been some rewriting before the book went to the printers. He began to read more quickly.

Adler ran through a series of theories about the real possibility that the planet was facing a period of serious cooling: sunspots, oceanic drifts, volcanic eruptions, slight changes to the orbit of the Earth around the sun, and so on. He argued plausibly about the dangers all these presented. After his immersion in the Schmiederhahn dossier, much of this was familiar to Chad.

Adler was clearly aware of anthropogenic climate heating, mostly from the burning of fossil fuels and the release of greenhouse gases which had begun in earnest during the Industrial Revolution, but he obviously had little conception of how the effect of these would expand drastically in the years after he wrote his book. All the way through Adler was seeking a turning point, an event in climate history which would tip the balance and set loose the one outcome he warned of: the catastrophic return of an ice age.

Chad was clear in his mind that the tipping point had been identified by the Schmiederhahn researchers as the melting of the Greenland ice cap, a result of the endless rise of the atmospheric heat, but Adler was not to know that. He preferred the thought of a major volcanic eruption, mountains sliding into the sea, tsunamis. In reality, few of these had occurred in the century and a half since his book was published, and where they had they lacked sufficient destructive power.

The real tipping point was more unobtrusive than that: a gradual, insistent warmth, too much for too long, a waiting ocean, a flood of cold fresh water, a benign and delicately balanced sea current doomed to be halted.

But Adler's prophetic effort, described by that internet bibliographer as 'unsubstantiated and variant', had been ignored not only by the popular audience at which it was aimed, but by the scientific establishment.

Brilliantly, he had foreseen the truth, by serious contemplation of the science, the facts as he saw them, the evidence they presented.

Chad came to the last chapter, described as a *Postscript*. A tiny white flower had been pressed between the pages, hidden by its unassuming place at the back of the book, and by its fragile thinness – it was as frail as a cobweb. There were ten petals, a slender pale-red stem, a single leaf. Chad slid it tenderly aside, so he could read the words it had been pressed against. The postscript was a short one, a single page. The words looked the same as all the rest – the paper was browning and slightly foxed, the print had faded – but as soon as Chad started reading he detected a different style, a revised intent:

Last night I had a dream. In this I was striding across a steep mountainside – above me the grey clouds were low, concealing the peak. A long way behind me, in the deep valley below, I could see the great white spread of a glacier.

I had no feelings of being cold in such a high place. I came across a stretch of rocky ground, and I saw that a large number of alpine flowers were growing there. They were creepers, hugging the barren ground. In my dream I bent down to look closely. They were small and modest: each flower had eight or ten creamy white petals, a cluster of yellow stamens, and small, shiny leaves. The reddish stalks of the flowers were thin and woody, almost too frail to hold up such a lovely flower.

I cupped the head of one of the simple little blooms between my fingers and I felt a surge of physical well-being, as if it could momentarily improve me and protect me. I did not understand how, but I became capable of many things. I was renewed and inspired. I knew it was what I had been searching for, all of my life. I let the flower go and straightened.

The dream ended as I stood beside the flowers, looking down at the glacier far below, the sense of bliss abruptly turning to the fear of what it might portend.

A. J. B. – London, 1904

Bibliography

Bjorngjeld, D. L. *Grand Solar Minimum*, 2019

Coates, Tim (editor) *The Strange Story of Adolph Beck*, 1999

Dow, Kirsten & Downing, Thomas E. *The Atlas of Climate Change*, 2006

Fagan, Brian *The Long Summer*, 2004

Foer, Jonathan Safran *We Are the Weather*, 2019

Goudie, Andrew *The Nature of the Environment*, 1993

Hoyle, Fred *Ice*, 1981

Klingaman, William K. & Klingaman, Nicholas P. *The Year Without Summer*, 2013

Lynas, Mark *High Tide*, 2004

Lynas, Mark *Six Degrees*, 2007

Lynas, Mark *Our Final Warning*, 2020

Mack, John *The Sea*, 2011

Murchie, Guy *Song of the Sky*, 1954

Rich, Nathaniel *Losing Earth*, 2019

Shah, Sonia *The Next Great Migration*, 2020

Sims, George R. *Two King's Pardons*, 1904

Smith, Laurence C. *The New North*, 2011

Taylor, Peter *Chill*, 2009

Wallace-Wells, David *The Uninhabitable Earth*, 2019

Watson, Eric R. *The Trial of Adolf Beck*, 1924